Dreamers and dealers, winners and losers . . .

FRIENDS AND FORTUNES

Kat Winter—raised in the brutal smoking mines of West Virginia, her magnificent good looks helped give her a shot at stardom. But she leaves an explosive secret behind her, a secret that not even her friends can ever know . . .

Samantha Devane—born to luxury and privilege, the daring director is addicted to danger, tempting the good fortune of her birth with near-lethal adventures. Restless, vital, this sultry temptress may test fate once too often . . .

Leah Sirk—despite its long Hollywood roots, her blacklisted family never helped her to establish her screenwriting career. She did it herself. But fighting to restore her father's reputation will bring her pain and broken friendships . . .

Pru Daniels—always torn between ambition and affairs of the heart, the producer's turbulent emotions spring from her rocky upbringing in the gambling halls of Tahoe. Her love connections have always raised her up—or torn her down . . .

FRIENDS AND FORTUNES

FRIENDS
AND
FORTUNES

Savannah Stewart

DIAMOND BOOKS, NEW YORK

FRIENDS AND FORTUNES

A Diamond Book / published by arrangement with
the author

PRINTING HISTORY
Diamond edition / February 1991

ISBN: 1-55773-456-9

Diamond Books are published by The Berkley Publishing
Group, 200 Madison Avenue, New York, New York 10016.
The name ''DIAMOND'' and its logo are trademarks
belonging to Charter Communications, Inc.

PRINTED IN THE UNITED STATES OF AMERICA

10 9 8 7 6 5 4 3 2 1

Prologue

April 1988

ACROSS THE DOROTHY Chandler Pavilion, crystal chandeliers threw a light as pink as the California dawn. On stage, a starry grove of lights twinkled against an amethyst sky. In the orchestra, silver cameras swayed gracefully on their dollies. They floated like swans, dipping and bobbing their long necks as they plucked famous faces from the sea of celebrities.

Slowly the houselights dimmed to a deep purple. In a rustle of silk and a flash of diamonds, the Oscar ceremony was about to begin. The distinguished members and guests of the Academy took their places among the plush velvet seats.

Several rows back from the orchestra, four young women sat together. Bathed in the warm glow of red and gold stage lights, they shifted nervously in their seats and exchanged lively glances.

Raven-haired Leah Sirk cast an appraising look at the famous, the infamous, and the mere wannabees.

"They've rounded up the usual suspects," she remarked dryly. Her gypsy eyes sparkled, and excitement dusted her olive skin with just a hint of rose. Her diminutive frame seemed even smaller than usual as Hollywood's latest, hottest hunk squeezed his bulging thighs into the seat behind her. "I hear he's got three legs," she whispered to her friend Prudence Daniels.

"Shh . . ." Pru scolded. "I can't take you anywhere!"

Sighing with exasperation, Pru swept her fiery red hair

high off her neck, hoping to cool down in the crowded theater. But, unfortunately, she had no such luck: here she was, on the biggest night of her life, reduced to a pool of sweat and soggy dress shields. Since her first Saturday matinee at the Tahoe Rialto, she'd dreamed of this evening and worked hard to make it happen. Finally, her dream had come true—and all she could think was that she glistened like Tyson stepping out of the ring.

"Relax, Pru."

An arm fell around her shoulder, and Pru looked up. Samantha Devane was watching her with a knowing look in her pewter-colored eyes. Her white-blond hair, shot through with silver and gold, fell against Pru's freckled cheek as Sam leaned close to her.

"I dare you to smile," she said, and of course Pru did.

Sam sat back in her seat then, her profile as regal as that of an empress on an ancient coin. Pru gazed at Sam's fine-boned body, elegant and reed-thin. How many times had that silhouette inspired Pru in all her harebrained diets? Thank God for beautiful, perfect Sam, who gave the world something to aspire to.

Next to Sam sat Kat Winter, the actress. From her voluptuous body to her violet eyes, everything about her was as artless as breathing. Under the halo of her honey-colored hair, she leaned forward in her seat, eager as a child for the ceremonies to begin.

The orchestra wrapped up its medley, and Chevy Chase, the evening's host, stepped from the wings. Thunderous applause, then deafening silence filled the theater. Pru looked at her friends one last time before darkness fell on their expectant faces.

Leah's breaths were quick and shallow, Kat was biting those famous ripe lips, and even Sam—the coolest of customers—was digging her fingernails into the armrest.

For her part, Pru had to go to the bathroom. It always happened at times like this.

"This is the worst night of my life," she groaned to Leah.

Leah's dark eyes widened in puzzlement. "What about the time we ran out of Mallomars?" she asked.

"I'll get you for that," Pru vowed under her breath. "But

not right this minute. I'm afraid if I move a single muscle, I just might flood the aisle.''

Finally Chevy crossed the stage and arrived at the podium. As he took a deep breath, so did the four friends. Each one looked to the others, and they all knew—without speaking a word—exactly what the others were thinking:

Here we are—and what a ride it's been . . .

One

IT WAS THE last night of the school year, and in their cramped apartment at 612 Weyburn Avenue, three of the four roommates busily prepared for their end-of-school blowout. They'd survived their first year as graduate students at the most famous and prestigious film school in the world, and with that under their belts, they were ready to kick back and disgrace themselves in style. But first they had to clear their bicycles out of the living room and stash the lingerie that was hanging up to dry all over the kitchen.

While they toiled, L.A.'s celebrated lavender sunset hung low on the horizon, and a pale moon climbed steadily above the date palms that surrounded the second-story apartment. Below the apartment and two blocks down the hill, dozens of theater marquees and restaurant signs twinkled to life: Westwood Village, L.A.'s bustling student mecca, was bracing itself for another night of undergraduate follies.

High above the Village—and trying hard not to look down—Leah stood on tiptoe and leaned halfway off the balcony to string Christmas lights in the azaleas. Gentle breezes ruffled her jet-black hair as she scolded Samantha for her latest in a long line of escapades.

"The next time you have a hot date, Sam, *please* don't wake me up at five A.M. to let you in."

"Was it that late, sweetie?" Sam asked innocently.

"The girl can't help it," Kat said, rising to her friend's

defense. "As my mama used to say, some little gals are just blind dogs in a butcher shop!"

"Well, that's no reason for her to bark at the door," Leah muttered.

"Give me a break," Sam moaned. "It's no picnic being a slave to love."

She sighed wearily and got back to the job at hand. With a toilet plunger in a garbage can, she was stirring a batch of Boomerangs, a punch she'd first tasted in Borneo.

"All killer, no filler," she promised.

"What's that stench?" Pru called from the front door. She wrinkled her freckled nose and sniffed as she trundled into the apartment and set a steaming, grease-soaked sack onto the table. "Tacos on the house."

"Hot damn," Kat said. "What are we celebrating?"

"I got the job!" Pru announced.

"Pru," Sam asked airily, "do you really think you should take a gig sweeping the floor of a TV studio?"

"If it gets me in the door, absolutely."

"But what about school?" Kat asked, digging into the bag.

"What about it? I came here from Tahoe to have a career, not to refine my mind. I'll gladly kiss UCLA good-bye if this job turns into something."

"But it's a television station. I thought you wanted to make movies," Leah protested.

"Right, but I've got to start somewhere," Pru said, licking her fingers. "Dee-lish. Come on, kids. Eat up, and let's throw a party!"

When the guests arrived, Sam's Borneo Boomerangs disappeared as fast as they were poured, and by the time the clock struck midnight, the room was spinning for most of the crowd. Students who weren't dancing were coupled off in corners like sideshow contortionists. Springsteen blared from the stereo, and the crumbled remains of finger food lay strewn across the surface of the dinette table.

Pru took one last pass at the California dip, washed it down with Tab, and made her way in semidarkness to the door of the bedroom she shared with Sam. She knocked, but there was no answer, so she turned the knob. The door was locked.

"Sam?" she called. "Can I come in?"

"You've got to be kidding," Sam groaned, and in the background Pru heard a man's amused laughter.

"Dammit, Sam, I want to go to bed."

There were snickers and groans and several yelps before Sam, naked and glistening, flung open the door.

"We're done," she said breathlessly.

On the bed, a good-looking aspiring actor sat propped up against a pillow.

"Sam," Prudence snapped, "I have to be at work in a few hours."

"Lighten up," Sam said huffily, climbing into a cotton jumpsuit. With her admirer stuck to her like a barnacle, she flounced down the hall.

Coming out of the bathroom, Leah saw them. She gasped out loud, and her eyes filled as the couple disappeared.

"What is it, sugar?" Kat came running. "Sweet heaven, you look like cold collard greens."

"It's nothing," Leah said. "I'm fine. I just overdid the Boomerangs." She flashed a feeble grin. "Is this the mug of a damsel in distress?"

Kat took Leah by the shoulders. "Don't give me any hooey," she said softly. "I saw how you looked at that fella with Sam."

Tossing her head defiantly, Leah walked away, but Kat caught her arm.

"You like him, don't you?"

"Of course not," Leah lied.

"You can't kid me," Kat told her gently.

"Oh, damn," Leah cried. She collapsed in tears against Kat. Propping her up, Kat led her to the bedroom they shared. She closed the door, and the sounds of the party were reduced to a murmur.

"Between you and me," Kat spoke confidentially, "that fella is beneath you."

"I wish," Leah moaned.

"Don't be crude, sugar."

"Why not? It's as close as I get to a sex life," Leah whined. "The damned thing is, he means nothing to Sam.

To her, he's just another banana in the bunch. But since I liked him all quarter, she had to have him. It's more predictable than my period. I meet a guy, I start to like him a little, and Sam moves in for the kill.''

''That's because you let her.''

''No! It's because she's gorgeous and brilliant and rich. Compared to her, I go over like a pork chop at a bar mitzvah.''

''Stop that,'' Kat scolded gently. ''I'll bet she didn't even know you liked that boy. You always act like you don't give a darn about anything. How could she realize he wasn't up for grabs?'' Kat pushed Leah's unruly mane from her eyes. ''You've got to stand up for what you want, sugar. Don't expect people to read your mind.''

''Then read my lips.'' Leah smiled. ''Make like a sheep and get the flock out of here. I'm going to bed.'' She swatted her friend's behind as Kat went out the door and back to the party.

Every male in the apartment felt his antennae twitch when Kat returned to circulation, but unfortunately for them, their mating calls were not to be answered. Kat had something else on her mind that night: her eight-year-old daughter, tucked away in the rolling hills of West Virginia. Kat had conceived Misti when she was just thirteen. She'd handed the child over to her mother when she'd left for California. Misti's father, Duane, was long dead—crashed in an Army flight exercise before he ever learned of Kat's pregnancy. She didn't miss him any longer, but her heart ached that he'd never laid eyes on his beautiful daughter.

She lived for the day when she would at last be able to protect Misti, and to care for her properly. She knew it was only a matter of time. She was talented and hardworking, and even during the worst moments, when she thought she couldn't stretch her scholarship another inch, or bear another night without her child, she gritted her teeth and somehow got by.

Every night when her golden head hit the pillow, she dreamed the same dream: she was walking down a palm-lined street, breathing deeply of the tingly scent of eucalyptus. She walked proudly, her head held high, while her lovely daughter skipped along at her side. But for now, Misti was far away, and the secret of her existence was safe with Kat. She knew that everyone—even her best friends—would only take pity on the little girl. And Misti deserved so much more than that.

Kat slipped out of the apartment as the party continued at full tilt. She walked downstairs to the moonlit street, where the air was fragrant with jasmine.

She walked a few blocks to an all-night diner, and took a seat in a back booth.

"Little Sugar," she wrote for the thousandth time: "Not one moment passes that I don't long for the touch of your cheek against mine . . ."

At dawn, Pru's alarm went off, and she awoke with a shiver in the chill morning air. She noticed Sam's bed was rumpled but empty as she walked to the bathroom to take a shower. She briefly wondered where her roommate had spent the night, but since Sam herself never gave it a second thought, there was certainly no reason for Pru to rack her brain about it. She was just thankful she'd gotten some sleep. After all, there had been plenty of nights when she'd lay facing the wall, with her Walkman going full blast, while Sam took the gold in the Olympics of love.

She went to the kitchen, and there, amidst the debris of last night's festivities, Leah sat at the kitchen table. She pecked away noisily on the prehistoric Olivetti that had once belonged to her father.

"I'll bet you thought it was my death rattle," Leah said cheerfully. She saluted Pru with a brandy snifter.

"Isn't it a little early for that?" Pru asked, wrinkling her freckled nose and pouring herself a glass of juice.

"*My* clock says it's late. I couldn't sleep."

"You should try," Pru said curtly. She left the apartment without another word.

When Leah was alone, she got up and went to the window. "Nice chatting with you," she whispered as she watched Pru get into her red Mustang. The sun rose cautiously above the foothills of the Santa Monica Mountains, and she downed her brandy. She was doing her best to forget that today was the anniversary of her father's death.

Poor Ray, she despaired. From the Bronx, he'd come to Hollywood with nothing more than his wits. For twenty years he'd dished out the best scripts that ever crossed Sam Goldwyn's desk. He never let the studio down. But they let him down. Hard . . .

Trembling in the cold, Leah wrapped her bathrobe tightly around her waiflike body. She shuddered as she remembered what he'd told her countless times.

The Cold War broke out, and the blacklist came. He'd been on the honor roll for almost a decade by the time she was born. The strain killed her mother. She died in childbirth.

Ray packed her up—diapers and all—and took her to London, where the sixties were swinging. He wrote for the BBC and the West End theaters, and even when Hollywood recovered from its madness and invited him home, he refused.

He never looked back.

They lived all over Europe for many years—Madrid, Zurich, Berlin—and he saw that her life was an endless banquet. It was wonderful to be with him, getting her education on the run, but it all fell apart on the Spanish Steps. His heart stopped, and she buried him in the Jewish cemetery in Rome.

His will provided for school in Switzerland, and after that, the Sorbonne. One evening, as she strolled the banks of the Seine, an idea took shape in her mind.

She returned to L.A. To the scene of the crime.

Cheers, she toasted him. *Rest in peace.*

She took a last, burning swallow.

All summer, Pru worked herself to the bone. In every way, she made herself indispensable to the news department at TWSP, a ramshackle outfit on Gower Street. Its news was basically all the stuff that wasn't fit to say out loud, but that's exactly what anchorperson Judy Spence did.

Squinting at the cue cards, she sat in her pancake makeup (which she did herself after the budget cuts), and read stories of canine heroes and space invaders in Pasadena. Then she did the weather, sports, and the Daily Astrologer.

For Pru, the whole pathetic business meant a long, hot

summer in the TV trenches, but she was grateful. She'd learned a lot in those three months, most importantly, she mused, how *not* to run a TV station.

One fine September afternoon, Judy Spence was propped up like the honored guest at a wake, and Pru was busily wiring her for sound, when the beeper went off in her pocket. It was the station manager, Shirley Sampson, calling Pru downstairs to her office.

Behind her desk, Shirley got right to the point.

''Harry's quitting, and I need a stage manager. You want it?''

Bobbing her head mutely like the village idiot, Prudence accepted the job.

As she floated out of Shirley's office, she realized that her brave new world was finally unfolding. She couldn't wait to call her brother, Tony. He, Pru, and their younger twin sisters had endured a childhood of neglect, and he alone understood how deeply Pru needed to put the rough times behind. As the oldest child, Pru had borne the brunt of her father's gambling and petty crime. She'd wiped away the little ones' tears when Hugh threw the family into poverty and despair. And she'd held her siblings close to her late at night, when Thelma's drunken rampages rocked the house.

Growing up, Pru had often wondered what it was like to live in a happy home. On the sitcoms, the kids didn't carry Mom to her bedroom and then scrub the couch where she'd urinated in her sleep. They weren't fat and unhappy like Pru. They didn't spend all night in coffee shops, ordering French fries and Cokes while Hugh rolled dice next door.

Finally he'd appear, his face drawn with defeat.

The two ugly scars that ran down his cheeks were deep purple against the ghostly pallor of his skin. They curved upward like fish hooks when he swore—as he always did— ''Better luck next time!''

But, of course, there seldom was better luck, and even when there was, the cash was squandered on witless scams before it ever found its way to the household coffers. That's why it so shocked Pru when Hugh came up with the money she needed for college.

It arrived one evening: a cashier's check delivered by messenger. It was enough to cover a year at Berkeley.

When Pru looked at her father incredulously, he gave her a little lopsided smile.

"I promised you could count on me!"

For the next three years, the cashier's checks arrived on a regular basis. Pru was grateful, but she never discussed the money with Hugh: she didn't want to know which line he'd crossed over for her.

On her twenty-first birthday, the bank sent a note—unsigned—along with the check.

"Ms. Daniels," the note read: "On the occasion of your enfranchisement, your patron wishes to assure you that, as long as you need assistance, it will be forthcoming."

Dad? It didn't sound like Hugh.

She went to her father and confronted him, and finally he confessed.

"The money was never from me, Pru. I only said it was so you'd respect me."

Pru went to the Tahoe bank where the checks were issued, but only the president himself knew where they came from, and he wasn't talking.

"The rules of the trust are quite explicit, Ms. Daniels. Your donor requests strict anonymity."

She left the bank stunned. For a woman like Pru, who had always had to look after herself, it was mind-boggling to think that a total stranger was looking after her.

She never went to the bank again. When she was accepted by UCLA, a check arrived—as she knew it would. So did a brand-new Mustang convertible.

Now, almost a year to the day later, the world was her oyster as the up-and-coming stage manager pulled out of the parking lot. She drove home happily, oblivious of the snarled traffic around her. As she inched her way down Sunset Boulevard, it seemed to her that the smog hung like cotton candy across L.A., and even the bus fumes that hit her in the face were as fragrant as Chanel No. 5. Prudence Daniels was on her way, and the smell of success was sweet.

* * *

In a peach satin bedroom in Beverly Hills, Samantha awoke to the determined nuzzling of something hot and hard in her back. Running her fingers through her white-blond hair, she turned over beneath the silk sheets, and her sleepy gray eyes widened appreciatively.

"I see lunch has arrived," she said huskily to her companion. She took the best part of him in her mouth and flicked her tongue across the tip as her fingers deftly stroked the inside of his thigh. When she had worked him to frenzied arousal, her mouth abruptly abandoned him, and he gasped helplessly.

"Patience, sweetie," she said, pushing his head down below her belly. She lay on her back, while his tongue obligingly flicked between her spread thighs. When she was close to orgasm, she knelt and put her lips to him again until he was begging to be inside her. Finally she straddled him and rode him slowly as he fingered her swollen nipples. By the time they were both drenched in sweat, a deep shudder coursed through her, and then through him.

"Samantha," he sighed, as she fell in a heap across his chest.

"Oh, sweetie," she answered, trying to recall his name. *You're good,* she thought. *But you're not the one. No one ever is. No one can make me forget . . .*

Sam grew up in posh Hillsborough, just south of San Francisco on the peninsula. In that tiny outpost of old money and young debs, she was given every conceivable advantage, and by rights she should have been the happiest little girl in the world. But she was miserable. She had everything that money could buy—and nothing it couldn't. There was no love, no passion, and not even a glimmer of warmth in her parents' home. Edward bought and sold small countries, and Polly—who came from missionary stock—was a one-woman Inquisition. "Captain Queeg," Andy had dubbed her.

He would be twenty-five if he had lived. From the very beginning, it was obvious that he wasn't the son the Devanes would have chosen. Artistically gifted and terribly shy, Andy quietly burned with a fire that threatened the dry brush of his parents' lives.

He was three when Samantha was born, and in the beginning, her birth took the pressure off him. Sam was a blue-eyed, athletic child whose noisy triumphs on the playing field afforded Andy his quiet, introverted life. He mastered the violin and taught himself photography while Sam pleased her parents by racking up trophies.

Despite their differences, brother and sister were best friends. She loved the afternoons they spent in his darkroom. He taught her everything he knew.

When he was fourteen, he was accepted at Juilliard, but Edward forbade it: he wanted "the real world" for his son. By the time Andy turned sixteen, Edward's Princeton pitch was in full swing, and finally, for the first time in his life, Andy stood up to his father.

He was quickly struck down. Father and son bellowed across the dining room table until Edward at last rose from his chair, walked to Andy, and backhanded him savagely across the face. Sam fled from the table, slamming the powder room door in rage before she vomited. Andy retreated to his room and hardly ever came out after that.

One spring afternoon in his senior year, he left school early, went home to an empty house, and threw his violin out the bedroom window. When Sam saw the splinters later, strewn across the wide lawn, she rushed upstairs, but it was too late. He was hanging from an overhead pipe in his bathroom.

When the police arrived, she sat cradling his cold body in her arms. They managed to pry her fingers loose, and they carried him away.

In her loneliness, Sam spent as much time as she could in the darkroom. At first, it was a good place to cry. Later, it was a place to feel his presence. She honored him in the strange red light, turning out pictures he would have been proud of.

She left home as soon as she could, attending six of the Seven Sisters. Each college was a miserable failure: she couldn't keep her mind on her classes. There were too many pictures out there in the world, begging to be taken. After a time, she stopped resisting them, and she circled the globe with her Nikon.

When she was in Rio shooting Carnaval, Vassar reluctantly awarded her a fine arts degree. They didn't know what else to do with her. She never came to class—or even to Pough-keepsie—but she sent back heart-stopping photos from her far-flung adventures.

In Sumatra, she had a brief fling with a photojournalist, and he advised her that UCLA Film School would teach her everything she needed to know about making pictures. He was right: on her first day of graduate school she cradled a 16mm movie camera in her arms, and even before she'd shot a roll of film, she was hooked.

"Samantha?"

A deep voice cut through her thoughts. Her lover—his name still escaped her—was kissing her neck. His hand slipped easily between her thighs, and she quivered beneath his touch.

Two

AFFECTIONATELY KNOWN AS ''the Hub,'' the student union was the focal point of campus life at UCLA. All over the grassy slopes that surrounded it, beautiful young women and equally gorgeous young men stretched out like cats to warm themselves in the autumn sunshine, but even in that extraordinary display, Kat stood out like a diamond in the dirt.

On the afternoons she worked in the Hub's yogurt bar, it did land-office business. There was just no keeping them away as soon as she donned her gingham apron and Dutch girl hat. Even in that uniform, Kat managed to look both sexy and sweet as she daintily pulled the udders of the frozen-yogurt maker, and pastel streams spiraled into Styrofoam cups.

Guys who didn't even like the stuff ate there two or three times during her shift. They stood around, trying to catch her eye, while Kat rang the register and silently ran lines for her acting class.

On the hot, smoggy day that Alex Hadley walked into the student union, he was tired and pleasantly achy with the muscle soreness he always got after a game of racquetball. He'd played with a Sigma Chi brother who was called Dr. No because no one ever beat him—no one, that is, until Alex.

Feeling profoundly pleased with himself, he strode into the Hub and immediately forgot his victory on the court. As if hypnotized, he slowly approached the yogurt bar, and Kat let loose with a klieg-light smile.

Alex, who was nobody's wallflower and had been known

to have his way with every girl at Tri Delta, was over his head this time, and he knew it. But, oddly enough, he didn't mind at all. Standing before him was the woman of his dreams.

"Kat," he read, staring at her name tag. He was suddenly tongue-tied for the first time in his life. "Uh . . . Gee, let's see, what'll I have?"

Make up your mind, sugar, Kat thought irritably. She was by nature a patient woman, but it had been a long day.

"Why don't you decide for me?" he suggested, and then it dawned on her that he was extremely good-looking. *And he doesn't drool when he talks. That puts him an evolutionary leap ahead of most of the bozos who hang around,* she thought.

He smiled winningly, and the monologue Kat had been memorizing for class flew from her head.

"I'm Alex Hadley," he said, extending his hand, "and— oh, hell, I don't want any yogurt. I want to take you to dinner!"

Boyish charm didn't usually do it for Kat—she'd been on the receiving end of that for as long as she could remember— but Alex caught her off guard. She was feeling a little homesick, and maybe dinner with a handsome stranger would be just the ticket for a quick trip out of her own head. She shook his hand warmly.

"I'll mosey on down to Mario's at seven o'clock," she said in answer.

"I love the way you talk!" he exclaimed.

Because Mario's was a popular spot, it was packed when Kat and Alex made their way inside. There wasn't a free table in the place, so Alex discreetly pulled a twenty from his wallet and was about to hand it to the maître d' when Kat took his hand in hers.

"Applesauce!" she said. "Put that money away. We can't eat the atmosphere, for heaven's sake!"

Holding his hand lightly, she led him out of the restaurant. As they walked down the street, a movie marquee flashed up ahead, and she turned to him excitedly.

"Can we go to the movies?" she begged.

"Anything you say, Dixie."

Before long, they were sitting dead center in the dark auditorium, happily wolfing down buttered popcorn and Atomic Fireballs. The movie was an arty European film with subtitles, but sitting close to Kat, Alex hardly minded. He just sat giddily in the dark, breathing in her grassy scent and watching the light dapple her skin as the film flickered on the screen. He barely noticed the movie.

Kat, on the other hand, watched it closely. She studied the actors' gestures and movements, and she tried to second-guess what they would do next as they reached inside themselves. She imagined herself in each of the roles, and it occurred to her more than once that she was as good as anyone she saw on the screen.

Later, at the front door of the Westwood apartment, Alex tried to kiss her lovely, full mouth, but she offered him her cheek instead. He was intrigued by the fact that this southern beauty knew her own mind. She was an old-fashioned hold-out.

"Kit Kat," he said, pointing his finger like a pistol at her. "I'll catch you later. Count on it."

Inside the apartment, Kat found Leah lying on the living room rug in leotard and tights, deep-breathing her way into creative energy. As Kat told her about the movie, Pru rushed in from the bathroom. She'd been washing her hair and, apparently, spying on Alex as his car pulled away in the street below.

"Who was that?" she demanded to know.

"A boy I met at the Hub."

"Well, he drives a Porsche, and if my cash register of a mind isn't sorely mistaken, he was wearing about two thousand dollars' worth of Bambi's mother across those strapping shoulders."

"Isn't it a crying shame," Kat sighed. "Those poor, defenseless animals—"

"You twit," Pru interrupted, furiously toweling her hair. "Now is not the time to moan and groan about our furry friends—"

"Now, Prudence," Leah stepped in. "Let's not crucify Kat just because she has feelings. They may not come in handy in the TV business, where you have to step over the bodies to get ahead, but Kat's an actress, for chrissake, and everyone knows they're a bunch of Albert Schweitzers.''

"You two are scrambled," Kat muttered. "I'm going to bed."

Pru blocked her at the door. "Not until you spill," she said. "Who *is* Mr. Megabucks?"

"His name is Alex, and he goes to the law school," Kat told her.

"Well, call me Juris Prudence!" Pru whooped. "*Please* give him to me," she pleaded, tearing into a package of Oreos. "He sounds like a man who could meet my every greed."

Kat, who was normally generous with her girl friends— she bequeathed them her cast-off suitors with hardly a second thought—surprised Pru with what she said next.

"Actually, I think I like this guy, sugar. Do you mind if I keep him?"

"Easy come, easy go," Pru sighed, wiping cookie crumbs from her mouth. "He won't be the first one who got away. I remember Mr. Douglas, my high school English teacher. What a hunk and a half—"

"Down, girl," Leah ordered. "You're drooling like a St. Bernard."

"I'll ignore that remark," Pru said. "I'm going to get my beauty rest." She took the Oreos with her.

Kat went to the kitchen, where scenes from *Streetcar* and *The Little Foxes* were taped to the window above the sink.

" 'I have been betrayed by a sexual streak in my nature,' " the actress recited as she warmed a pan of milk for her evening drink. "Can I make you a Bo Peep?" she asked Leah, stirring in the cinnamon.

"I'd sooner take a swig of Mr. Clean," Leah replied, making a face. "Watch it. That stuff's good for you."

She shooed Kat out of the kitchen and quickly assumed her working position like a jockey climbing his mount. She faced the keyboard, took a deep breath, and made the sign of the cross.

The brown stench that passed for air finally cleared in late September, just in time for the Santa Ana winds to blast their heat across the county. Even Westwood, which was usually cooled by ocean breezes, was an oven that fall.

"Adiós," said Sam as she hightailed it out of town one morning before the heat set in. She took off from the small private airport in Santa Monica. The horizon was teeming with other planes, all trying to beat the heat, but Sam was a competent pilot, and crowded skies didn't bother her a bit.

She gracefully guided the *Annabelle* past the smog layer, and when she'd reached her designated altitude, she pulled off her pigskin jacket, rolled up the sleeves of her silk blouse, and looked down at the dusty nipples of the Diablo Mountains.

At two thousand feet above Imperial County, she cruised and let her mind wander to the upcoming weekend in Puerto Vallarta. She'd booked a suite at the tropical hotspot, Hotel Oceana, and she was looking forward to prowling its trendy bars in search of some charming señor to keep her company.

That tantalizing prospect was beginning to bring a little color to her cheeks when suddenly, a thousand feet below her, she saw two Cessnas shoot through the air on a collision course. Sam watched helplessly from above; there was no preventing the imminent disaster. She grabbed her camcorder and, at the moment of impact, recorded the screaming fireball. The video camera purred away as black smoke streamed across the empty sky, turning day into night.

Her hands shook as she piloted the *Annabelle* away from the explosion. Every channel on her radio was jammed, and she was on her own as she mindlessly, mechanically flew back to Santa Monica. She circled in a holding pattern for what seemed like forever, and when the tower finally gave her permission to land, her palms were sweaty and her silk shirt was drenched.

She drove straight to TWSP TV.

"I thought you were twitching your tail in Puerto Vallarta," Pru said when Sam showed up at her office. "I was hoping to get some rest with you gone—"

"Shut up, Pru." She dropped the cassette into Pru's hands.

That evening, the horrifying footage of the midair collision ran exclusively on TWSP's six o'clock news. TWSP scooped every station in Southern California, and it beat out the num-

ber two station in the Basin by three to one. The tape ran
again at eleven, and Kat and Leah sat in grim silence as they
watched TV in the living room.

Sam couldn't watch. She moved like a zombie into her
bedroom and went through the motions of undressing. Immediately she fell into a deep, heavy sleep. At one point, she
thought she might be dreaming, but she couldn't be sure.

Why, that's not a dream, she told herself calmly at the
sight of Andy loping toward her. The wind was up, sweet
and warm, as they climbed into the *Annabelle.* Once aloft,
they soared higher and higher, admiring the huge clouds
above and the rugged landscape below. Finally they were too
high up to see anything at all. *What is this bizarre terrain,
like the inside of emptiness?* Sam's heart beat wildly as she
saw panic creeping into Andy's face. He clutched his seat
and opened his mouth as Sam suddenly lost control. The
Annabelle dived and blew a path into Andy's old bedroom.
She could see the rope, and she reached to her brother to
hold him back, but his seat was empty . . .

"Sam, wake up!" Pru shook her awake. Sam's body
jerked, and her eyes flew open in terror.

"It was just a dream," Pru said soothingly. Sam's skin
was clammy, her breathing ragged, her hair lank with sweat.
"Are you all right?"

"I'm fine," Sam whispered.

"Good girl." Pru pulled the damp locks away from Sam's
high, fine brow. "I wanted to thank you for the tape," she
said. "TWSP's not used to reporting real news. I owe you
one."

Sam smiled faintly and sank back into darkness.

To celebrate their three-week anniversary, Alex made reser-
vations at Rex, one of L.A.'s fanciest restaurants. When he
picked Kat up, she floated out of the apartment in a white
kimono she'd borrowed from Sam, and she looked so beautiful that Alex decided to stop at home on the way to the
restaurant. He wanted to pick an orchid for her hair.

He lived in the guesthouse on the family estate in Bel Air.
His little house stood next to the tennis courts, far behind the
main house with its wooded grounds and iron gate. Kat loved

the place. It was like being in a treehouse, she said—and so private. In all the nights she'd spent there, she'd never even caught a glimpse of his parents.

This evening, however, they were having drinks by the pool when Kat and Alex arrived. As Alex introduced Kat to his mother, Althea limply offered a diamond-studded hand to the younger woman, and Kat could see in her withering glance that she didn't approve. Without another word, she lost no time finding her place in the novel on her lap.

Next it was Anthony Hadley's turn to be introduced. He held forth his liver-spotted hand with studied indifference.

"I sure am pleased to meet you, Mr. Hadley," Kat drawled, and the old man winced. To him, her voice sounded like a banjo being plucked. And that godawful kimono! *Geisha's just another word for whore,* he thought.

"The pleasure's all mine," he said tonelessly as he stalked off to pour himself a stiff drink. "Swampbait," he muttered under his breath.

"Make mine moonshine," Kat called after him.

"Stop it," Alex whispered.

She kissed his ear and strolled to the greenhouse in search of her orchid. Through the shaded window, she watched Althea Hadley pull herself up from her chaise longue and wag an accusing finger at her only son. Kat watched to see if his lips moved, but to her disappointment, he said nothing. He merely stood in silence before his mother, his head hanging, his eyes on the ground.

The drive to the restaurant was uncomfortable. Kat fiddled with the orchid in her hair as Alex parked and led her into the imposing Art Deco restaurant. In a spacious booth, they made small talk throughout dinner.

Finally, after the waiter had taken their plates, Kat decided to clear the air.

"So. Are your folks as all fired up about me as I am about them?" she asked with a twinkle in her eye.

"My parents are jerks," he muttered.

"It did feel a little like *Tammy Tell Me True,*" she said.

"Don't give those idiots a second thought, Dixie."

"I don't. But I think you do."

Alex studied the dessert menu the waiter had brought. "So. What's for dessert?"

"Something sinful," she suggested. She looked him in the eye, and her mouth curved slowly into a wide smile. On the table, her fingernails brushed the back of his hand. He reached into the pocket of his jacket and pulled out a hotel key engraved with the word "Otani."

They didn't waste another moment, but walked quickly, hand in hand, through the deserted steel-and-glass skyways of downtown L.A. The city's lights twinkled below them as if they were high above the heavens, in a place where even the stars couldn't reach.

Their gaze met, and then their lips. The billowing silk of her kimono sleeves fell protectively around both of them as they kissed in their private dark corner of the universe.

Three

THE PHONE RANG shrilly several times before Kat groggily pulled it to her ear.

"Wake up, kiddo!"

"Who is this?" the actress mumbled. Bleary-eyed, she looked at the clock. Five A.M.

"It's me. Pru. You've got to come down to TWSP on the double!"

"Sugar, what is it? Are you all right?"

"Yeah, yeah—just get your ass down here pronto!"

While Kat dressed quickly, got into her Bug, and drove through the dark streets toward Hollywood, Pru ran upstairs to the booth, where chaos reigned and the whole crew was in an uproar.

"We're covered, Shirley," she assured the tyrannical station manager. "Kat's on her way, and she's perfect."

"Well, as long as she's not in a coma, we'll use her. God, I'd like to wring Judy's neck. How dare that bitch walk out on me?"

"We should have seen it coming," Pru said. "She's been griping about her salary and schedule for months now—"

"Hold the phones!" the assistant director exclaimed. "Is that her?"

All eyes looked below the glass booth at the statuesque blonde who crossed the sound stage as if she owned it.

Pru scrambled downstairs to the stage and gave Kat a quick squeeze.

"You're doing the news," she explained as she clipped a mike to her collar. "And the weather, and sports."

Kat's violet eyes opened wide as Pru plunked a black witch's hat on her head.

"I look ridiculous," Kat protested.

"I know, but it's Shirley's orders. Happy Halloween!"

Kat scowled unhappily, and Shirley shouted from the booth, "This is your big break! Don't blow it or I'll throttle you!"

Pru quickly powdered Kat's nose and showed her where to watch the prompter.

"Just watch the red light on camera one, over there, and don't be nervous," Pru coached as she settled Kat behind the news desk.

"Don't *you* be nervous." Kat smiled serenely.

"Okay, boys," Pru whispered into her headphones. "Ready to roll."

As she backed away from Kat and the cameras dollied in, Pru shook like a leaf and fervently wished she had time to go to the bathroom. But when the director called places, and the On the Air sign lit up, she realized there was no need for anxiety: Kat took to the camera—as she herself would phrase it—like a hog to mud.

In the entire "hard news" segment, she never missed a beat as she reported a tiff between Mrs. Reagan and Oscar de la Renta, then moved on to an in-depth analysis of Vanessa Williams's career. When they broke for a commercial, Pru rushed to the desk and pulled Kat over to her next mark.

She handled the weather like a seasoned meteorologist, and up in the booth, the savvy assistant director told camera one to move back and get a full-body shot as she stood against the weather map.

When she moved on to sports, there was genuine sorrow in her close-up as she reported a Rams defeat. When the broadcast was over, Pru threw her arms around her.

"You were terrific—even with that dopey hat!"

Apparently the viewers thought so too. By seven in the morning, the switchboard was lit up with calls from the public. When would that new anchor appear again? What was her name? Was she single?

Pru wanted to tell Kat about all the calls, but Kat was long gone from the station. She'd dashed off to school to make her eight o'clock acting workshop with her beloved professor, Krysta Bennett. As she sat in the classroom and absorbed Krysta's lecture on Stanislavski's sense memory, she hardly gave TWSP a second thought.

But later that night, when Pru came home and filled her in, Kat began to realize that she'd caused quite a stir at the station.

"They loved you, Kat. We got a hundred calls asking about you. Do you realize that's a hundred more than Judy's ever gotten?"

"That's nice, sugar—"

"And TWSP has me to thank," Pru said, "a fact I certainly won't let them forget!"

"Good for you."

"And good for you, kiddo, because here comes the *big* news. You're hired!"

"Hired! But I was just helping out, for heaven's sake!"

"No, Kat. The Dragon Lady wants you on the payroll. Such as it is."

"Well, thanks very much, but it's out of the question."

Pru shook her head incredulously.

"I don't get it, Kat. I thought you came here to *succeed*."

"I sure did—but on my own terms." She shrugged apologetically. "Right now I'm studying with one of the world's greatest actresses. She's sharing everything she knows with me, Pru. I can't give that up to report the weather."

"Lots of actresses have started out as weathergirls."

"Maybe, but I'm not lots of actresses. I'm me, and I've got to stick to my guns."

Pru threw up her hands in frustration. "Boy, did I get a wrong number!" she said angrily as she stalked out of Kat's room and slammed the door behind her.

The holiday season was fast approaching, but a festive mood had not yet cheered the occupants of the Westwood apartment. Pru was working impossible hours, Leah's constant tap dance across the typewriter keys had everyone a little frazzled, and Kat was a bundle of nerves at the thought of spending Thanksgiving with Alex and his parents.

But as it turned out, Kat need not have lost any sleep over it. On Thanksgiving eve, Alex called and announced that he'd suddenly come down with the flu. He begged off for the following day, and when Kat offered to run right over with a pot of chicken soup, he said no, he needed to rest. Disappointed, Kat wished him well and returned to the letter she was writing. Meanwhile, Leah was sharpening every pencil in the apartment, then chewing off all their erasers.

"Jesus, I wish I could get a handle on this thing," she said, ripping a page from the typewriter. "I hope you're having more luck with what you're writing."

Kat looked at her letter.

"This?" She quickly folded it over.

"Have you got yourself a sweetheart stashed away in them thar hills?" Leah asked slyly.

Kat blushed. "Just my mama," she said.

"You must miss her a lot."

"You're right about that, but I do my darnedest not to let it run me ragged." She pointed to her monologues taped above the sink. "This is where my life is now. I love the folks I left behind, but I wouldn't be doing them any favors if I stayed in West Virginia and rotted away like an old tree stump."

She tucked the letter into her jeans and gave it a dismissive little pat. "Now, how's about we talk turkey, sugar? It's Thanksgiving tomorrow, and I for one intend to do it up right."

They drove to Ralph's and bought the biggest tom turkey Leah had ever seen. It was frozen solid, and with Thanksgiving only hours away, Kat took her hair dryer to it, full blast. Sometime after midnight, the bird was finally thawed, and Kat grabbed a couple of hours' rest.

In Hillsborough, the Devanes' drawing room was polished to a high gloss. The mahogany woodwork gleamed, and the Kerman rug muted the sounds of the hundred guests who were gathered. An elegant Thanksgiving buffet was in progress.. A Paul Revere platter cradled the proud bird, and a Lalique chandelier bathed it in golden light.

But among all the fine silver and antique crystal, something was out of place. It was the stunning display of African artifacts on the wall above the lavish buffet. Most arresting were the masks, whose black faces spoke of a world unknown to Hillsborough. Crowned in beads and feathers, the strange, eloquent masks stood like silent sentries above the feast. They were the bounty Sam's grandparents had sent back from Africa, and they had always fascinated her.

As Edward and Polly's friends spoke in low voices at the sumptuous buffet, Sam felt like a stranger, completely ill at ease. There didn't seem to be a pulse in the whole crowd. She tried a little small talk with a couple of her mother's friends, but after a few short rounds, she knew that she couldn't bear another second. Impulsively, without so much as a ''See you later,'' she slipped out of the dining room and then out of the great house.

Three hours later she brought the *Annabelle* to a flawless touchdown in Santa Monica.

Kat was mashing potatoes, and Leah was whipping cream by hand when Sam breezed through the door.

''Diggety damn,'' Kat exclaimed. ''Aren't you a sight for sore eyes!''

''I thought you'd be at Alex's,'' Sam said, munching a stalk of celery.

''The poor thing has the flu,'' Kat explained as she led the others to the table. Pru lit the candles, and they all sat down.

''The flu,'' Sam scoffed. ''Who does he think he's kidding!'' Snagging a yam, she sighed. ''What a jerk.''

''Applesauce,'' Kat scolded. ''Alex is sweet and supportive and kind.''

''He's a *child*,'' Sam insisted.

''Samantha,'' Leah cried in, ''you are hardly in a position to talk. Your so-called men are a lineup of matadors, polo players, tennis bums, and other assorted riffraff.''

''My point exactly,'' said Sam. ''I know these Peter Pans inside out, and I can promise you—Kat's wasting her time.''

''That's great!'' Leah laughed, heaping a mound of cranberry sauce onto her plate. ''Now Sam's the judge of who's wasting time. Actually, maybe she should be the judge—she's certainly the expert.''

''I resent that,'' Sam said. ''What about the footage I got of the collision? Was I wasting time then?''

''Those shots you got were an accident, and you know it.''

''Well, you're jealous,'' Sam hissed, ''because you sit all day in front of your typewriter, and nothing comes out but drivel.''

Leah ran from the room, and Kat chased after her in hot pursuit. Pru glared at Sam as Leah's sobs echoed through the apartment. Her green eyes flashed angrily as she whispered, ''Get in there and apologize!'' Sam scowled and threw down her napkin. She padded down the hall to Leah's room and stood poised in the doorway.

''May I come in?''

Her eyes shining with tears, Leah nodded and gripped Kat's hand.

''What I said was rotten. I'm sorry.''

Leah's response sounded as though it were coming up from the bottom of a well. ''You didn't say anything that wasn't true, Sam. It *is* all drivel.'' She started to cry again as Sam sat down on the bed.

''That's ridiculous,'' she said gently. ''All those pages you throw out give you away. You're too good to settle for anything less than the best.''

Leah brightened. ''You wouldn't bullshit me, would you?''

''I won't even dignify that with an answer. Now, wash your face, and let's eat.''

Kat insisted that they begin the meal over again, starting with a long, drawn-out grace. She might have gone on all day, thanking God for every blade of grass, if Pru's stomach hadn't growled so loudly it couldn't be ignored. Finally the friends tore into their feast.

They were just polishing off Kat's sweet potato pie when the phone rang.

Pru handled it to Kat with a guilty look. ''It's for you.''

As Kat listened to the voice on the other end, she looked at Pru reproachfully.

''Yes, ma'am,'' she said finally, in exasperation. ''I'm on my way.'' She hung up and wagged a finger at Pru as she grabbed her sweater from the closet. "You knew all along, didn't you?"

"I told Shirley you *might* do it," Pru said, getting up from the table. "But I didn't promise her anything. I swear!"

"Pru, you're hopeless," Kat sighed as she picked up the keys to her Bug. "Come on," she said, pushing her toward the door. "I don't have much time to slip into my Pilgrim outfit before we air."

"Count your blessings," Pru retorted. "I talked Shirley out of the turkey costume." As Kat gave her a little shove through the door, Pru called to Sam and Leah, "Film at eleven!"

Later that evening, for the second time, the TWSP switchboard was jammed, and the next morning, the overnights confirmed what Shirley Sampson already knew: TWSP owed its minuscule success to Kat Winter. She phoned Kat with an offer.

"Just fill in on weekends and holidays," she proposed. "Two hundred a week."

"That's awfully nice of you, but I don't think so—"

"All right, three hundred."

"Shoot, I sure am sorry—"

"Don't toy with me, Kat. Five's the limit!"

"With an extra thousand for Christmas week?"

"All right, but that's my final offer—"

"I gratefully accept," Kat said sweetly.

As she hung up the phone, Shirley turned to Pru.

"Your hillbilly friend's no Daisy Mae, is she?"

"I guess not," Pru answered. She waited until she got out of Shirley's earshot to whoop with delight over Kat's coup.

Four

KAT'S BREATH QUICKENED as she lay on her back, her honey-colored hair a tangle of curls. In the dark, he touched her insistently, and she opened her legs.

She trembled beneath him as she guided him inside. Moving to his rhythm, she devoured him with each stroke. He bent his head to take a nipple between his teeth, and she moved more urgently, her breath coming in gasps as he licked the tiny beads of perspiration from her lip.

"I love you, Dixie," he whispered as her cries subsided. She reached up to kiss him, and when the sweet perfume of her hair hit his senses, he hastened his own climax, coming as she caressed his glistening back and thighs.

"I'm sure going to miss you," she murmured when they lay together afterward.

"Without you," he said, twirling a strand of her golden hair, "Aspen will be a total bummer."

"Do you promise to pine for me every single second?"

"Let's put it this way. We'll have ourselves a New Year's Eve reunion that will make you wish I'd leave town more often."

"Merry Christmas, Alex."

"Merry Christmas, Kit Kat."

As soon as she got off work on Christmas Eve, Pru started the long drive to Tahoe. It was almost dawn when she rounded the crest of the highway and got her first glimpse of her hometown. Christmas morning broke in shades of pink across the sparkling emerald lake.

This will be a great trip, she enthused. *They're not going to get to me this time. No way!*

But as it turned out, they did. Thelma was drunk when Pru arrived, and she stayed drunk the whole time. On Christmas night, in a stupor, she knocked over the tree and came close to burning down the apartment building.

Hugh didn't make it home at all. When Pru asked where he was, Thelma mumbled something about "seeking financing." That was her standard euphemism, and as always, it enraged Pru.

The amazing thing, in this domestic hell, was the way her fifteen-year-old sisters survived. Both twins got excellent grades and held part-time jobs. When Prudence asked them—as she always did—how they coped, they answered in unison, "We have each other."

Tony was doing very well too. With a degree in accounting, he'd landed a job at Harrah's, the biggest hotel in Tahoe, and he was now the proud owner of a stunning lake-front condo. He made it a second home for the twins, and Pru was grateful.

She had lunch with Tony the day she left. They ate in Harrah's elegant, glass-enclosed restaurant, the Summit. It offered a spectacle of snow-capped mountains and powder-blue sky that took Pru's breath away.

"What a magnificent view," she sighed.

"The view from here is pretty magnificent too, Sis. You look fantastic," Tony told her. "You must be doing great in L.A."

"You don't look as if you're doing too badly yourself."

He grinned. "I can't complain. I like the hotel racket, and my boss is great. Anytime you get fed up with the Dragon Lady, you can always come and work for Mercer."

"Thanks," Pru said, "but L.A.'s for me. I can't get enough of that dirty rotten town—"

She was interrupted when a red-suited messenger suddenly appeared at her side. He handed her an envelope, and inside was a cashier's check for two thousand dollars.

"Merry Christmas," the note said. Pru showed it to Tony, who offered a low whistle.

"You have no idea who it's from?" he asked.

"Not a clue, and that suits me fine." She dropped the check in her shoulder bag and reluctantly pushed her chair from the table. "I hate to eat and run," she said. "I'd rather eat and eat. But duty calls. It's time to head south." She stood up, and Tony walked her out to the Mustang.

Alex had promised to be home for New Year's, but by five o'clock on New Year's Eve, there still wasn't any sign of him. Kat paced the apartment nervously until it was time to go to TWSP and tape the special ten o'clock edition of the news.

"Have him call me when he gets in," Kat instructed Leah as she left.

But he never did call, and by ten-thirty, Kat began to worry. She drove to the airport and met all three flights coming in from Colorado. He *had* to be on one of them. But he wasn't.

When the midnight hour struck, she was alone on the freeway, crying like a baby.

At home, she collapsed in Leah's arms. "Where is he?" she wailed.

"You know where," Leah answered gently. "Imprisoned in an international playpen. Come on, let's take a walk."

But even a stroll through Westwood couldn't hearten Kat. Date palms and primrose jasmine were a far cry from the rolling hills of West Virginia, and homesickness sank in her stomach like a stone.

"I'm never missing another Christmas at home," she vowed.

The next morning, bright and early, Alex called and yammered away about a storm in the Rockies. He blithely explained that the airport had been closed and the phone lines were down. Kat—who knew better—quietly hung up and left him talking to himself.

The new semester began, and even though Alex called every day without fail, Kat refused to speak with him. Her classes with Krysta Bennett helped take her mind off her estranged boyfriend.

Kat could listen to Krysta for hours on end. Her fine-boned beauty and delicate frame belied the enormity of her passion for acting. She'd been greatly successful in her own right on the stage, but after spending a summer teaching at Carnegie-Mellon as a favor to a friend, she realized she loved the job of working with young actors.

In her six years at UCLA, she'd never had a student as gifted as Kat. When she invited her into her advanced lab, it was the greatest thrill in Kat's young life.

"I don't know why," Leah said, when Kat bounded in with the news. "Krysta's a bitch."

"Oh, Leah, that's just not so."

"Kat, don't you remember her in Acting Fundamentals, that required course? She used to glare at me every chance she got."

"That was just your imagination. Krysta liked you—she still does. She's always asking after you. As a matter of fact, just last week she was asking about your writing."

"Go figure," Leah said, shaking her head. "You know, it seems like every Tom, Dick, and Harry on campus has taken a sudden interest in my work. Red Foley's accepted me into his writing seminar."

"That's terrific, sugar!"

"Maybe," Leah said slowly. "The thing is, he's a big fan of my dad's, and he gets kind of carried away on the subject. It's pretty obnoxious. Especially"—she paused, a gleam in her eye—"when we go to bed."

"No!" Kat said, wide-eyed.

Leah shrugged. "It's no big thing. And I mean that—literally. But this is as near as I've gotten to a social life in ages, so why not?"

"Well, gee, as long as you're enjoying yourself," Kat gulped. She thought Red was as creepy as all get-out, but she kept her opinion to herself.

"Actually, I'm not really enjoying myself," Leah mused. "I mean, he hates the script I'm working on, and he's always saying, 'Ray would do it this way,' or 'Ray would do it like that.' He rags me constantly to write 'closer to home,' whatever that means. So, all things considered, he's a pain in the

ass. But he's my pain in the ass.'' Leah managed a grin.
''Beggars can't be choosers. Can we?''

On Valentine's Day, Alex showed up at the apartment with
enough white roses to fill a hearse.

''Long time no see,'' he said humbly, his eyes downcast.

In spite of herself, Kat was touched. She smiled, and he
took a step toward her. She didn't stop him, so he kissed her.

''I'm so sorry, Kit Kat,'' he whispered. ''Will you ever
forgive me?''

She answered with a shiver as he dropped the delicately
wrapped bouquets to reach around her and press her body to
his. He released her momentarily to close the door behind
him, then fell to his knees and began to undo her jeans.

''No, not here, sugar,'' she whispered huskily.

He picked her up; she was lighter than a summer breeze.
As they made their way to her bedroom, they left a trail of
rose petals along the carpet. An hour later Leah came in and
entertained herself on the couch playing ''He loves me/He
loves me not'' with four dozen long-stemmed beauties.

Sam was showering for a date one evening when she heard
the phone ringing in the bedroom. She dashed to the nightstand and picked it up.

''Miss Devane?''

''In the flesh.''

''This is Curtis Sharpe, with Cable News Network. We
liked your tape last fall of that midair collision.''

Sam stood naked and dripping water onto the carpet as she
listened breathlessly to what he had to say.

''Are you interested in doing a job for us?''

Her heart skipped a beat. ''Of course.''

''Do you shoot film as well as tape?''

''Better,'' she replied with confidence.

''Well, there's a problem with some miners in West Virginia, and we thought we'd put a crew on it.''

''I'm as good as there!''

On her way to the airport, she dashed into the Theater Arts
Library and pulled Kat away from *The Night of the Iguana*.

"Get the lead out," she ordered. "We're going to West Virginia."

The Lear jet she'd leased was ready and waiting when the women arrived at Burbank, and in no time at all they were climbing into the pitch-black sky.

"I can't believe I'm going home!" Kat exclaimed as her eyes began to fill.

"Don't get all gooey or I'll throw you out," Sam threatened.

They landed in Charleston, where a sound man and reporter were waiting. Sam loaded up the rental van with the crew's gear, and they drove north to Buckhannon. On the way, in a tiny hamlet called Frenchton, they dropped Kat off at the gate of a trailer park. Sam volunteered to drive her right up to the front door, but Kat refused.

"You folks had better shake a leg," she told them. "It's another half hour to Buckhannon."

The sun was just clearing the red horizon as Sam and her crew pulled up at the Sutton Mine. The situation was heating up fast as the strikers used a bull horn to shout out their grievances. Scabs, on their way to work, cut through the picket lines and—egged on by Sutton's hired goons—screamed obscenities at the strikers.

While Sam and her crew were preparing to shoot, a tall stranger approached.

"You be careful," he said. His dark eyes were shadowed with fatigue.

"Don't tell me how to do my job," Sam answered curtly.

"No offense intended, ma'am. But there's going to be trouble."

More scabs arrived, shouting and throwing balloon bombs at the strikers.

Someone handed the tall man a bull horn, and he strode into the fray.

With her minicam whirring away, Sam moved into the thick of things. She shot the tall miner as he raised the bull horn and instantly silenced the strikers.

"Stay calm," he told them in his deep, unfaltering voice. "We'll win this thing as long as we keep our heads and hold our ground."

Suddenly a shot rang out. Colts were pulled on both sides and bullets ripped back and forth. Those who weren't carrying guns brandished knives and threw rocks. The miners and the scabs raged against each other until the blue grass of Buckhannon was covered with a blanket of blood.

Sam and her sound man kept shooting while they ran for cover, but as they scrambled toward their van, they were caught in crossfire, and the sound man went down.

Sam fell to her knees, loosened the sound man's jacket, and struggled to lift him as sirens screamed in the distance. He was far too big for her to carry, but the bloodstain on his shoulder was spreading, and she had to find the strength. Somehow she'd managed to drag him a few feet when the tall miner appeared at her side. Effortlessly he carried the injured man to safety.

The state police arrived, the medics carted away the wounded, and an eerie calm resounded through the valley as the strike leader neatly bandaged the sound man.

"You're lucky," he told him. "Barely a nick."

The reporter helped the sound man to the van, and Sam reached out to shake the miner's hand.

"I want to thank you for all you did."

He studied her with clear contempt, and she felt his burning gaze of disapproval. "You almost got a man killed today."

"I was doing my job—"

"So you said, lady."

A shadow of disgust fell across his face, and he turned his back on Sam.

"I'm sorry," she said quickly. "I was wrong. If anything had happened to him . . ." Her voice faded to silence, and she realized she was trembling.

"I know," he said, not unkindly. He started to walk away, but she grabbed the sleeve of his denim jacket.

"Wait! May I interview you?"

"I don't think so." He considered her warily. "One of my men got pretty messed up. He'll make it, but I'd like to sit with his wife for a spell."

"Of course. I won't bother you anymore."

She picked up the minicam and walked alone toward the

van. She was about to climb in when someone tapped her on the shoulder. She turned around, and the miner handed her a matchbook from the Dew Drop Inn.

"Meet me there. Six o'clock."

"Wait," she called out as he set off for his truck. "I didn't catch your name."

"Frank," he answered over his shoulder. "Frank Steele."

"I'm Sam," she said, but she knew he wasn't listening. She filmed him as he walked away.

In the cramped trailer, Kat warmed up a can of tomato soup and set a chipped bowl in front of Marie. The silence between them was broken only by the sound of Saltines being crushed into the soup.

"Mama, we've got to talk."

"Talk is cheap, Kathleen."

"Please, Mama. I need you to listen. As soon as I'm settled, with work and a home—"

"You have a home," Marie snapped. She pushed her soup away. "Come back, Kathleen. Get a job at the mill and raise your daughter right. Think of *her* for once in your life."

"I do, Mama. The reason I'm at school, and the reason I'm going to be somebody, is for her," She looked outside at the bleak landscape of strip mines and a poisoned sky. "This is no place for her," she said.

"Well, aren't you Miss High and Mighty. You always were, weren't you. You had to have your fancy soldier boy, and look what that got you. A girl you don't pay no mind to."

"Shush, Mama. I love Misti."

"Not enough to come home for Christmas."

"I had to work."

Tears suddenly sprang from Marie's eyes. With a weathered hand, she wiped them away.

"Time's moving on, miss. A girl needs her mother *now*, not later. Come home where you belong."

"Los Angeles is where I belong."

Marie's forehead knotted in anguish, and Kat reached for her hand across the cracked Formica. They sat in silence, a silence that neither of them wanted—and neither knew how to break. There was no relief from their mutual despair until finally Misti's school bus bounced down the road.

When the towheaded child saw her mother, she dropped her lunch box and whooped with delight.

"Mama!"

Kat scooped her daughter into her arms and held her in a fierce embrace.

Five

"MIND IF WE turn that thing off now?" Frank asked.

"By all means."

As Sam reached across the table to turn off her tape recorder, she let her hand brush against his. She'd been wanting to touch him since they first sat down in the Dew Drop Inn. After everything he'd told her about himself, she felt that she knew him from the inside out. Now all that was left was to see if his strong hands were as interesting as his life story.

She paid the check, and her rental car followed his truck over the winding country roads that led back to her motel, the Wagon Wheel. She could have easily negotiated the roads by herself, but when he'd asked her if she'd wanted a guide, she'd been quick to agree.

They parked in front of her bungalow, and she walked over to his truck to say good night. They shook hands awkwardly through the window.

"I'll make sure your side of the story is told," she promised.

"I know you will, ma'am."

"Samantha," she corrected, and smoothly added, "I'd ask you in for a nightcap, but there's only a hot pot and a jar of instant coffee."

"That sounds fine, Samantha."

As he took her arm and steered her to her bungalow, she memorized his clean, piney scent. Fumbling with her key, she felt his penetrating gaze on the back of her neck, and slowly she turned to him in the dark.

By the time the water was boiling, their clothes were strewn across the floor, and the bedsprings sighed as he plunged deep inside her. Together they quickly established a tender rhythm, and after a few minutes, Frank withdrew. Sam started to protest, but he silenced her with a kiss. Then his mouth and hands began their slow, careful journey over her skin. His tongue fluttered across her nipples, and she stroked his coal-black hair as he made his way to the warm curve of flesh below her belly. Soon her breathing was shallow and, looking up to see that she was ready, he entered her again, moving insistently until, he, too, had come. Afterward he pulled her into the circle of his arms, and they held each other quietly until their breathing returned to normal.

"It's good to get lost like that," Sam said, stroking the soft hairs on his chest.

"Careful," Frank teased, biting one of her fingers. "You'll have me ready to go again in no time."

"That's just what I'd hoped you'd say," she laughed, pulling back the sheet to see that he was, indeed, ready.

Just after dawn, Kat helped Misti dress for school. Outside, frost clung to the bright patches of daffodils that were already in bloom. Whippoorwills greeted the morning as mother and child walked to the gate. Misti held Kat's hand easily. Unlike Marie, the eight-year-old girl understood that long separations did not diminish love.

"I miss you when you're gone, Mama. But I know we'll be together soon."

"That's right, baby."

Kat choked back tears as they waited for the school bus.

"Don't be sad, Mama. I'm not."

"You're a very brave girl." Kat looked steadily at her daughter. "How's school? Honestly."

"It's okay."

Searching her daughter's violet eyes, Kat didn't know whether to believe her. It couldn't be easy for the fatherless child. Kat knew the names they called her.

"I bet you can't spell 'pneumonia,' " Misti said suddenly.

"Let's see—"

"I can!"

As she proudly recited the letters, the bus appeared.

"Wish me luck, Mama. The county spelling bee is two weeks away."

"You'll ace it, Misti."

"I know," the child replied solemnly. She leaped into Kat's arms and held her tight for an instant. Then she was gone, and Kat was left all alone.

At the Wagon Wheel, Sam slipped out of bed and dressed quietly. As she left the motel, she took care not to look back: something about the sight of Frank asleep would make her want to stay, but she had business to attend to. And besides, she knew from experience that once she hit the road, she'd forget all about the previous night. Even if it had been a hell of a lot of fun, she mused.

Out of sight, out of mind, she told herself breezily as she drove to Frenchton. She picked up Kat, who was waiting in front of the trailer park.

"You look fabulous," Sam said as she opened the door for Kat. "Good visit?"

"Great."

Kat didn't want to say any more, and fortunately, she didn't have to. All the way to the Charleston airport, Sam spoke of nothing but the exciting work she'd done for CNN.

Anger raised the color in her porcelain complexion as Krysta Bennett approached Red Foley's office in the Theater Arts Building. She knocked loudly on Red's door.

"Red," she said sharply, "let me in."

"It's open."

She closed the door behind her and got right to the point. "I want you to leave Leah Sirk alone."

"I beg your pardon?" he said. He scratched his scruffy red beard and pushed his wire-rimmed glasses up on his nose.

"You heard me," she said.

"Loud and clear. But the last time I checked, Leah was a consenting adult."

Krysta just glared at him.

"Look, Krysta, my extracurricular activities are my business," he said coolly. "What's it to you, anyway?"

"You've hurt too many young, impressionable women. Leah's the last straw, and I want you to know that I'll file a complaint with the administration if you don't leave her alone."

"You know damn well you haven't got a case, Krysta. I don't fuck minors, and the rest is—as I've already said—*my* business."

"We'll leave that up to the dean, Red. One step out of line, and I'm in his office faster than you can say 'sexual harassment.' "

She left Red sitting at his desk, vaguely puzzled by her sudden interest in his love life. *She probably has the hots for me herself,* he thought. But he decided he'd better watch his step just in case.

When Leah stopped by later that afternoon, he kept the door open during their appointment. And the plans they made to see each other later that night were, he said, strictly between them. Leah, who loved a little intrigue, readily agreed. They talked briefly about the new pages she'd written, and he advised her as he always did.

"Find your voice, Leah. Write the story that only you can write."

"Here we go again," she said irritably. "Quit spinning your record, Red. I'm history." She rose and made a silly face at him, then smiled and blew a kiss whose heat hit him like a flashfire set to his beard.

Later that evening, he couldn't stop rhapsodizing about Leah's father as they watched one of his old films on the VCR.

"Give it a rest, will you?"

"What are you talking about?"

"Stop idolizing him."

"That's ridiculous, Leah. I don't 'idolize' your father." He started rubbing the back of her neck. "It's you I worship . . ."

"Forget it, Red. I'm going home."

Back at the apartment, she poured herself a shot of brandy,

then sat down at the typewriter and forgot all about her anger as one word led to another.

Sam was a sudden sensation—with offers pouring in from everywhere—when her CNN story scooped the three networks. She followed up the first tape with a background piece on the miners' history, and in her third spot, she used outtakes from the Buckhannon shoot to profile Frank Steele.

All three pieces did well in the ratings, and immediately the networks flocked into Buckhannon. Overnight Frank found himself a welcome guest in living rooms across America. There was something about his quiet strength that touched even the hardest hearts. Millions of dollars in donations found their way to the miners and their families.

In Beverly Hills, a fund-raiser for the miners was hastily thrown together by a rich liberal contingent. Frank flew out to be the keynote speaker, and the words flowed easily from his heart to the audience. But when the speech was finished and the crowd rose up in a standing ovation, Frank hardly noticed. His mind was on Samantha.

Hoping against hope, he scanned the crowd for her face, but she was nowhere to be seen. He left the podium wearily. As he went backstage, a statuesque blonde approached him, and when she opened her mouth, she spoke with the familiar cadence of a West Virginian.

"Sam's sure sorry she couldn't meet you," Kat said. "She left for Africa this afternoon."

The news hit him like a punch in the stomach. He'd had so much to ask Sam. Why had she left that morning without a word? His mind was reeling as Kat said kindly, "You probably want to catch the Red Eye . . . I think we can still make it."

But they didn't. Frank's flight had lifted off by the time they got to the airport.

"Why, you'll just have to stay with us," Kat told him, and he found himself heading for the Westwood apartment.

As Kat drove, she and Frank talked easily about the rolling hills they both loved, and by the time they pulled up at the Westwood apartment, Frank felt comfortable enough to ask her, "What did Sam say about me?"

"She said you don't know anybody in L.A., and it might be nice if I sort of looked after you. So I am," she said brightly. "We're home."

"Hi," called a voice from above, and Frank and Kat looked up at the patio, where Leah was sitting in the lotus position. When they came upstairs, she met them at the door and boldly looked Frank up and down.

"You're even better-looking than I thought," she said.

"Than you thought . . . Did Sam say something?" he asked eagerly.

"No—I meant you're better-looking in person than on TV."

"Oh," Frank said, disappointed. Kat took his jacket, then found him sheets and towels in the linen closet.

"I'm afraid the couch is the best we can offer you," she apologized.

"I consider it an honor," he answered gallantly.

"You country boys." Kat smiled approvingly. Then she turned to Leah. "Where's Pru?"

"Already in bed. If she's not at work, she's resting up for it."

"I think I'll go rest up myself," Kat said after she'd made up the couch. "Sweet dreams, you two." She disappeared down the hallway.

Leah turned to Frank. "How about a nightcap?"

The first warming mouthful made him want another. He knew that he was drinking to forget, but he figured he had a lot worth forgetting. Sam had hardly mentioned him, even to her roommates. That cut him to the quick, and the only thing that could kill the pain was a shot of whiskey, and then another.

Prattling away about her school and her work—about everything but Sam—Leah matched him drink for drink. With each swallow, she edged closer to him on the sofa. When they finally finished off the bottle, they made drunken, awkward love on the couch, and then Leah stumbled into her own bed while Frank tossed and turned, dreaming of that night at the Wagon Wheel.

When he awoke in the morning, his head was aching, and the vile aftertaste of Jack Daniel's brought back the entire wretched evening. He'd come to Los Angeles to find Sam, and he would leave with a case of cottonmouth and his heart in a sling. Facing himself in the bathroom mirror, he despised what he saw.

While he was shaving, Leah appeared with coffee and a shy smile.

"Mum's the word," she whispered pointedly to Frank as she set the mug down on the sink. "We really tied one on last night, didn't we?"

"I want to apologize," he stammered.

"Forget it. These things happen." She patted his shoulder like a sister, then called a cab to take him to the airport.

Togo was the most beautiful place Sam had ever seen. Dense belts of graceful reeds surrounded the coastal lagoons, and along the river valleys, tropical forests echoed with the screeches of monkeys and birds. As she flew her Cessna close to the ground, she felt as if she were inside the skin of Africa. Soaring across vast coffee plantations, she surveyed the young shrubs that blanketed the fields in rich green velvet. Farther on lay rows of cocoa trees, their branches laden with delicate pink blossoms.

Although her decision to come to Africa had been an impulsive one, she was glad she'd made it. Her assignment—for Time-Life Films—took her deep into the highlands of the north, where rebels from Ghana were hiding out.

She met with the rebel leader for three days, and despite her high tolerance for excitement, she was happy to leave his camp once she'd gotten her footage. Bunking down in a bomb factory was okay for a night or two, she decided, but as a life-style, it left a lot to be desired.

So, once *Rebels* was in the can, she took off for some R and R. As sunlight scattered like gold dust across the bush, she drove south to Skobode, and from there drove the winding road that led to a cluster of wooden houses—the John Wesley Mission.

The caretaker, Vonga, came out to greet her. When he spoke, his English carried the musical lilt of his native tongue.

"What brings you here?" he asked.

When she told him that her grandparents had founded the

mission, he insisted she stay for dinner. As they feasted on roast quail and plantains, Vonga explained that Clayton Warner, the head missionary, was off to Lagos for a church conference.

"He'll be sorry he missed you," Vonga said.

After dinner, when Sam got ready to leave, Vonga insisted that she stay. A recent rainstorm had left the roads washed out and too treacherous for night travel, so Sam bedded down in a simple wooden bungalow. It was full of antique furniture that must have been brought from Europe decades ago. There were paintings on the walls, too, including one of the Golden Gate Bridge.

"Was this my grandparents' house?" Sam asked. Vonga smiled and nodded.

"Sleep well," he told her, then vanished into the darkness.

Maybe it was the exotic foods, or perhaps it was simply the intoxicating African air, but as Sam slept, she dreamed of her grandparents. Young and strong, they cleared a forest with two machetes and built a chapel with their bare hands. Wary at first, African faces watched the missionaries' hard-won triumph, and after a time, the sweet strains of juju mingled with Methodist hymns into a great, throbbing chorus that resounded across the bush . . .

Sam awoke, got out of bed, and walked to the veranda. Dawn was breaking, and the fog was so thick she might have been in Hillsborough. But she wasn't. She was deep in the heart of West Africa, wanting to learn everything she could about her grandparents' life in this fascinating place. Vonga had mentioned Clayton Warner, and as Sam stood shivering in the cool morning air, she watched the fog rise and disappear, and she hoped Clayton could tell her what she needed to know.

In the second-floor ladies' room in MacGowan Hall, Leah glowered into the mirror. She coaxed her unruly black mane into a businesslike topknot, then marched out of the bathroom and down the corridor. She knocked on Red's office door and found him alone, reading scripts.

"To what do I owe the pleasure of this visit?" he asked

coldly; he hadn't seen her since the night she walked out on him.

"I'm getting a new advisor," she said. "I thought you should know."

Red was taken aback. He wasn't used to his adoring students leaving the nest until he kicked them out. Now that it was happening, he had to admit it turned him on.

"Let's talk," he told her as he pulled her into his office and locked the door. "God, you smell great," he murmured.

Nuzzling her neck through her bulky sweater, he reached under her denim skirt. He kissed her roughly, and as he tugged down her panties, she felt her will bending, and then her knees. When she was moaning so hard they must have heard her in the dean's office, he drove loud into her. As she cried out for more, he obliged. She came quickly and, laughing, threw him off.

Still swollen and throbbing, with his pants gathered around his ankles, he lay struggling like a beetle turned on its back as she straightened her skirt and strolled out of his office.

When she got home, the taste of his kiss was still in her mouth, and she poured herself a brandy to wash it away. Then she fired up the Olivetti.

Long into the night, she drank and wrote, oblivious of the concerned looks of Kat and Pru as they stopped by the kitchen on their way to bed. When she woke up in the morning on the living room couch, she didn't have any idea how she'd gotten there.

In spite of rave reviews for her *Rebels* piece, Sam was restless and dissatisfied. Her producer at Time-Life tried to talk her into other projects, and she ended up doing a travelogue on Hawaii. She hoped she'd be distracted by a scuba diver or two, and she was—but not distracted enough.

The afternoon she returned to L.A., she impulsively picked up the phone. The number she called rang several times before a harried voice answered, "Coal Miners of America. Can you hold?"

"No, I can't. Is Frank Steele there?" Sam demanded.

"He's not, ma'am, but I can take a message."

Sam left her name and number, and several days later she

was still smarting that he hadn't called her back. She thought about calling him again, but her pride wouldn't let her.

Instead, she twisted her silver and gold hair into a chignon, donned a little black dress that clung to her like snakeskin, and went out on a one-woman search party. At Trumps, she found just what she was looking for: a well-built young lawyer who smelled of Bijan and old money.

They went to his place in the Marina and made love until she was exhausted enough to sleep for a few hours. She slipped out in the morning while he took his shower, and she didn't leave a note.

Meanwhile, in the clutter and chaos of the miners' headquarters, more messages got lost than delivered, and Frank never knew that the woman he couldn't forget had tried in vain to reach him.

Six

AFTER THREE WEEKS of intense rehearsal under Krysta Bennett's direction, Kat opened in *Hurly-Burly* at UCLA's Mac-Gowan Theater. In general, college productions don't attract much attention outside their ivy-covered walls, but UCLA is the exception to the rule. MacGowan's stage has given birth to many stars, and consequently, agents flock to each opening.

The night that *Hurly-Burly* opened, every agent in the audience was glad to be there. Kat was remarkable, and even in her smallish part as an oversexed hitchhiker, she stole the show. Her staggering beauty and finely tuned performance brought down the house. By the time the curtain fell, every agent in the audience had left a card for her.

Pru's first anniversary at TWSP was fast approaching, and she decided it was high time to make her move. Late Friday afternoon she marched herself into Shirley Sampson's office and demanded a promotion to assistant director. She was flabbergasted when the Dragon Lady laughed out loud.

"Get real," she guffawed.

"But I'm good," declared Pru.

"Maybe—but you're still too green to move up to assistant director. Check back in six months."

Her phone rang, and while Pru seethed, Shirley waved her off impatiently.

Furious, Pru turned on her heel, marched out of the building, and drove home. When she arrived back at 612 Weyburn, she found Kat in tears on the couch, with Sam and Leah standing helplessly by.

"What is it?" she asked.

Over Kat's sobs, Leah answered. "Alex's parents are throwing a party to celebrate his graduation from law school—and Kat's not even invited."

"Can you imagine?" Sam hissed. "Two hundred guests—and Kat didn't even make the first cut!"

"It's not the end of the world, kiddo," Pru said, sitting down beside her friend.

"I wish it were!" Kat sobbed.

"Kat," Leah admonished, "you've known all along what you were getting into with Alex. His parents keep him on a twenty-four-carat leash."

"But I love him!" Kat cried.

"Too bad he doesn't deserve it," Leah muttered.

"Hey, ladies, I've got an idea." Sam trotted into the kitchen and emerged with a one-gallon jug of Tide. Kat looked at her quizzically, and then, for the first time all evening, her violet eyes sparkled and she even cracked a smile.

"Sam," she said with a wicked grin. "You wouldn't."

"This is just the beginning," Sam replied. She patted a bulge in her breast pocket.

Without another word, the giggling foursome piled into Sam's silver Audi, and as they sped down Sunset into Bel Air, they began to get into the spirit of their mission. Led by Kat, who knew her way around the grounds, they crept onto the Hadley estate, and before they were through that night, the swimming pool was a foaming bubble bath and the carp in the Japanese gardens had been dyed hospital green. On the wide front lawn, two marble cherubs shone menacingly in the moonlight, spitting blood-red water from their fat little cheeks.

Long after the women had left, Alex Hadley awoke to his mother's screams.

When Prudence arrived at TWSP on Monday morning, the office was in turmoil. Rumors were flying that the station had been sold, and by noon those rumors were confirmed. A posse of lawyers arrived after lunch, and they escorted Shirley, kicking and screaming, from the premises.

Up in the booth, Pru was unaware that the Dragon Lady had been fired. She was finishing a sound check when the phone rang and a deep voice told her to get downstairs on the double.

The lawyers were waiting, and they didn't mince words.

"We need a director of programming. Now. You game?"

Stunned beyond words, she nodded dumbly as one of the lawyers produced a contract. He explained that TWSP had been purchased that morning by the New York conglomerate Fischler and Associates. Fischler wanted new blood, to the tune of an enormous raise with a two-year guarantee. Pru signed on the dotted line, and by four o'clock that afternoon she was running a television station.

Congratulations poured in from all over town, but Pru was too swamped to pay much attention. Late in the day, when she finally had a minute to spare, she called home.

"Leah," she ordered. "Gather the troops and meet me at the Bistro. We're going to see just how many chocolate soufflés I can gag down."

Kat, who'd dropped by the station for a fitting, hugged Pru when she heard the good news. But with congratulations out of the way, the actress got down to business.

"I can't wear this," she groaned.

Stepping back for the full effect, she modeled her costume for the upcoming Fourth of July. It was a star-spangled Uncle Sam suit, complete with tails and a long gray beard, which she held aloft like a dead possum.

"I like it," Pru countered.

"Please don't make me wear it. I feel like an idiot," Kat pleaded, doing a little tap dance in her satin stars and stripes. "*Why,* Pru? Why *me*?"

"Ratings, my dear."

"Oh, Pru—you're as bad as Shirley. Can't I do the news seriously?"

"The news is too important to be done seriously," Pru philosophized. Kat looked at her skeptically and, with a toss of her golden curls, went back to Wardrobe and changed.

Afterward, she drove across town to pick up some clothes she'd left at Alex's. She hadn't seen him in over a week, and she didn't want to see him ever again, so she made sure his car was gone, then used her key to enter the guesthouse.

She was almost finished collecting her things when he suddenly appeared in the doorway.

"Hello there, Dixie," he said. "What a nice surprise."

She glared, but he didn't seem to notice.

"Between your play and my finals," he said, "we've been apart too long. Come here, Kit Kat."

She drew back as he opened his arms.

"I know all about your party!" she accused.

"Let me explain—"

"Explain what? That you can't stand up to your parents, not even for the woman you supposedly love?"

"Whoa, Kat. Calm down."

He brushed past her and plucked a pair of airline tickets from his desk drawer.

"One week in Maui, making wowee." He grinned.

Kat grabbed the tickets and ripped them in half. Her violet eyes were as hard and shiny as amethysts as she dropped the torn tickets at his feet.

"I'm not someone you can just stash away between fucks!"

"God, you're beautiful when you're pissed off, Kit Kat. You should flare up more often." He moved to kiss her, but she slapped his face. "Bitch," he snarled. He yanked her shining hair. She ducked away, but he came right back at her.

"Get away from me!"

He lunged forward, and she clawed his face. Her nails drew blood.

"Cunt!"

He smashed her face with the back of his fist, and her head hit the wall behind her. She sank to the floor, and the next thing she knew, Alex was on top of her, tearing off her clothes. She screamed until she realized that no one was listening.

Blood trickled into her eyes, and she couldn't see as he rammed himself inside her. She bit his shoulder, and he hit her with the heel of his hand, sending her flying deep into a long, black tunnel . . .

When she came to, it was after dark. The room was empty, and as she slowly, painfully, raised herself up, she felt the sticky wetness of her own blood on the carpet beneath her face.

Somehow she managed to get to her car, and at home she

took a long shower and had a good cry. Naked, she stared at herself in the full-length mirror. Her hair covered the gash on her head, but nothing could conceal the bruises on her arms, and one eye had swollen halfway shut.

Is there enough pancake makeup in all of Hollywood to cover this up? she wondered dully. As she held an ice pack against her eye, she remembered she was due at the Bistro.

She drove there quickly, and when her friends saw what had happened, they insisted she go to the police.

"He committed a felony," Sam told her gently.

"It's no use," Kat responded almost inaudibly. "I took a shower. I washed away the evidence."

"But what about your bruises?" Leah asked. "He assaulted you, for chrissake!"

Kat shrugged and stared emptily into the distance.

"It's his word against mine. I've been sleeping with him for almost a year. Why would he rape me? I'm his girl friend."

"So what?" Leah cried. "The bastard is guilty!"

"Leah," Kat told her patiently. "I don't have a prayer. Can you imagine the kind of defense his parents would buy? They'd roast me like a pig on a spit, and after they were through, no jury in the world would convict him."

Leah started to speak again, but sat back silently when Pru and Sam caught her eye. Kat raised a glass of wine to her trembling lips. After taking a healthy slug, she shuddered, and her eyes narrowed like a laser.

"But don't get me wrong," she said. "Alex Hadley will pay for this."

T-H-E E-N-D

My two favorite words, Leah thought as she ripped the pages from her typewriter. Here it was at last: *The Mother Who Ate Her Young*.

Red-eyed and bone-weary, she looked out the window. The stars were fading as a pale cerulean dawn hovered along the edges of the horizon. When the streetlights had blinked off and she heard the racket of a garbage truck on the next block, she trudged wearily to bed and fell asleep with her screenplay in her arms.

Seven

AFTER *HURLY-BURLY* FINISHED its run, Kat sorted through her pile of agents' business cards and began making calls. Unfortunately, each call was more discouraging than the last. The same agents who'd scrawled enthusiastic messages on their cards just weeks earlier had already forgotten her. They were never in, their secretaries were always rude, and the "assistants" who were supposed to get back to her never did.

Kat phoned her teacher Krysta for moral support, but all Krysta could say was, "Hang in there. The problem is, talent's not enough. Now you need to get lucky."

Kat was weighing Krysta's words and wondering if she'd ever get lucky when the telephone finally rang.

"Ms. Winter?" a woman barked.

"Yes?"

"Michele Gendelman."

Kat promptly dropped the phone. Michele Gendelman headed the best agency in town.

"Are you there, Ms. Winter?"

After some fumbling, Kat spoke breathlessly into the mouthpiece. "Yes, ma'am, I sure am here!"

"Jesus, that accent is really something. I guess you tone it down for TWSP."

"I can sound like Barbara Walters," Kat assured her.

"No, thanks, dear! Anyway, I like it. No one's going to forget it, that's for sure."

"Gee . . . It's awfully nice of you to say so—"

"Save it, hon. The meter's running! All I wanted to say was, my assistant caught your performance the other night—"

"But you didn't leave your card."

"For chrissake, those things are worth about as much as Confederate dollars. No offense. Anyway, I've got a couple of calls you might be interested in . . ."

The following week, Kat landed her first movie role. She was cast as a hooker in an Eastwood film that was already shooting at Warner's. She didn't have a single line, but she got to lick her lips in a close-up, show off a few square miles of fishnet, and wag her fanny until the crew members were falling off their dollies.

The next afternoon, an independent producer, Mel Walter, was watching the Eastwood dailies in a screening room on the lot. He was with the director and some junior brass, and as the frame counter clicked toward Kat's scene, the director announced, "Here she comes."

Even in her scant few seconds on the screen, Kat's face stood out like a lighthouse in a storm. Her body, however, was a different story: no lighthouse at all, it was pure siren. Any man who saw Kat on film could only wonder, Will she save me—or will she devour me? The question suggested a high-risk venture—that was obvious—but there wasn't a man alive who wouldn't fall all over himself to take the gamble.

"I want her for *Somersault*," Mel Walter ordered.

By the end of the week, he had her. Michele and the studio hammered out a contract, and Kat won her first speaking role in the thriller that Mel was shooting at Universal.

Unlike many productions, which are shrouded in secrecy, the *Somersault* set wasn't closed. In fact, it was swarming with press. This was because Mel secretly believed that the picture was a piece of garbage that desperately needed propping up in the media. If the writer and director couldn't save it, then the paparazzi would have to. And so they were invited.

Originally, most of them came aboard to interview the has-been leading man, but he quickly got lost in the shuffle when reporters noticed the blond actress with the spectacular orchid-colored eyes. Only a few of them had seen her before, those who got their news from TWSP TV.

Right away, the reporters sensed a story. Like sharks smelling blood, they moved in on Kat, and, as if to oblige them, she lit up the sound stage whenever she smiled.

A stringer for *People* really got the ball rolling. He asked her a couple of questions and—much to his consternation— discovered that she could actually put one word ahead of the other. Not only that: she had one of those cute little down-home accents *and* she was smart.

Among the legmen, this was big news indeed. Here was someone you could talk to! Kat sparkled with intelligence and folksy humor. Free of pretense, but no Ma Kettle, she was the kind of woman who would one day have all of Hollywood eating corn bread out of her hand. In short, she was a fairy tale just waiting to be told.

The eager press offered her their microphones. Film and tape rolled, cameras shot hundreds of stills, and before the week was up, Kat found herself staring out from newsstands all over L.A.

She waited several days until her mother would have seen *Us* and *People* at the A&P; then she called home. Marie answered, and after a long uncomfortable pause, Kat asked, "Did you see my pictures?"

"How could I miss them?" Marie screeched. "You were halfway undressed on every cover at the checkout. I was mortified."

"Oh, Mama, that's just publicity. I thought you'd be happy for me. I'm not doing anything wrong."

"Hogfeed, Kathleen. Now, what did you want?"

Kat exhaled deeply before she took the plunge. "Mama, will you bring Misti out for a visit? I can send you the tickets tomorrow."

"What's come over you? Of course I won't pull her out of school just so you can drag her all over Hollywood. If you want to see Misti, you'll have to come home."

"Mama, that's not fair. You know I can't stop working just like that."

"Then I guess you've made your choice, Kathleen."

Kat flinched when Marie slammed down the phone.

* * *

Six weeks after she submitted her screenplay, Leah finally got a call from the literary agency of Elizabeth Bloom. Ms. Bloom's assistant told Leah to come in at five on Friday afternoon, and Leah spent the next four days chewing her fingernails, wondering if her script would be accepted. Elizabeth Bloom was renowned as a great negotiator, and she had a very prestigious stable of clients. The fact that she'd offered to meet with Leah gave hope to the young writer. Hope was a luxury that Leah usually felt she could not afford, but just this once, she allowed herself a glimmer.

She spent all of Friday trying on clothes in an effort to come up with the right outfit. After a few dozen costume changes, she decided on her usual denim skirt and sweater.

Elizabeth Bloom saw her promptly at five, and spent exactly four minutes with her. She had two things to say:

First, *The Mother Who Ate Her Young* was a nice try, but nothing special. Leah should get back in the saddle and have another go.

Second, what about changing her name? "Sirk" was a name that sent up flags: while some people thought he was a hero, others felt quite the opposite. Perhaps Leah should try on another one. What about her mother's maiden name? . . .

Leah managed not to cry until she was alone in the elevator, but once the doors closed, she wept for her script that was a "nice try," and for the father she'd been advised to discard like an unfashionable dress. Most of all, she wept for her mother's name—a name she didn't even know.

When she got downstairs, she hurried out of the glass-and-steel tower and crossed the street to the Century Plaza. She took a seat in the darkest corner of the bar, and she didn't leave until they threw her out.

Eight

ON THE UNIVERSAL lot, Mel Walter found himself watching Kat's *Somersault* over and over. Even in a tiny role, she walked away with the picture.

That gave Mel an idea. Although *Somersault* was already half completed, he brought in a script doctor to make some changes, and Kat's part suddenly grew. It went from a walk-on to a supporting lead. As Kat performed her new scenes, the cast and crew watched *Somersault* improve before their eyes. With each line that she spoke, the mediocre thriller shot up a notch.

When the shoot wrapped, Mel decided that his best move would be to sell it as Kat's showcase, and he put together a catch-a-rising-star campaign that he took to the studio brass. They thought he was crazy; no one sells a picture on the strength of an unknown, they said.

But when *Somersault* opened, they were proven wrong: the public flocked to the picture. At openings across the country, box-office records were set. When reporters asked the people on line why they were there, the answer was always the same: Kat Winter.

She promptly resigned from TWSP and watched the scripts pour into her agent's office. Michele passed them along, and Kat sat in her apartment, reading until she couldn't focus on another word. Most of the parts designated for her were purely decorative, but she knew she could handle a real role, so she plugged away through the mountains of paper, searching for that elusive script that asked her to do more than flash bedroom eyes at the camera.

"More tootsie roles," Leah announced cheerfully one afternoon as she handed Kat the latest delivery from Michele. Then she retreated back to the kitchen. After being shot down by Elizabeth Bloom, she refused to talk about what she was up to, but from the almost unceasing clatter of her typewriter, it had to be *something*, and her roommates had their fingers crossed.

Fischler and Associates made no secret of the fact that they were highly pleased with Pru. In record time, she'd turned the station into a minor, if not a mega-moneymaker. It was slowly but surely claiming viewers, and on the welcome day that it hit number one in the local overnights, Pru invited her roommates to lunch at the Polo Lounge.

Sam was in Fresno, shooting a piece on farmworkers, but Kat and Leah were thrilled at the prospect of dining in the same room where DiMaggio lost his heart to Marilyn.

The women met early, before the hordes swarmed in, and they found they had the posh restaurant all to themselves.

They'd no sooner ordered their seafood chiffonades than Pru noticed a flurry of activity at the bar. With her newly acquired nose for news, she caught a whiff of a story in the making and decided to check it out.

Under the pretext of going to the ladies' room, she drifted toward the bar and eavesdropped on a tense, tight-lipped conversation among members of the restaurant staff.

"I think we should call the cops," a busboy whispered.

Cops?

The busboy picked up the bar phone, and when the manager yanked it from his hand, Pru knew that something big was up.

It's now or never! she told herself as she headed for the pay phone to call her office.

That done, she returned to the bar, where the restaurant manager and two burly security guards crouched beneath the gleaming counter. They were too busy to notice her as they spoke in low, frightened voices that were barely audible. But even though she couldn't make out what they were saying, she could see exactly what they were doing. Behind the bar, in tense silence, they were frantically looking for something.

The hair on Pru's neck stood straight up. All this secret panic could mean only one thing: a bomb. She rushed to the table where Leah and Kat were sitting.

"Get out," she commanded in a calm voice.

"Are you kidding?" Leah asked, surprised.

"Now," said Pru. "Don't argue."

They didn't, and Pru returned to the bar, only to be deflected by the bartender. As she struggled in vain in his strong grip, she heard a huge sigh of relief. Suddenly the manager rose from behind the bar. In his hands he held a small alarm clock, and Pru saw the note that was taped to its face: FOOLED YA! The manager pocketed the evidence and scurried away with his security guards. Pru tried to follow, but the bartender held her back.

"I'm sorry, miss. This is what they pay me for," he apologized.

"Prudence!" a voice yelled. Her news crew had arrived. Pru struggled free of the barman and ran to meet them.

"A hoax ain't news," the cameraman said irritably when Pru told him what had happened. "I was filming a perfectly good story in Culver City, and you dragged me up here for a false alarm!"

"It looked major," Pru said curtly. "Come on, let's go find the manager and get to the bottom of this."

She felt a hand on her shoulder and spun around; the manager looked at her coldly.

"This is private property," he said. "You're welcome to stay and finish your lunch, but the camera crew will have to leave."

"I want to know what happened," Pru said.

"Nothing happened," the manager answered. "Please don't force me to call the police."

Her crew got the message and took off, but when the manager had disappeared, Pru sneaked back to the bar and handed the bartender her business card.

"What's your name?" she asked him.

"Jim," he responded, glancing nervously in the direction of the manager's office.

"Well, Jim, any time you want to talk—"

He waved her away and, with shaky hands, resumed his task of slicing limes.

"See you," she said. He didn't answer, and she left.

Outside, Leah and Kat were waiting. "What the hell is going on?" Leah asked when Pru had led them back inside to their table.

"A big fish," Pru said. "But it got away, so let's forget it. I'm famished."

She started on her chiffonade, and her mystified friends followed suit, but they'd hardly snagged their first shrimp when an overfed fan from across the room spotted Kat. She waddled over with a napkin for her to sign, and the young actress hastily scrawled her name. As the fan gushed her thanks and lumbered away, Pru looked exasperated.

"I chose this place because I thought it was too discreet for that sort of thing," she said.

"Are you teasing?" Kat exclaimed, her amethyst eyes sparkling. "I love it! But I don't think I'll ever get used to it," she added modestly.

"You'd better," Leah said. "You're not in this for the privacy, you know."

"Speaking of privacy," Pru asked, swallowing a mouthful of king crab, "how's life after Red?"

"Running on empty." Leah signaled the waiter for another glass of wine.

"Uh-oh," said Pru. "We'll have to carry you out of here."

Leah laughed. "I'm just greasing the gears for another long afternoon behind the wheel."

That evening, as Pru was calling it a day at TWSP, she got a call from Jim at the Polo Lounge.

"I don't know why I'm calling you," he said. "But I had to talk to someone. There's been another bomb threat. My boss won't call the police—he says it's just a crank—but I'm not so sure . . ."

"I'm coming over."

Pru hung up and pulled together a news crew. Unfortunately, the crew didn't arrive at the hotel in time to film the manager as he removed a second clock from the ladies' room. However, the crew *did* get coverage of the cops who showed up, thanks to Pru's tip. The footage of the cops, plus later film of Pru chasing after the elusive manager, made a dandy scoop for the eleven o'clock news.

At one point, Pru considered not running the spot, because a bomb squad detective told her that these stories sometimes inspired copycats. "You don't want to plant the suggestion in some weirdo's mind," he warned. Pru heard him out, but she wasn't buying. She felt that the public deserved to know the truth: a prominent hotel was covering up bomb threats at the possible expense of the public.

She went on the air with her story, then sat back and watched her ratings climb.

The following day, a bomb tore through the heart of the Polo Lounge, demolishing the bar and shattering almost every window in sight. Tables and chairs lay strewn across the floor in splinters, and the white linen tablecloths were spattered with blood. Jim was killed, and seven others were seriously injured.

Pru received a note from the bomber:

"I'll be in touch when I'm ready for my close-up."

Pru called her assistant in and dictated her resignation. She signed it with a trembling hand; then, like someone in a dream, she boxed up her office and packed her car.

She got home but could not remember driving there.

In the empty apartment, she swallowed a Valium, then went back to her car. Mechanically, she put it in gear and drifted like a ghost through the L.A. traffic.

Blind and dumb to the world around her, she felt no trepidation as she merged onto the freeway doing sixty. She neither knew nor cared how long she'd been driving when suddenly, on the hood of the Mustang, Jim the bartender appeared before her, pounding his fists on the windshield. His skin was flying like streamers from his body, and he screamed Pru's name over and over as his charred fists smashed the glass in front of her.

The Mustang careened across three lanes of traffic and sailed through the air, then bounced into a field as it gathered flames. When it finally exploded, it burned like some peculiar sun, bright in the blackness of the night.

* * *

Sam flew Leah and Kat up to the hospital in Tahoe, where the twins and Tony kept vigil at Pru's bedside. She was comatose, and with tubes leading in and out of her, she seemed to be cradled in the arms of a giant octopus. Under the oxygen mask, accompanied by the gentle gurgle of the life-support system, her battered body breathed almost imperceptibly.

As her friends stood in silence around her bed, Pru's mother came weaving in, clutching her husband. No one spoke; the only thing now was to wait and hope. When a nurse appeared and told everyone to leave, the women silently filed out of the room. At the door, Leah blew a kiss across the room.

Sam and Kat bought a month's worth of groceries for the family, and while Kat baked casseroles and froze them, Sam and Leah cleaned. They dusted, vacuumed, and cleared out all the empty whiskey bottles that cluttered the apartment. As Leah piled them into the garbage can, she stood in the chill evening air and a series of shivers danced along her spine.

When the house was in order and the soothing aroma of Kat's chicken soup wafted through the rooms, the women knew they had done all they could. Whatever happened now, it was out of their hands. They flew back to Los Angeles, where Leah hit the typewriter with everything she had, as if the clatter of keys could drown out her fears for Pru. Kat continued to read scripts, but the words on the pages ran together as she wept for her friend.

A week passed. Late one night, the women were morosely picking through containers of Chinese takeout when the phone rang. Kat picked it up. Sam and Leah watched guardedly as she listened for a long time. Finally her face broke into a smile. She thanked the caller and hung up.

"That was Tony," she said, her voice breaking with emotion. "Pru's going to make it."

Unaware that her friends in Westwood were tearfully embracing each other with joy, Pru slowly opened her eyes in her hospital room. For the first time since the accident, she could actually focus them. And what she saw was a handsome, dark-haired man standing at the foot of her bed. His cornflower eyes looked familiar, but it wasn't until a wide grin lit up his suntanned face that she pushed through the cobwebs of her mind and remembered who he was.

"John Douglas," she whispered incredulously. Her voice sounded strange to her, as if it belonged to someone else. And, in a sense, it did. She was different now.

He moved closer toward her, knelt beside her, and took her hand in his. His touch was knowing, like a blind man's.

"I love you," he said almost fiercely. "I always have." She squeezed his hand, and as tears drew shiny ribbons down her face, he gently brushed them away with his lips.

Nine

Fall 1984

WITH JOHN DOUGLAS cheering her on, Pru began to recover. Her fractured leg and collarbone started to mend nicely, and as the weeks went by, the headaches brought on by her concussion had all but disappeared. And on top of her rapid recovery, she had lost so much weight on the hospital diet that she was practically svelte.

"It's a miracle," the therapist exclaimed one morning as she witnessed Pru's long, sure strokes in the hospital pool. "You're swimming like a mermaid."

As she spun through the water, Pru's mind floated back to that day in the hospital when John stood before her after a six-year absence.

Fresh out of college, he had been her English teacher in her senior year of high school, and she'd had a schoolgirl crush on him from the moment she set foot in his classroom. She was inspired by him to work hard and set her sights high, and when it came time to choose a college, she took his advice and applied to Berkeley. When she got her letter of acceptance in the mail, it was John she sought out to share the good news.

When she left Tahoe for Berkeley, and during the following years while she was busy at school, she often thought fondly of John. The innocent crush she'd had on him was one of the happier experiences she'd known while growing up.

She'd never dreamed that her feelings were returned, but they had been all along, and when John read about her accident in the *Tahoe Tribune*, he realized he could no longer deny them. As he rushed to her bedside and boldly confessed his love, he knew right away that he'd done the right thing. A flicker of light sparked in Pru's green eyes, and after her long darkness, she burned once again with life and hope.

By late October she was out of the hospital and recuperating at her brother Tony's lakefront condo. Sitting on his deck and listening to the waves lap gently against the pier, she thrived. Pine-scented breezes renewed her, and the lake's sparkling surface filled her with serenity. In the hush of the woods, she waited each day for John's visit.

He'd practically moved into Tony's with her. He came over every day after school and made simple suppers, then graded papers while she read books he brought from his library. Afterward, they talked late into the night.

She was not yet allowed to make love, but John said he didn't mind; he could wait as long as it took. Pru, however, wasn't sure she could wait that long, and one evening she asked John to carry her from the living room to her bed. He carefully laid her down among the pillows, then tenderly used his tongue to explore between her legs. His cautious kisses grew bolder and deeper until at last she shuddered in his arms and fell into a deep, healing slumber.

With days and nights like this, Pru felt she couldn't possibly be happier. But one thing was missing from her life: she was dying to get back to work. Her counselor at the hospital had helped her to realize that the bombing at the restaurant wasn't her fault, and Pru was eager to do something challenging. Even though she had John, she missed her career. She missed her friends, too, and her phone bills to 612 Weyburn were staggering, but at least she kept up with news from the home front.

Kat was in *As You Like It* at the Westwood Playhouse. Shakespeare wasn't exactly a "career move"—at least that's what her agent said repeatedly—but the actress had gotten sick and tired of waiting for the perfect script to come her way. Besides, Kat's heart was in live theater, and every moment that she spent onstage utterly fulfilled her.

Sam seemed to be in a state of limbo. In spite of her success with *Rebels* and a host of other pieces, she was clearly at loose ends, and as Leah gravely confided to Pru, "She seems awfully depressed. I don't think she's picked up anyone in at least at week."

Pru's roommates were thrilled by the progress reports on her burgeoning romance with John, and they were equally thrilled by her news in early November that she'd been hired by Harrah's to produce an industrial film. The hotel wanted something that would teach employees how to spot card counters at the blackjack tables.

Pru was getting around on crutches by now, and she hired a crew, leased a sound stage, arranged for some location shooting at the hotel, and cast her actors.

Suddenly it seemed as if everything was going to be all right again. Two days into production, John dropped by the set late one afternoon, and Pru took him into her makeshift office adjoining the Stateline Cabaret. They sat drinking coffee from a thermos and listened to the orchestra as dancers warmed up on stage for the early show. Pru rambled on excitedly about the film, and midway through a sentence, John silenced her with a kiss.

"Will you marry me?" he asked.

She said "yes" practically before the words were out of his mouth, and then she added with a smile, "Will you please lock the door?"

"Are you sure?" he asked.

"Doctor's orders. All systems go."

He turned the lock, then eased her down onto the plush carpet. Tenderly they undressed each other. She took him in her mouth and aroused him slowly. When gooseflesh appeared on his thighs, she covered his body with hers. As she guided him inside her, he moaned urgently, then paused.

"I don't want to hurt you," he said softly.

"You won't," she breathed. Her hips moved to the tempo of his thrusts.

Groaning with pleasure, he lifted his head to kiss her hair, eyes, and throat. Then slowly he withdrew from her, and inching his way down her alabaster skin, he left a trail of tiny kisses from between her breasts to the satin-smooth skin of her inner thighs. She writhed against his mouth, and when she knew she could not wait a second longer, she pulled him on top of her and he entered her again. Over her passion-filled cries, the cabaret orchestra launched into an overture, and they came together as "Evergreen" faded to a single note.

The day before Christmas, Sam phoned Pru from the airport. Feeling footloose and fancy free—her parents were at their Santorini villa for the holidays—she'd decided to check out the one-armed bandits.

When Pru met her at the airport, she didn't like the way Sam looked. She was pale and drawn, and even her dazzling mane had lost some of its luster.

"So, kiddo," Pru said as they sat down at a table in the Sky Room Bar. "What's up? You look awful."

Sam sighed miserably. "I can't believe it," she said. "I've got man trouble."

"The only man trouble you could possibly have is if the supply ran out," Pru teased, glancing around at the airport travelers. Even though Sam was wan and tired-looking, every male eye in the place was giving her the twice-over.

"I'm not kidding, Pru. This is serious. It's that guy in West Virginia—Frank Steele. I just can't get him out of my mind."

"Then why try?"

"Because it's nowhere, Pru. I haven't seem him in eight months, and he's never even called." She paused and then added, "It's worse than that. He didn't return the call I made to him in August."

"So call him again."

"But he ignored my last call."

"No one in his right mind ignores you, Sam. There must be some mistake. Call him again. What have you got to lose?" Sam hemmed and hawed, and suddenly the freckles danced on Pru's nose as she laughed merrily. *"You're scared,"* she chortled.

"I am not," Sam protested.

"Honestly, Sam, you're the only person I know who climbs glaciers, jumps out of airplanes, and snorkels in shark-infested waters. But when it comes to dialing some guy's number, you act like a wimp."

"I am *not* a wimp," Sam said huffily.

"Prove it," Pru challenged.

Sam gave her friend's hand a squeeze. "I'll do just that," she said.

Little did she know as she flew across Kentucky, hours later, that Frank Steele lay in a pool of blood. A Sutton Company goon had shot him in the back, and the bullet was lodged in his spine. His oldest friend and union brother, Patrick Adkins, died on the spot.

At the same moment that Sam landed in Charleston, Frank was wheeled into surgery. The medical team did what it could, but they couldn't remove the bullet with the patient in such trauma. His blood loss was profound, he'd lapsed into a coma, and the doctors were almost certain he would be paralyzed from the waist down.

While Sam sped along the icy mountain roads, heading toward Buckhannon, Frank's sister Nora was informed that he probably would not survive the night. Nora sat as still as a stone, staring at Frank's broken body through the glass window of the intensive care unit.

As Sam drove into Buckhannon, the news of the shooting came over the radio, and she whipped frenziedly through the streets until she found the hospital.

She wept at the sight of Frank, his face gray as death. She beat her fists against the hospital wall, sobbing inconsolably. Before her lay the only man she desperately wanted to love, and he was slipping through her fingers . . .

"Don't die," she whispered. "You have to fight."

Suddenly a bony finger bore like a bullet into her shoulder.

"Murderer!" Nora snarled. "Haven't you done enough?"

"Me?"

"You think I can't smell one of your kind?" Nora growled. "You reporters got him shot! If you hadn't made him a hero, Sutton would have had no reason to kill him."

"That's not true!" Sam cried.

Nora grabbed her by the throat, and it took two orderlies to pull her off. Sam ran from the hospital with Nora's shrieks echoing in her skull. *Murderer! Murderer!*

She drove blindly to the airport and flew home.

Three days later, she saw the news on TV: Frank had

beaten the odds. He would live. Sam was overcome with relief, but she quickly changed the channel; she didn't want to hear any more about him. That chapter in her life was over. As far as she was concerned, Nora was right. Sam *was* poison, and whatever got close to her could only suffer for it.

In late January 1985, Pru wrapped the film she'd made for the casino, and with the cast off her leg and her physical therapy completed, she was just marking time until she and John moved to L.A. at the end of the school year.

Even though the film had been a small project, making it had taught her something she already knew: her heart was in movies, not TV. She'd paid her dues at TWSP by turning a laughingstock into a moneymaker, and now she was ready for the truly big time: the silver screen. But unfortunately, she had to wait until John's teaching contract was up.

She tried to be patient, but day-old copies of *Variety* couldn't satisfy her. On the phone, her friends sensed her increasing anxiety, and finally they decided to surprise her with a visit. They flew to Tahoe in Sam's plane, and Pru was delighted to see them. She sympathized with Leah's travails at the typewriter, and was pleased to hear that Kat had at last found a script she wanted to do. It was something set in the buckle of the Corn Belt, and Kat hoped it would make her a success.

"You're already a success," Pru laughed. But Kat seemed a little bit down in the dumps, despite the fact that *As You Like It* had moved downtown to the prestigious Mark Taper Forum. Moreover, Kat had recently won the award for best actress from the L.A. Drama Critics Circle.

"So, what's the beef?" Pru asked her.

"No beef," Kat said.

"Not true," Sam sighed. She draped an elegant arm around Kat. "We're sob sisters," she informed Pru. "Both looking for love!"

"And one of you is finding it in all the wrong places. Right, Sam?" Leah asked pointedly. She turned to Pru. "Without you keeping tabs on her, Sam's moved the Rams into your old room."

"I have not," Sam protested. "Besides, my affairs are none of your business. You're just jealous—"

"Now, ladies," Pru reproved. "Knock it off."

"Pru's right," Kat declared. "I hate it when we fight." She had all the fighting she could stand with Marie. "Truce," she decreed, and she pushed Sam and Leah into each other's arms.

Valentine's Day finally came, and the wedding took place in a tiny chapel overlooking the lake. After her weight loss in the hospital, Pru looked stunning in a floor-length gown. The white silk lovingly caressed her new, slinky figure, and it hugged her slim thighs as it flowed to the floor.

Surrounded by hundreds of gardenias, she and John stood at the altar, their hands entwined through the bridal bouquet of tiny white roses. As the minister began to speak, Pru was touched to see tears fall silently down John's cheeks.

In the front pew, her friends were crying, too, but not as silently as the groom. No matter how hard they tried to control themselves, Kat and Leah couldn't quell their sobs. Even Sam fell apart at the kiss and sniffled loudly as the newlyweds sailed out of the church.

The reception was held at Harrah's. Tony's boss had generously donated a banquet room, use of the staff, and even a lavish dinner. Pru was stunned by the kindness of this man she'd never met, and she stole up to the executive suites right after dessert to thank him in person. He wasn't around, so she left a note with his secretary. Then she returned to her party and danced until after midnight.

When it was time for the newlyweds to leave their guests and depart for a brief honeymoon, the wedding party gathered around Pru as she giddily threw her bouquet into the air. Strangely, as it sailed overhead, it managed somehow to snag itself on the chandelier.

The women booed with fervor, but in truth their heckling was all an act. None of them was ready to catch the bouquet, and each was secretly relieved that it hadn't landed in her lap.

Ten

SHORTLY AFTER PRU'S wedding, Sam turned down a plum of a job at CNN. She was thrilled when they called, but as soon as the producer told her what he had in mind, she immediately bowed out. He wanted an hour-long special on the miner's strike, which had emerged as the red-hot labor issue from coast to coast. He offered Sam her choice of crew and a flattering salary, but her answer was firm: "No, thanks."

Every night since seeing Frank in the hospital, she'd dreamed of the shooting. And every night she awoke to the sound of his sister's accusation. *Murderer!*

Her only recourse was to forget him completely. The night Dan Rather announced to the nation that Frank Steele would soon leave the hospital, on his own two feet, Sam switched off the set.

"Hey—" Leah protested. But the look on Sam's face told her to forget it.

In Tahoe, it dawned on Pru that her previous job producing Harrah's industrial film had been a one-time godsend. There wasn't any other film work around, and she found herself to be a lady of leisure. At first it was a novelty, and she had a wonderful time. She lunched every day with Tony at the Summit, and she took the twins shopping whenever they were free. By March, she knew the inside of every mall from Reno to Sacramento—and by April, she wished she didn't.

In the interest of self-improvement, she enrolled at the local community college. She took bonsai classes, pottery classes, and several cooking classes with menus from around the world.

Her favorite class was Mastering Viennese Pastry, and she quickly got into the habit of presenting John with those whipped-cream-topped extravaganzas that make men happy—and women fat. They looked as if they were filled with air, but Pru knew better; they were really filled with calories, and each one settled on her expanding hips.

Pru cursed under her breath as she assessed the return of her Rubenesque figure in the bathroom mirror. She felt defeated, but John, like all new husbands, said, ''Now there's more of you to love.''

And he proved it in bed. As empty as Pru's days were, her nights with John were overflowing with the taste and touch of bodies that belonged together. For both of them, the long search was over.

Leah could no longer avoid the unwelcome truth. The small estate her father had left her was dwindling, and she needed money. She took a job as a cocktail waitress at Ports.

The trendy bar and grill was right across the street from Sam Goldwyn Studios, so it was frequented by Industry types—producers, agents, actors, and writers. As Leah brought their drinks and eavesdropped on their conversations, she envied her customers. There were the glitterati who turned their merest fantasies into million-dollar movies. They were living their dreams, and even if—for the most part—their dreams were profoundly pedestrian, at least they weren't the nightmare her own life had become. She wrote and rewrote all day long, revising sentences practically before they were put down. It was a lonely, endless process. Nothing she did satisfied her, and every day she came to work in a state of frustration. Things didn't improve much on the job, where drunks hassled her and Industry high-rollers often left meager tips.

One balmy evening in May, after taking abuse all night, Leah finally served last call and left the bar with a sigh of relief.

She stood on the corner of Santa Monica and Formosa,

waiting for the light to change. Her beat-up Volvo was parked a block away, on a side street, and as she walked to it, she had the oddest sensation that someone was following her in the dark. She spun around quickly but saw no one behind her. She thought about running back to Ports and asking the bartender to escort her, but by then she was more than half-way to her car.

Picking up the pace, she moved into the middle of the dimly lit street and struggled to get her keys out of her purse. She heard footsteps behind her, and she started to trot, but suddenly the footsteps were upon her, and she felt an arm encircling her throat. A steel blade glinted in the darkness, and a deep voice warned in her ear, "Give me your money, or I'll kill you." Instinctively she bit into the wrist in front of her face, and as the mugger yelped in pain, she ran for her life.

Screaming for help, she tore down the middle of the street, and she'd almost made it to the bright lights of Santa Monica Boulevard when her attacker overtook her and shoved her to the ground.

"Bitch!" he spat. Behind his ski mask, his eyes burned her like a branding iron, and she knew she was about to die.

Only later, when a strong hand gripped her arm and pulled her to her feet, did she realize that she was still alive. Her heart was beating so rapidly it hurt, and slowly she understood: the terrible chime that was ringing in her ears—the chime she'd taken for death's knell—was the sound of the shot that had killed her attacker. He lay in the street, blood rushing from his chest into a sewer drain.

"You're safe now," a voice told her. Trembling, she looked up, and a rugged, sandy-haired man stood before her.

"L.A.P.D.," he said kindly. As he showed her his photo ID, her body quaked with the memory of terror.

"Thank you," she stammered, reading the ID. "You saved my life, Officer O'Reilly."

"Mick," he told her.

He led her to his car, settled her in the front seat, and then radioed his precinct. As they waited for the ambulance, Leah gradually began to comprehend what had just happened, and once she did, she passed out and fell against the dashboard.

When she came to, Mick was cradling her, and there was a vial of smelling salts in his hand.

"I wondered when it would hit you," he said gently. He rocked her in his arms and told her, "That's the ticket. Let it out."

When she'd cried herself dry, he took off his sports jacket. He swept her shining black hair off her neck and covered her shoulders with the jacket.

"Where to?" he asked. "I'm taking you home."

When they pulled up in front of her apartment, she stared into the shadows and gripped his arm in fear. He understood, and he walked her up the stairs to her door. While he held her steady, she unlocked it.

"Is your husband here?" he asked as they entered the silent apartment.

"Roommates," Leah answered shakily. She sank into the sofa.

He turned on a lamp, then disappeared into the kitchen and came back with a bottle of bourbon. He poured a shot and placed it carefully in her hands. She downed it quickly, and as soon as the fiery liquid hit the back of her throat, she felt a sudden dizziness and her body went limp. She surrendered to fatigue, and as she slumped against Mick, he kneaded the tension from her frail neck and shoulders. She fell easily into a deep slumber.

When her breathing grew regular, and he was sure she was asleep, he tucked a pillow under her head, and pushed the black ringlets from her pale face. Then he turned out the light and made sure the door was locked behind him as he left.

Kat finished her run at the Mark Taper Forum, and with just three weeks left before shooting *Hawkeye* in Iowa, she decided to take action. It was time to buy a house.

She spent all of her spare time searching, and finally she found the perfect one. It was an elegant Spanish hacienda perched high on the steep slope of Nichols Canyon. There was a hot tub and a Swedish sauna, and every window in the house offered a breathtaking view. As she stood in the back doorway, she could just picture Misti splashing in the pool and Marie puttering in the garden.

She made an offer, and it was readily accepted. The deal closed just a few days before she was scheduled to leave for Des Moines. Her starstruck broker hand-delivered the papers.

"I want you to know," she told Kat, "we can put you in touch with a highly reliable and discreet security management team."

"Well, that's sure nice of you, but I don't think so," Kat replied with a smile.

"But, Ms. Winter, a star of your stature—"

"Can't live like a billy goat, can I?" Kat said. "All fenced in, that's not for me!"

That night, she sat with Leah and Sam on the tiny balcony of the Westwood apartment. As usual, it was flying a colorful assortment of lingerie. Kat looked down the hill at Westwood Village, and when she spoke, her voice was laced with melancholy.

"I can't believe I won't be coming home to you all," she said. As she gazed inside the cramped apartment where she'd had so many good times, a tear rolled down her cheek. "I'm sure going to miss this place."

"Then, honey, you've got lambswool between your ears," Leah drawled. "I'll bet where you come from they've got outhouses nicer than this."

"Well, now that you mention it, Mt. Vernon it ain't . . . You know," Kat said, getting an idea, "I'd be awfully obliged if you two wanted to move into Nichols Canyon and keep an eye on things while I'm gone."

"I'll pass," Sam said promptly. "No house-sitting for me. I like to be ready to take off at a moment's notice."

"Take off what?" Leah asked. She turned to Kat. "Maybe I could do it. I never go anywhere, and I could certainly use some peace and quiet." She gave Sam a sidelong glance. "Miss Roundheels here has a revolving door in her room."

"Better that than the life of a saint," Sam shot back.

"You know," Leah told her with a narrowed gaze, "I'm . . . I'm going to miss the hell out of you!"

She gave her a hug, then went to her room to pack.

Eleven

SAM DECIDED TO throw a two-pronged dinner party. She wanted to welcome Pru and John to L.A., and also to bid farewell to Kat on the eve of her venture into the heartland. She chose Yamashiro's for its sheer beauty. The Japanese restaurant was nestled on a graceful crest of the Hollywood Hills, and from its candlelit terrace, all of L.A. shone brightly at its feet.

"Cheers!" toasted Sam, pouring glasses of Schramsberg.

"Amen," said Leah, greedily gulping hers down.

"Enough," said Kat pointedly. "Why don't you switch to sassafras tea, sugar?"

Leah was about to tell Kat why when Pru and John returned from the dance floor. Arm in arm with her handsome husband and haloed by the light of Japanese lanterns, Pru had never looked lovelier.

"It's good to be home," she said. "Even though I never thought I'd call Weyburn Avenue home again."

"Someone has to look after Sam," Leah remarked. "Without you two patrolling the area, her sex life could set the place on fire."

"I don't know about that," Pru said, "but John and I are happy not to have to house-hunt right now. Job hunting will be enough of a headache for a while."

While the others nibbled at tempura and sashimi, Leah leaned over the balcony railing and studied the city below. Night fog was just beginning to roll in from Santa Monica, and almost before her eyes, L.A. sank into a misty golden haze.

"It looks so unreal," she said. "Like a dream."

" 'A dream in the sleep of the gods,' " John quoted.

"And goddesses," Leah added.

"Of course," said John.

"Of course," Leah mimicked.

"Leah," Sam scolded under her breath. "Back off."

Ignoring her, Leah reached for the bottle and splashed more Schramsberg in each person's glass.

"I propose a toast to tomcats and studs," she said, staring coldly at John, "to cowboys and cool jerks and manly men."

She took a long swallow directly from the bottle, and immediately Kat and Sam were on their feet. They each took an arm and "helped" Leah up from the table.

"Excuse us," Kat murmured as they carted her off. Moments later, they returned without her.

"We put her in a cab," Sam said. "She was heading for disaster."

"I'm sorry if she offended anyone," Kat apologized.

"No way," John answered promptly. He knew Kat's apology was meant for him.

"You're a sport," Sam said with a rueful smile. "A lot of people find her pretty hard to take."

"*Sometimes,*" Kat emphasized. "Most of the time she's a wonderful person."

"Wonderful, maybe," said Sam. "But happy? Not a chance. She does nothing but write. She never goes anywhere or sees anyone."

"No men?" Pru asked.

"One of L.A.'s finest calls her a lot." Sam shrugged.

"He sounds really nice on the phone," Kat said, "but I don't think Leah's interested. One time I heard her tell him, 'When I need a cop, I'll call 911.' "

"Charming," Pru sighed.

Sam's face rested on her palms as she frowned.

"It pisses me off that someone so fantastic is so fucked up," she said.

The next day, stepping off the DC-10 with the rest of the film production company, Kat was startled by the vastness of the Iowa sky. She'd gotten so used to L.A. smog that she'd forgotten what fresh air felt like. When she took a deep breath and it tickled her nose, she knew then and there that she would spend a happy summer in Iowa.

The Iowa Film Commission, which was eager to please its high-rolling guests, treated the *Hawkeye* cast and crew like royalty. In hotel and restaurant tabs alone, the Hollywood presence was very lucrative for the state, and the Film Commission did everything it could to make Iowa seem like a patch of heaven right here on earth. For her part, Kat had no trouble believing it. As her hired limo cruised the freeway toward downtown Des Moines, the yellow fields turned into shining high-rises, and Kat realized that the state of Iowa was a lot more than a king-size corncrib.

On her first night, she was the guest of honor at a cocktail party at the governor's home. The estate was palatial, and the ballroom as opulent as anything she'd ever seen in Beverly Hills. But even so, there was a down-to-earth quality about the Iowans she met at the party. She liked their openness. They seemed a lot like the folks she knew in Frenchton.

She was ruminating on this, and nibbling on a chicken wing, when a helicopter noisily touched down right behind the mansion. She looked out the window and saw a very tall, rather lean man loping across the lawn.

She opened the door for him, and the man smiled broadly.

"You're even prettier than your pictures," he said ingenuously.

"Thanks," she said, blushing, as he bowed like a schoolboy before the Queen of England. He even kissed her hand.

"On behalf of the State of Iowa, let me welcome you," he said. "I'm Governor Robert Rice, and it's my job to see that you enjoy your stay in the Hawkeye State."

"Thank you, Governor," Kat purred.

"My friends call me Bob, and believe me, the pleasure's all mine. Would you like to see my garden? I'm very proud of it."

"I'd love to."

Bob offered his arm, and as they strolled outside through the rose garden, Bob kept looking at her wonderingly.

"What is it?" she finally asked. "Is something wrong?"

"I just can't get over it," he said. "I assumed you'd be just Hollywood hype, but you're so real!"

Kat didn't know quite how to respond to this, but it didn't seem to matter. She and Bob roamed among the roses in a comfortable silence, and they might have gone on like that all evening, except that a sudden thundershower burst from the sky, and before they knew it, they were drenched.

As they stood under the cover of a wide elm tree, Kat looked up at Bob's deep brown eyes. He was worlds away from the pretty boys she met in L.A.

"Are your folks farmers?" she asked him.

"For six generations," he said. "I broke with tradition and went to law school, but my brother still grows corn over on our spread in Webster County. What about you? Have those Hollywood kingpins taken the country out of the girl? I'll bet you could tell me stories that would make me blush!"

She started to set him straight, but chattering teeth got in the way.

"Good heavens," he cried. "Here you are, soaking wet, and I'm talking your ear off."

Gallantly, he put his arm around her shoulders and led her in a quick sprint across the lawn back to the house. She stopped in the foyer to catch her breath, and as her chest rose and fell beneath her wet, clinging dress, Bob graciously looked away.

"I think my guests have vamoosed," he said. Cocking an ear, he added, "I don't hear revelers in the drawing room."

"I'm sorry I took you away from them," Kat said.

"I'm not. It was a real pleasure."

He asked her to stay for supper, and she readily accepted. When she'd had a bath and snuggled into the robe he offered, they sat before the fireplace and wolfed down rib-eye steaks and French fries.

Afterward, Kat, who had to be up at five, finally excused herself. She was surprised by her reluctance to leave the governor. He escorted her to the front hall, and when he bashfully asked if he might kiss her good-night, she answered with slightly parted lips. Chastely his mouth brushed her cheek, but in that innocent moment Kat felt the desire that ran through him like blood through a bull. Her heart was pounding as she stepped into her limo and took off into the night.

* * *

Sam stopped by the Time-Life offices to have lunch with her friend Sharon, who was a film editor there. Sharon was in a meeting when she arrived, so Sam made herself comfortable in the tiny editing room, where raw, chaotic footage was cut and pasted into Emmy-winning documentaries.

As Sam sat down to wait, she flipped the switch on Sharon's moviola, hoping to be entertained while she killed time.

The moviola groaned into action, the screen began to glow, and suddenly Sam felt her world give way.

Frank Steele was staring out from the frozen frame of the moviola. He was decked out in a black tuxedo, and the woman on his arm wore a peach-colored dress—and a veil.

Sam blinked, and tears welled up in her eyes, but even out of focus, the picture was all too clear.

Just then Sharon appeared. "You look as if you've seen a ghost," she exclaimed.

"Look," Sam said distractedly, "can we do lunch some other time?"

"Sure," Sharon replied, and before she could ask what was wrong with her friend, Sam had bolted.

For hours she aimlessly cruised the maze of L.A. freeways. Dodging trucks and low riders, she lapsed into automatic pilot as images of Frank's wedding fluttered like confetti in her mind. As she drove in circles around the Basin, an idea started to take shape in the turbulent skies of her mind. She swung by the apartment, grabbed the bag she always kept packed, and headed for the airport.

Later, as she leaned back into her first-class seat on the Pan Am flight, she closed her eyes tightly, and it hit her with resounding force that, no matter how hard she tried, she would not be able to shut out the face that haunted her. But she'd sure as hell try.

From Dakar she flew to Lomé, where she rented a Rover and began her journey out of the capital. As she drove, the musky scent of coffee plantations laced the air, and birds of paradise decorated the trees with brilliant shades of orange.

When she got to the mission, Vonga greeted her warmly. "Samantha," he said, "it's good to see you. How long has it been?"

"Over a year." She looked around at the bush and the hills rising gently in the distance. "I've missed this place."

"Then will you stay with us awhile?" a deep voice asked.

Sam looked up to see a man clad only in cut-off dungarees. Even with shaggy, sun-bleached hair, there was a natural elegance about him.

"Clayton Warner," he said, and as he shook her hand, the only thought that ran through her head was, *This guy's too gorgeous to be wasted on God!*

"I'm Samantha Devane," she said with a smile.

"I know. I'm pleased to meet you. Listen, why don't we take a ride?"

Without waiting for an answer, he squired her into his Jeep. As they bounced down a dirt road, giraffes and brightly plumed cranes dotted the watery landscape. In the distance, the Queen's Crown rose majestically above the other snow-capped mountains to the north.

"I'd forgotten how glorious it is," Sam said.

He smiled, and they drove as deep into the jungle as they could. When it wasn't possible to go any further by car, they backpacked into the teeming paradise.

In a clearing, a village appeared. Smoke from chimneys rose into the sky, and children ran to greet Clayton. As he embraced each one, he spoke to them in the strange, percussive language that rolled off their tongues in a series of short clicks. Clayton introduced Sam, and her smiles were as bashful as the Africans'.

While he chatted and joked with the villagers, Sam wandered around and was overwhelmed by the beauty of what she saw. The women wore paint on their breasts and faces, and the children seemed to be covered from head to foot with elaborate and brightly colored beadwork. Everywhere Sam looked there were hand-carved fetishes and woven baskets similar to the ones in her parents' Hillsborough home.

Welcome home, she thought.

"What did you think of my congregation?" Clayton asked later as they bumped along over potholes and through washed-out patches of road.

"I envy them."

As the Jeep passed beneath a canopy of palm fronds, she

realized that she hadn't felt so untroubled, or so free, in months. With the wind blowing through her white-blond hair and the sun warming her face, she closed her eyes and thanked her lucky stars to be back in Africa, rocking in the cradle of civilization.

But suddenly the cradle fell. Clayton's Jeep veered off the road as an antelope flew out of the bush. Skidding sideways across the mud, the Jeep upended. Sam was thrown to the ground, and only a dense growth of underbrush broke her fall. Clayton, who had managed to hang on to the steering wheel, was unscratched in the upset. He leaped to Sam's side and helped her to her feet.

"Are you all right?"

Disheveled but unhurt, she nodded.

He pulled a few briars from her khaki jumpsuit, then went to work on her tangled hair, running his fingers through the soft strands as he gently dislodged the thistles.

His hands work miracles, she thought blasphemously.

She looked at him boldly—daring him to meet her gaze—but instead he stared straight into the sun as he gestured to her to board the Jeep.

They headed back to the mission in an awkward silence that lasted until dinner. Then, over a bottle of rich Kenyan wine, Clayton showed Sam an album of photographs of the mission in its early days.

"Your grandmother was beautiful," Clayton observed as he studied a sepia portrait.

"And is there a family resemblance?" Sam asked.

Abruptly Clayton closed the album and handed it to her.

"I think I'll turn in," he said quietly. "Good night, Samantha. Sleep well."

She sat on the cool veranda alone, and after examining every photo in the album, she took the kerosene lamp into the guest room. When she was comfortable between the sheets, she lay in the dark and listened to a pair of parrots shrilly calling to each other. At one point she thought she heard her door opening, but when she raised herself expectantly onto her elbows, she realized it was only the wind, whistling faintly through the open fingers of the coconut palms.

Twelve

KAT PUT IN long, grueling days on the *Hawkeye* set. Since it was her first starring role, there was a lot riding on her performance, and she wanted it to be her best work. For the most difficult scenes, she felt she needed coaching, and one morning she called Krysta Bennett.

"I need your advice," she said. "I'm just not sure I can pull off a farmer's daughter."

"Of course you can, dear. Get to know the kind of people you're playing. Watch them carefully, learn from them. As my own teacher used to tell me, 'People are great. *Use* them.' And Kat? Try to *care* about them. Empathy does wonders for building roles."

"I'll remember that, Krysta. Thank you."

"You're very welcome," she said, pausing as if she were searching for words. "How's that crowd you run with? Are you ladies still thick as thieves?"

"We sure are. As a matter of fact, Leah's taking care of my house while I'm away."

"How *is* Leah?"

"Pretty good. Obsessive as ever. When that girl works, she gets positively feverish."

"Sounds like someone else I know," Krysta said sagely. "You both have big talents, and you've been lucky. You've gotten the chance to make your mark."

"I know. I wish Leah would get *her* chance, too."

"She will—if she hangs in there. My fingers are crossed for her . . ." Krysta's voice dwindled away.

Suddenly there was an insistent buzzing on the line, and Kat had to apologize. "They want me on the set. I'd better run, Krysta. And thanks again."

Moments later, as the stylist brushed her hair, Kat regretted hanging up so abruptly on her teacher. Krysta had sounded a little bit lonely, and Kat vowed to call her back that evening.

"Places," a voice yelled.

Kat found her mark and got to work.

Following Krysta's advice, Kat spent her free time getting to know the locals. In this endeavor, she was indebted to the governor, who graciously spent his weekends showing her around the state. He took her to a county fair and a church social, and one night they played Bingo in a nursing home. For Bob, these visits with the voters were just good politics, but for Kat, they were a way of getting in touch with the character she was playing.

On weekend mornings, Bob's driver, Chuck, a freckle-faced kid with a sunny disposition, would pick up Kat at her hotel, and she'd join Bob for breakfast at the mansion. Although these breakfasts were strictly ham and eggs and good conversation, Kat sometimes wished for more. Ever since their first meeting, when she'd felt a current of electricity pass between them, she wondered when he'd make a pass. But so far he'd been a perfect gentleman, and part of her was pleased by that. After all, she was no stranger to men who stared longingly, and the fact that Bob didn't, she had to admit, was a refreshing change. But even so, his perfect chivalry sometimes made her wonder.

One evening, driving back from a barn dance, she got her answer. In a fit of boldness, she snuggled up next to Bob in the limo. Taking his hand in hers, she brought his fingertips to her lips, and the look in his eyes told her almost everything she needed to know. She discreetly glanced downward, and the bulge in his trousers confirmed her suspicion that there was no time like the present.

As if reading her mind, Bob immediately raised the window separating the back of the car from the front seat. He pulled Kat into his arms with bone-crushing strength. He buried his face in her breasts, then kissed the skin of her throat and neck.

Kat unbuckled his belt and unzipped his fly. Her fingers had barely begun to caress him, when he threw back his head, shut his eyes, and groaned a gutteral curse as his body shuddered in her delicate hands. Embarrassed, Bob retreated miserably to his corner of the back seat. He didn't even look at her as he zipped up his trousers. He was thoroughly humiliated, and Kat's heart went out to him.

She moved next to him and laced her fingers through his. They remained like that, rigid and silent, all the way to Kat's hotel. As the car stopped, she asked quietly, "Will I see you tomorrow?"

"Are you sure you want to?"

"I'm sure." Her guileless smile convinced him.

"As long as you can stand making time with an old apple-knocker like me, I'm rarin' to oblige. I'll see you in the morning, Kat."

The next morning, the car was waiting when Kat came down to the lobby, but Bob wasn't in it.

"The governor got called to Washington," Chuck explained apologetically. When he saw how disappointed she was, he stammered, "I'm real sorry, Ms. Winter."

That week they wrapped the film and the moment it was in the can, the cast threw a party at a local club. Kat danced all night with gofers and best boys. She was jitterbugging with the assistant director when suddenly Bob strode into the club. She flew into his arms, and he lifted her off the floor and twirled her in the air, shouting, "We're *both* celebrating tonight!"

They went to the bar, where he told her he'd had a successful trip to Washington—and the night was all theirs. They slipped away from the party, and Chuck drove them to an all-night diner where they held hands and drank coffee. They talked breathlessly about her work and his, and it was four in the morning before they glanced at a clock.

"I'll take you home," he said.

"We could go to your place," she suggested demurely.

"Nice try, Cinderella, but your flight leaves at eight A.M. That's four hours from now—and four hours wouldn't be enough time to rev our engines."

"We could give it our best shot," she challenged with a gleam in her violet eyes.

"Let's wait, Kat. Let's wait until it's perfect."

"But I'm *leaving*, Bob."

"You'll be back."

"What makes you so sure?" she giggled.

"This."

He kissed her long and deep, and he didn't stop as they got in the limo and drove to the hotel. His mouth eagerly explored every inch of skin he could find, and she thought she'd explode by the time they arrived at her hotel.

"You're cruel to leave me like this," she whispered as Chuck—with politely averted eyes—helped her out of the car.

Bob looked at her solemnly. "Get some shut-eye, honey. You've got the rest of your life with me."

Before his words had a chance to sink in, he handed her a package through the window.

It was a small box.

"Marry me, Kat."

Not waiting for her answer, he raised the window and signaled for Chuck to drive. The limo snaked away into the night, leaving Kat to contemplate a two-carat diamond solitaire.

Since moving back to L.A., Pru had been looking for work at a studio, but nothing came along. It grew increasingly clear to her that she'd have to pay more dues in TV before she got her shot at the big screen. Finally, after a month of pounding the pavement, she landed a job as producer for a syndicated talk show called *Cupid's Arrow*. The show was hosted by portly Marvin Reinhart, a gold-chained psychotherapist who'd had a radio show in L.A. before he moved up to television. On each half-hour program, he talked with a couple who were having problems with their relationship. First he grilled the man, then the woman, and afterward he brought them together for a joint session. Psychiatry in thirty minutes—with six commercial breaks—was no small trick, but Marvin was a fast talker and a showbiz natural. Whatever else his mind-healing did, it made beautiful music with the Nielsen families.

However, Marvin was hitting sour notes with the rest of the world. He'd lost four producers in eighteen months, because, as he told Pru, "No one understands my ideas." As far as Pru could tell, Marvin didn't *have* any ideas, but she decided to defer judgment and give him the benefit of the doubt. She did her job well, and the set ran smoothly for two weeks before Pru realized why all those producers before her had quit.

One Friday afternoon, Marvin became involved in an unusual case: a biker couple. They were having problems because the husband wanted to cut his hair—or wash it, at any rate—and earn an M.B.A. It was a sticky situation, and unfortunately, it ended abruptly when the biker's hell-on-wheels old lady produced a switchblade and brandished it at her husband.

"Cut!" yelled the director, and Pru had to act fast to break up the brawl. After she narrowly escaped getting cut herself, she had security escort the guests to their Harleys. Then she sent the whole staff home for the day. Only she and Marvin—who needed an hour to chip off his makeup—stayed late.

In the cutting room, Pru patched together "Easy Rider II" and saw, to her delight, that the entire bizarre episode made a good show. When she stopped by Marvin's dressing room to convey this surprising news, he was carefully peeling the hairpiece from his receding hairline. Not possessing the stomach to watch, she was turning to leave when Marvin said, "Pru, you and I ought to get together sometime. Why don't you go with me to my book signing at Esalen next weekend?"

"No, thank you, Marvin," Pru politely declined.

"But I'd like to get to know you better," he said, resting his manicured, short-fingered hand on Pru's shoulder. She quickly ducked away.

"I don't think so," she said firmly. She bid her leering star a perfunctory good night.

At home, she found John upset—as usual—by his inability to find a job in L.A. The public schools had an endless wait-

ing list, and the private schools weren't hiring at all. Pru
assured her husband that there was no problem with money—
after all, she was pulling down a pirate's ransom at *Cupid's
Arrow*—but even so, it depressed John to be jobless.

Pru had encouraged him to use his "leisure" for something he'd always wanted to try—writing poetry—and he'd
been doing that. He was grateful for the chance to write, but
he found that writing was terribly lonely, and he was so hungry for company at the end of each day that he talked Pru's
ear off from the moment she walked in the door. After nine
hours at the studio, Pru would have preferred a little less
conversation, but that wasn't in the cards, at least not until
she and John finally turned out the light and sought each
other in the dark. There, words were unnecessary.

When Kat arrived back in Nichols Canyon, she found that
Leah had taken her house-sitting job very seriously. She'd
pruned the garden and painted the pool house a brilliant fus-
chia. She'd sanded and stained all the kitchen cabinets and
even built one of those wood-burning pizza ovens that were
rapidly becoming *de rigueur* up and down the West Coast.

Everything looked wonderful, but Kat quickly realized that
all Leah's handiwork could mean only one thing.

"You've got writer's block, sugar."

"How'd you guess? Could it have been the fact that I laid
parquet in the garage?"

"Poor Leah," Kat sighed.

"It's not so terrible." Leah shrugged. "Maybe I'm just
not a writer. Remember that old folk song, 'If I had a Ham-
mer'? Well, I do—and I've done okay with it, right?"

"You've done *great*!" Kat marveled as she opened a door,
and what had been a shabby little den was now a library
complete with hand-built bookshelves.

She was running her fingers along the polished cherry-
wood when the phone rang. As she headed toward it, Leah
grabbed her arm.

"Could we just let it go?" she pleaded. There was panic
in her eyes.

"Why?" Kat asked. The phone continued ringing, and

with Kat's bewildered eyes upon her, Leah finally marched over to the desk and picked it up.

"Hello?" she answered weakly. She looked over at Kat and mouthed, "It's for me." Kat discreetly left the room and shut the door behind her.

"Leah," a low voice said, "I'm glad you didn't hang up."

"What do you want, Mick?"

"Can we talk?"

"What do you think we're doing?"

"You know what I mean. I wonder how you are, Leah."

"Perfecto. I don't dream about ski masks anymore, and I'm not even afraid to raise the shades at high noon."

"Then don't be afraid to have dinner with me."

"I'm not afraid—I'm just not interested."

"I don't believe you, Leah."

"Well, believe this." She slammed down the receiver.

Immediately the phone rang again, and when she resignedly picked it up, Mick went right on talking. "Have dinner with me," he insisted. "Give us a chance."

"Oh, Christ," she sighed wearily. "I'll think about it." Then she hung up.

Thirteen

August 1985

IN TOGO, SAM and Clayton waited out a thunderstorm under the shelter of an immense baobab tree. Exhausted and hungry after spending the morning digging a well with the local villagers, they greedily devoured the spicy groundnut stew that Vonga had sent along.

As they settled back with a steaming thermos of mint tea, Sam studied Clayton's tanned, craggy features.

"You seem distracted," she said. "Is something wrong?"

"I was just thinking about the villagers. Some of them didn't look well. I hope there's not something going around. An outbreak of the wrong thing can wipe out an entire village."

"Aren't there doctors?" Sam asked.

"There's a mission doc up north, but the fighting's so bad up there, she's got her hands full. Everywhere you look, there's so much to do." Suddenly he jumped to his feet. "You know what your grandmother used to say? 'If there's so much to do, then why are we sitting here exercising our backsides?' "

He pulled Sam up.

"What a woman," he said. "Of course, I was just a kid when she was around, but I remember my father used to say about her, 'She's the kind of Christian lady who could make Lucifer himself see the light.' "

"I wish I'd known her," Sam said wistfully.

"*Known* her?" Clayton asked incredulously. "You're car-

rying her around right inside there,'' he said, brushing her
breast with his fingers. Quickly he withdrew his hand, and
the two of them hastily busied themselves gathering together
the remains of their lunch.

As she packed the wooden hamper, Sam noticed a slow
ripple in the tall grasses of the savannah. She nudged Clayton, who looked up in time to see a wild boar creeping toward them.

''Freeze,'' ordered Clayton in a low voice. They stood like
statues as the savage creature stared them down. It snarled as
it dug its hooves into the ground.

Sweat poured down Sam's face, and adrenaline pumped
through her as the boar moved in closer, its shiny snout covered with saliva. Its black fur stood up on its back while its
beady eyes roved back and forth from Sam to Clayton.

Suddenly it charged, and as it shot through the air toward
Clayton, Sam pulled the hunting knife from her belt and
lunged. She sliced through the boar's jugular in a single, sure
stroke. The animal seemed to freeze in midair, and with a
bloodcurdling cry, it fell to the ground, its life over. Sam
screamed, and Clayton held her as she sobbed.

That evening, Sam and Clayton invited the whole community to a barbecue. As Sam bit into the succulent flesh that
she'd provided with her own bare hands, she turned to Clayton, her silvery eyes twinkling.

''I've always wanted to kill a bore,'' she chuckled.

After dinner, Clayton broke out the palm wine, but Sam
refused to indulge. Wine made her think about places—and
people—she was better off forgetting. Instead, she concen-
trated on the music the Africans made. As they sang their
heartrending harmonies, accompanying themselves on tongas
and flutes, she leaned back, closed her eyes, and knew that
she was as happy as her torn heart would allow.

Back in L.A., with looping and other postproduction headaches behind her, Kat decided to throw a dinner party. She
invited Pru and John, and she assumed that Leah, now her
housemate, would also come and bring her mystery man.
Mick was still an unknown quantity to Leah's friends, because as she put it, ''I don't want to jinx things.''

On the day of the party, Kat was going through cookbooks when she asked Leah if this was the night she'd finally unveil her masterpiece. Leah surprised her by answering that, no, Mick wasn't coming—and neither was she.

"But why?" Kat asked. "I thought you liked my shrimp creole."

"I love it, and there'd better be leftovers or I'll tell the *Enquirer* that you date aliens. But I just can't make it to-night."

Kat looked her friend squarely in the eye. "What's shaking, sugar?"

"If you must know, I'm trying not to drink—"

"That's great, Leah—"

"And I don't want to be in a situation where I'll be tempted."

"But we're your *friends*. You don't have to drink to have fun with us."

"Look, Kat, when I'm at a party, I have this urge to get loaded—that's just the way I am—so I think I'll sit this one out."

"Where will you go?"

"The movies. The library. Any place that doesn't have a bar. I'll be fine, Kat. Trust me."

"Trust you? You don't even trust me enough to let me be with you and help you."

"Maybe I don't." Leah paused and added, "Why should I? You don't trust me enough to tell me what's going on with you. Every month you rack up a few million dollars in calls to West Virginia, and yet you never say a word about that part of your life. Something must be going on. But do I pester you to find out?"

"Okay, okay," Kat sighed. As she slumped into an Eames chair, her honey-blond hair spread like a fan against the dark leather. "I get your point."

"Fine. From now on, let's just give each other a little space."

With her violet eyes averted, Kat nodded.

Since returning from Iowa, she'd hardly enjoyed one moment in her beautiful new home. Without her family around her, how could she? Marie still refused to come to L.A., and it was obvious she did her best to keep Kat from even *talking* to Misti.

At times like this, Kat was grateful for Leah's company, and she wished she could tell her the truth about her past, but she couldn't. She hadn't even been able to tell Bob—and he wanted to marry her! If he wouldn't understand, who would? An illegitimate daughter—and a decade of lies.

At dinner that night, she told Pru and John that her Hawkeye governor had proposed. She wasn't wearing his ring because she hadn't made up her mind yet, but she was sure of one thing: she missed him and thought about him constantly.

"Great! Go for it!" Pru advised, but John kept his own counsel. He himself was having problems adjusting to Hollywood, and he didn't wish similar problems on anyone else. What kind of life would Bob have if he left Iowa politics?

As crazy as John was about Pru, he had to admit he was miserable in L.A. A friend of Pru's had helped him get a job tutoring on the set of a network sitcom. The "school" was a sham, and John was disgusted with the general attitude: the network, the studio, and even the parents didn't care whether the kids could spell their names as long as they pulled down a twenty-five share. John despised the cynicism and opportunism he saw all around him.

And Pru wasn't much help. Even as she denounced *Cupid's Arrow* for its instant fixes, she was nevertheless completely absorbed by it. That was Pru's nature: whatever the job was, she gave it her best shot. Of course she had her ear to the ground about other opportunities, but even so, *Cupid's Arrow* received a lot more of her time and energy than it deserved.

Like all workaholics, Pru brought her job home at night, and for John, who just wanted to forget his work at the end of the day, it was a challenge to get Pru to relax and have fun. They cooked together, they went to the movies, and they made love until they couldn't walk, but John knew that Pru was happy to go to work each morning. And when he tried to explain how unhappy he was at the studio, she just didn't get it. Advising him to seize the reins at work, she didn't seem to realize that he wasn't even holding them. It was a frustrating situation, and as he thought about it, he couldn't help frowning.

"What's bothering you?" Pru asked.

"Nothing," he answered. He raised his glass to Kat. "Whatever decision you make about Bob will be the right one," he said, and he hoped that no one else noticed the hollow ring in his voice.

"Thank you," said Kat. "I go back and forth. He's a great guy, but we live in different worlds."

"Good," said Pru. "You'll be like foreign countries to each other—exotic, stimulating, and never dull."

Pru took John's hand as she spoke, and it gave her pause to realize that her own beloved husband wasn't as exotic or stimulating as he had been in the beginning. It shamed her to admit it, but she was tired of his constant complaints.

"Listen up, y'all." Kat tapped on her wineglass with her spoon. "I almost forgot, my producer's throwing a big bash tomorrow evening, and I hope you'll come."

"But we're such deadbeats," Pru protested. "I mean, we don't freebase cocaine or sleep with Dalmatians or anything."

"That's why I hope you'll come," Kat said. "For moral support."

"Of course we'll be there," Pru answered. "And we'll really cut up. I'll try to stay awake past nine-thirty, and John will recite his poetry. We'll have Hollywood standing on its ear."

John winced at Pru's joke about his poetry. Even though he knew she didn't mean anything by it, it still made him feel an inch tall.

"By the way," said Kat, changing the subject when she saw John's pained expression, "I got a letter from Sam. She says that Togo's spectacular, and she's learning a lot because there's some missionary there who's taken her under his wing."

Pru chuckled. "I'll bet he's trying every which way to convert her. Can you imagine any greater challenge to a man of God than the salvation of Sam's soul?"

* * *

In the African evening, the moonlight's silvery reflection shined in Sam's eyes.

"It's strange," she told Clayton. "All my life I've hated who I was. When I was a little girl, I used to stand on my balcony late at night and pray that a meteor would come crashing to earth. If only it would land on my big white house! I imagined my family going up in flames, and me right along with them. How I wanted that. I prayed that Andy and I wouldn't have to grow up if it meant we'd be like our parents—"

"Shhh . . ." he said softly. "Look." He pointed skyward, and they watched a shower of stars burn its golden path across the black sky.

She took it as an omen and reached for Clayton's hand. "When I came to Africa, do you know what I found? A past I can be proud of. I had to reach back a generation, beyond my parents and their self-centered little lives, but when I did, I discovered who I really am. And I have you to thank for that."

Impulsively she drew him to her. When he didn't turn away, but instead met her bold gaze, she reached out and stroked his cheek. He was hot beneath her fingertips, and when his lips touched hers, she felt as disoriented as a child in the throes of a fever. As he kissed her, he undid the buttons on her khaki shirt and lowered his head to press his lips to the pulse in her neck. She breathed deeply of his scent and let the now familiar sounds of the jungle rock her in a loving rhythm. Finally, she closed her eyes and leaned back as his capable hands took over, dispelling uncertainty wherever his fingers caressed her tawny skin.

Fourteen

ED HYATT, KAT'S *Hawkeye* producer, threw the sort of parties that would have made the Marquis de Sade run for cover. And because Ed had spent the long hot summer in Iowa, then weathered two months of postproduction in L.A., he was ready to cut up when the harvest moon rose in the sky and a cold snap bit the October air.

The Day of the Dead brought out the best in him. Unlike his usual soirées, the Halloween ball would not be strictly A-list; in fact, he instructed his A-team—the white-hot guests like Kat—to bring whoever they fancied. Ed could be a very democratic guy.

In the spirit of democracy, Leah and Pru, along with John, accompanied Kat to Ed's Spanish Colonial high above Beverly Hills. John and Pru went as Sonny and Cher, since Pru was in a thin phase. Leah bopped around in beatnik black, and Kat dressed up as Sadie Hawkins in a tight-fitting ruffled blouse. She was not unaware that a few people in Hollywood found her too ''white trash'' for their sophisticated tastes, so she decided to show them just how down-home she could be. It was all good-natured on her part, but it served to let the snobs know that their prejudices were no secret.

Ed insisted on leading her around the party, so her friends soon realized they were on their own. Pru acted quickly, chatting up people in film production. Her relentless networking left John and Leah to fend for themselves, which irritated Leah. She wasn't in a great mood to begin with, and everywhere she turned there was a waiter poised with a bottle of Chandon.

The fiftieth time she shook her head no, John tapped her on the shoulder. "Having a ball?" he asked wryly.

"Sure. I mean, it could be worse—we could be in Beirut. What about you?" she asked. "Is your mojo working?"

"I hate this stuff," he answered with a laugh.

"That puts us on the same team. The Z-list."

"Well, you won't be for long," he said.

"What makes you think that?" she asked curiously.

"I know. That's all. It's just a matter of time."

"Well, don't hold your breath. Save it for your own work. Pru tells me you're a poet."

"I didn't think she'd noticed." He frowned, then asked quickly, "You like poetry?"

"Do rough winds shake the darling buds of May? You betcha. I'd like to read yours sometime."

"Just as soon as you show me a screenplay."

"Enough playing doctor!" Leah hedged. She looked around miserably at the high-flying crowd. "So . . . how are we going to get our girls out of here?"

"I don't think we are," John said. "Pru can't get enough of this 'Industry' business, and Kat's producer won't let her out of his sight."

"Kat can hold her own," Leah said, and she looked across the room at her friend, who was mixing and mingling like a pro. Even the most elite guests were fawning all over her, and she in turn appeared to find them fascinating, but Leah knew otherwise. Kat was acting.

When Kat looked across the room and saw Leah and John chatting, she was pleased. After the debacle at Yamashiro's, she hadn't entertained high hopes that Leah and John would strike up a friendship, but it looked as if they had. That was terrific, since John needed to make friends in L.A. Pru complained that he was still very much a fish out of water, but maybe that would change.

Kat scanned the crowd and saw Pru huddled in a corner with a couple of line producers for Paramount.

She's in hog heaven, Kat thought happily.

"Kat?" Leah startled her. "John and I are going to catch

a cab and go play some Scrabble." Across the room, John made the same announcement to Pru, who pecked him on the cheek and sent him on his way, then quickly returned to her powwow.

As Kat watched them leave, she wished she were going with them, but just then Ed showed up with Catwoman—who turned out to be Rona Barrett—and Kat got back to the serious business of partying.

When she returned home late that night, there was a message from Bob on the answering machine. He wanted her to call him back, no matter how late she got in. When she did, he picked up on the first ring.

"I'll bet you were at one of those wild Hollywood orgies," he teased.

"You know me better than that," she said.

"I'm not so sure, honey. We hayseeds are always the last to know. Why, I believe you glamorous movie stars keep us in the dark just to amuse yourselves."

"Sugar, you make my life sound a lot more exciting than it is."

"Well, you make my life a lot more exciting, period." He paused, and when he spoke again there was gravity in his tone. "Will you come and visit, Kat? I miss you so much I can't stand it."

"I miss you, too, but I'm tied up here with publicity obligations. I'll come as soon as I have a chance to catch my breath."

"I like you breathless, lovely lady—and I'll like you even more with that ring on your finger."

Kat looked at her hand. There *was* no ring: it wasn't time.

"Soon," she promised. They kissed across the Rockies before they hung up. It was late by then, but Kat couldn't sleep. She stayed up all night, searching her soul, and when morning finally came, she called her agent.

"Hold on to your hat, Michele. There's something I have to tell you."

"Sock it to me, toots."

"I have a ten-year-old daughter," Kat said. She hesitated, then added guiltily, "Her father and I were never married."

"I'm shocked." Michele laughed. "So, what do you

want—a press conference? This is the eighties, for chrissake. Everyone from Goldie Hawn to Jessica Lange has an illegitimate kid. It may not be hip in West Virginia, but in L.A. it's almost required.''

After hanging up, Kat dressed, packed a bag, and caught a cab to the airport. So, it wasn't as bad as she'd thought it would be. Well, okay, she'd hold that press conference and introduce her beautiful daughter to the world. But first she'd go to Des Moines and tell Bob about Misti before he heard it from someone else.

She caught a midmorning flight to Des Moines and phoned the governor's mansion from the air. Chuck was waiting with the governor's limo when she landed. He was glad to see her. She was easily the nicest person who'd ever graced his back seat.

When she arrived at the mansion, Bob was in the library, waiting with champagne on ice. As he offered her a glass, he saw her ringless hand.

''Does this mean the answer is no?'' he asked cautiously.

She smiled. ''I wanted to make sure the offer is still good.''

''Honey, the offer's good as long as it takes to get to yes.''

''First, there's something I have to tell you.''

''This is Iowa.'' Bob grinned. ''I'm all ears.''

Her violet eyes were watchful as she took his hand. ''I have a daughter. Her name is Misti, and she's the most important thing in my life.''

Bob frowned. ''I didn't realize you'd been married before—''

Kat bit her bottom lip. ''I wasn't.''

''I see.'' He withdrew his hand from hers, drained his champagne, and stood up. He walked out of the library. ''Chuck will drive you to the airport,'' he said without looking over his shoulder.

Kat rose and ran after him. ''So that's it?''

''That's it,'' he said with his back to her.

''You won't let me explain?''

Suddenly he whirled around, and his eyes were filled with rage. ''What will you explain?'' he asked furiously.

''I made a mistake,'' she said.

''So did I,'' he said. ''I thought you were a cut above the usual tramp.''

She slapped him so hard that her fingers left red marks on his cheek. She ran from the library, and she didn't stop running until she hurled herself into the limo and asked Chuck to take her to the airport.

In the rearview mirror, he watched her cry softly. He hated to see anyone so upset, especially her, but he couldn't say he was surprised. Where the governor was concerned, crying women were a fact of life. Bob called them the Hanky Patrol.

"I want to thank you for all you've done," Kat said when they pulled up at the airport. She reached into her purse and handed him a gaily wrapped present. "This is for you. I'd intended to give it to you under happier circumstances—" She sniffled loudly, dabbing at her eyes as they began to fill again.

"You shouldn't have—" Chuck said, but she cut him off with a quick peck on the cheek. Then she dashed inside the terminal.

As she disappeared, he unwrapped her present: a beautiful pair of Maserati driving glasses. Trying them on, he wondered how Bob could have let such a wonderful woman get away.

As the first frost dusted the rolling hills of Buckhannon, Grace Adkins Steele made a decision. She'd seen the other woman behind Frank's eyes, and she knew more certainly with each passing day that the woman wasn't about to disappear. If anything, she was pulling Frank deeper inside himself.

Grace's first husband, Patrick Adkins, had been slain in the same shooting that nearly killed Frank. Out of a sense of honor and responsibility, Frank had married Grace. But no matter how hard they both tried, it wasn't working. Frank's loyalty and kindness couldn't make up for the fact that he didn't love her.

One snowy evening, Grace confronted him. She asked him about the other woman, and the more he denied it, the more she knew it was the truth. When he saw at last that it was useless to pretend, he told her everything.

Afterward, she did what she knew was right. She filed for divorce. She wished her husband well; he deserved to have what he yearned for. She prayed that he'd find a second chance at happiness.

Fifteen

PRU AND JOHN almost didn't go to the *Cupid's Arrow* Christmas party. For John's sake, Pru was trying to spend more time at home, and she saw no reason to kick up her heels at the annual office festivities. The prospect of Marvin in a Santa suit was almost more than she could bear, and she knew that if he were swilling eggnog, he'd be even more obnoxious than usual.

In the end, it was John who insisted they go to the party.

"I've got to see this guy in the flesh," he said.

"Let's just hope he's not in the buff," she replied. "I wouldn't put it past him."

"It'll be fun," John said, grinning, and even though she raised an eyebrow, she was touched by his insistence. She knew how he hated shindigs, especially Hollywood shindigs, and she was fully aware that his party-animal act was a kind-hearted expression of support for her career.

When they arrived at the Formosa, the Chinese restaurant where the party was being held, Marvin was busy handing out presents to his staff and crew. No one bothered to open them; everyone knew they were autographed copies of Marvin's new book, *Itching to Love*.

When Marvin caught sight of Pru and John, he ambled over to their table.

"Ho, ho, ho, Pru. May I offer you a glass of Christmas cheer?" he asked, expressly ignoring John. His flowing white beard was spotted with eggnog.

"Marvin, I'd like you to meet my husband—John Douglas."

"My pleasure," said Marvin, his eyes never leaving their permanent post at Pru's décolletage. John glared.

"Eggnogs all around?" Pru asked brightly, as she rose quickly to go to the bar.

"I'll come too," John said, and they made their way to the punch bowl. "God, talk about creatures low on the food chain . . ."

"Shhh,—" whispered Pru, "he's my boss, so please try to put up with him—"

"While he's nosing around you like that?"

"He's laughable, darling."

"Well, I'm not laughing."

While the waiter ladled their eggnogs, Marvin cosied up behind them, and his red velvet paunch brushed Pru's derrière. He produced a sprig of mistletoe and raised it in the air above her head.

"Jingle, jingle, jingle," he said. "I have a proposition: I think I can persuade the brass to make you *executive* producer." He leaned toward her and snatched a kiss. "How would you like that, little lady?"

"And how would you like this?" John asked. He decked Marvin with a clean right hook. "Let's leave," he told Pru as he stepped over Marvin, who lay sputtering on the floor.

To his surprise, she refused. "How could you do that?" she asked shrilly. "Marvin signs my paychecks!"

"That doesn't give him the right to insult you. I had to step in."

"No, you didn't," she seethed. "I can take care of myself, thank you very much!"

He looked at her incredulously, then shook his head slowly. Without another word, he turned and walked out of the restaurant. Pru ran to the ladies' room and spent the rest of the evening there, sobbing.

When she finally ventured back to the party, Marvin was once again out cold, but this time, she was told, it was the eggnog that had put him under. Pru downed a goblet or two to catch up with everyone else, and then she joined the entire crew in their drunken rendition of "Fuck the Halls with Balls of Folly." By the time she drove home at two, she was thoroughly depressed. Climbing into bed, she realized that John was only pretending to be asleep. She did the same. They lay all night like that, their eyes closed as tightly as clenched fists.

After Bob Rice's reaction to the news of her daughter, Kat backed down from her resolve to tell the world about Misti. *If Bob couldn't handle it, how could strangers?* she wondered. Or at least she did at first. But eventually she realized that Bob was wrong. She was proud of Misti, and if Bob objected, that was his problem.

Her problem was that she hadn't shared her secret with her three best friends. It was silly, she now realized, to shut them out. They'd been supportive in the past, and she hoped they'd be supportive now. Bearing that in mind, she brought together Leah and Pru for dinner at a beachfront restaurant in Malibu.

There, with the silvery ocean shimmering in the distance, she told her friends about Misti. Just as she'd hoped, they were delighted to learn they had a "niece," and they pressed Kat for photos, which she proudly pulled from their hiding-place in her wallet.

After dinner, Leah insisted that they phone Sam right away. The overseas connection crackled with static, but Sam got the message anyway, and she too was thrilled. No one was as thrilled as Kat, though. She went to sleep that night with the certain knowledge that Misti had three new allies in the world—allies who would never waver.

The week before Christmas, she went to West Virginia to be with her family, and while she was there, she held a press conference. From the Grange Hall in Frenchton, she introduced Misti to a barrage of reporters.

Although she hadn't planned it that way, her announcement coincided with the Christmas release of *Hawkeye*, and upon its opening, the film shot to the number one position in the box-office sweepstakes.

On Christmas Eve, Michele called her to state the obvious: her public hadn't abandoned her, the critics called her "sensational," and new scripts were pouring in. There was even a million-dollar offer from Sony to do a mother-daughter commercial, an exclusive for Japanese TV.

"No, thanks," Kat laughed. "Now, you have yourself a

Merry Christmas, Michele. And for heaven's sake, take the day off!''

"How can I with deadbeat clients like you?" Michele griped. "Oh, well, maybe '86 will be better."

On Christmas night, Kat was cleaning up the last of the torn wrapping paper when the phone rang.

"Kat?" the voice asked. It was Bob. "I called to wish you a Merry Christmas," he said. "And to apologize. I'll walk on my knees all the way to West Virginia if you'll just promise to listen to me."

"I'm listening," she said coolly.

"What I said that night was hateful. I was jealous, that's all. It was the old green monster, plain and simple. I thought you were all mine, and when I found out . . . about your daughter . . . I blew up."

Kat remained silent.

"Oh, Lord, I've been a shit," Bob continued, "and I'm sorry every goddamned minute of my life. I'm sorry for what I said and did, and I'm sorry I didn't run off and elope with you the night we met. I want you, I want your daughter to be *our* daughter, and I want us to be a family this time next year. Will you think about it?"

"I don't know," she said wearily, but she knew she would think about it. Something inside her told her the winter would be a short one. Already her heart was melting like an icicle on the first day of spring.

On New Year's Eve, Leah drove downtown to Mort's, the Clara Street bar favored by cops. It was an old-fashioned tavern, with blue-plate specials and boilermakers for a buck and a half, and since it was right around the corner from police headquarters, it was always packed with off-duty members of the L.A.P.D. who were winding down.

As Leah took a seat at the bar, she wasn't surprised that Mick wasn't there yet. As usual on their handful of dates, he was right on schedule—running late. Minutes turned into hours, and it was ten o'clock when Mort finally handed her the phone.

"I could have had more fun with Guy Lombardo," she said when she heard Mick's voice.

"Babe," he said dully, "you think I plan the drive-bys in this shithole?"

Leah softened. "Sorry. Just get here when you can, okay?"

"You bet, babe—Christ, there's the radio." The line went dead.

As she handed the phone back to Mort, a handsome young stranger sauntered over. The closer he got, the more he resembled the poster boy for Gold's Gym. There were bulges in his chinos that made her blush, and when he offered her a glass of cold duck, she voted with her hormones.

One glass turned into another, and her hand rested lightly on Poster Boy's thigh as she listened avidly to his life story and kept an eye out for Mick. Eventually, however, both eyes were on the hunk before her. He'd just discovered—to their mutual delight—that he could easily encircle her tiny waist with his large hands.

When it was almost midnight and Mick still hadn't appeared, Leah threw herself with full force into her newfound friendship. By the time 1986 finally rang in, she'd savored more than a few wine-sweetened kisses. At one in the morning, when she left the bar, she wasn't alone, and she wasn't lonely.

Just before last call, Mick showed up, looking like hell. He asked after Leah, and he could tell by Mort's evasive answer that she hadn't gone home to pine.

His temples were pounding, his face ashen, as he swallowed a scorpion that was so strong it made his back teeth float. He gave Mort a grateful look, then popped two aspirin and drove home to Silverlake.

Leah was waiting on his front steps.

A little unsteadily, she walked to his driveway to meet him. "Happy New Year," she giggled. Her lipstick was smeared.

"Hey, kid." Wearily he walked her to his front door.

"You ready to party?" she asked, and she tooted a little horn she'd picked up at Mort's.

"Babe," he said in a dead voice, "one of my squad went down tonight."

"Oh, Mick," she said, "I'm so sorry. Will he be all right?"

"He died on the table." Mick slumped down on the front

stoop and crumpled against her breasts. She cradled him in her arms as his body shook and he tried unsuccessfully to choke back his tears.

Holding him, she thanked God she hadn't gone home with Poster Boy. Almost, but not quite. They'd gotten all the way to his cul-de-sac before she came to her senses.

"Mick?" she said softly.

When his sobbing subsided, she helped him to his feet and led him inside the house. He let her undress him, and in the silent darkness, she offered what small comfort she could.

In the morning, as she fried bacon and eggs for him, the size of her hangover made it easy for her to figure out her New Year's resolution.

The funeral was held two days later, in the first downpour of the rainy season. As the widow dropped dahlia petals onto the casket, Leah knit her fingers through Mick's.

She thought sadly of the way they'd met—through an act of terrible violence. And now, for the past two nights, it was another act of violence that bound them together, clinging helplessly to each other. She wondered if all they would ever manage as a couple would be simply to double their losses.

She didn't stay with him that night, and when she kissed him good-bye and told him she would call, they both knew she was lying.

Pru was in her office, working late as usual, when Marvin invited himself in.

"Born to party," he announced.

In one hand he held a tiny glass vial and a sterling spoon, and in the other, a Styrofoam cup of Bacardi 151.

"Care for a hit?" he asked Pru.

She waved him away irritably. "Get that stuff out of here, Marvin. And make it snappy—I'm going home." As she shut her briefcase and grabbed her keys, he hadn't yet moved, and she glowered in exasperation. "You heard me," she scolded. "Amscray!"

She marched to her door, but he got there first and blocked the way.

"I think we'd better have a little chat," he said.

"Marvin, you're way out of your league here."

He stared at her with an imbecilic look on his face. "I've been nicey-nice for six months," he said in what he clearly intended to be a tough-guy tone. "Now it's time for you to be nice back."

"You think so?" she asked, smiling. She took a step toward him, and then another. When they were almost touching, beads of sweat sprang to his brow. He leered with anticipation.

"Keep your eyes on the prize," she told him, and he obediently moved in for a surgical inspection of her breasts. While he ogled her, she reached for the vial, and after unscrewing its cap, in a single graceful sweep of her arm, she scattered it like fairy dust across the carpet.

"You bitch," Marvin moaned.

"You ain't seen nothing yet," she told him.

She retrieved the cup of Bacardi from her desk, made tracks to him, and yanked open his fly. Then she gave him a christening he wouldn't soon forget.

"It burns!" he yelped.

He was still hopping around frantically when Pru left the building.

The next day she handed in her letter of resignation to the brass. She included a full and detailed explanation of her grievances, and she messengered a copy to the American Psychiatric Association. Then she telephoned the L.A.P.D., and late that afternoon Marvin was arrested—for possession of cocaine—in the midst of taping a show. His last show, as it turned out.

When the dust finally settled, John suggested to Pru that they take a few days off and drive up the coast.

"I don't need a vacation," she told him. "I need to find a better job."

Not for the first time, John wondered if his wife needed to work more than she needed to be married. The closer he looked, the harder she was to see, and each passing day seemed to add another brick in the ever-growing wall between them. Sometimes it seemed that more than the honeymoon was over. Maybe the marriage was finished too.

Sixteen

ONCE KAT LET Bob back into her life, he began calling and sending flowers daily. On Valentine's Day, he even found time to join her for an impromptu rendezvous in West Virginia. Somehow the press got wind of their meeting, but Bob—who was an expert at slipping through reporters' nets—managed to keep them at bay and spend a quiet day with Kat and her family.

After dinner, he dashed off to Washington, and Kat stayed with Marie and Misti until the child fell asleep, clutching the Valentine locket that Kat had given her.

"Don't let Bob get away," Marie told her daughter that night. "He's a fine one, Kathleen. You hook yourself up with him, and I won't have to worry about you and all those polecats out there in Hollywood. Why, if you were married to that fella, it's just possible Misti and I would come visit you in Des Moines."

"That's the problem right there. I can't live in Des Moines, and Bob can't live in California. We're oil and water, Mama."

"Where there's a will, there's a way," her mother intoned.

"Well, how about this," said Kat diplomatically. "I'll think about marrying Bob—if you'll think about bringing Misti to L.A."

"When you gave her to me to raise, Kathleen, you promised that you wouldn't interfere—"

"But that was before things happened for me . . . Mama, are you listening?"

Kat looked hard at Marie's lined face. She was searching for love, but it was hard to see, buried beneath years of bitter disappointment. Marie had been young once, too, but a handsome traveling salesman had turned her old in a hurry. He'd disappeared without a trace, leaving her alone and pregnant. Fourteen years later, she'd seen the same thing happen to Kat—and she wasn't about to let it happen to Misti.

"No grandchild of mine is going out there to that Sodom," she vowed.

"Oh, Mama, please. Think about it. Will you?"

Marie's thin lips cracked open and revealed a mouthful of bad teeth as she rose from the couch.

"You've got a plane to catch," she said.

"I love you, Mama."

Marie turned away. Blinded by tears, Kat stumbled out of the trailer toward her car.

Every morning when Leah sat down to work on her "secret project," she made a silent promise.

If I don't have a good time writing this, she swore, *no one else will have a good time reading it.*

Then she hit the keys.

Kat occasionally wondered what her housemate was up to— Leah sat at her typewriter all day, chuckling away—but she figured it was all to the good. Leah's disposition was sunnier than it had been since UCLA. She was a pleasure to live with, and on the weekends she worked hard on what she called "Misti's room." She was turning it into a showplace because, as she insisted, "Your mother will come around, Kat. She and Misti will be out here any day now. Mark my words!"

"I don't know, sugar. Valentine's Day was really awful."

"Then it can only get better," Leah said. "Come on, we'll sand Misti's floor and you'll feel like a million bucks."

They were upstairs, trying to master an automatic sanding machine, when Pru dropped by. As the huge contraption led the giggling friends in a dance across the unfinished floor, Pru stood with her hands on her ample hips.

"Hi, you two," she said. "Aside from the fact that you're trying to steer a machine with a will of its own, what's up?"

"We were just discussing Kat's boyfriend," said Leah. "I was asking Kat if there's an ear of corn growing between his legs."

"Leah!" Kat scolded.

"Well, honestly, Kat, I'm only trying to figure out what you could possibly see in some Bible Belt guy with the body of Abe Lincoln and the smile of Mr. Ed."

"How can you say that?" Pru asked in Kat's defense. "You've never even met Bob."

"No, but I've seen him on C-SPAN, and frankly, I think Kat should graze closer to home. Do you want her moving to some cornfield?" Leah asked.

"That will never happen!" Kat answered.

"I don't know," Leah sighed. "I don't see your boyfriend moving to Hollywood and capturing the hearts of the cocaine crowd. He's not the type."

"Which is precisely why I'm crazy about him," Kat stated firmly.

"But aren't you worried about how different you are?" Pru finally ventured. "I mean, look at John and me. We've got some pretty insurmountable problems, and I'm afraid you will too."

"I'm not saying it'll be a walk in the park, Pru. But I know we'll be able to compromise."

"That's what John and I thought," said Pru, and the pain in her voice was hard to argue with. "Change the subject before I cry."

Leah saw that she meant it. She turned quickly to Kat.

"So, what's he like in the hay, so to speak? Is he bigger than a silo?"

Kat blushed. "You two aren't going to believe this," she said, "but we haven't slept together."

"*What?*" Pru and Leah gasped in unison.

"It hasn't come *up*?" Leah asked in distress, then laughed at the double entendre. "I can't believe you're practically engaged to a guy who might be a Vienna Choir Boy for all you know."

"He's not," declared Kat. "And listen up, ladies. If I'm not worried, there's no need for you to be."

"I'm glad for that," Pru said. "I've got my own sex life to worry about."

She fell silent, and Kat quickly excused herself. When she came back a second later, she laid a heap of negligees and teddies at Pru's feet.

"What's this?" Pru asked.

"Presents from fans."

Pru looked askance at the lingerie, but finally the shimmering silks and handmade laces were too much to resist.

"These things are beautiful," she said as a magenta satin camisole ran through her fingers like wine. "Your fans have good taste."

"Take them," Kat said. "You, too, Leah. They're all yours."

"Are you sure you don't want them?" asked Pru.

"They wear flannel Mother Hubbards in Des Moines," quipped Leah.

"Or they wear nothing at all," Kat answered with a wink.

"Well, thanks," Pru said. She walked to the full-length mirror, and as she held up one of the skimpier articles, she sighed miserably.

"There's no way this is going to fit. I've been indulging in too many midnight rendezvous with my refrigerator. I'm one step away from a serious case of sleep-*eating*. Oh, hell, I'll take them anyway—you never can tell when my flab will turn back into fab."

"Thank God you've got curves," Leah said. "My boobs would fit handily into Tom Thumb's thimble. Let's see, I'll take one of these," she said, selecting a black lace merry widow. "Unfortunately, it'll probably be the year 2000 before I get laid again, and we'll all be wearing space suits by then."

"Thanks a lot," Pru told Kat as she threw her bounty into her oversize purse. "You've saved my marriage! Now, if you could just find me a job in the Biz."

"No luck?" asked Kat. Pru shook her head.

"I've got résumés in all over town, but not so much as a nibble yet."

"I can't believe that," Leah said. "You've got a great track record."

"Only in TV. This time I'm aiming higher. Really, don't you think I'd be a great film producer?"

"Produce some elbow grease, and I'll get back to you," Leah said. She handed Pru a sheet of sandpaper, and the trio spent the afternoon on their hands and knees. Afterward they took turns in the shower, and as they stood together before the bathroom mirror, it was like old times—almost.

"I wonder what Sam's up to right now?" Leah asked the other faces in the mirror.

"She's probably wondering what we're doing," Kat said.

"I miss her," Pru mused.

"Ditto," answered Leah. "No one else could hog a mirror quite like Sam." They giggled at the memory of their friend climbing all over the sink in Westwood as she struggled for enough turf to do her eye makeup.

"Good old Sam," Leah sighed. "Do you think she brought leg wax to Africa?"

By the middle of March, Leah had finished her project. She'd had a lot of laughs writing it, and even if it wasn't any good, she didn't begrudge a second of the time she'd spent on it. Neither, however, did she look forward to showing it to anyone—especially an agent. She was still smarting from Elizabeth Bloom.

As she switched off her Olivetti, she remembered it was St. Patrick's Day, and Mick O'Reilly popped into her mind. Maybe it was loneliness, maybe it was horniness, and maybe it was just cheap sentiment inspired by Ireland's patron saint, but something made her miss her big Mick terribly.

She wandered into the bathroom, and as she ran a comb through her wild black mane, she wondered how long it had been since she'd ventured out into the world. She'd been snug in the cocoon of her work for over two months, and she'd almost forgotten there was a universe beyond the clatter of her typewriter. But here she was, dabbing Magie Noire on her wrists. Apparently she was preparing to set foot in the big cruel world. And it was scary.

She wished Kat were around to talk to, but the actress was at Michele's office, discussing a new project. She picked up the phone and dialed Pru's number, but she got the machine. *Damn,* she thought. *Where are my friends when I need them?*

Smoothing on lip gloss, she wondered what it would be like to see Mick again, just for old times' sake. She decided to drive downtown to Mort's.

"Erin go bragh," Mort greeted her when she took a seat at the bar. "What'll it be?"

"Irish coffee," she said. "Hold the Irish."

She made her way through the crowd of revelers, searching for Mick. When she finally saw him, she was sorry she'd looked. A blonde was wrapped around him like a boa constrictor. Leah ducked away before he saw her. She marched up to the bar and ordered another Irish coffee. No special requests this time.

She'd just paid for her third drink when Mick spotted her. He was on his way to the men's room when all that lustrous hair—on that tiny frame—caught his eye.

"Leah," he said as he tapped her on the shoulder. When he spun her around, her eyes were spinning, too.

"Imagine running into you," Leah said icily.

"It's been a while, hasn't it. I've thought about you."

"Sure," Leah scoffed. "What about the Barbie doll?"

"She's no one," he answered.

"In that case"—Leah paused to signal the bartender—"why don't you join me?"

"I'll join you, but not for a drink." He gently pulled her off the barstool. "Come on, I'll take you home."

She twisted away. "How dare you patronize me," she said coldly. As he reached for her drink, she downed it in a swallow. "I'll do what I want," she said, her eyes gleaming darkly.

"What's that, Leah?"

"I want to get laid," she said.

"You always wanted that."

"So did you, Mick."

"So did I. That's right. But I wanted more, babe. I wanted you, and you weren't interested. Whenever I came around, you made sure there was nobody home behind those big brown eyes."

"Give me another chance," she pleaded.

"Let's get you home."

"That sounds perfectly divine," she said slowly. She lurched forward and started to undo his tie.

"Stop it," he said. He gripped her shoulders hard and steered her toward the door, but she spun away from him.

"Bastard!" she cried. "Leave me alone!"

She raced out of the bar and staggered through the dark to her car. She ran two stop signs before she got to Hollywood, where she stopped off at the Liquor Locker and bought a fifth of Jack Daniel's. She drank from the bottle as she spun down Santa Monica, then made the turn for Nichols Canyon.

The house was dark when she got home. With the Jack Daniel's under her arm, she padded down the hall and into the bathroom. She turned on the bathtub faucet and stared at her face until, at last, it came into focus in the bathroom mirror.

Slowly, as the tub filled, the air grew heavy with steam, and Leah's reflection clouded over. Other faces came and went, swimming before her in the foggy mirror. Her father, Red Foley, that bastard Mick, and a shadowy mask that bore a woman's features. Her mother?

She took a long swallow of whiskey, and Sam, then Pru, and finally Kat floated before her. But as she reached to the glass to touch them, they rose like genies, one by one, and dissolved into mist.

She drained the bottle, then stepped languidly into the tub. She groped for her razor in the soap dish and started shaving under her arms before she got a better idea. She unscrewed the razor. Carefully she carved a tiny heart into her left wrist. Scarlet ribbons ran from the wound. They unfurled in the bath like streamers at a child's birthday party.

In her other wrist, she cut the letters *L-O-V*, and then stopped to inspect her work. *This,* she thought, *is the best damned thing I've ever written.*

She never got around to the last letter.

Seventeen

SHE OPENED HER eyes slowly, and before her stood two angels. "Am I in heaven?" she murmured.

"Try again," Pru said softly.

As Kat reached out to take her hand, Leah saw that her wrists were bandaged. She noticed the dull throbbing behind her eyes, and her pain told her that she must be alive.

"You're in the hospital," Pru told her.

"How do you feel, sugar?" Kat asked.

"Aces," Leah muttered. Her throat was so dry it burned. She looked at Kat. "You found me?" she asked.

Kat nodded.

"It was an accident," Leah blurted. "I got carried away—"

"The doctors are surprised you made it," Kat said quietly.

"The luck of the Jewish," Leah blithered, and suddenly the tears shot from her eyes. "God, I can't tell you how embarrassed I am."

"Well, you ought to be proud," Pru said.

Leah looked confused.

"Not about this bullshit," Pru said, waving her hand around the hospital room. "I mean *this*—" She pulled a folder from her bag. "*College Craze* is something to boast about!"

"That's my script!" Leah cried. "Where did you get it?"

"It was on the bathroom floor when the medics arrived. And seriously, Leah, anyone who writes this well and wants to kill herself has got to be crazy."

"I'm not crazy, and I don't want to die."

"Good, because I'm going to produce your script, and I'll need you alive for the rewrite."

"Not so fast, ladies," Kat said. She shot Pru a questioning look, then sat down on the edge of the bed and looked into Leah's deep brown eyes. "Sugar, you've got a few things to work out. You say that what happened was an accident, but that doesn't change the fact that you drink too much—"

"That's all behind me," Leah promised.

"We've heard that before," Kat answered. "Anyway, the doctor says you have to see a psychiatrist."

"I understand Marvin's available," Leah remarked dryly.

"Be serious," Kat ordered.

Leah nodded solemnly, but her mind was elsewhere. *Pru likes my script!*

"Listen, here's the plan," Pru said briskly, sitting down on the other side of the bed. "You'll do some time with a shrink, and then we're going to haul ass on this script of yours. Copacetic?"

Leah nodded. "I hope I don't let you two down again—"

"The only one you can let down is yourself," Kat said.

She and Pru stood up to leave as an orderly appeared with a dinner tray.

"I'm so hungry I could eat a horse," Leah said.

"I'm sure they serve it here," Pru laughed. "We're going to take off now. Eat up."

In the elevator, Kat turned angrily to Pru. "Why did you bring up her script?"

"Because she needs to know how good she is. She needs to believe in herself."

"I know that, but you've gone and filled her head with big plans, and what if they don't happen? She'll be so disappointed—"

"They will happen. I guarantee it."

"And then what? In the shape she's in, how will she respond to deadlines? To criticism?"

"She'll do fine. Just watch."

Kat shuddered. "I hope you're doing the right thing, getting her all riled up."

"She needs to get riled up. Believe me, Kat—she'll rise to the occasion. Work will make her happy."

"Like it's made you happy, sugar?"

"Don't be bitchy. The point is, Leah won't get any better by sitting around contemplating her navel."

"But aren't you just a little afraid that you might be throwing her to the wolves?"

"No. Now, stop mothering her."

"I do *not* mother her," Kat protested.

"You mother everyone," Pru said. "But where Leah's concerned, it's time she grew up. You can't breastfeed her 'til she's forty!" Kat looked stricken, and Pru reached out impulsively to take her hand. "You're the best damned mother any of us ever had," she said softly. "Promise me you'll never change."

Through her tears, Kat hiccuped and smiled. "On my word of honor," she vowed. They left the hospital arm in arm.

After an exhausting week downriver, rebuilding a school that rebels had blown up, Sam and Clayton came home a few days early. The mosquitoes had gotten so bad that work was impossible.

After unloading the Jeep, Sam had just settled into a comfortable wicker chair on the veranda when Vonga brought her a cool drink and a cable. She read Pru's terse account of Leah's misadventure, and immediately she booked a flight for the following day.

That night, she lay with Clayton under mosquito netting, and they listened to a flock of starlings settle into their cacophonous nighttime ritual. For Sam, who'd never known peace of mind until she came to Togo, the sounds of the jungle were a symphony.

She turned toward Clayton, and he kissed her. She felt a stirring of desire and pressed her mouth more urgently against his.

"Do you think we might just lie together for a while?" he asked apologetically. "I'm beat."

"Of course," she told him. She closed her eyes as the starlings quieted down in the trees. She let her mind travel to where it often went at this hour.

Two years had passed since she'd first met Frank Steele, but even so—even in Africa—he was so much a part of her, he may as well have been living inside her. And yet . . .

Clayton stirred and turned over on his side.

Sam tried to be philosophical. So what if Frank would never be hers again? She'd had more in a single night with him than many women got in an entire lifetime. Wasn't that something to be grateful for?

She moved her body against Clayton's. He felt feverish; he was working too hard. She put her cool lips to his back and fell asleep with her arms around him.

Forty hours later, when she walked through the arrival gate at LAX and into the welcoming arms of her friends, she was frazzled and exhausted. But not for long. By the time she threw her bags into Pru's trunk, their cheerful company had restored her. She was glad to be back with her best friends, and the chatter that began on the way from the airport didn't wind down until well past dawn.

Slowly but surely, Kat and Bob's relationship began to mend. They hadn't seen each other since West Virginia, but they talked on the phone frequently, and Bob was the first person to hear Kat's big news: she'd found a film project, *Gambit*, a film she really wanted to do, and her agent had already set up talks with the writer and his agent.

"I'm surprised," Bob said. "I thought you were going to do a *Hawkeye* sequel right here in Iowa, where I can keep my eye on you!"

"That would tickle me to death, Bob, but I can't say no to this. I've always wanted to do a thriller, and my role's an absolute plum. But the best part is, we're shooting in L.A., so I won't even have to leave home."

"Does that mean I'll have to come there if I want to see my gal?"

"I'll visit you, too, sugar!"

"That's what I like to hear. How about tomorrow?"

"But tomorrow's Thursday—"

"Make it a long weekend. We'll have a late afternoon picnic down by the river, and I'll pick you a bouquet of spring's first flowers—"

"Don't tell me it's already spring in Iowa," Kat exclaimed. "I'd love to spend a spring day on the riverbank," she mused.

"Chuck will meet your plane, and I'll pack a hamper. You like ham salad? Deviled eggs?"

"You wicked man, you've talked me into it." She laughed.

"Okay, sweetheart, I'll see you tomorrow afternoon, and we'll have ourselves a touch of spring fever."

The first hitch in the *Gambit* negotiations occurred bright and early the next morning. Kat was awakened by a phone call from Michele. "They want you in on this," her agent told her. Kat dressed quickly and hurried down to Michele's office in Century City. The writer and his agent were already there, devouring a platter of bagels and smoked salmon.

"To make a long story short," Michele told Kat in the outer office, "that punk's got terms you wouldn't believe, and he says he'll walk if we don't play ball."

"Batter up," Kat drawled, and she strolled with Michele into the inner sanctum.

Tommy O'Toole, the writer, was an abrasive, self-confident man, and his agent, Chaz, was one of the new breed of Hollywood agents—Ivy League, understated, and slick. In his Boston accent, Chaz laid it on the line: Tommy was the hottest young writer around. He'd sold three features while still at USC, and now he was ready for the Triple Crown.

"Write *and* produce *and* direct?" Michele hooted. "Hold on, fellas—"

Before they knew it, the two parties had spent the entire morning in hot debate, but the discussion was getting nowhere fast when Kat suddenly remembered Bob. She looked at her watch, groaned inwardly, and quickly excused herself.

In the outer office, she found Michele's assistant.

"Will you please call Governor Rice and tell him that I can't make the five o'clock flight?" she asked. "But I promise to be on the late one."

When Bob got her message, he was none too pleased. Why couldn't she stick to her plans? he thought. They sure were flakes out there in La-La Land. Flakes—and worse. Maybe she was playing games with him.

He tried to work, but found he couldn't concentrate.

Meanwhile, in Century City, Kat and Michele tangled with Tommy and Chaz until long past six, when they decided to call it a day. Tommy suggested the foursome go to Trader Vic's for a drink.

"I think we could all use one," he said. "Right?"

"Wrong," Kat apologized. "I'm awfully sorry, but I have a plane to catch."

When she landed in Des Moines at one-thirty in the morning, Chuck was waiting. He drove her to the mansion, and she rang the doorbell several times before Bob appeared in his bathrobe.

"Let me guess," he said coldly. "You were in the neighborhood."

"Didn't you get my message?"

"Yes, I got your message. But not until *after* you'd spoiled our plans."

"Sugar, I was stuck in the middle of negotiations—"

"Negotiations?" he snorted. "Does that mean you were laid out on some producer's casting couch?"

"You know better than that," she said evenly. "I'm sorry, Bob. Honestly. Go to bed."

"Are you coming with me?"

She looked at his face, gray and haggard with exhaustion. Her heart went out to him: she *had* wrecked his evening, and she shouldn't be surprised to find him angry and defensive. What man wouldn't be? Her picture was plastered all over the tabloids, and every new issue had her hooked up with some young stud. Bob would be crazy not to be jealous.

"You need to sleep," she said tenderly. "I'll call you tomorrow."

Wearily he nodded. He ran his fingers through his sleep-mussed hair as he closed the door on her.

Chuck took her back to the airport; she chartered a plane home and called Michele in the morning to say she was ready for another round of talks.

Eighteen

LEAH STARTED THERAPY three times a week, and she also joined the Sports Connection to put her abused body back together. She depended on Pru and Sam for their frequent visits, and she was grateful that Kat was such a doting housemate.

Mick phoned often just to say hello, but Leah told Kat that she wasn't ready to talk to him yet. As Kat diplomatically conveyed this message, she was impressed by Mick's genuine concern for her friend.

Gradually, her brief chats with him grew longer as she discovered she could talk with him about anything. She also discovered that, after long days of tough negotiations, it was pure pleasure to have a phone pal whose friendly voice was as comforting as an afghan across her lap.

On a handshake, Leah and Pru became partners, and Pru began the difficult task of selling *College Craze*. The script made waves wherever it went, but unfortunately, no one had made a hard offer yet. Even so, Pru knew she had a winner.

Buoyed by the svelte new figure she was acquiring through hours of nonstop rewrites and discussions with Leah, and doubly encouraged by the nibbles she'd already garnered, she took *College Craze* to the one studio she'd so far avoided. Heliotrope was the star player in a constellation of heavy hitters. Everyone told Pru it was way out of her league, but that wasn't why she'd held off. She'd simply saved the best for last.

For weeks she tried to wangle an appointment with the head of Project Development, but his secretary shot her down every time. Finally, she got up one morning at the crack of dawn and sneaked onto the lot. Dressed as a cleaning woman, she managed to enter the offices where the *real* cleaning staff was hard at work. Looking as if she knew her way around, she found the offices of the head of Project Development, where she'd intended to leave the script on his desk. But then she had a better idea.

She filched a piece of his letterhead, rifled his desk for a sample of his handwriting, and carefully forged a note.

"Mo," she wrote: "We're talking MEGA with this one!" She signed the head of Project Development's name and, keeping an eye out for security guards, quietly padded down the plush hallway to the enormous office of Mo Blake, Heliotrope's commander-in-chief. She flung Leah's script, along with the forged note, onto his desk; then she stealthily made her way off the studio lot.

She said nothing to Leah about her shenanigans at Heliotrope: she didn't want to give her friend any false hope. But one night when Leah was killing herself at the Sports Connection, Pru told Kat what she'd done.

Kat was delighted. "You're a slyboots," she laughed. "Now listen up, Pru, if there's any little thing I can do to help you out—"

"There just might be, kiddo," Pru said, and she laid out the second phase of her plan.

The next day, she got the call she'd been hoping for—but not daring to expect.

"Ms. Daniels," said a woman's voice, "Mr. Blake would like to meet with you. When can you come in?"

They made a date for the next day at five o'clock, and Pru breezed in on the stroke of the hour, then cooled her jets until nearly six. Finally, the secretary said, "He'll see you now," and Pru was ushered into Mo Blake's office.

For the most powerful mogul in Hollywood, fifty-year-old Mo looked decidedly ordinary. From his ebbing hairline to his slight paunch, everything about him said Nothing Special—except for his eyes. They were a rich sable color, and his eyelids were so heavy that he almost looked asleep. But Pru had a feeling he never slept.

"Ms. Daniels," he said. "Thank you for dropping by. Here's your script. Good luck with it." He handed her the screenplay. "And next time," he added, "be sure to go through proper channels—or I'll see you in court."

In a gesture meant to dismiss her, he picked up the phone, but Pru planted herself in front of his desk and hovered there like a vulture until he had no choice but to meet her narrowed gaze.

"I think we've finished our conversation," he said.

"The only reason you're passing is that you don't like my style."

"To say the least, Ms. Daniels."

"But, Mr. Blake, it's bad business to let a good script get away just because you don't approve of the way it was delivered."

"It's bad business to form a working relationship with a young woman who shows contempt for other people's property. I don't like your methods."

"And I don't like your studio rules! But you *do* like this script, and you're crazy to let our differences interfere with making it. We both know it's blockbuster material."

"Possibly. But I didn't get where I am by allowing would-be producers to ride roughshod over me."

"Well, you certainly didn't get where you are by turning down monster hits that land in your lap."

"Ms. Daniels, if you'll kindly show yourself out—"

Suddenly the intercom buzzed. "Yes, Roz, what is it?" Mo's eyebrow raised in puzzlement. "Kat Winter?"

Perfect timing, Pru thought as he took the call.

"Hello, Kat, how are you?" he said warmly. "I see. Mm-hmmm." He listened for a long time, then bid Kat the standard Hollywood sign-off: "Of course, doll. We'll do lunch. *Ciao!*" He put the receiver back on the hook.

"Name your terms," he said curtly, without so much as looking at Pru.

"What are you talking about?" she asked innocently.

"Kat Winter says she wants to option *College Craze* if it's still available."

"And is it still available?"

"Not if it means she snags it and takes it to Warner's," he said, buzzing Roz. "Get the legal eagles up here, please."

Pru suppressed a shout of joy as she looked Mo squarely in the face and wondered for a fleeting second if his chocolate eyes were melting. She decided to strike while the iron was hot.

"These are my terms, Mr. Blake. Two hundred fifty thousand—and four points. I produce, you're executive producer."

"I can live with that," Mo said evenly.

Twenty minutes later, the contracts were signed, and Mo and Pru shook hands.

"You won't be sorry," she told him.

"I won't hold my breath, either," he said, and suddenly it occurred to them both that they'd been shaking hands just a tiny bit longer than protocol demanded. They moved apart quickly, and Pru started to leave.

"By the way," Mo called after her, "tell your friend Kat that she deserves an Oscar for best actress in a leading role on the telephone."

"You knew!" Pru blushed, her eyes greener than twin pieces of jasper.

"Of course."

"But if you knew she was bluffing, why did you make the deal?"

Mo grinned. "I love that script! It's an all-girl *Animal House*. I haven't laughed so hard in months. Right from the setup, I knew I had to have it. But I was so mad at you for diddling with me that I almost talked myself out of it. Then your pal called with her outrageous bluff, and I realized that if you can inspire that kind of loyalty in your friends, *and* you're running with the funniest script I've read in ages, then I can forget your guerrilla tactics and give you a shot at making some money for Heliotrope."

"Thank you very much, Mr. Blake—"

"Mo."

"May I use your phone, Mo?"

He tactfully disappeared while Pru called Leah with the good news. She chattered on about terms and points, but the money talk meant nothing to Leah. All that mattered to her was that someone out there liked what she'd written. Listening to Pru, she looked past her window at the lavender- and orchid-streaked sunset. If anything that beautiful could be real, then maybe—finally—her dreams would come true.

Nineteen

AFTER A LONG, exhausting day posing for publicity shots, Kat was feeling pretty wrung-out as she drove up Nichols Canyon, but she got her second wind in a hurry when Leah told her that Michele had called: Tommy O'Toole and Chaz were ready to make some major concessions on the *Gambit* deal.

An hour later, when Kat swept into Michele's office, her hair floating after her like a golden cloud, everyone was waiting. After hemming and hawing for an hour and a half, Chaz conceded that Tommy would not insist on directing. That didn't mean the deal was sealed—there were still a lot of terms to haggle over—but the biggest hurdles had been overcome, and Kat was delighted.

When she got back to the house, Sam and Leah were out on the deck doing a dance Sam had learned in Togo, but they cut their gyrations short when they saw Kat coming.

"Wait right here," Leah said.

She went into the kitchen and returned with a steaming lobster bisque and a baby asparagus soufflé. She set them down on the redwood table and motioned to the others to come and eat.

"In Pru's honor," she said resignedly, "I slaved over a hot stove all afternoon—and she stood us up."

"Why?" Kat asked.

"She forgot she had a date to save her marriage tonight. She went with John to a poetry reading."

"What a good idea," Kat said stoutly, sampling the perfect soufflé.

"Please," Leah scoffed. "Pru hanging out with would-be bohemians? I can't imagine what she'll make of Allen Ginsberg . . . Sam, will you please pass the soufflé?"

"It's delicious," Kat said.

"If I say so myself," Leah agreed, closing her eyes as she swallowed a forkful. "Sex doesn't hold a candle to this!"

"How would you know?" Sam grinned.

"Don't start," Kat scolded. "You two!"

"Sam's right," Leah said magnanimously, "and come to think of it, none of us is exactly burning down any beds, are we?"

"In my dreams," Kat sighed.

Leah directed her gaze to Sam. "Correct me if I'm wrong, but hasn't it been ages since the last time you shocked us with one of your sordid escapades?"

Sam shrugged. "I got bored with wild abandon."

"A likely story," Leah said. "I'll bet John and Pru sent the Rams back out to pasture. Right?"

"John and Pru don't exactly inspire romance," Sam said. "And now that you mention it, most of the men I know don't either." She stifled a yawn and stood up, stretching her lean body. "I'm out of here," she announced. "I need my eight hours."

After she'd left, Leah said under her breath, "That woman looks like hell on the half shell, doesn't she?"

"Frank hit her a lot harder than she lets on," Kat said.

"Amen. I never thought I'd see the day when a man got through the armor that surrounds her heart. Why, I think a two-ton blast has blown her whole M.O. to smithereens."

Kat shook her head in agreement as they cleared away the dinner things.

While they were loading the dishwasher, Leah remembered what she'd been meaning to tell Kat.

"You got a message from Krysta Bennett."

"Oh? What did she want?"

"Just to shoot the breeze, I guess. And she even stooped so low as to chat with yours truly. She congratulated me on *College Craze*. I was shocked."

"Why?" Kat asked.

Leah rolled her big brown eyes. "It's not every day that the bane of my academic life calls up to heap praise."

"Why wouldn't she, Leah? She always liked you."

"Ha! Remember that scene I wrote for her acting class? Christ, she did everything but wipe her ass with it."

"She was only being tough, Leah."

"She was being *toxic*."

"Fiddlesticks. She just wanted you to write a better scene, and as I recall, that's exactly what you did. Right?"

"I guess," Leah replied, scowling. "But only after enduring extreme humiliation." Suddenly she brightened. "Anyway, I got back at her. I told her she's in the movie. That shut her up in a hurry. She probably thinks I really toasted her."

"But you didn't," Kat said.

"That's for me to know and her to find out—after she's suffered the way she made me suffer."

"You sure do carry a grudge," Kat sighed.

"Like Hercules," Leah said, bending her elbow and showing off a puny bicep.

Kat shook her head, and as she put the leftover bisque in the refrigerator, her lavender eyes widened.

"Leah Sirk, you shouldn't have!" she gushed. "You angel!"

She pulled out a mile-high banana cream pie, and they both reached for soup spoons.

With negotiations past the crisis point, Kat decided one evening to surprise Bob with a late-night visit. She called the governor's mansion from Des Moines International, and at two in the morning, Chuck picked her up.

As they drove through the dark, he realized that one of his tires had a slow leak, and even though she was decked out in honey-colored silk, she volunteered to help him change it.

An hour later, she walked into the foyer, where Bob waited under the chandelier. She dropped her overnight case and ran to embrace him, but when she wrapped her arms around him, he pulled back and stared down at her coldly.

"What is it, sugar?"

"Where have you been all night?"

"We had a flat tire. Chuck had to fix it."

"Is that all he had to fix?"

"Bob, what are you talking about?"

"Oh, I think you understand what I'm talking about."

He took her into his arms and kissed her roughly. Then he lifted her and carried her up the staircase and down the hallway to his bedroom. He kicked the door open and marched through the darkness to the bed. He dropped her onto the satin comforter.

As he clicked on the bedside lamp, she saw several weekly tabloids and magazines strewn across the carpet. One of the magazines contained a publicity still of Kat on the arm of a well-known Hollywood mogul. Another showed her at Disneyland with Tom Cruise and a group of handicapped kids.

"Is this why you're so upset?" she asked incredulously. "It's only public relations, sugar." She looked up at him. He was tearing off his shirt and breathing hard. "Are you listening to me?" she asked softly.

He answered by lunging at her. He covered her mouth with his own, and—consumed with a jealous lover's passion—kissed her so deeply that she could hardly breathe. His hands flew down her belly to her crotch, and as he pulled down her panties, his fingers forced their way inside her.

"No. Not like this."

"You love it like this," he groaned. "This is exactly what you've always wanted. To be mine, Kat. *Mine!*"

He pinned her shoulders to the bed and once more tunneled his way down her throat with his tongue. He swallowed her protests as she struggled in vain. Then he suddenly stopped. He reared back and unzipped his fly as his restless gaze devoured her. He fell on top of her, and parting her legs with his knee, he whispered fiercely, "I'm in charge here."

His weight was oppressive, and she fought her way from under him, but his arms clamped down hard on her shoulders.

"I want you," he insisted.

She shook her head defiantly. Then with all her might she shoved him away and rolled off the bed as he lost his balance. Quickly she stepped into her shoes and hurried from the bedroom.

As she hastened down the stairs, angry that he'd come on so strong, she glanced over her shoulder and saw him standing in the bedroom doorway, watching helplessly as she left. In the foyer, she grabbed her overnight case as she pushed open the front door.

She hurried to the garage, where a light burned in the window.

"Please," she said to Chuck as she stepped inside, "if it's not any trouble, I'd like to leave now. I'd like to find a hotel."

Noting her disheveled clothes and mussed hair, he nodded. She climbed into the limo while he put it in gear. As he drove through the dark to a downtown hotel, she tidied her hair, slipped a scarf over it, and perched a pair of sunglasses on her nose. By the time they pulled up at the hotel entrance, she looked anonymous—and perfectly composed. For privacy's sake, Chuck booked her a room while she stayed in the car. Then she thanked him and headed into the elevator.

Driving away from the hotel, Chuck wondered what had happened in the mansion. Poor Kat must have been subjected to one of the boss's tantrums. Governor Rice was too temperamental, and Chuck vowed he wouldn't put up with him very much longer. Just as soon as he found another job, he'd be out of there.

Kat slept for thirteen hours, and when she awoke, her first thoughts were of Bob. For all his impeccable manners and courtly behavior, he was really just another macho creep. Kat had known too many men like that, and she wasn't about to put up with another one. As she threw open the drapes and let the sunlight warm her, she relegated Bob to the past, where she knew he belonged. Then she dressed and went downstairs to catch a cab to the airport. As she climbed into the taxi and closed the door behind her, Robert Rice was all but forgotten.

When she arrived back in Nichols Canyon late that afternoon, there was a long apology from him on the answering machine. He sounded subdued and very sincere, but Kat wasn't fooled. With a flick of her wrist, she erased Bob's voice forever.

Twenty

In the offices of Time-Life, Sam collapsed.

When she came to, her friend Sharon was standing over her, pushing the lank, sweat-soaked hair out of her eyes.

"You're on fire," she said worriedly.

Sam shook her head and sat up slowly. She felt fine. "It's nothing."

"I wouldn't be so sure, Sam. I think you've got a touch of flu. Go home and get some rest."

"Okay, but I'll call you later. I got the green light for a follow-up to *Rebels*, and I want your ideas."

"I'm honored," Sharon said. "Now, scram!"

Sam started down the corridor feeling slightly light-headed, and the next thing she knew, she was flat out on a gurney, staring up at the glaring lights of a hospital room. A concerned face loomed overhead.

"What's wrong with me?" she asked weakly.

"You have a virus," the doctor replied.

"Well, I hope it's the twenty-four-hour type." As she raised herself on her elbows, she realized she felt perfectly all right. "Whatever it was, it's burned itself out," she said, sitting up and smiling.

"I'm afraid not, Ms. Devane." He hesitated. "Your bloodwork indicates a parasite. Have you been out of the country—in the jungle, perhaps?"

"Dammit," Sam said. "I've been in Africa. In Togo. I always get something when I travel. What is it this time?"

she asked, only half listening. She swung her legs over the side of the gurney and looked around for her shoes.

"You have what's called the Ivory Coast Sleeper," the doctor said carefully, as if he were splicing the words together in an editing room.

"Well, zap it with penicillin and get me out of here!"

"We can't do that," he said in a voice so low she could hardly hear him.

"Pardon me?"

"We can't help you, Ms. Devane. I'm sorry." He paused, and the only sound in the room was the ominous ticking of the wall clock. "It's not good," he said. "The prognosis . . . Ms. Devane, what you have is incurable."

The room spun, and she found it hard to breathe.

"You mean it's fatal," she said. Her tongue was thick in her mouth as she asked him vaguely, "No drugs? No treatment? That's impossible."

He shook his head. "I'm afraid not."

"I see . . . What will happen to me, Doctor?"

"The kind of thing you've just experienced. Sudden fever. Fainting. Over the course of time, your heart will weaken—"

She cut him off. "How long?" she asked dully.

"Two years at the outside . . ." The words seemed to crumble in his mouth.

"Thank you." She rose, and as she shook his hand, her silver eyes were flecked with light. "I'm going to beat this thing," she said. "Or die trying."

"This is just like old times," Pru sighed, moving in on her third slice of pizza.

"I love it," Leah agreed. "The four of us, chowing down at Chez Bimbo, where it all began."

Kat contentedly surveyed the Westwood apartment. Pru and John had fixed it up nicely. Pru's salary had paid for an Italian leather couch, and John's enormous library covered the walls with books.

"Where is that sweet old man of yours?" Kat asked.

"At the library." She plainly didn't wish to discuss it.

"Well, that's his tough luck," Sam said heartily. "He's

going to have to eat cold plantains flambé. Which reminds
me . . .'' She dashed into the kitchen.

"Sam's in a good mood," Leah remarked. "I've never
known her to cook before."

"And clean!" Pru laughed. "You haven't lived 'til you've
seen her wield a broom."

"Africa really changed her stripes," Leah said, and the
others groaned their appreciation.

In the kitchen, Sam flipped the bananas in the frying pan
and marveled at how well she felt. It was difficult to believe
what the doctor had said, but he'd carefully explained what
to expect. First the episodes would be mild, but they'd
worsen, and intensify, and eventually . . .

She pushed the thought away. She'd made her decision.
She would carry on as if nothing were wrong. She'd work,
and play, and above all, she'd keep her illness to herself. She
didn't want pity, and more importantly, she couldn't bear the
thought of being a burden to her friends.

"How about those fritters?" she heard Pru shout.

"Coming right up!" She brought them in, flaming like a
small forest fire. The women dug in, and as the last sweet mor-
sel slid down Pru's throat, she looked guiltily at the others.

"I forgot to save some for John."

"John who?" Leah quipped, but Pru didn't smile.

"I'm wondering that myself." Pru looked away. "Sometimes I think he and I don't have the faintest idea who the
other one is. Can you believe that I once thought he'd love
my exciting Hollywood life-style?"

"And he pegged you for Anne Hathaway," Leah reflected.

"Who's that?" Pru asked.

"I rest my case. Shakespeare's wife."

"You're on to something there, Leah. I think what happened
was, I used to be the only person who managed to stay awake
in his English classes, so he decided that I was the literary type.
He never knew that I crammed like hell to earn those A's."

"And I'll bet you left a few dog-eared Cliff's Notes in your
wake," Leah remarked.

"Guilty as charged," Pru admitted. "For the longest time,
I thought it wasn't Shakespeare if it didn't have black and
yellow stripes on the cover."

"And now you sit across from him at the dinner table, and he recites the Dark Lady sonnets while your head bobs in your soup. Right?" asked Leah. Pru nodded balefully.

"Don't you and John have things you both like?" asked Kat.

"If we do, we haven't found them. Except, of course, divorce. Now, *that's* something we both might like. A lot."

"Oh, Pru, don't talk like that," Kat said as she ruffled her flaming hair.

"It's not that bad, is it?" Leah asked.

"Nothing a pint of Ben and Jerry's won't cure," Pru said as she sprinted for the kitchen.

Much later that night, Kat was back home, looking for her briefcase, when she remembered where it was. She'd gone to Westwood straight from a meeting with Tommy O'Toole, and she'd left her briefcase on Pru's dining room table.

Exasperated with herself, but wanting to go over some points Tommy had raised, she drove to the Westwood apartment. She found her old key on her key ring and let herself in.

Stealthily she retrieved the briefcase. Then, as she tiptoed out of the apartment, she noticed a light on in Sam's room. She'd assumed everyone was fast asleep, but—always ready for some late-night talk—she quietly approached Sam's door. It was ajar.

"Are you awake?" she whispered.

There wasn't any response, so she crept in to turn off the light. As she reached across her sleeping friend to switch off the lamp, she saw that Sam's face was wet with tears. In her hands she held a crumpled sheet of paper.

Curiosity got the best of Kat. She opened the paper and read what Sam had written.

"Dearest Frank," it began. "I'm writing to say that I love you. I've always loved you, and now that I'm sick with no hope for recovery—"

It stopped there. What was she talking about? She knew Sam had been feeling ill—some kind of virus—but no hope for recovery . . . ?

Nausea lodged inside Kat's belly.

With clammy hands, she put back the tear-stained letter. Covering her mouth, she staggered out of the dark apartment.

When she got inside the Saab, her screams began.

Bob couldn't get Kat off his mind, and he regretted having lost his temper that night. Things had really gotten out of hand, and now it looked as if Kat might *never* come around.

"What's the story, chief? Have you reached her?"

Bob looked up. His recently hired campaign manager waited impatiently for an answer. "Not yet," Bob answered.

"Well, put the pedal to the metal," Freddy chided. "My figures say you need her on your arm if you intend to be re-elected. The public can't get enough of that angelic face of hers. And if you're thinking Oval Office, you'd better have some babies too."

"She's not sure about me," Bob hedged.

"Well, make her sure, chief. Get her thinking with her twat, ya know what I mean?"

Bob reddened and Freddy sighed in exasperation.

"Look," he said, "the bottom line is, voters like *her* more than they like *you*, so let's bang those wedding bells already."

"Soon," Bob promised.

"Very soon. My man in L.A. says you're not the only stud sniffin' around. There's some other dude—"

"Who?" Bob glowered.

"Simmer down, big fella."

"Who, goddamnit?" Bob's eyes narrowed to slits.

Freddy checked through the hefty file he was holding until he pulled out a Xerox of Kat's last phone bill. He read what the private investigator had scribbled across the top.

"Here it is . . . Mick O'Reilly." Freddy looked up and smirked. "Think she'll dump you for some Irish cop?"

"Shut up, you idiot." As Freddy gave a little salute and left, Bob punched Kat's number into his phone. But when he reached her answering machine, he slammed the receiver down. For a long time afterward, he sat staring at the framed photo of Kat on his desk.

"Bitch," he said softly. With his fist, he shattered the glass.

Twenty-One

UNDER MO BLAKE'S wing, Pru was learning how to package a film. The process thrilled her, but when she tried to share her excitement with John, it was all he could do not to recoil in revulsion. As far as he was concerned, Hollywood was the pond where guppies grew into piranhas. He saw it every day at the studio school, and it made him feel as if he were swimming in quicksand.

He needed to talk, but when he voiced his disturbing feelings, Pru's response was pure irritation. She couldn't believe what a complainer he'd become. Two days before Christmas, he started up again, and she found she'd had enough.

"Will you please give it a rest?" she snapped. "Find something else, why don't you!"

"I'm stuck where I am until the school district lifts its hiring freeze."

"Well, maybe you shouldn't work at all, then," she said. "I make plenty of money. Quit your job."

"Come on, Pru. You, of all people, know how important it is to do meaningful work. But teaching those snakes in training isn't meaningful—"

"Oh, for God's sake!" she interrupted. "Stop griping about meaning, will you? Who the hell knows what meaning is, anyway? Just write your poems, or get a real estate license, or do something—but don't bother me about it."

John looked at her in stunned silence, and Pru softened.

"I'm sorry," she said. "That wasn't fair."

"It's all right," he told her. "I know you're under a lot of pressure . . ."

He put his arms around her, and he was about to kiss her when suddenly she reared back.

"My God!" she cried. "I'm late!"

She ducked his embrace, grabbed her briefcase, and blew him a kiss as she flew out the door.

"We'll talk later," she promised on the run. Her words were muffled by the sound of the Mustang roaring into gear.

Watching from the window as she disappeared in a cloud of exhaust, John made his decision. He needed time to think. He packed a bag and headed north.

That night, when Pru discovered his absence, she threw herself into the rewrite with Leah.

"You never let up, do you?" Leah said. "You'll be schmoozing at your own funeral."

"Only if the right people show up—and they'd better," Pru remarked. "Besides, look who's talking. You're not exactly a slug yourself. These pages are great," she said as she stuffed the revisions into her briefcase.

The next morning, she delivered them to her production manager, then met with Mo. As always, she was impressed by Mo's business acumen. He asked all the right questions and came up with endless tricks for cutting costs. Moreover, he was a great teacher and seemed eager to pass on his wisdom to Pru. But the thing that mattered most to her was that he treated her as an equal. In a town teeming with men who patronized women under the best of circumstances, she was grateful not to be working for one of the kind who called women B-girls—for bimbo—behind their backs.

As she left his office, he cautioned her to drive safely in the holiday traffic.

"I will," she promised.

"I'll bet you and your husband really deck the halls and roast the chestnuts. The whole bit," he said with a smile.

Her freckled brow furrowed as she thought of the Scotch pine standing naked and bedraggled in her living room. John had brought it home and asked her to help him decorate it, but she'd been too busy.

"Are you all right?" she heard Mo ask. He looked genuinely concerned, and it occurred to Pru that maybe he wasn't the simple, studio-stamped dynamo he appeared to be. Maybe there was more to him than nerves of steel and a mind like a silicon chip.

"I've never been better!" she answered gaily. Impulsively, she kissed his cheek. "Happy holidays, Mo!"

As she dashed out the door, red hair flying, he watched her like a smitten schoolboy.

"Happy holidays," he wished her softly. He traced the place where her lips had brushed his cheek.

While Leah spent Christmas under Pru's thumb, hammering out the rewrite, Kat flew home to West Virginia for some much-needed rest. Concern over Sam plagued her. She wanted to confront her, but she wasn't sure how. So far, she'd kept Sam's secret from Leah and Pru, but that didn't feel right either.

Kat didn't know what to do. Her nights were sleepless—wrestling with her dilemma—which made her days with Misti all the more necessary. For a whole week she indulged herself in the pleasure of her daughter's company. She marveled at what a young lady Misti was becoming. She'd always had her mother's extraordinary violet eyes, but now her body was beginning to fill out, and it looked as if it would mirror her mother's curves.

Gazing at her child, grieving for the years they'd been apart, Kat made her New Year's resolution.

"Marie Winter," she announced the night before she left, "it's time to put the trailer up for sale."

The authority in her voice jolted Marie.

"Kathleen," she said, "let's talk about this later."

"No, Mama. I've let you order me around long enough, and now I'm giving the orders. You and Misti are coming to live with me, and I won't take no for an answer."

"Since when do you talk to your mother that way?"

"Since I grew up, Mama, and realized that life's too short for the kind of hash you've been slinging."

To Kat's great surprise, and for the first time in her life, she heard not one syllable of argument from her mother.

She flew back to L.A. in a state of giddy exhilaration.

Marie was finally coming around—and Misti would be coming home. Now all that was left was the matter of Sam, and Kat knew exactly what she had to do. It was time to face her. Sam needed to know that her friends would be with her—no matter where the future led.

Sam spent Christmas at her parents' estate, regaling them with tales of her African adventures. She didn't tell them about her illness; there was no reason to make them suffer so early in the game. Instead, she stuck to the lighter side of her travels. Her stories meant a great deal to her mother: raised by an aunt in San Francisco, Polly Devane knew little about her parents' life. She was grateful to Sam, and even if it was difficult for her to express her gratitude, Sam sensed it, and was touched. She knew well what it was like to be grateful; she herself was immensely thankful for all that Africa had given her.

On Christmas Eve, she put a call through to the mission, and from the sound of Vonga's voice, she knew instantly that something wasn't right.

"Clayton's in England," Vonga said. "He hasn't been well. He needed a holiday . . ."

Sam's hands were trembling as she put down the phone. She didn't have to guess what was wrong with her friend. Across the vast space between them, her heart reached out to touch him.

The day after Christmas, she drove into San Francisco and dug in her heels at the Africa Center. Painstakingly she began the research on the follow-up to *Rebels*. She screened countless films from the center's archive, searching for footage she might borrow.

The work was good for her. It gave her strength and the will to go on. It occupied her thoughts and left her no time to brood about the next bout of chills and heart palpitations. Luckily, she hadn't had any symptoms in weeks. She was remarkably free of light-headedness—unless she counted the times, late at night, when her mind wandered into terrain she'd vowed not to enter. Fever gripped her then, and her heart raced uncontrollably as hot tears burst from her burning eyes.

* * *

"Sam?"

In the post-Christmas rush at LAX, Sam was waiting at the baggage carousel when she heard her name being called.

"Over here, Sam!"

She searched the crowd and finally spotted Kat, in dark glasses and a paisley scarf, waving frantically from the far side of the turnstile. She grabbed her luggage and ran to meet her.

"To what do I owe this honor?" she asked, hugging Kat.

"Can't a girl offer her buddy a lift?" Kat answered, taking Sam's bag. "Or would you rather call a cab?"

The two women linked arms and made their way to Kat's Saab.

"It's good to be home," Sam sighed happily as Kat drove west on Olympic. "Hey, wait a minute. You missed the turn for Westwood. Where are we going?"

Kat pulled into a parking lot and pointed to a nearby coffee shop. "Come on," she said, and from the tone of her voice, Sam knew better than to argue. They went inside and took a booth at the back.

Sam quickly opened the menu and studied it avidly, avoiding eye contact with Kat. Finally Kat reached out and took the menu away from her.

"Look at me, Sam." She paused, and her voice was barely a whisper. "I know how sick you are."

Biding her time, Sam blew the frost-colored bangs off her forehead. "I don't have the slightest idea what you're talking about," she said evenly, but she wasn't as much of an actress as her friend, and under the scrutiny of Kat's relentless gaze, she stopped pretending. Her lower lip quivered, and her silver eyes were varnished with tears. In a few terse sentences, she explained about the virus and her prognosis. "Promise me you won't tell," she begged.

Kat's silence was her answer.

"Dammit!" Sam's beautiful face was contorted with anguish. "Promise me, Kat. For God's sake, give me that much." She shuddered and burst into tears, and Kat quickly circled around the table and sat down next to her. She pressed

Sam's cheek against her heart and held her like that for a long time.

Finally Sam was able to speak. "Don't you understand?" she asked. "Pru and Leah both have so many problems, and Leah isn't very strong to begin with. I can't tell them."

"If you don't, they'll never forgive you," Kat said. "Don't you know how much they love you, Sam? If you keep this a secret, you might as well spit in their faces."

"That isn't fair!" Sam cried. "I don't know how to tell them."

Kat clutched her friend's arm. "I'll help you," she promised. "We'll find a way."

That night, in a driving thunderstorm, the four friends met at Kat's. As soon as they'd hung up their raincoats, Kat seated them at the kitchen table and served steaming mugs of cocoa.

"What's up?" asked Leah, settling back in her chair.

"I hope we're going to talk about whoever it is that Sam's been keeping under wraps," teased Pru. "You can't fool me. I smell a hunk, and I'm right, aren't I? I've always been able to pinpoint the reason for that distracted look—"

Sam looked beseechingly at Kat, and the panic on her face struck Leah and Pru with horror.

"Oh, Jesus, what is it?" breathed Leah.

As silence filled the kitchen, Sam buried her face in her hands. Her shoulders shook as if she'd caught a chill, and Pru quickly threw her sweater around her arms. Outside, the wind rose and slapped torrents of rain against the window.

Pru looked at Kat desperately. "What's going on?"

Kat started to speak, but when the words crumbled and turned to dust in her mouth, Sam looked up at her and shook her head.

"You don't have to tell them," she said. She stared past the window at a palm branch flapping wildly in the storm. "I think I should say this."

"Say what?" Pru asked so sharply that her hand flew up to cover her mouth.

"I'm sick," Sam said in a faraway voice. Outside, the branch smacked so hard against the window that the glass rattled in its frame. Sam closed her eyes and breathed deeply.

"I picked up a virus in Africa," she said, "and there's no cure."

"What do you mean 'there's no cure'?" Leah asked, incredulous.

Sam turned to face her. "I'm going to die," she said. She heard her own voice as if someone else were talking, but she knew that the words were hers alone. She was amazed at how easy it was to reach out and speak to her friends. She clasped both of their hands. They in turn reached out to Kat and laced their fingers through hers. Among the four friends, love surged as powerfully as life.

Sam began to cry once more, and for the first time ever, she cried without self-consciousness or shame. The others took turns cradling her and stroking her hair as she wept to the soft accompaniment of the storm that was just beginning to wane.

After a time, when the rain had finally stopped and Sam's tears had subsided, Kat rose to refill their mugs.

"This is good," Sam said as she sipped her cocoa. "It's strange how everything tastes better now that I know I won't taste it forever." She smiled bravely, her face still shiny with the last remaining tears.

She gazed steadily at the other three women and spoke in a voice whose softness belied its strength. "Promise me you'll keep this confidential," she said. "I don't want anyone to know. Do you understand? Not anyone."

They didn't have to ask who "anyone" was.

"It's a deal," Leah whispered. Pru solemnly bobbed her head, and Kat, who found she couldn't speak, mouthed the single syllable, "Yes."

Thunder clapped far off in the distance, and together the women turned to the window. Above the luminous glow of the city, a jagged edge of crescent moon had broken through the inky clouds. The thunderstorm was finally past. In its deep black wake hung a glittering web of stars.

Twenty-Two

"SAM. GET YOUR skinny ass over to Kat's. *Before* 1987."

The note was taped to the front door at 612 Weyburn. It was New Year's Eve, and Sam had just returned from the Time-Life archive, where she was gathering background footage for the *Rebels* follow-up. She drove across town to Nichols Canyon, where her three friends greeted her in party hats.

"Happy New Year," they clamored as they brought her into the fold.

It was a nutritionist's nightmare. Every preservative, artificial ingredient, and saturated fat that had ever been processed was heaped on the coffee table. Mallomars, Butterfingers, Cheez-its, and all their relatives filled bowls everywhere. An ice chest overflowing with champagne and Diet Coke stood next to the fireplace.

"I thought you'd never get here," Pru said. She turned to Kat. "Now can we dig in?"

"Be my guest," Kat drawled.

"I hardly know where to begin," Pru said, but that wasn't quite the truth; she was already halfway through a Nutty Buddy.

"I don't think I can watch this," Sam laughed.

"You must have seen worse," Leah said. "Didn't you meet any cannibals in your travels?"

"Very funny," Pru said. "But honestly, I feel that I owe

this to myself. After all, it's New Year's Eve, and my husband is off somewhere, probably with his nose buried in a book.''

"Better a book than a broad," Leah said.

"Oh, I don't know," Pru replied. "But enough," she said resolutely. "I'm absolutely ecstatic to be here with you three. Period. End of story."

"Right," Kat affirmed. "No persons of the male persuasion are going to deflate our happiness this evening. This party is strictly Ladies Only."

"Except for Mr. Salty," Pru corrected, chewing a handful.

"Hear, hear," said Leah. She cleared her throat dramatically. "I'd like to make the first toast of the evening." She raised her Diet Coke. "To hell—and back."

"To good times," added Kat.

"To good food," said Pru.

"To friends forever," Sam declared, her voice breaking. The others stared at her silently. For once, even Leah was speechless as Sam sipped her champagne.

From the mantelpiece, the sound of the ticking clock punctuated the silence. Sam's upturned face was full of fascination as she studied the sweeping motion of the clock's second hand.

When, after a moment, she looked back at the others, her eyes were dewy. "I mean it," she vowed. "I couldn't ask for three better friends. Whatever I have to go through, I damn well want to go through it with you."

"I'll drink to that," Leah said faintly, and took a slug of Diet Coke.

"Amen," Kat sniffled. As she blew her nose, Pru set down the bowl of Doritos she'd been clutching.

"I'd like to amend my toast," she said thoughtfully. "Forget the chow." She reached out and clinked her glass against Sam's. "Let's drink to tomorrow."

"And tomorrow," Sam smiled.

The toasts continued, and everyone from Mel Gibson to Alf was honored as the night wore on.

Long before the clock struck midnight and the New Year finally rolled in, the women were already ushering out the old one.

"Let's eighty-six '86," Leah declared. "Good riddance."

"How can you say that?" Sam asked. She requisitioned herself a bottle of Mumm's and sat demurely on the couch, legs folded like a swami's, as she took dainty sips. "This has been a great year—for each and every one of us. Honestly, can any of us say we didn't make serious inroads in 1986?" She scanned her friends' faces. "For example, Pru," she began with a twinkle in her eye. "Look at the inroads you've made in that box of Milanos!"

"Touché," Pru said, and she raised the last Milano in a gracious toast, then bit it in half. "I've got no complaints. Leah and I are giving birth to a major motion picture that will undoubtedly prove boffo at the box office. So, I for one am counting my blessings. Although I'd rather count box of-fice receipts. And while I'm counting, so should you, Leah."

"Right, Pru. I'm an alcoholic, I've got souvenir scars on my wrists, and I haven't had a date in nine months."

"But," said Sam, "what about the fact that you sold your screenplay for an obscene price, and your creative juices are flowing like mother's milk?"

"Yuck." Leah grimaced, hugging her tiny frame.

"Sweetie," Sam continued, "you are looking at a fabulous future, and all you have to do is show up."

"Sam's right," Pru told Leah, then she turned to Kat. "What about you, kiddo? Haven't you had a pretty incredible year?"

"Beyond my wildest dreams," Kat smiled. She turned a lock of honey-blond hair. "I've got my family in West Virginia—and my family here. I love my work, I love my house, and I love the way you all fill it up."

"Speaking of filling it up," said Pru, "we'd better do just that. It's almost midnight."

As the clock struck twelve, they raised their glasses and wished each other health and happiness. Through the win-dows, they listened while all of Los Angeles welcomed in the New Year. Together they walked out to the deck and linked arms, watching the fireworks light up the sky. Scarlet and pink showers danced across the dark as the women stood together, facing their future. When a chill set in, they moved back into the house.

"I'm starving," Pru whined. "Isn't there anything to eat around here?"

"There is," said Leah, "but you made me promise I wouldn't let you near it once the old, fat year was behind us."

"Oh, Leah, can't you take a joke?" Pru said. "I was only kidding. I'll start my diet tomorrow."

"It is tomorrow, and I'm afraid I'll have to make a citizen's arrest if you open that fridge."

"Please," Pru begged.

"Forget it. You made me promise to be a cop for the first five pounds. Which reminds me"—Leah raised an eyebrow at Kat—"how's L.A.'s finest, Officer O'Reilly?"

"Gee, I'm not sure." Kat felt the color rising in her cheeks.

"You talk to him every day, don't you?" Leah asked slyly.

"On the phone, you mean?"

"No. By mental telepathy. Of course I mean by phone!"

Kat blushed deeply, and Leah reached out to put an arm around her.

"I just want you to know I think it's great," she said.

"I don't know what you mean," Kat stammered.

"I mean I'm not carrying a torch for Mick. Okay?"

As Kat smiled and hugged Leah, Sam looked at her watch and frowned.

"If you're ready, Pru, I've got to run," she said.

"So soon?" Kat asked.

"I've got loads to do before I start filming."

"Now?" Leah asked. "It's New Year's Day!"

Sam smiled faintly. "My New Year's resolution is never to put off until tomorrow what I can do today."

A silence fell over the others. With downcast eyes, they walked outside to Sam's car.

"Be happy," she told them. "I am."

When she and Pru were gone, Leah and Kat began tidying up the living room until suddenly Leah stopped in her tracks.

"I've got an idea," she said. "Let's invite Mick over."

"Leah, it's two o'clock in the morning!"

"Great, he's probably off by now," Leah said as she went to the phone.

"Wait. Do you really think we should?"

"I think you two have been phone pals long enough," Leah said. "It's high time you met in person. And I'll even spring for the lox and bagels."

"Gee, I don't know—" Kat answered, smoothing her hair uncertainly.

"If you're worried about how you look—"

"Of course not! Don't be silly."

"Good. Remember, two hundred million Americans can't be wrong," Leah said dryly.

"Are you sure?" Kat asked.

"For God's sake," Leah rasped. "Even if you weren't the most beautiful woman between two oceans, you'd be a sight for sore eyes to a guy like Mick. He spends his life with murderers, for chrissake. Those guys don't even shave."

She picked up the phone, and Kat raced up to her room, afraid to listen to the conversation that was about to transpire. She was sitting on her bed, trying not to bite her nails, when Leah bounded up the stairs and called out, "He'll be here in half an hour. I'm going out to get the bagels."

When Leah returned, Mick was about to ring the bell. He turned and waited for her, and when she caught up with him, he lifted her off her feet, swung her through the air, and laughed heartily.

"Happy New Year!" she cried, and as he set her down, she realized with relief that it was no problem seeing Mick again. They were still friends. Just friends.

"Come on," she said. "Kat's dying to meet you." As she unlocked the door, Kat stood waiting, radiant beneath the light in the foyer. She smiled at Mick as she gripped his hand. "I'm so glad to meet you at last, even though I feel as if I've known you for a long time."

"You have," he said. "For six months now, I've told you things I wouldn't tell my dog."

"I'm flattered," she laughed.

Leah scooted past them, muttering something about getting the spread together, but Kat and Mick weren't listening. While Leah sliced onions and toasted the bagels, Kat showed Mick around the house. In the study, he picked up a framed photograph of Misti and inspected it closely.

"She's got your eyes," he said. "Prettier than the L.A. sunset."

He followed her out onto the deck, and the first thing they saw was a shooting star.

"Make a wish," he said, and they simultaneously closed their eyes. Impulsively they reached for each other's hand, then let go when they heard Leah's voice.

"Chow's on," she called from the kitchen, killing the mood.

They marched back into the house with their hands at their sides like tin soldiers, and Leah shook her head. Didn't they realize she was setting them up because she knew they were perfect for each other? Love could be stupid as well as blind.

Once they'd gone through the bagels, Leah beat a hasty retreat to give the pair some time alone. But unfortunately, Mick couldn't stay: he was working a split shift.

"So," he said as Kat walked him to the door. "May I call you?"

"That would be nice," Kat answered. "But if it's all right with you, I'd like to take things a little bit slowly—"

"I understand. We're not running a race here. We've got nothing but time."

She smiled gratefully and rose on tiptoe to brush her lips against his. Then she ducked into the house, quietly closing the door behind her.

As he walked to his car, Mick was lost in such heady thoughts of Kat that he didn't pay any attention to the Honda that was parked down the street, shrouded in darkness.

Whore!

Inflamed with jealousy, the governor of Iowa sat alone in the Honda he'd rented just hours earlier. Renting a car discreetly hadn't been easy—he'd had to first buy phony ID at a Chinatown bar—but there was no point in taking any chances. He'd planned this trip carefully. He was supposed to be vacationing in Nassau, working on a tan that would see him through the long Iowa winter, but unbeknownst to anyone, he'd slipped off the island for a brief jaunt to L.A.

He hit the steering wheel hard with his fist while he watched the last light go out in Kat's house. Then he turned on the ignition, and as he caught a glimpse of himself in the rearview mirror, he was pleased with the week-old beard and dyed-blond hair. His own mother wouldn't recognize him.

He drove down the canyon to the Hollywood motel room he'd paid for with cash. As he pulled into the parking lot, he chuckled at the name he'd signed on the register—I. Hawk. What a gag. He ambled into his sleazy little room, hit the floor immediately, and did a hundred push-ups to calm himself down. When that didn't work, he did a hundred more.

Twenty-Three

NIGHTMARES RACKED BOB Rice's sleep. Relentless gales rocked the boat of his mind, and when he finally awoke, he lay exhausted and drenched in a pool of sweat.

He showered and left his motel for a nearby Denny's. Dressed like everyone else in L.A.—in sunglasses and a jogging suit—he sat at a back booth. He ordered steak and eggs, and when they arrived, he ate heartily as he weighed his options. Part of him still longed for Kat and wanted to marry her, but after what he'd witnessed the night before, he had to face the unpleasant truth: she simply didn't measure up to his standards. In that case . . .

He picked up his steak knife and ran his fingers across its jagged blade. Then sipping his coffee, he pondered the two different plans he'd formulated. Unfortunately, the plan for love and marriage had been scuttled by Kat's unforgivable behavior. That left him no choice, Bob realized with reluctance. He'd have to set Plan Two in motion.

Kat was dreaming of a tall, broad-shouldered policeman when the phone woke her. By the time she answered it, Leah had already picked up the extension.

"Hello?" mumbled Kat.

"I've got it," Leah answered.

"Hi, I've got a problem," Pru said. She sounded terrible, her voice shaky and trembling. Kat sat bolt upright in bed.

"Pru! What's the matter?" Kat asked.

There was a snuffling noise.

"I'm sick as a dog."

Both Leah and Kat giggled.

"What's so funny?" Pru asked miserably.

"Well, honestly, Prudence, after everything you ate last night—"

"This is the flu, Leah—not indigestion. I've been up all night tossing my tacos, and my temperature's a hundred and one!"

"We're coming over," Kat announced.

"No, I'll be okay, really, but could you do me a huge favor?"

"Name it," said Kat.

"John's flight comes in at noon. Could one of you pick him up?"

"We'll take care of it," Kat promised. "Now, go back to bed and get some rest."

"You're an angel, Kat."

"What about me?" Leah quizzed her.

"The jury's still out," Pru answered, "and I'm about to be. 'Bye, ladies," she said, and the phone went dead.

Kat wrapped herself in a peach silk robe and padded down to the kitchen. "I'll get John," she said. "I feel like a drive."

"Got something to think about?" Leah asked slyly, buttering a piece of toast. "An officer and a gentleman, perhaps?"

"Perhaps," Kat answered, and blushed. She went upstairs to change.

Later, as her Saab peeled out of the driveway, Bob was right behind her in his rented Honda. He trailed her as she made her way down the winding canyon road, onto the freeway, and south to the airport.

When she swung into the PSA terminal a half hour later, Bob was still on her tail. He waited outside, and in a few minutes, she emerged on the arm of a handsome man. They got into her car, and Bob was once again in hot pursuit of the Saab.

In a patch of heavy traffic on La Cienega, Bob almost lost Kat, but eventually he tracked her to Westwood. When she parked across from the Weyburn apartment, Bob kept on driving. Two blocks later, he parked, then walked back to Kat's car. Her dirty little rendezvous was probably in full swing by now . . .

Furtively he glanced up and down the street, and when he was sure that no one was looking, he climbed into the back seat of the Saab, where Kat had left a pile of dry cleaning on the floor. He buried himself beneath it and waited patiently.

In Pru's kitchen, Kat sliced the last carrot into her famous chicken soup and left it to simmer under John's supervision. Then she checked in on Pru one last time, blew her a kiss, and left the apartment.

She drove all the way to Nichols Canyon and pulled into her garage without ever suspecting that there was a stowaway in her car. When she entered the house through the kitchen door, Leah glanced up from her typewriter.

"You've had three messages from Tommy O'Toole," she reported. "He wants you to meet him at the Polo Lounge."

"Shoot, I get so tired of meetings," Kat said. She looked at her watch. It was six forty-five. She sighed deeply. "Well, like my mama says, root hog or die."

Leah looked at her in bewilderment. "I suppose that's real Pig Latin?" she asked.

"For your information," Kat explained, "it means there's no rest for the weary."

"I could have told you that in English," Leah said with a grin as she waved Kat out the door.

Driving down Sunset, Kat was lost in delicious, lingering thoughts of Mick. She was totally unaware that her wheat-colored mane and lavender cologne were fueling a terrible energy in the back seat. Each moment that Bob spent in her presence fanned the fires of his wrath.

She pulled into the driveway of the Beverly Hills Hotel, left the Saab at the valet station, and headed into the Polo Lounge. Stealthily Bob rose up and peeked through the back seat window. He saw that the valet was busy parking a Bentley, so he climbed out of the Saab and strolled into the bar.

It was jammed with the privileged and the famous, but even in that dazzling crowd, Bob had no trouble spotting Kat. She was all the way across the room, this time with yet another lover. He took a table behind a potted palm and ordered a double scotch. As he gulped the drink, and then another, his jealousy ebbed. Calm resolve set in.

When Kat and Tommy O'Toole finally left the bar, Bob was way ahead of them. He caught a cab and headed east to Nichols Canyon. At Laurel Drive, he paid the driver. He walked the rest of the way to Kat's house. It was dark, and he had no trouble hiding himself in a rhododendron bush next to her garage. Then he knelt down, prepared to wait as long as it took.

In the end, that wasn't long at all. Kat drove up the street just a few minutes later, and she parked the Saab in the garage, then began the short walk to the back door.

Suddenly Bob leaped from the bushes behind her and locked her throat between his arm and chest. With a swift karate chop, he hit her skull so hard that she slumped noiselessly to the ground.

He fished in his pocket for the razor blades he'd picked up at Thrifty's that morning. He carved deep, crisscrossed ravines into each of her cheeks, then etched a zigzag across her forehead. Smiling as he pocketed the bloodied razor blade, he took off into the night.

He sprinted down the canyon all the way to Sunset. Somewhat disheveled but none the worse for wear, he walked a couple of blocks to the Imperial Gardens Restaurant, where he grabbed a cab for Westwood.

Two blocks from the Weyburn apartment, he picked up his rental car, then hightailed it for the airport and a return flight to Nassau. In all, his California trip had lasted only a little more than twenty-four hours. No one would even notice he'd been gone.

As he found his seat in the DC-10, he patted the pocket of his jogging suit. Through the fabric, he could feel the blade he'd carefully wrapped in a handkerchief. It was a comforting reminder of his firm resolve to keep the upper hand with Kat—even if she didn't know it.

His plane was close to lifting off by the time Leah stepped out the back door with a plastic bag full of garbage. When she heard faint moans, she tore across the yard. Kat lay crumpled like a broken kite on the lawn.

"It's all right," Leah sobbed, cradling her friend in her

arms. Vermillion streamers were running down Kat's face and into the grass, and when Leah felt the faint pulse in her throat, she knew that Kat was close to death.

Less than a week later, in a blinding blizzard, Bob Rice's limousine overturned on Interstate 80. Bob wasn't in the car at the time. His chauffeur, Chuck, was the sole fatality.

The governor was upstate when he got the news—and what a good piece of news it was. He'd begun to have serious doubts about Chuck's loyalty, and just a day earlier, he'd even caught him sneaking around in the mansion. That hadn't set well with Bob at all. He was accustomed to surrounding himself with fiercely protective staffers like Freddy. Chuck had never been that caliber of employee, and as far as Bob was concerned, his collision with a semi was the best thing that could've happened.

The limo was totaled and sold for scrap to a junkyard in Des Moines. There it would sit until piece by piece it was stripped down for parts. It might be weeks or months—or even years—before the package in the glove compartment would finally be discovered . . .

For Kat, the next few weeks were like an underwater ballet. The world was silent and languid. Her breathing tube rose and fell like gills, and each time she would rise from unconsciousness, the excruciating pain in her head plunged her back into darkness. Whenever she thought she might finally break through the surface of the water, something warm flowed into her arm, and she sank once more.

The nurses and doctors floated in and out of dreamlike scenes like actors in her private play. She longed to follow the action, but she couldn't concentrate; the stage lights were blinding, and the cues made no sense. *"Two hundred cc's."* *"Full serum count."*

And then one day, *"She's coming around!"*

With four operations behind her, and the swelling in her brain finally brought down, she woke up one sunny morning to see her friends standing above her. She tried to smile, but the pain in her face made her cry out.

Sam gripped her hands tightly. "It's all right, sweetie. You'll be fine."

Pru patted her knee under the thin hospital bedspread. "Looking good, kiddo."

"I don't understand," Kat whispered, but she couldn't say more; it hurt too much. Something was wrong, very wrong, with her face. She gripped Sam's hand, and a look of panic shot through her eyes.

"You're going to make it," Sam said firmly. When Kat tried to touch her face, Pru pulled her hand back.

"Don't do that. You got hurt—"

What happened? she tried to ask, but all that came forth was a guttural moan.

"You've got a face full of stitches," Leah told her. "They'll be out before you know it."

I don't believe you! Kat's mouth twisted and gaped like a wound.

"You've been here more than a month," Leah said. "Your family came. I'm sorry you missed them. Marie's a pistol. She really kept the surgeons on their toes. And Misti! What a beauty."

Leah prattled on as Pru swung the bed table across Kat's chest. On the table, there was a menagerie of tiny wooden animals. Kat reached out and picked up a miniature horse. She turned it over in her fingers, as awestruck as if it were a diamond.

"They're from Misti," Pru explained. "They're supposed to keep you company, since she had to go back to school."

"She didn't want to leave," Sam said, "but Marie said that's what you would have wanted."

Slowly, almost imperceptibly, Kat nodded.

Just then the doctor came striding in, and the women moved away from Kat to give him room.

"How are you feeling?" he asked, not waiting for her answer. He pulled up a chair and sat down. "You are a very strong young woman," he said. "And a very lucky one."

Lucky? she thought, despairingly.

As if he read the words behind her bruised violet eyes, he told her, "You're in good shape. Your CAT scan's fine. Unfortunately, the facial wounds are severe. We've done as much as we can for now. All we can do at this point is wait and see.''

Her body shook uncontrollably, and the bile rose in her throat as she tried to imagine what she must look like.

He patted her trembling hand. ''With microsurgery we can help you a good deal more, but skin tissue heals very slowly, and it will take time before your face is . . . as good as we can make it. I want you to know, though—we can work wonders.'' The doctor gave her a tight-lipped smile and rose.

When he'd left the room, Kat shook her head violently and struggled to sit up.

The mirror, she thought, *I have to see the mirror.*

Her friends looked at her blankly. She brought her hands toward her face, pointing frantically, and suddenly Leah understood.

''You want to see, don't you?''

Kat closed her eyes, grateful to be understood. Slowly Sam opened her purse and took a small mirror from her cosmetic bag. She placed the mirror in Kat's hand, then turned on the light above her bed. Slowly, with shaking fingers, Kat brought the mirror to her face.

Quickly she opened her eyes.

Nausea gripped her as she confronted the swollen, discolored, bandaged mass that had once been her face. She looked like animals she'd seen on the road, smashed to a bloody, unrecognizable pulp. With a wail that rose from the marrow of her bones, she hurled the mirror across the room, and it broke, like her face, into a million pieces. Silently Pru and Sam picked them up.

Kat motioned to Leah for a pen and a piece of paper. ''What happened?'' she scrawled.

Leah began to tell her the little that she knew, but she was soon interrupted.

''Mick!'' said Pru.

He stood shyly in the doorway, holding a bunch of daisies.

Make him go away, Kat thought helplessly. Instead, the others made a space for him on the bed, and his hand reached across the blanket to hers.

''Long time no see, babe.''

''He's kidding,'' Leah told Kat. ''He's been here every day

for a month now and, frankly, we're all getting pretty tired of him—''

"Kat, listen to me," Mick interrupted. He looked squarely at her mangled face, and she wanted to hide, but there was nowhere to go. And now there never would be. "You are going to get well," he said. "A hundred percent. And I'm going to catch the bastard who did this." He held out his hand to her. "Will you shake on it?"

As she squeezed his hand weakly, her three friends tactfully rose from the bed and busied themselves elsewhere, straightening flowers and flipping through magazines.

He leaned in so close to her that she could feel his breath against her ravaged face.

"They tell me I can't kiss you, or I might spread infection," he said softly. "But if I could, would you want that?"

Her eyes shone with the answer she couldn't speak. Her steady gaze said all there was to say in any language. By the time he kissed her hand and pressed it to his heart, she was taking her first small steps on the road to recovery.

Twenty-Four

BY MARCH, KAT was feeling strong enough to recuperate at home, and the doctor discharged her from the hospital. As Mick drove her up Nichols Canyon Road to her house, she stared despairingly at the security gate and electric fences; the place looked like a fortress. Leah was waiting at the gate, and she showed them how to use the alarm keys.

"It's for the best," she said as she led them inside. "And once we have the dogs—"

"No dogs, Leah. I will not live in a prison," Kat stated flatly. She sat down on the sofa while Mick paced the floor, fuming.

"Whoever attacked you is still out there," he said, "and we can't afford to take any chances."

"I won't take any chances, Mick—but I can't live like an inmate in my own house."

"Kat," Leah said in a brittle voice, "you were almost killed."

"Leah's right," said Mick. "The fact that you're alive is an accident. How do you know he won't come back to finish the job?"

"I don't," said Kat. "So I've got my fence, and I've got my alarm—but I won't have vicious dogs running loose."

A buzzer sounded, announcing that someone was at the security gate. Leah jumped up and went into the foyer.

"Who is it?" she asked into the intercom.

"Pru."

Leah pressed the button to open the gate. "Was that so awful?" she asked Kat. "Not exactly San Quentin, is it?"

"I suppose not . . ."

"There's no other way," Mick said. "Not with the attacker still at large."

"I'm sorry I wasn't any help there," Kat said miserably. "I didn't see a thing."

"I know, babe," he said. "I wasn't criticizing you. I'm just frustrated, that's all. It's been three months, for chrissake. My people have interviewed all your old boyfriends, and we've talked to every goddamned person you've ever spent more than five minutes with. They all have alibis."

Pru came up the walk and into the house. She hugged Kat briefly, then retreated to the kitchen with Leah. Mick ran his fingers through his disheveled hair. He looked as if he hadn't slept in weeks.

"We're up against a wall," he said dejectedly. Kat kneaded his shoulders and spoke softly in his ear.

"You've gone through a million fan letters," she said, "and you've rounded up every kook in L.A. You've done your best."

"Then my best ain't good enough." He looked at her wearily. "Sometimes I think I shouldn't have taken your case. Maybe it's too close. Maybe my judgment's impaired."

"Your judgment's fine. It's just like the other detectives said: psychos aren't easy to pin down, because they don't have logical motives like most criminals. That gives them the advantage."

"So what?" Mick snapped. "Dammit, he's out there, and I want him." He got up and walked to the huge plate glass window overlooking the canyon.

"Mick, you may never get him. We both know that."

"Bullshit. I'll get him if it's the last goddamned thing I do."

"But what if you don't? How long do we hang in suspense? I've got to get on with my life, Mick."

He turned on her. "Listen to yourself! You're willing to let him walk away scot-free because you want to get on with your life. You're a textbook case. You think that if we stop looking, then maybe it just never happened."

"How dare you talk to me like that! Do you think I can't see the scars on my face? I don't deny what happened, but unlike you, I intend to put it behind me. I can't start healing until I've gotten past it."

"Well, I can't get past it until I've got him by the balls. Can't you understand that?"

She looked at him defiantly. "Here's what I understand," she said. "I need you to be with me. Not with him. *I* want your time."

"But that's playing into his hand."

"You're already playing into his hand. He may as well have killed me for all the life you and I have together."

"That's how you feel?" His voice was dangerously quiet.

"Yes. You're letting him drive a wedge between us. He's winning, Mick. He's driving you crazy. You're living and breathing for him."

"I'm a cop. It's my job."

"It's not your job to abandon me when I need you."

"Is that what you think, Kat?"

"I think you've only got time for one of us. And you've made your choice, Mick."

He left, and when Pru and Leah heard the front door slam, they hurried in to comfort Kat.

"It'll all blow over," Pru assured her. "You're both under incredible pressure."

Kat's scarred face looked even redder and more swollen after she'd cried. Pru massaged her shoulders while Leah set a steaming mug before her.

"Drink," she ordered. "It'll help you sleep."

"I really am tired," Kat admitted.

"Well, then, get those famous gams outta here," Leah ordered.

Kat obediently went upstairs. When she was out of earshot, Leah said, "I'm glad she's moving her family here. She needs their support."

"Marie really came through, didn't she?" Pru mused. "I guess you wise up fast when you almost lose someone."

Leah nodded. "Now let's just cross our fingers that Mick doesn't stay away. Even with all this *mishegas*, he's good for her."

"That's what John says," Pru remarked. "He thinks they were made for each other. John's such a romantic."

"Hopeless," sighed Leah. "You think you can clone him? Or at least have him make a deposit at the sperm bank?"

Pru rolled her eyes and stood up. "I can see this conversation is deteriorating rapidly. I think I'll check my messages."

On her way to Leah's office to use the phone, she looked in on Kat, who was fast asleep. As she studied the wreckage of the actress's face, she thought of her own father, who'd also been badly scarred. His wounds had never healed, inside or outside. As she thought of him, she was flooded with sadness.

"Hang in there," she whispered to her sleeping friend.

She rearranged the quilt around Kat's shoulders, then walked heavily to the office and settled into a long afternoon of telephoning. As she gabbed and brainstormed with various members of her preproduction staff, her melancholy passed. Soon she was back in the thick of things, right where she belonged.

Days turned into weeks since their quarrel, and still Kat didn't see Mick. She tried to accept the fact that it was over between them, but she couldn't. There were times when she picked up the phone—only to slam it back down again.

If he wants me, he knows where to find me, she thought stubbornly. *I have my pride.*

Unfortunately, Mick had his, too. From where he was sitting, Kat had given him the old heave-ho, and he wasn't about to grovel where he wasn't welcome. Instead, he worked day and night to break the case. He dreamed of the moment when he'd pick up the phone and tell her the son of a bitch was off the streets. But until then, he wouldn't bother her. That was the way she wanted it.

When she was well enough to travel, Kat flew to West Virginia. Arriving in Frenchton, she wore a beret pulled low on her forehead, oversize dark glasses, pancake makeup, and blond tendrils framing her face. Her wounds had been much worse in the hospital, and Marie was stunned at how well the microsurgery had taken. She threw her arms around Kat, wishing she could absorb her pain. Instead, she handed her a broom, and for the next few days, the Winter women prepared for the move west.

There was packing to do, and Marie scrubbed and scoured the trailer for its new owners while Misti bid tearful farewells to her friends. Misti, who was getting used to the idea that her mother was rich and famous, decided to strike a bargain with Kat.

"Can I have a pony in California?" she asked.

"We'll see," Kat laughed, hugging her daughter and winking at Marie.

On their last night in Frenchton, Marie finished pin-curling her hair and rose from the sagging, threadbare couch. "I must be getting old," she complained. "Here it is, barely half past eight, and I'm as dead as a skinned muskrat." She headed down the short, narrow hall to her bedroom, then looked back at Kat. "We've got a big day tomorrow, don't we?" She looked small and fragile in the shadowy light of the trailer.

"Are you scared, Mama?"

"Stiff," Marie answered. "I haven't been so scared since the night you were born—but I guess that didn't turn out so bad."

"Quit your gushing, Mama, and go on to bed."

Marie nodded and shuffled down the hall. Kat picked up a novel she'd been reading, but she couldn't concentrate. For weeks now, she'd been torn up inside, wondering what to do about Sam. It was only right that Frank know about her condition. After all, she loved him. Quickly, before she could talk herself out of it, she picked up the phone and dialed. A man answered.

"Frank Steele?" she asked.

"Speaking. What can I do for you?"

"Frank, I don't know if you remember me. My name is Kat Winter—"

"Kat, sure. I heard about what happened to you. I'm real sorry."

"Thanks. Look, I'm in town until tomorrow, and I was

wondering if we could get together tonight.'' She hesitated. ''I wouldn't bother you if it weren't important.''

''You know the Dew Drop Inn?''

''I can be there in half an hour. Thank you,'' she said, but he'd already hung up.

The tavern was lit like a cave, which was fortunate, because Kat didn't want to be recognized. Now was not the time to sign autographs. She slipped into a back booth and waited.

Am I doing the right thing? she asked herself. Sam had sworn her friends to secrecy, and here was Kat, about to break her vow. But she had to. Sam was wrong.

''Hello, there.'' Frank's voice shook her free of her thoughts. He sat down, and she took a deep breath.

''I want to talk to you about Sam Devane.''

''There's nothing to talk about,'' Frank said, and the temperature in his voice dropped a few degrees.

''Do you love her?''

''What gives you that idea?''

''I'm asking, that's all.''

''Why?''

''Because it's important, Frank. Please tell me the truth. Do you love Sam?''

''Yes, I do.''

Kat didn't know whether to feel relief or sorrow.

''Has she said something?'' he asked tremulously.

Kat smiled gravely. ''She didn't have to. She loves you, Frank. But she's convinced that you don't care—''

''Where is she?''

Slowly Kat shook her head. ''I'm afraid it's not that simple. Let's go outside.'' She steered him out of the noisy bar, and they walked beneath the cottonwood trees while nightingales trilled in the branches. Kat looked ahead as she spoke.

''She won't like my telling you this—''

''What?'' he begged. She stopped in her tracks and looked him in the eye.

''Sam's very sick.''

''What do you mean? What's wrong?''

''She's dying.''

"But she can't be!" Frank cried out. "I don't believe you! It's a mistake!"

"No," she said sadly. "It's not a mistake."

Kat told him the story and as her words sank in, his eyes caught fire. They burned with determination. He gripped her shoulders, and his voice cracked with urgency. "I have to see her," he said hoarsely.

Kat put her arms around him as he sobbed on her shoulder.

Twenty-Five

IN SAN FRANCISCO, Sam was staying at her parents' pied-à-terre on Russian Hill. It was close to the Africa Center, where she was filming interviews with a Ghanian rebel leader in exile. The guy talked a blue streak, and Sam's workdays were marathons.

Late one evening, as she rode the elevator in the Victorian building, she happily anticipated a long soak in her antique, claw-footed bathtub.

At her door, her mind was preoccupied with the heady prospect of peach-scented bubbles—until a shadowy figure appeared before her. She froze in fear, and then, when the figure stepped into the light, she felt something worse than fear.

Her keys clattered to the floor.

''Frank!'' she gasped. Her heart pounded, and she swayed unsteadily, but it didn't matter: he was there to catch her. He held her close as he lifted her face to the light.

''I love you, Samantha.''

She twisted away from him and stood at arm's length. It took every muscle in her body to resist the impulse to rush into his arms, but she stood her ground.

''Good-bye, Frank. I'm sorry.''

She turned to go inside her apartment, but when her fingers trembled too much to turn the key, he brushed past her and unlocked the door himself. It swung open, and he gathered her effortlessly into his arms. He carried her across the threshold, into the living room, and to the bedroom beyond.

As she struggled in his arms, he held her more tightly, and when she felt herself longing to give in, she acted quickly, before she lost her resolve.

She slapped him hard across the face.

"Get out of here!" she yelled, but he didn't budge.

"We've got to talk," he said quietly. "About us."

" 'Us' was just a meaningless fling." Her lies tasted like sand in her mouth as she looked away from him.

"The night we had together wasn't meaningless, Sam. Not until we both acted like idiots."

"We weren't idiots, we were realists. We had nothing in common and no possible future. For God's sake, Frank, forget it."

"I can't forget you any more than you can forget me."

"You got married, Frank, and I wasn't exactly cloistered." She whipped around and faced him coldly. "I never gave you a second thought," she said. "And I'd like you to leave now, before I call the police."

He reached toward her, but she turned away, shaking her head. When she heard the door close behind him, she muffled her sobs in a pillow.

Somehow she slept. It was raining when she awoke. She sat bolt upright in bed when she saw Frank standing at the window.

"You left your key in the lock," he said. "You should be more careful."

"Get out of here. Now!"

"After you answer one question."

He looked out the window. High above the Golden Gate Bridge, the sun poked through between a pair of storm clouds.

"Have you ever been able to forget me?" he asked.

Sam was silent. He turned to face her, his eyes smoldering. "Swear that you don't love me, and I'll be out of your life forever."

She tried, but the words wouldn't form in her mouth, and he reached across the bed for her hand.

"I know you're sick," he said quietly.

"I don't want your pity," she choked.

"Pity?" He stared at her blankly, utterly devoid of comprehension, and suddenly relief opened up inside her like a small caged bird set free.

Never taking his eyes from hers, he fished around in his pocket and pulled out a modest diamond ring.

"My grandmother's," he said. "She'd be proud to have you wear it."

Sam burst into tears. She fled to the bathroom where she locked the door. Her sobs drowned out Frank's pleas to let him in, and all she felt as she sagged to the tile floor was her death engulfing her, pulling her down.

When Frank finally burst through the door, he brought her to her feet and spoke briskly.

"Get dressed," he commanded. He steered her back to her bedroom. "You and I have a date with the judge."

She shook her head. "I can't put you through this."

He smiled. "You can't stop me. Here—" He handed her her jacket. Helping her on with it, his fingers brushed her shoulders, and the blood pounded in her temples as she fought back desire. But it was no use. She let the jacket drop to the floor as she met his intense gaze. His mouth closed over hers, and their tongues found each other.

With one hand, he supported the small of her back, and with the other, he caressed the softness of her breasts. She pulled him down with her onto the bed, unzipping his fly as he buried his head in the lemony scent of her hair. When her hand found him, she touched him lovingly and stroked him until he was begging to be inside her.

Their clothes seemed to peel away from their bodies, and she wrapped her long legs around him. They fell into a single, pulsating rhythm, then, to her surprise, he slowed down his thrusts, and as her body tightened its grip on him, he inhaled sharply.

He picked up the diamond ring from her nightstand.

"Marry me, Samantha." As he slipped it over her trembling finger, she cried, *"Yes!"*

She arched her back to draw him in deeper, and the further he plunged, the more she needed him. She bucked beneath him as they came together, and afterward, when she lay in his arms, she twisted the ring on her slender finger and thought with pleasure, *I'm a married woman*. The rest was just a formality.

The next morning, as she piloted their aircraft toward Las Vegas, she and Frank got a few things out in the open. Frank confessed that almost three years earlier, while blind drunk, he and Leah had made rather sloppy love on the couch at 612 Weyburn.

"I can live with that," Sam told him. She paused uneasily, then gave Frank a somewhat condensed version of her own liaisons. Even in its shortened form, the chronicle took an hour, and she'd barely wrapped it up when the plane touched down at McCarren International. Unbuckling her seat belt, she turned and looked at him.

"Are you sure you want to go through with this?" Her heart stuck like a fishbone in her throat as the plane cruised to a stop.

He answered her by pulling her against him. Under her leather jacket, his hands unbuttoned her blouse and cupped her breasts. His tongue darted from one nipple to the other until she was flushed and breathless.

"Not here," she whispered, kissing the top of his head. But then she took a look around the empty runway, hung her jacket across her window, and let the boys in the tower think what they might. Smiling mischievously, she leaned back in her pilot's seat as Frank unzipped her leather pants. Soon his mouth was moving over her belly and into the warm, eager wetness between her legs.

Leah packed the last load of clothes into her Rabbit and wound down the canyon to Westwood. She'd decided to move back to Weyburn. Now that Marie and Misti had moved in with Kat, she felt a little like a fifth wheel. Besides, Sam was a married lady now and working in San Francisco, so Leah's old room was free. And what's more, Pru was lonely. She and John were spending most of their time avoiding each other, and since he practically lived at the library, Pru wanted Leah's company.

Pru also wanted to keep an eye on her. The partners were practically joined at the hip now that they were clearing the home stretch on polishing *College Craze*. The project was close to production, and the pressure was on to get a shooting script finished as soon as possible.

"Thank God I don't have a social life," Leah sighed one evening as they worked late in her office at the studio. "I'd sure miss it about now."

"Shoot, that reminds me." Pru looked at her guiltily. "We got so busy, I forgot to tell you: Krysta Bennett called. She invited us to a party."

Leah shrugged. "That might be fun. When is it?"

Pru shifted uneasily. "Tonight," she answered.

"And you didn't tell me?"

"We're swamped, Leah. You know that. Besides, you hate parties."

"But this one's different. I like Krysta."

"You do? That's a switch."

"Well, I wouldn't mind rubbing it in about *College Craze*. She always thought I was such a flake—"

"No, she didn't. She thought you were very talented. She told me so herself."

Leah raised an eyebrow. "A likely story. Anyway, the next time I get invited somewhere, will you please let me decide? You don't have to give me your answer now. You'll probably have a few years to think about it."

"Stop that, Leah. Let's get to work. Now, where's that party scene . . . ?"

They started reading some dialogue aloud, but after just a few minutes, Pru abruptly put down her script.

"It's ten o'clock," she said, glancing at her watch. "We could still drop by Krysta's."

"Are you kidding?" Leah asked. She tugged at the mass of black curls hanging down her back. "It takes me an hour just to blow dry this beast. By the time we get to the party, everyone will be gone—or unconscious. You can include me out."

"Really?" Pru asked with relief in her voice.

"Really, Cap'n." With a theatrical sigh of resignation, Leah hit the keys and made her typewriter sing.

Twenty-Six

ON HIS BIRTHDAY, John was a party of one.

Sitting in the bar at El Cholo, working on his third bowl of chips, he looked at his watch. It was 9:45. Their reservation had been for 7:15. Pru still had half an hour to go before she broke her own record. And probably the world's.

If only she didn't pull this all the time. Maybe then he'd feel a little bit worried. Call the hospitals. Check the morgue. But no, he wasn't worried at all. Just pissed.

He looked at his watch again. Ten o'clock. He thought about ordering another Tecate, then decided he wouldn't. Hurricane Pru wasn't worth a hangover.

He went to the lobby and called her office. It rang and rang, but she didn't pick up. Maybe they were in Leah's office. He started to dial that number, then stopped. What was the point? Pru would race across town, smother him with apologies, and make all the same promises he'd heard a hundred times before.

He went back to the bar and paid his check to the lovely señorita who'd brought him his drinks. As she flashed her automatic smile, he felt closer to her than he'd felt to Pru in months.

Driving home, he reached a decision.

He packed his things quickly and piled them into his van.

Later, when Pru burst through the door, his bookshelves were clear, his clothes gone. There wasn't a trace of him anywhere. It was as if he had never existed.

* * *

Returning home from a late meeting at Michele's, Kat found a small package on the table in the foyer. It was a postal mailer stamped in the left-hand corner with the logo of a Des Moines, Iowa, junkyard.

Thinking the package was a gift from a fan, Kat opened it distractedly. But once she saw what was buried inside the wrapping, she froze.

Nestled in several layers of tissue paper and a plastic sandwich bag was a single razor blade. It was wrapped in a handkerchief and accompanied by a note.

"Dear Kat, I thought you should have this. I found it in the governor's closet and put a different one in its place. I think it's what you're looking for. Your friend, Chuck Sorenson."

Kat took deep breaths. When she finally felt confident that she could walk without her legs giving way, she went upstairs to her bedroom. She closed the door and dialed the phone number on the logo of the Des Moines junkyard.

She spoke briefly with the man who'd found the mailer just days earlier, locked in the glove compartment of a wrecked limousine.

"I didn't know what else to do," he told Kat, "so I dropped it in the mail."

"Thank you," Kat said, her voice on the verge of breaking. "Thank you very much."

"No problem," the man answered cheerfully. "The wife will be tickled pink I talked to you!"

As soon as she'd hung up, Kat called Mick at police headquarters. It was the first time she'd heard his voice in almost three months.

"Please come," she begged him after she'd told him as much as she knew. She didn't have to ask twice.

He arrived with an L.A.P.D. evidence pouch and gingerly dropped the razor inside.

"I'll get this to the lab tonight," he said, tagging it.

She nodded stiffly, and as she held the front door open for him, he noticed that her face was almost completely healed.

"You look good," he said gruffly.

"Thank you. My doctor swears she'll make me look better than God did in the first place."

"I'll believe that when I see it," he mumbled.

"Oh, Mick . . ."

"I'm so sorry," they both said at once. They smiled shyly at each other.

"I was thinking," she paused uncertainly. "I could drive downtown with you." When he didn't argue, her pulse quickened. "We could . . . discuss my case."

They drove in silence for the first mile, and then, instead of discussing her case, they talked about more pleasant things, including Kat's brand-new domestic happiness.

"Misti and my mother are fitting right in. Misti loves everything about L.A., and Marie loves two things: Chinese food and freeways. She tears up and down the city all day, and at night she comes home with a big sack of Szechuan takeout."

"Me, I prefer lox and bagels," he said, with a sidelong glance at her.

"Keep your eyes on the road, sugar," she giggled. "I was making a point. Marie's happier than a dog with two tails. I was so afraid she'd raise the roof out here in the belly of the beast, but it's just the opposite: she seems to have left all that righteous hellfire back in Frenchton."

"Maybe her hellfire was just a bad case of loneliness."

"You sure are one smart cop," Kat said, and smiled at him.

He pulled into the parking lot at headquarters, ran the evidence into the lab, and hurried back to the car. Even though it was late and he was tired, he felt energized as he approached her. It was funny how the old spring in his step returned when Kat was around.

As he opened the car door and climbed in, Kat boldly spoke the words she'd been practicing since he left.

"I know it's late, but about those bagels . . ." she said. "At your place?"

As the last stars faded in the sky, they picnicked on his living room rug. When he finally leaned forward tentatively to wipe some cream cheese from her chin, she expressed her thanks with a long, deeply felt kiss. After they parted, he lifted her to her feet and guided her to the bedroom. They undressed quickly, sank onto the mattress, and his hands and tongue were simultaneously gentle and insistent as he explored her body. When he put his lips between her legs, she moaned and felt her pleasure ripple up from her loins. He stood up and led her to the window. Outside, the sky was as violet as her eyes. He wrapped her legs around his waist and stood erect inside her. With circular movements, he made love to her slowly, almost leisurely, until she came for the second time.

Then he took her back to the bed. He tenderly kissed her most sensitive flesh again before turning her over and entering her from behind. He moved cautiously at first, and then, as her moans grew louder and their passion climbed, the power of his thrusts increased. When he was about to come, she pulled away and dipped below his flat belly. Opening her mouth greedily, she took him inside her as far as he would go.

She was still savoring his salty taste when the LED on his bedside clock blinked six o'clock.

"Oh, no," she murmured, and he nuzzled the small of her back.

"I have to go," she whispered. He understood. They dressed quickly, and he drove her home. As they headed up the canyon road, the sky lightened from violet to a hazy pink, and he walked her to her door just moments before Marie and Misti woke up. She kissed him deeply, then waved goodbye as he headed down the canyon. Watching until he was out of sight, she wondered how she'd ever spend another night without him.

Twenty-Seven

DEW WAS STILL clinging to the grass when Mick returned from Forensics. His face was as hard as an ax handle, and Kat knew at once what he'd discovered.

"It's him, isn't it?"

"His prints are all over the blade. Along with your blood and skin tissue."

She fell against him and shuddered in his arms.

"It's over," he said, stroking her cornsilk hair.

She looked up at him, wide-eyed. "Are you sure?" She longed to share his confidence.

"He's history, babe. We'll fire up the warrant this morning. There'll be a hearing in Des Moines, and we'll have him extradited within twenty-four hours. With the kind of lab report we've got, no judge—not even one who's eating out of the bastard's hand—is going to sandbag this."

"But extradition doesn't guarantee anything, does it? He still has to get convicted."

"No sweat, babe. We've got the weapon."

"But couldn't a good defense attorney convince the jury that it wasn't a weapon? After all, I stayed in his house. I could have borrowed his razor and nicked myself. Don't forget, he's the Prince, and I'm the Showgirl. Who do you think they'll believe?"

Mick punched his fist into the back of the couch. Kat took his hand, and a sly smile slid across her face as a plan took shape in her mind.

"Forget the extradition, Mick. Let me bring him in. I guarantee, I'll serve him up like a tom turkey with all the trimmings."

"I won't even pretend to consider an idea like that," he scoffed.

She let her fingers drift to the knot in his tie. His breathing grew shallow as she loosened it.

"I promise I'll reel him in faster than any warrant."

"Are you crazy? The guy's a psychopath!"

"I'll be perfectly safe," she purred in his ear. "You'll see to that."

She laid her head against his chest and described her scheme. When he found he couldn't argue with its brilliant simplicity, he reluctantly agreed to go along with it. Immediately she reached for the phone and dialed the governor's mansion.

"Bob," she said breathlessly. "It's good to hear your voice. . . . It's been too long, you're right. . . . Yes, I got the flowers you sent. They were lovely. Thank you so much. . . . Well, yes, it's been a very rough time, but I think I'm coming around. . . ."

Kat looked nauseated as her eyes met Mick's. She groped for his hand and clutched it tightly while her phone conversation continued.

"Sugar," she cooed, her face grim, "do you suppose I could ask a really huge favor? . . . Oh, you are a naughty boy! . . . Listen, I've decided to go ahead with the *Hawkeye* sequel, and there's a press conference this evening. I know it's awfully spur of the moment . . . You *can*? You wonderful man!"

She covered the phone and took a deep breath. She was choking on the words coming out of her mouth. Nervously she twisted a flaxen strand of hair as Mick stood by, listening intently.

"I'll see you when you get here, darlin'," she cooed into the mouthpiece. "Maybe we can start all over again."

She hung up the phone. "Cut and print," she said bitterly.

She walked Mick to the door, and he held her tightly. "Are you sure you want to do this, Kat?"

"I'd like to do worse," she answered gravely. She tousled

his sandy hair and pushed him gently out the door. "There's a lot to get ready. I'll see you tonight, sugar."

When the caterer arrived, the *College Craze* set shut down for lunch. All things considered, the first morning of shooting had gone smoothly. Pru handled herself like a pro, and from the sidelines, Mo was pleased.

He asked her to have lunch with him in his trailer, and they carefully plotted the rest of the week's shoot. So far, things were in such good shape that it didn't take long, and as they polished off their pastrami sandwiches, Mo found the courage he'd been looking for all morning.

"Tell me where to go if I'm out of line here, but are you feeling okay?"

Pru sighed deeply. "I got served with divorce papers yesterday."

"Ouch."

"You bet. I had no idea it would hurt like this. My husband and I were in trouble almost from the word go, so it's not as if I didn't see the writing on the wall, but still . . ." She sighed miserably.

"I'm sorry," Mo said. "If you ever need someone to talk to, I'm here."

With a timid smile, he reached out and patted her knee.

Oh, swell, Pru thought. *Is this guy on the make?*

Her cynical streak told her he was indeed, but why? He could have any cupcake he wanted, so why mess with her? she wondered. In the last few months of her marriage, she'd blown up like a beachball, and she couldn't believe Mo was actually interested. It couldn't be *that* lonely at the top.

". . . I've never been divorced," she heard him saying, "but I've seen other people go through it, and it seems real bad."

She found herself genuinely puzzled. "How did you manage to get this far without a divorce?" she asked impulsively. "Not that it's any of my business—"

"My wife died."

"Oh, God, I'm sorry . . ."

"I've had time to come to terms with it. It happened thirteen years ago."

"And you've never remarried?"

He shook his head. "I threw myself into Heliotrope. That didn't leave time for much else."

"No kids?"

"Two. Sarah died with her mother. Lucien is eighteen. Sometimes I think he's never forgiven me for what happened."

"But surely he doesn't blame you."

"Not directly, no. But maybe if I'd been around more . . ." He paused. "My wife was driving the kids to a ball game. I'd promised to take them, but I got hung up at the studio. A drunk hit them head-on."

Reflexively Pru reached out and clutched his hand. His deep brown eyes filled with gratitude.

"You must be awfully strong," she said. "A lot of people wouldn't be walking around after that."

"I do all right," he answered stoically. He let go of her hand. "I go to work, build an empire, and live like a god-damned pharaoh. The only trouble is, none of it matters." Abruptly he rose. "Come on, we'd better get back to the set."

Dusk fell like primrose gossamer across the Hollywood Hills as Bob's limousine pulled up in front of Kat's. He waited for the electronic gate to open, and as he walked up the drive, her words echoed in his mind. *"Maybe we can start all over again."* It was true, he realized. They *were* being given a second chance! His heart soared with anticipation as he rang the doorbell and a butler showed him in.

Kat was waiting in the foyer, smiling. He was touched by how beautiful she looked in a strapless gown that showed off her creamy shoulders. And she was wearing his ring! He moved quickly toward her, but an inept waiter cut between them with a tray of drinks. Bob took a glass of champagne and followed Kat into the living room.

It was packed with press. Waiters were everywhere, serving drinks and canapés, and in all the commotion, Bob hadn't even had a chance to properly kiss his fiancée when he lost her in the crowd.

Then he saw her, walking regally toward the fireplace.

Daintily she tapped her glass, and the room came to attention. Cameras rolled, lightbulbs flashed, and reporters thrust their mikes at her as she smiled warmly and thanked everyone for coming.

"I know you're all very busy," she began, "and I won't take up too much of your time." With a gracious sweep of her arm, she gestured at Bob. "I'd like to introduce my honored guest, Governor Robert Rice."

He grinned and took a modest bow before Kat continued. "As many of you know, I've made a film in Bob's home state of Iowa."

A round of applause sounded for *Hawkeye*. Kat waited patiently for the cheers to subside before she continued.

"*Hawkeye* was a great experience, and it's no secret that I've been considering making a sequel. The sequel would also be produced in Iowa." She smiled directly at Bob, who blushed with pride.

"The Hawkeye State has been good to me. The Iowa Film Commission did everything in its power to make our stay a pleasant one, and it often seemed that the entire state lent its support. The extras, the caterers, the fans—everyone was wonderful."

She looked at Bob, and as he grinned humbly, the cameras trained on him for a second, then returned to Kat.

"Because Iowa has treated me so well, I feel it's only fair that I return the favor." She paused, and her lavender eyes sought out Bob. "Governor Rice, will you come up, please?"

He quickly joined her in front of the fireplace, and he would have linked arms with her, but a cameraman was wedged between them, filming.

"I would like to show my appreciation to the people of Iowa by taking this opportunity"—she paused dramatically—"to tell them the truth about their chief executive."

Bob frowned as Kat's words sank in.

She looked dead-on at the dark gleam in his eyes. "Over there, sugar." She indicated Mick, who was approaching the fireplace. In his upraised hand, he held the clear plastic evidence pouch.

Bob lurched forward to grab it, but instantly two waiters tackled him. They pulled out their guns.

"Freeze! L.A.P.D." As they wrestled him to the ground while reciting his rights, Kat moved quickly into Mick's arms. She gazed calmly at the press corps as she pointed at Bob.

"I give you the animal who left me for dead."

"Cunt!" Bob shouted. "You deserved it!"

Shutters clicked and video cameras purred as he twisted in his leg restraints and swore, "I'll finish the job!" Trembling against Mick, Kat watched the governor being dragged away.

She pulled the diamond ring from her finger and threw it into the fireplace.

Reporters scrambled to phone in their stories, and Kat went upstairs with Mick, where he held her as she sobbed with relief that it was finally over. On the landing, Michele held her ground and kept even the most aggressive press at arm's length.

When Marie and Misti arrived home moments later, Marie let loose with her mountain manners and shooed everyone out of the house.

"The coast is clear," she finally announced, and Kat and Mick came downstairs. Marie opened steaming cartons from Ah Fong's and inhaled deeply of the peppery aromas.

"This'll clean your pores," she said. She turned to Kat. "It'll also save you a bundle at Miss Fancy Pants Georgette Klinger's."

During dinner, Marie showed off her newfound skills with chopsticks, and the act was better than the late show at the Comedy Club. Misti, who'd been blissfully unaware of the day's proceedings, laughed until she cried, then excused herself to do her homework.

She came downstairs a little later, rubbing her eyes.

"Tired, sweetheart?" Kat asked. "Come on, I'll tuck you in."

As they climbed the stairs, Misti turned back and looked at Mick. "Do you want to come?" she asked him shyly.

By way of an answer, he barreled up the stairs two at a time.

Watching him disappear, Marie had to smile.

He's not half bad, she thought. *And he likes Chinese!*

Twenty-Eight

SAM'S DOCTOR REFUSED to let her make a trip to Africa to shoot the *Rebels* follow-up. Her fevers were only occasional, and they never topped 102 degrees, but even so, he was adamant. He told her the trip would only wear her down.

In the end, she was forced to send a second-unit team to get the footage she needed. She gave her friend Sharon the job of heading the team, and she knew that the film was in good hands. Meanwhile, she made contacts through the African embassies in San Francisco, and she shot several key interviews without ever having to leave the city.

She saw Frank every weekend. He flew in on Friday evenings from Charleston, and they holed up in the Russian Hill pied-à-terre with nothing but their passion to entertain them. It was plenty.

One Sunday, they awoke to such a crystalline morning that they decided to leave the city for a drive in the country. They were heading south on the sun-warmed peninsula when Sam had an idea.

"Why don't I show you Tara?" she suggested.

"I thought you didn't like to set foot there."

"Not usually, but Edward and Polly are in Santorini—no doubt driving the poor Greeks crazy—so this is the perfect time to show you around."

He looked skeptical.

"Oh, come on," she said wickedly. "What do you say we

fuck our brains out in the library, under the penetrating gaze of my missionary forefathers?''

He smiled and squeezed her thigh. ''Drive on, lady.''

As they passed through the gates and approached the house, Sam suddenly giggled. ''Did I tell you I wrote them when we eloped? Polly shot right back with a nasty telex: 'Isn't he the Communist?' We haven't been in touch since.''

She led him to the front door and punched in her code. ''They'd be mortified to know you're in their house,'' she said with a grin.

''Don't let me leave the toilet seat up.''

When they got inside, she led him to the drawing room. ''This is why I brought you here,'' she said, turning on the lights. She pointed to the wall of African artifacts.

''They're beautiful,'' he said softly.

Standing close to him, surrounded by such loveliness, she suddenly had to have more. She looked up at him, and her breasts heaved gently as she drew him to her. He leaned down to kiss her full, ready mouth, and then he lowered her tenderly to the Persian carpet. The great white house, which had always been so silent, echoed with their cries.

Afterward, they lay together, and he told her he had good news.

''Better than what you just delivered?'' she asked dreamily.

''We're going to be together, Sam.''

She looked at him warily. ''No more of this bicoastal crap?''

He shook his head and grinned. ''The Sutton Company's caving in,'' he said. ''The union's got them on the run, and the word coming down is, they're going to meet every one of our demands by the end of next week. This time, it's *our* contract, not theirs.''

''Frank, that's wonderful!'' She threw her arms around him. ''You've worked long and hard for this,'' she said huskily. ''What are you going to do, now that you've won?''

He reached for her silver and gold hair, and he buried his face in it. ''We'll think of something,'' she heard him murmur. His fingers wandered lazily down from her breasts, past her belly, to the heat between her thighs. . . .

* * *

The night wind off Malibu was high and wild. The surf pounded at Pru's feet as she strolled with Mo along the ocean in front of his beach house.

She trembled, and he gallantly dropped his tuxedo jacket over her shoulders. He closed the lapels across her ample bosom, and when she shivered again—this time not from the cold—he fussily arranged his cummerbund like a muffler around her neck.

"Next I'll be taking off my pants," he laughed.

Here's hoping, she thought.

"Thanks for asking me tonight, Mo. I'm always up for a banquet."

"Not me. I know it's part of the job, but Christ, those rubber chickens give me heartburn. I gotta tell you, Pru, I would've been miserable without you. You really lit up the joint, that's for sure. You were the prettiest woman there."

"Well, I wouldn't say that. Maybe the second prettiest."

They ambled in companionable silence as phosphorescent waves broke rythmically against the shore.

What's wrong with this picture? Pru wondered at one point, and then it hit her: Mo didn't have a phone stuck to his ear.

It's nice to see him so relaxed, she thought, stealing glimpses of his faintly Roman profile.

Finally, he spoke. "I can't remember the last time I took a midnight stroll on the beach. I feel like a kid again." He cast a bashful smile at her.

"You know," she remarked, "right now you're awfully different from that guy at the studio."

"You mean the ruthless, cold-hearted s.o.b.?" he asked.

She looked at him earnestly. "Just because you go after what you want," she said in a torrent of emotion, "people get all bent out of shape. They say you're hard-driven and screwed-up in your values—"

"I know," he said quietly. He looked at her for a long moment, and she saw her reflection in his deep brown eyes. "We're a lot alike, Pru." They walked on until suddenly he turned and faced her. "Most women find me—distracted," he said.

"Not me," she blurted.

''That's because you and I are distracted in the same direction.''

''Two sides of the same coin,'' she said softly.

Luminous in the moonlight, she tilted her face toward his, and he kissed her. In that lingering moment, a decision was reached. The evening would end in his bed.

They walked back to his house expectant but not in a hurry, and when they finally went upstairs together, Mo made love with consideration and skill. It wasn't the conquering of Everest, but Pru was grateful for that. She wasn't ready for another long fall.

Twenty-Nine

THE LONG HOT summer of '87 hit L.A. like a slap in the face, and every scorching day seemed to break yet another record. The Westwood apartment was unbearably hot, and Leah and Pru were constantly at each other's throats as the heat wave dragged into its third week. Fortunately, *College Craze* had finally finished shooting, and the pressure was off a little, but even so, there were postproduction problems plaguing Pru that made her less than easy to live with.

"Why don't you go stay with Mo?" Leah finally asked her in exasperation. "He's been begging you to move in—and I'm about to kill you here."

"Are you sure?"

"You'd better believe it. Where is that ax, anyway? Go on—get outta here!"

Pru wasn't about to argue. She'd been hankering to live with Mo, but she hadn't wanted to abandon ship. As it was, Leah had thrown her out—and Pru wasted no time packing.

The tiny Westwood apartment would have served nicely as a closet in Mo's spacious Holmby Hills mansion. Situated in the middle of several acres of manicured lawns, and flanked by a cool birch grove, the spread was the perfect place for Pru and Mo to feather their love nest.

Upon moving in, Pru began to gain valuable perspective on herself. Although she'd always felt guilty as charged of being a workaholic, she discovered that—compared to Mo—

she was about as hard-driven as a dozing cat. Mo *never* stopped, and even Pru found it slightly exhausting at times. Exhausting, that is, when it wasn't exhilarating.

Part of the exhilaration was seeing the way she satisfied Mo. He often told her that working side by side with her, then spending nights in her bountiful arms, was making him feel young all over again. One night he confessed that if he'd written down a detailed model for his ideal woman and then ordered the Property Department to build her from scratch, they couldn't have come up with a better piece of work than Prudence Daniels.

"Mo?" she asked one Saturday afternoon—their first day off in weeks—"How does trout almondine sound?"

Sitting poolside, she waited for him to glance up from the script he was reading. The light from the aquamarine water danced across her freckles and made her green eyes sparkle as she looked at him expectantly.

"Delicious, darling," he said, then returned to the screenplay.

Leah was coming for dinner, and Mo's son, Lucien, who'd been attending summer school in Europe, would be flying in to join them. Pru was anxious about meeting Lucien because she wasn't sure what they'd talk about. And when she asked Mo for suggestions, he was no help.

"Don't worry about it. Lucien will talk enough for both of you. He's the original bullshit artist."

As it turned out, he was right. Pru needn't have troubled herself unduly, because Lucien made things very easy. With his neat ponytail and the discreet diamond stud in one earlobe, he was every bit the engaging young man. His manners were impeccable, and as he helped toss the salad with a practiced hand, Pru was baffled that Mo had called him "a pain in the butt."

Whatever he was, one thing was clear: he was a dead ringer for Mo, except for the fact that he was taller and leaner. They both had the same dark eyes, full mouth, and restless gaze. Lucien, however, was missing his father's love handles. Instead he had the kind of rock-hard, aggressively muscled body that made most women take a second look.

When Leah waltzed in, she took one look at him, prowling

the pool area like a panther, and thought, *This party could get interesting!*

By the time dinner was served, she and Lucien had developed quite a rapport. It turned out they'd attended the same school—the Lycée Divonne in Switzerland—and they chattered away like old friends about various teachers they'd both had. Mo was happy to see their friendship blossom because he had very little to say to his son. It would be good to get him out of his hair. When dinner was over and Lucien politely asked for the keys to the Lamborghini, Mo quickly slid them down the table.

"Be my guest," he said.

"Staggering, Dad. Thanks." Lucien turned to Leah. "Would you like to take a ride?"

Leah nodded, her black hair bouncing. She was excited at the prospect of listening to the music that Lucien had told her about during dinner. He'd played drums in a rock band in Divonne, and he'd brought along a tape of the band's songs. Even if the tape proved to be uninteresting, it couldn't be any duller than Mo and Pru's endless studio talk.

Lucien slipped the tape into the deck as they tore down Sunset toward the beach, and Leah jumped in her seat when the first song jackhammered out of the speakers. What the band lacked in talent, it made up for in volume.

"I love it," she shouted as her hair flew in all directions and the wind burned her cheeks.

They parked and walked down to the empty beach.

"Are you happy to be home?" Leah asked.

"I could do without my father—he's an asshole."

They sat down on some driftwood, and he pulled a sterling silver flask from the pocket of his leather jacket. He held it out to her, and she quickly declined with a nervous smile.

"You don't drink?"

She shook her head.

"Staggering." Tactfully he put away the flask. Then he took her hand and lifted her to her feet. "Come on. I'll race you," he challenged. He charged down the beach, and she galloped along right next to him. They ran a mile, and when they finally collapsed together on the sand, they lay on their backs laughing and catching their breath in the moonlight.

The air was turning cool as Lucien pointed out the constellations—Orion, Andromeda, the Big Dipper.

"You know them all?" she asked.

"My mother did. I can still remember the night she showed me the Centaur." He lapsed into silence, and when Leah looked over at him, his face was pale and drawn in the moonlight.

"Maybe we should get home," she said quietly.

"Why? My father doesn't miss us. He has everything he wants. God, he and Pru are made for each other."

The wind blew hard across the water and sent a chill up Leah's back. Her thin shoulders shook.

"Are you cold?" he asked anxiously, and without waiting for an answer, he threw his leather jacket over her shoulders and pulled her to her feet.

"I'd better take you home."

They raced into town with the top down and the music cranked up. When they got to Weyburn Avenue, Lucien walked her upstairs, insisting that she wear his jacket until she got inside. She gave it back to him at the door and said good night. They shook hands solemnly, and she watched him drive off, swallowed up by the encroaching fog.

With Leah and Lucien out of the house, Mo had used his privacy with Pru to the utmost advantage: after leisurely spoonfuls of trifle followed by coffee and Kahlua, he presented her with a four-carat diamond engagement ring.

"Liz Taylor, eat your heart out," she gushed. "This thing could sink the *Queen Mary*."

As Mo held the ring box open before her, it seemed to light up the whole backyard. Pru just stared at it, shaking her head.

"I hope that doesn't mean no," Mo said. "Listen, Pru, I know it's kind of sudden, and I sure as hell don't expect an answer before you've had time to think about it. But . . . you will think about it, won't you?"

"Of course," she said, smiling. "I just need some time. That's all." When she saw the disappointment on his face, she quickly added, "I'm crazy about you, Mo. That's the bottom line."

"I'll show you the bottom line," he winked. "Let's go upstairs."

Eager to make love, she followed him to the master bedroom. But when they got there, he grabbed two scripts from the pile next to the bed. He handed one to Pru, and they both climbed under the covers. Unfortunately, Pru found that she couldn't keep her mind on the page. All she could think of was that flashing diamond she'd be a fool not to wear.

Leah, Kat, and Pru met early the next morning, at Pru's request, to brainstorm what she'd referred to over the phone as "fast-breaking news." On the breezy deck at Mirabel, Kat just about fell off her chair as Pru demurely pulled off a white glove and revealed the rock on her ring finger.

"My God, it's like looking straight into the sun," Leah moaned, and she rubbed her eyes as if blinded.

"I know," Pru sighed happily.

"Christ, if you weren't rich and famous—"

"Which I'm not—"

"—I'd swear that thing was hot," Leah declared. "Maybe you should call the Duchess of Windsor and see if anything's missing . . ."

"Isn't that just the berries," Kat said dreamily. "You're engaged, sugar."

"But what about your husband?" Leah asked. "I hope we're not talking bigamy here. It's a felony, and pardon my saying so, but you'd look awful in horizontal stripes."

"First of all, I'm not engaged. I'm only thinking about it."

"I see," said Leah. "You're just hoisting that rock around for the exercise."

"No," Pru said.

"What, then?"

"I need advice—"

"Don't ask me anything about romance or sex," said Leah. "I haven't been laid since the years had B.C. after the numbers."

"Sugar," said Kat, "we think Mo's a wonderful man—"

"Just say you'll marry him," Leah begged, as a waiter

passed by with a steaming plate of Belgian waffles. "Then we can finally order."

"I want to be sure this time," Pru answered. "Besides, like you said, Leah—there's no hurry. My divorce isn't even final." She looked intently at Kat. "What would you do if you were me?"

"She'd eat," Leah said pointedly. "So let's order already."

"Gee, I think this is the first time in our long association that you've been the one begging me to eat," Pru laughed. "Maybe this really is true love," she sighed. "I haven't even glanced at the menu . . ."

"So much for true love," Leah said later, when Pru had plowed through a pile of blintzes. She topped them off with a side of hash browns, and then finished Kat's omelette before she wiped her mouth daintily and turned to Leah.

"So. Where did Lucien take you last night?"

"To the beach. We had fun. He's very nice."

"I thought so, too," Pru said. "But Mo says he's a pain."

"Mo should know," Leah muttered.

"And just what is that supposed to mean?"

"Nothing," Leah said, and shrugged. "It's just that when he goes on and on with those wheeling and dealing stories, it's all I can do to keep from snoring in my soup."

"Well, excuse me," Pru said huffily. "Do you think I didn't have my snout in my trout when Lucien was describing his punk music?"

"Maybe that's the crux of the matter," Kat philosophized. "If they have such different interests, it makes sense that they'd bore each other to distraction."

Pru nodded. "That's probably true," she agreed. She looked hard at Leah. "Do you really find Mo—uninteresting?" she asked.

"Of course not," Leah fibbed.

Satisfied, Pru turned to Kat. "How about you, kiddo?"

"I think he's cute," Kat answered ingenuously. "And smarter than my cousin Joe Bob's Pendleton sow."

"You always say just the right thing," Leah told her, "even if no one knows what the hell you're talking about."

Thirty

SAM COULDN'T RUN from the truth any longer. Her heart was weakening. She'd seen the EKG with her own eyes, and even though the deterioration was barely measurable, she had to face the facts. It was time to tell Edward and Polly. They'd already been dealt the blow of a lifetime when their son died, and they needed to be prepared for their next loss.

Against her doctor's wishes, and while Frank tied up loose ends in Buckhannon, she flew to Athens. Frank had begged to go with her, but she'd stood her ground. This trip had to be solo.

From Athens, it was a quick flight to Crete, and then a rocky boat ride to the white and cobalt cliffs of Santorini. Olive trees clung to the ravaged marble island that reared up from the Sea of Crete. Gulls flew in lazy circles high overhead, and Sam breathed deeply of the salty air.

She'd wired her parents that she was coming, but she couldn't be sure they'd received the message: communication was unreliable between the islands. She was pleased, then, as she helped the captain tie up his boat, to see her father standing before her.

"We certainly were surprised to get your cable," he said as she stepped onto the rickety dock. "It's not often you deign to visit us."

"I've missed you," she said. She smiled up at him. His eyes were hidden behind sunglasses, but his mouth stayed tightly drawn, and she panicked to think that coming here might have been a mistake. Her legs felt weak as she scrambled up the cliffs after him. They walked through the bustling village in tense silence, and even the warm sun on her back was cold comfort. As they neared the cobblestone path that led up the hill to her parents' villa, Sam stopped. She grabbed her father's arm. It was the first time they'd touched since she arrived.

"I have to talk to you—" she faltered.

"What is it?" he asked, and his body stiffened. "Money?"

"No, not money," she choked. Her mouth was dry, but she forced herself to speak. "Just please listen to me."

"No, young lady. You listen to *me.*" When Edward removed his sunglasses, his eyes were as cold and hard as ice. "Whatever you've done this time, I don't want to hear about it. I've had enough bad news from you to last a lifetime."

She looked at him, stunned, as she saw that he meant every word. She felt light-headed and backed away. "I haven't done anything," she stammered. "I just wanted . . . to see you."

"You just wanted to *see* us?" He laughed unpleasantly and put his glasses back on. "Samantha, I'm not a moron. You have your reasons for coming here. What's the matter? It is money, isn't it? Is your Bolshevik stealing you blind? How very like you to marry a Communist *and* a gold-digger, all in one."

"Don't be hateful," she said softly.

"I think you'd better leave, Samantha. Whatever bed you're sleeping in, you've made it." He turned away from her.

"What about Mother?" she asked desperately. "Can't I see her?"

Already climbing the tangled footpath, Edward didn't answer.

"Father!" she cried out one last time, but he was gone. She walked blindly back to the boat.

Frank met her at San Francisco International, and they cleared her things from the apartment on Russian Hill.

"Good riddance," she said as she locked the door behind her. She marched angrily down the hall.

"Let it go," Frank told her. "I've got a surprise for you."

They drove to the Top of the Mark, where Pru was waiting at a window table overlooking the city lights.

"You look wonderful," Sam told her. "Do I detect the rosy blush of love on your cheeks?"

"That or swine flu," Pru answered amiably.

"Well, sweetie, that bigmouth Kat already spilled the beans," Sam told her, "and we're really happy for you."

"What's he like?" Frank asked.

"Me!" Pru exclaimed delightedly. "We're totally sympatico. He loves work, hates kids, and eats me under the table. So to speak." She grinned. "We're a match made in Hamburger Heaven."

"So when do we get to meet him?" Sam asked.

"I was going to bring him along tonight, but he couldn't get away. It's just as well, I suppose. It might have been awkward in Tahoe."

"You're on your way to Tahoe?"

"I'm taking a nine o'clock flight. John and I are finalizing the divorce. I want to wrap it up pronto, just in case—" She hesitated, blushing.

"In case of what?"

"In case I decide to marry Mo."

"But I thought you had decided," Sam said. "What have we just been talking about?"

"Love, Sam—not the M-word."

"The M-word is the best," said Sam, clasping hands with Frank.

"For you kids, absolutely. But for me, I'm not so sure."

"Why?"

"It's probably nothing, but—well, I just don't want a rerun of the John and Pru Show. Maybe I'm overreacting, but I'd like to take things a little bit slowly."

"Not too slowly," Sam said. She looked at Frank. "I hate to think of all the time we were apart when we should have been together."

"You don't have to worry about that with Mo and me. We're together twenty-four hours a day. Sometimes it feels as if we always have been. Mo's the most exciting person I've ever met." *Except in bed,* she thought. "Our days fly by like the Concorde." *Even if our nights aren't quite up to speed.*

"Our days fly by, too," Sam said thoughtfully. "It's amazing how they rush right past, and then they're gone."

''Oh, God, Sam, I'm such a thoughtless lug,'' Pru apologized. ''Here I am going on and on about my petty little problems, and you're . . . you're—''

''In the pink,'' Sam said firmly. She glanced at her watch and smiled. ''You have a plane to catch.''

When Pru arrived in Tahoe, it was too late to go to John's. Instead, she headed straight to Harrah's to say hello to Tony.

She noted with pride that her kid brother was really coming up in the world. He had a plush office with a dazzling view of South Lake Tahoe, which throbbed below like a giant pinball game. He planted a kiss on her cheek, and when she hugged him and felt the rub of Italian silk in his suit, she smiled approvingly.

''Well, little brother, I can tell you're doing just fine,'' she said.

''Can't complain.'' He smiled. ''How about you? The twins tell me you're getting hitched again.''

''Maybe, kiddo.''

''It's not for sure?''

''Mo wants to, but the more I think about it, the more I want to think about it.''

''So what's the rush? You're not pregnant, are you?'' he teased. ''I'd hate to think of my respectable, hard-working sister having herself a shotgun wedding.''

''Not on your life, Tony. It's just that Mo thinks there's no reason to dally. He says we might as well get the tax break before they change the law!''

''Christ, he sounds like a sentimental fool.''

''He's a wonderful man,'' she insisted.

Suddenly there was a soft knocking on Tony's door. ''It's open,'' he called out.

A tall, athletic man entered the room, and in that moment, as Mercer Vaughn stood before her, Pru knew what it was to be struck by lightning.

''I didn't mean to interrupt—'' Mercer said.

''Mercer, I'd like you to meet my sister, Prudence Daniels . . . my boss, Mercer Vaughn.''

''At last, we meet,'' Mercer said as his hand reached out for Pru's. When he smiled at her, his suntanned face revealed the deep lines of a life lived fully. His shaggy salt-and-pepper hair, swept off his face, dramatically revealed his chiseled bone structure. "Your brother has told me a lot about you," he said.

And why hasn't he told me a lot about you? Pru thought dizzily as Mercer shook her hand.

"What brings you to Tahoe?" he asked politely.

"My divorce," Pru said.

"I'm sorry—"

"Oh, don't be. I'm not," Pru said, shocked by her own honesty. "I mean, I am," she added hastily.

"Sis," Tony interrupted, cupping his hand over the telephone receiver, "what do you want for dinner?"

"You decide."

"Can I order you anything, Mercer?" He shook his head and walked over to Tony's computer, where he tore a sheet of paper from the printer.

"Thanks for pulling these figures," he said when the younger man was off the phone.

"You bet," Tony said. "I'll have the rest in the morning. Are you sure you don't want a bite to eat with Pru and me?"

"I'd like that—but I've got a meeting." He turned to Pru. "Maybe some other time." She could have sworn his eyes held a question mark for her, but she decided it was just her imagination. "Nice to meet you," he said crisply as he walked out of the room. "Enjoy your dinner."

As soon as Mercer was gone, Pru turned to Tony. "Why have you been keeping your boss under wraps? He's gorgeous!"

"Don't get your hopes up, Pru. Mercer doesn't like women."

"You mean he's gay?"

"No, he doesn't like men, either."

"Well, what does he like? Dachshunds? Seriously, Tony, what's with him?"

"He keeps to himself, that's all. In the four years I've worked for him, I've never seen him socialize with anyone. So forget it, Pru. Here's your dinner."

A waiter presented their meal: rack of lamb, a spinach soufflé, and a bottle of prize Bordeaux that made Pru giddy just reading the label. She got giddier when she drank the stuff—a whole bottle all by herself.

"Where does he live?" she asked dreamily.

"Who?"

"Mercer. Who else?"

"The penthouse. Why?"

She shrugged indifferently, but Tony wasn't fooled. He looked at her suspiciously.

"He's a lost cause, Pru."

"And I'm engaged to be engaged," she said.

"You're also engaged to get divorced," Tony reminded her. "You'd better get some rest," He handed her a key. "I've booked a room here. Three-fourteen."

"Thanks, Tony." She kissed his cheek. "You don't have to tuck me in."

The penthouse, she thought happily as she rode down the elevator, right past the third floor and room 314.

She left Harrah's, walked across the street to Harvey's, and booked their penthouse. According to her calculations, it faced Mercer's. She bought a few things in the lobby shops and then went upstairs to her base camp.

"D-Day," she exclaimed. "Perfecto." She called room service and ran a bath. When her order arrived, she sank contentedly into the fragrant bubbles with a split of Moët and a headful of fantasies—all of which cast Mercer Vaughn in a starring role.

She indulged herself in her risqué imaginings, and it felt wonderful to let go so completely. She stroked herself with her soapy fingers and thrilled to the havoc she wreaked between her thighs as she brought herself to easy underwater orgasms.

She finished the champagne and dried herself languidly, then powdered and perfumed every creamy inch of her ample body. For the coup de grace, she wiggled into the black silk teddy she'd bought downstairs.

Finally, she flung open the curtains on her eight-foot windows, and she gazed across the velvety night at Mercer's penthouse. There was a light on in only one of the rooms, and there, with his head bowed, Mercer sat at a desk, working.

She picked up the phone and dialed Harrah's switchboard. "This is Tony Daniels's sister," she said. "I'm trying to reach Tony, and I think he's in the penthouse—with Mr. Vaughn."

"I'll try," said the operator.

Before she'd thought of what to say, Mercer's unmistakable voice asked, "Yes? Ms. Daniels?"

"Why don't you look out your window," she whispered—and then put the phone down.

She walked to her balcony and threw back her fiery hair with an arrogant toss of her head. Haloed by the soft illumination in her penthouse, her pale skin glowed in the moonlit sky.

She watched unblinking as Mercer stepped onto his balcony, and slowly she slipped the straps of her teddy from her shoulders.

With a brief nod he disappeared inside his penthouse.

She hardly had time to turn back the covers and spray perfume down her ample cleavage before there was a rapping at her door. Breathless with expectation, she flung it open.

Thirty-One

HE AVERTED HIS gaze from her body.

"This can't happen," Mercer said. He didn't look back as he turned and retreated down the hallway to the elevator. Pru ran to her bathroom and retched until she was empty. Then she staggered to bed and fell into a stupor.

She woke up at seven, left the hotel, and taxied to John's house overlooking the lake. Surprised at seeing her so early, he was kind enough not to ask any questions. They drove to their lawyer's office to sign the final divorce decree, and in a matter of minutes, their marriage was dissolved. John insisted on driving her to the airport.

"I almost forgot," he said at the terminal, reaching into the back seat. "Give these to Leah, will you?"

She nodded and stuffed several books into her purse. She was reaching to open the car door when she burst into tears.

He held her as she sobbed, blubbering, "Goddamnit, I can't do anything right!"

"Shhh," he said in his low, soothing voice. "We were right for a while there."

"Sure, and look how I screwed that up!" she wailed.

"Not by yourself, Pru. We were just spinning in different orbits. It was no one's fault. Okay?"

"Okay," she mumbled as she blew her nose and climbed from the car. With intense determination, she began to compose herself and gather her forces. "Thanks for everything," she said as she hurried to make her plane.

Sick with self-loathing, she shriveled up in her first-class seat and wondered, *How could I?* Tidal waves of disgust sent her wobbling to the toilet, where she locked the door and brought her face close to the mirror. She felt every bit as ugly on the outside as she felt inside. She tried to cover the face in the mirror with a spread palm.

When she touched down in L.A., she called Mo from the airport. "Darling," she told him breathlessly, "the answer is yes."

Kat was back in the hospital, recovering from her fifth—and final—operation. It wasn't much, just a couple of tucks and a deep peel. Her scars were fading like shadows in the sunlight, and she was thrilled to know that once these last stitches came out in the morning, she'd seen her last scalpel.

"You look real good," Marie said as she walked in with Chinese food. This time she'd made it herself: Marie had bought woks, cleavers, and steamers, and was stir-frying her way through half a dozen Oriental cookbooks.

"Mmmm," sighed Kat. "Delicious."

"I'm glad you like it. Misti made the won tons."

"Where is Misti?"

"Riding," Marie said, setting down her chopsticks. "That child sure loves horses—"

She was interrupted by the ringing of the phone. Kat picked it up.

"Oh, God, I'm such a wreck," Pru said desperately. "We're announcing the engagement in an hour! I'm beside myself."

"You wouldn't be a normal human being if you weren't," Kat said. "It's not every night a woman declares her love for a man in front of two hundred close personal friends. Just thinking about it puts me in the hospital."

"It isn't funny, Kat. The entire showbiz community is about to arrive and descend on a mountain of shrimp that even Evil Knievel couldn't climb."

"Gee, sugar, do you think you'll have enough?"

There was a long pause followed by some curious crunching sounds, and Kat knew that Pru was eating something. She waited patiently for the conversation to resume.

"Sorry, Kat. I had to have a chicken wing to tide me over."

"No problem, sugar."

"Easy for you to say. You're not wearing double dress shields!"

"Oh, come on, Pru. Relax a little. Mo's a doll, and you two should be fit to bust."

"I hope that's nicer than it sounds," Pru said skeptically.

"Sugar, you know what I mean."

"Of course I do. Mo and I go together like a pair of old slippers."

"You could do worse, Pru."

"Don't remind me," she said. She was still stinging with secret shame after Tahoe. "Kat," she said quickly, "you're right. I'm going to throw a wonderful party."

"That's the spirit, Pru. Break a leg! I wish I could be there."

Pru was just hanging up when Leah rang the doorbell. In the soft glow of the porch light, with her black hair braided down her back, she could have passed for sixteen.

"Thank God you're here." Pru pulled her in. "Sam's fogged-in in San Francisco, so it's just you and me."

"Can I help?" Leah asked, but the bell was ringing again, and it continued ringing until all two hundred guests had shown up. Pru and Mo were swept up in the bustle of hosting, and Leah wandered off to check out the scene.

It wasn't her kind of party—too many strangers—so she wandered off to the greenhouse, where she knew she'd have a moment's peace. Unfortunately, an obnoxious young producer who'd had too much to drink followed her. As she ambled through the greenhouse, admiring Mo's orchids, the producer was right behind her.

She inspected the delicate blooms while he buzzed around her like a fly, and she was starting to warm to the idea of swatting him when she heard the unmistakable roar of Lucien's Lamborghini in the driveway.

She walked out to the driveway to say hello. Lucien waved enthusiastically when he saw her, and she was quickly crossing the lawn toward him when she noticed that her one-man fan club wasn't far behind.

Before she reached Lucien, the producer stepped in.

Flushed and unsteady, his jaw went slack and his eyes bulged when he took one look at Lucien, who wore beat-up jeans and a black T-shirt.

"You'd better get out of here," the producer slurred, "before I call security."

"You're drunk," Lucien remarked.

"You're outta here—you and your hot car."

"I live here, man—and the car is mine. So, if you'd step aside—"

As he spoke, he took Leah's arm, and they almost succeeded in brushing past the producer. But suddenly he lurched forward to grab Leah, and in doing so he made her lose her balance. Lucien caught her and steered her away from the drunk, but he wouldn't be ignored.

"Hey, you fuckin' punk—"

Lucien whipped around, and his eyes narrowed as he picked up the drunk by the shoulders, pushed him against the Lamborghini, and landed an expert punch to his jaw. The drunk buckled in defeat, but Lucien hit him again and landed a blow to his groin that made him fall backward in agony—and then silence.

"Don't mess with me, motherfucker!"

Leah looked away in revulsion as Lucien hoisted the producer high above his shoulders and marched him like a slain deer across the lawn. The defeated man vomited all over Lucien, and by the time Lucien dumped him into the fishpond, he looked far worse than the drunk.

Not sure what else to do, Leah giggled.

"Shit," said Lucien as he surveyed himself.

"Get Mr. Blackwell on the horn," Leah agreed. "Listen, is there some discreet way we can get you inside and changed?"

"My bedroom's at the top of the stairs. People will see me if I try to go up there."

"Then how about this? We go to my place and clean you up."

"But what about clothes?"

"We'll figure something out. Let's just get you out of here."

They climbed into the Lamborghini and sped toward Westwood. On the way, he played her another tape of his band. The songs needed work, and Leah had to admit that the band's musicianship wasn't very original, but for all its rough edges, the tape had a lot of energy. Like Lucien, it was long on overdrive.

When they got to the apartment, she led him upstairs and pointed him toward the bathroom, and while he showered, she hunted for something he could wear. Her own clothes were too small, so she went to Pru's old closet. She still kept a few things there—fat clothes, thin clothes, and in-between clothes, all neatly organized—and Leah quickly found a pair of black pants that would fit Lucien nicely. She matched them up with an oversize white shirt.

When she heard the shower go off, she called out that she had clothes ready. He stepped stark naked out of the bathroom and stood before her. One look at him was enough to make her blush.

"What have you got?" he asked easily, as if unaware of his nudity or her surprise. Leah marveled at his natural, casual attitude toward his body. She felt embarrassed undressing at the Sports Connection.

The black pants she gave him hugged him tightly, but the white shirt was loose and billowy, and when he'd put it all together, Leah thought he looked like a pirate.

"Very dashing," she said appreciatively.

"Thanks for finding this stuff. Is it yours?"

Leah shook her head. "Pru's . . . but she'll be only too happy to contribute to the cause."

Lucien looked puzzled. "What cause?"

"The party. She'll be grateful that you look so nice."

"Why should she care?"

"Well, it isn't every day she gets engaged—"

"Engaged?" Lucien looked stunned.

"Well, yes. What did you think the party was for?"

"I thought it was Dad's annual Labor Day blowout! It's the only party the cheapskate ever gives—and he's given it every year for as long as I can remember."

"Christ," Leah said in bewilderment. "I'm sorry he didn't tell you. It must have slipped his mind."

"*I* slipped his mind," Lucien said, sitting on the edge of

Leah's bed. "My goddamned father can't even remember to send a fucking memo!" He jumped up and pounded his fist on the night table and sent a lamp flying. "Goddamnit!" he cried, picking up shards of the broken light bulb.

Afraid that he might break the glass and cut himself, Leah pulled him back. As she grabbed his arms, she could feel the anger rippling through him. She stroked his shoulders and his back, trying to calm him down, and finally he let her massage his neck.

His breathing eased up, his muscles relaxed, then he turned and faced her. "Thank you, Leah."

He leaned down and kissed her sweetly, darting his tongue into her mouth and then gently biting her lower lip. She undid his shirt and kissed his chest. He tasted of salt and youth.

His hands roved down her back and cupped her buttocks. She fell on the comforter, and standing above her, he lifted her skirt deftly. Then he slid her bikini pants down over her ankles and, tossing them to the corner, sighed when she spread her legs.

"Oh, baby, I'm afraid I'm too big for you . . ."

Leah sat up and pulled him toward her, unzipping his pants feverishly as the color rose in her cheeks. When he was free, she brought him to her lips.

"That's it . . . Oh, baby, I love fucking your mouth . . . You're staggering."

His thrusts were deep, and when she thought she was about to taste him, he withdrew abruptly. He pushed her back on the bed with a low growl. His tongue teased hers again as he groped under her silk blouse and found the inside of her bra. Her breasts strained and quivered at his touch, and as his strokes became sure and steady, he pinched her nipples until she thought she would cry out.

"Is that good?" he asked, pausing to look at her. "Is that what you like?"

"Yessss . . ." she moaned as he reached beneath her and boldly kneaded her open from behind. He'd barely begun to arouse her with his fingertip, when she climaxed with a pounding in her eardrums.

He drove himself into her, shuddering and gasping, the

sweat from his body drenching them both. Leah had never seen anyone climax so violently.

Later, as he lay peacefully in her arms, it was hard to believe that this was the same young man who'd nearly torn her apart with his passion. She fell asleep with him inside her, but when she awoke, he was gone—and the sun was up.

Shit! I slept through the party! She'll kill me!

Suddenly Pru burst into the room.

"Oh, Leah, I'm so sorry," she apologized before Leah had a chance to speak.

"What for?" Leah asked groggily.

"Weren't you sick?" Pru asked. Anxiously she sat down on the edge of the bed. Leah rubbed her eyes.

"Poor baby," said Pru, throwing a plump white arm around Leah's thin shoulders. Leah looked at her bleary-eyed.

"I knew I should have gone with the other caterer! Two hundred people sick from the shrimp. I can't believe it."

Leah sat up. "I'm okay," she said.

"You're over the worst part," Pru assured her. "It's not supposed to last long. The public health people said it would be quick and violent. God, I could have told them that. We had guests puking on the baby grand by ten o'clock!"

Leah glanced quickly around the room, hoping there weren't any telltale signs of Lucien. She didn't want to open that can of worms. Pru wouldn't approve of her going to bed with teen-agers. Especially the particular teen-ager who would one day become her stepson. She could hear Pru now: "Cradle-robber!"

He's just a kid, Leah thought. *I ought to be ashamed*. But she wasn't, not in the least.

"When did you get sick?" she heard Pru ask. She shrugged noncommittally. "Well, anyway," Pru clucked, "it's all over now."

Leah nodded, and as she started to wake up fully she had just one question. "Why aren't you sick, Pru? You love shrimp."

Pru hung her head in shame. "Some little starfucker with an eighteen-inch waist gave me cocaine," she said. "She told me it would kill my appetite. Which it did, thank God. But it also made me a real bitcheroo. After everyone had gone home sick as dogs, I threw a fit about what a bust the party was, and how we hadn't even had a chance to announce the engagement. I was raving all night. I swear I'm never touching cocaine again as long as I live. I can't believe how much I screamed at Mo.''

''And what did he do?''

''The prince! He just listened and stayed up half the night with me, holding my hand while I screamed my lungs out. And this morning right before I left . . ,'' She paused dramatically and grinned.

''Spill, Pru.''

Her green eyes sparkled. ''He said we ought to forget about an engagement and just get married. Like that. So guess what, Leah. We're doing it tonight! Can you come?''

''You're out of your mind,'' Leah laughed as she threw her pillow at Pru. Pru threw it back, along with another, and before long, Leah's bedroom was a riot of girlish squeals and high-flying goosedown. The melee didn't end until the phone rang. It was Kat, calling to say she'd checked out of the hospital.

''That means you can come to the wedding!'' Pru exclaimed happily, sitting like a snowman beneath a white blanket of feathers.

Thirty-Two

PRU HAD EXACTLY ten hours to plan her wedding, and she got right to it. Her biggest fear was the food—she didn't want a repeat of the previous night—but after making a dozen calls, she discovered that no caterer was available on such short notice.

"Hire Marie," Leah suggested. "I'll bet she hasn't poisoned anyone in months."

While Leah showered, Pru called Marie, and together they came up with a menu. When Leah emerged from the bathroom, toweling her jet-black hair, Pru stood in the kitchen with a guilty look on her face.

"All right," Leah said suspiciously. "Come clean."

"Congratulations," Pru said weakly. "You're going to be Marie's assistant."

"Nice of you to ask first."

Shaking her head, Leah dressed while Pru called florists, wine shops, and a string quartet. She was on the phone trying to bribe Michel Richard into selling her someone else's wedding cake when Leah left for Kat's. Driving to Nichols Canyon, she actually looked forward to helping out with the food: it would keep her mind off Lucien. Every time she thought of their night together, she felt a little faint.

When she got to Kat's, Marie threw her an apron and told her to start chopping. "Or I'll skin your hide," she threatened, "and add it to the egg rolls."

"Now, you be nice," Kat told her mother as she poked her blond head into the kitchen.

"In a pig's eye," Marie scoffed. "Her Royal Highness of Holmby Hills didn't leave me time to be nice." She offered Kat a cleaver, but Kat declined.

"I've gotta scoot," she said. "I have to get dressed."

"You mean you're not helping?" Marie asked.

"Sorry. Some folks from Infinity—our distributor—are dropping by. Afterward, I'm taking Pru to the Rodeo Collection to pick out a dress."

"Off the rack?" Leah said sorrowfully. "What's the world coming to?"

As she returned to chopping onions, Kat whispered in her ear, "If you're looking for some amusement, stay tuned to the living room."

"What's that supposed to mean?" Leah asked, but Kat only smiled mysteriously.

A little later, she came back downstairs, dressed in a lavender cashmere tunic that matched her eyes perfectly.

When the buzzer for the outside gate sounded, she winked at Leah. "Right on time."

Leah wiped her hands and followed Kat as she went to the intercom and buzzed her guests inside. When she swung the door open, there stood Roger Meyer, the head of Infinity. Roger was one of the biggest players in town, but he wasn't too big to be thrilled at the prospect of distributing Kat's next film.

"Thank you kindly for coming by," Kat told him, her voice dripping honey.

"My pleasure, Kat." He pecked her cheek. "I don't think I have to tell you how eagerly we look forward to working with you."

"Well, there's a little bit of a problem there," Kat drawled.

"Oh?" Roger asked, working hard to maintain his cool.

Just then a second man walked into the foyer. When Leah saw who it was, she felt her hackles rise.

"Alex Hadley," Kat said to her guest. Stiffly he held out his hand. Kat refused it, and Roger looked back and forth between them.

"You've met?" he asked.

"A long time ago," said Kat. "Sit yourself down," she told Alex with a withering glance.

As he sat down awkwardly on the edge of the sofa, his eyes darted nervously around the room, looking everywhere but at Kat. She, however, looked directly at him—and her gaze was lethal.

Alex Hadley, this is your life, Leah thought as she watched from a distance.

While Alex squirmed on the couch, Kat sat down across from him and crossed her legs regally.

"Leah," she called. Her lips were painted the color of blood, and a faint bruise from her final operation reminded Leah of how she'd looked the night Alex raped her. "Come and sit down," she said. She introduced Leah to Roger, and then she went to her desk and returned with a sheaf of contracts. She handed them to Roger with an apologetic look. "I'm sorry, but I can't sign these."

"I beg your pardon?" Roger looked confused.

"I'm afraid there's no way I can do business with Infinity," Kat continued.

Roger was puzzled. "I don't understand. We had everything worked out."

"When the messenger dropped these by," Kat said, "I noticed Alex's name on the contract, and . . . under the circumstances, I just can't work with you."

Roger looked totally bewildered. Kat turned to Alex, who had sunk as far back into the couch cushions as possible.

"Alex?" she said. "Would you care to explain?"

"Stop it," he begged. Sweat ran down his suntanned face, and his fingernails dug into his trouser legs. Ignoring him, Kat looked at the studio chief. "Apparently Alex doesn't wish to discuss it, and I myself find it unspeakable." Her lavender eyes were wistful. "I guess we'll have to let it go at that," she said. "Thank you again for stopping by, Roger."

As she rose from the couch, she looked calm and composed, but Leah knew that beneath the cool exterior, she was trembling like a leaf.

"Please, Kat. Wait," Roger called. Slowly she turned and raised an arched eyebrow. "It's my attorney you object to?"

"I sure do."

"Now, hold on," Alex cried, jumping to his feet. "I can't believe you'd do this—"

Roger cut him off. "No problem. He's out. Take a hike, Hadley." He made a meaningful gesture toward the front door, and all eyes were on Alex as he walked out. The door closed quietly behind him, and Kat quickly swept back into the middle of the living room and took her seat.

Marie appeared with a tray of plum wine and some steaming dim sum, and Roger ate every one while Kat signed the contracts. She smiled as she handed them back. "I hope you'll excuse me," she said, "but one of my dearest friends in the world is getting married in a few hours, and she hasn't got a thing to wear."

"Say no more," Roger said with a broad grin, snapping shut his briefcase. As he prepared to leave, he paused at the door and said, "Do you mind if I ask you— No, I don't want to know what Hadley did to you."

"No, sugar. You don't."

"Well, if it's any consolation, I promise you that he'll never work in this town again."

"Thank you, Roger. I appreciate that." They chatted about more pleasant things as she saw him to his car.

In the library—where Pru and Mo would exchange their vows—Lucien sat down at the baby grand. He ran his fingers through his hair and dragged on a cigarette while the judge took her place. As he looked at her, he wondered how much she'd been bought for: it wasn't legal to marry people without a blood test—any idiot knew that—but somehow Mo had managed to find someone to do it.

As the guests settled in their seats, Lucien languidly fanned himself with the sheet music for the Bridal March from Lohengrin. With great élan he put out his cigarette in a Baccarat ashtray.

From her seat in the first row, Leah thought he looked good enough to eat—in more ways than one—in his charcoal Claude Montana suit. She shifted uncomfortably and crossed her legs when a stirring deep inside her brought back a flood of memories from last night's lovemaking.

As he raised his hands to play, she remembered how he'd

played *her* just hours earlier. He'd been wild in bed, and she could still taste his mouth. Even now, her skin felt warm where he'd kissed her.

Suddenly a chord crashed through the library. An eerie melody rose like smoke as Lucien improvised a jazzed-up version of a march from Saint-Saëns's *Carnival of the Animals*. The guests, who'd been expecting a more traditional wedding march, rustled and looked quizzically at each other. Mo appeared in the doorway, glaring at his son. Lucien caught the look, winked at Mo, and immediately switched to Wagner. Unfortunately, even though all the notes were in place, the tempo was just half a beat too fast, and when Pru entered the library—dressed in ivory silk—she stumbled to keep up with the slightly skewed rhythm.

Sam, who'd finally made it down from San Francisco, nudged Leah. "Shoot the piano player," she whispered.

"Didn't he say he was a musician?" Kat asked incredulously.

"Yes, but not a good one." Leah shrugged. She didn't mind in the least how he played. She was perfectly content just to watch him and indulge in last night's reruns.

Once the bride and groom were in front of the judge, the simple ceremony began. In spike-heeled Maud Frizons, with her red hair piled high on her head, Pru towered over Mo as they swore their undying love, then kissed and linked arms for their walk down the aisle. This time, Lucien managed a serviceable, if uninspired, version of a Bach suite that saw the newlyweds out of the library.

Guests headed gaily to the back lawn to feast on Marie's tantalizing Chinese banquet. Leah put down her Diet Coke and sneaked away after the first toast was offered. She wasn't up for temptation and instead headed off to the greenhouse.

She was reveling in the strange allure of Mo's orchids when Lucien silently entered the greenhouse behind her. Unaware of his presence, she didn't turn around until she felt his warm breath on the back of her neck.

"You startled me," she laughed, looking up into his blazing brown eyes.

He put his hands on her breasts and gently guided her

backward until she was resting against the trunk of a Philippine water palm.

"I thought I'd come in my pants, watching you in that outfit," he said as he slid his hand down her satin dress until his palm rested on her pelvic bone. She leaned into his taut body and felt his hardness against her belly. "I missed you this morning," she said, her heart pounding.

"How much?" he smiled.

She reached up to bite his lip.

He fell to his knees and urgently shoved her slim skirt up her thighs until it was gathered above her pantyhose.

"We've got to get you some garters and *real* stockings," he told her, pulling her pantyhose down and pushing his tongue inside her.

She leaned back against the trunk of the palm and closed her eyes. Less than a hundred yards away, dozens of guests were milling about in the garden with their glasses of champagne and their showbiz banter. If only they knew.

Suddenly she pulled him up and kissed him. His tongue was cool, and he tasted like tobacco. She struggled to unzip his pants, and he helped her by working the zipper down in a single, graceful stroke. Leah pulled him close.

"There isn't much time," she said breathlessly. "Someone may come—"

Lucien silenced her by pressing her back against the palm tree. When he was inside her, he moved gently at first, then rammed her with such power it lifted her from the ground. As the rough bark of the tree brushed her thighs she undulated against him, and their now familiar rhythm brought them speedily to gasping heights of pleasure.

"Oh . . . baby . . . you're . . . a . . . staggering fuck—" Lucien groaned as he jerked to a finish. Still locked together, catching their breaths, they heard Kat's voice.

"Leah! Le-ah?"

"Oh, shit!" Leah giggled, frantically pulling her pantyhose up and her dress down.

"Relax," Lucien whispered, zipping up his fly and smoothing back his ponytail.

Through the frosted glass of the greenhouse, they saw Kat's

shadow moving outside. Then they heard Misti calling out, "Come on, Mom. It's time to cut the cake."

"Please," Leah moaned. "We'd better go."

"Jesus, I can't keep my hands off you," he answered, grabbing her arm and pulling her against his chest. She felt his body against her, eager, ready.

He nibbled her earlobe, and she began to ache for him all over again. But she felt guilty about missing the party, and reluctantly she led him to the door. They made their way back to the reception and found they hadn't missed much. Toasts were still in progress, and everyone was a little tipsy.

Lucien impulsively took a glass of champagne from a passing waiter, and with a wide smile, he raised it and faced the newlyweds.

"I'd like to propose a toast," he said. "To your everlasting happiness." The guests clapped as Lucien, Mo, and Pru put their arms around each other and posed for a photo.

Watching them, Leah suddenly wondered if maybe she'd been wrong about Mo. If Lucien was a chip off the old block, then there just might be hope for his father—and for Pru!

You minx, she thought, looking up at the bride. *No wonder you're blushing.*

"There you are!" Sam said, coming up behind her. "We've been looking all over for you."

"Aren't you enjoying yourself?" Kat asked worriedly.

"You bet," Leah declared. She was, too. She was thinking about her sensuous young lover and his promise of *real* stockings.

Thirty-Three

ON THE WIDE, white beach of Oahu, Pru wriggled her toes in the powdery sand. She sipped her mai tai and popped the cherry into her mouth. Twirling an orchid Mo had tucked behind her ear, she gazed up at the sun that was splintered into dazzling blades of light by the huge branches of a coconut palm. As porpoises leaped across the sparkling waters of the bay, she vowed to give Mo a honeymoon he'd never forget, and sure enough, under her tutelage, he became calm, relaxed, and carefree.

His only task was to rub sunblock into Pru's white shoulders, and his sole obligation was the snorkeling class she'd enrolled him in. His pared-down life did him a world of good, and after just a couple of days of rigorous vacationing, it was hard to believe he was the same driven executive who'd never been able to tear himself away from the studio. Pru was pleased and told him so, even though she realized she wasn't one to talk: not exactly laid-back in her own right, she knew that her own schedule was often equally frantic.

On the sixth day of their honeymoon, just as she was getting used to the new Mo, he surprised her and kicked right back into high gear. Only balmy afternoon, over a mouthwatering lunch of butterfly shrimp, he looked at Pru across the table, and she saw in his eyes the old familiar fire.

"Baby," he said, "it's time I gave you your wedding present."

Her jaw dropped when he handed her the newest script by

the hottest writer in Hollywood. *Tropic of Danger* was a coming-of-age tale set in the Florida Everglades, and it featured a plum of a role for a young leading-man type. Whoever played the part would become a star, there was no question of that.

As Pru looked dumbfounded at Mo, he surprised her one step further by laying a check in her hands. It was a cashier's check for five million dollars, made out to Pru.

"This ought to get the ball rolling," he declared.

"Mo, I can't accept this."

"Don't worry. There are lots of strings attached."

"You're giving me five million dollars and a priceless script?"

"I'm not exactly giving it. I'll executive produce, and Heliotrope distributes. No ifs, ands, or buts."

"But—"

"You heard me, baby."

"I heard you. It's just that I don't think I'm ready for this."

"Bullshit. You brought in *College Craze* under budget, under schedule, and in goddamned good shape. Such goddamned good shape that we're staking it for a Christmas release."

"Thank you."

"Thank yourself. You're the one who charged into my office, bluffed me into a deal, then took over on the set like a goddamned animal trainer. And between you and me, pulling a script out of that flaky pal of yours was like milking a bat."

"That's not fair," Pru protested. "Leah's a big talent."

"She's also a big pain in the caboose. I've heard the stories."

"Well," Pru said archly, "do you believe every rumor you hear?"

"I don't know, doll. But where there's smoke"—he paused and grinned—"there's usually fire." Pru bristled, and Mo looked suddenly contrite. "Baby, I'm sorry. Besides, your pal's not the point here. The point is, you're as ready as anybody ever gets. It's time for you to make a movie that will kick the rest of 'em right off the screen!"

"Gee, Mo, since you put it that way, what can I say?"

"Say you'll do it, and tomorrow morning let's blow this island."

"Are you telling me the honeymoon's over?"

"Do you mind?" he asked cautiously.

"Good God, no. If I never see another pineapple it will be too soon. Besides, I'm dying to get to work."

On their last night in Hawaii, they took a long walk on the beach and began discussing *Tropic of Danger*.

"I know how you feel about Leah," Pru said, "but I've been thinking it over, and I'm going to ask her to do the polish on the script."

Mo stopped in the wet sand and turned to her. "Are you crazy?"

"She came through the last time."

"Only because you poked her with a cattle prod twenty-four hours a day. She's just not plugged in. I'll give you that she's got talent, but the rest of her is pure liability."

"It's my picture," Pru snapped. "Right?"

Mo scowled and kicked up a cloud of sand. "Right, god-damnit!"

"Thank you," she said, resting her red mane on his shoulder.

As they walked along the beach, she told him that she wanted to get going on *Tropic of Danger* right away, because it would involve a lot of location shooting in the Everglades. Weather would be a problem: if they didn't shoot in the up-coming fall, they'd have to wait all winter, sitting out the rainy season.

"But do you think I can get it together that fast?" she asked Mo.

"The script is in good shape, which helps a lot. But scouting locations is no picnic, and your biggest headache will be finding your star. A lot depends on him."

"I think I want an unknown," Pru mused. "And you know, we could always turn the arboretum into the Ever-glades."

"What arboretum?"

"The one in the San Gabriel Valley. By the racetrack. Think of the money we'd save."

"That's my girl." Mo laughed heartily as a wave broke over their bare feet. "You're a quick study, doll."

After spending six days and nights in bed with Lucien, Leah was still amazed. He was an incredible lover, and every time she thought they'd reached the absolute ceiling of pleasure, he took her right through it. Their sex was the most powerful drug she'd ever known; alcohol paled beside it.

Finally, after almost a week in the apartment, Lucien suggested that they go out. There was a band, St. Vitus, that he wanted to catch at the Veil. St. Vitus was looking for a keyboardist, and Lucien wanted the gig.

When they got to the seedy punk club in Hollywood, Leah was wide-eyed: stoned young men wore kilts and prisoner of war haircuts, while women with shaved heads sported merry widow corsets and a fringe of Day-Glo pubic hair. In the eerie play of black lights and strobes, the shadowy, slow-moving figures looked like the undead dancing on their graves.

Without much fanfare, St. Vitus took the stage, which was really nothing more than a couple of planks. Looking at the band, Leah felt like an alien in her simple black shift and freshly washed hair that cascaded down her shoulders.

"They're amazing," she yelled to Lucien over the din of the crowd. As she studied their kohl-rimmed eyes, Lucien suddenly grabbed her arm so hard it hurt.

"Goddamnit!" he exclaimed, barely audible as the band played. "Those losers hired that dipstick from the Stains. Shit, that poker doesn't know squat!"

"Come on, Lucien, let's dance," Leah shouted. She pulled him through the pulsing crowd and let herself go with wild abandon. She liked the fact that it was four in the morning and she was learning to do the rapture while most of Los Angeles slept.

As they danced, Lucien downed a beer and started in on the band again.

"Get a fucking piano player!" he screamed.

"What's your problem?" she yelled in his ear, but he shook his head and ignored her question. Deftly he spun her around in a high-speed jitterbug.

"Uncle!" she cried when she'd danced until she was dizzy. They slow-danced their way down a dark hallway, where he writhed around her, snaking up and down her body as he led her into the shadows. He lifted her skirt, slid her panties down her slim legs, and made love to her slowly as St. Vitus groaned onstage.

Afterward, Leah danced alone, weak-kneed, while Lucien went to the bar. When he returned, he kissed her tenderly and handed her a cup of coffee. Hoping for a second wind, she chugged it fast, but it tasted bitter—it was probably overbrewed—and when he told her to drink more, she shook her head.

"Too bad," he shrugged. "You could use some loosening up." She wondered briefly what he meant by that, but he kissed her before she had a chance to ask. And by the time the kiss was over, she didn't have a thought in her head.

They danced again in the dark hallway, and her body felt strangely buoyant, her head light as the music swirled around her. She closed her eyes, basking in the waves of sensation that broke against her. Lucien smiled as he twirled her slowly, cheek to cheek like Fred and Ginger—except that Leah's dress was up around her waist, and Lucien was igniting an almost unbearable fire between her legs with his skilled fingers.

When she could take no more, he led her, gasping, to a table close to the stage. Smiling woozily, she ordered a glass of wine. She knew she should be ashamed of herself for breaking her abstinence, but she wasn't, not in the least. If anything, she felt a profound, delirious sense of well-being. Surrendering to it completely, she ordered another glass of wine, and after that, a carafe.

Lucien disappeared at one point; she supposed he was saying hello to friends. While she happily drank and awaited his return, she looked around the club, but she was barely able to see anything at all between the strobes, the smoke, and her own clouded vision. At one point she thought she saw Lucien over by the stage, but she kept losing focus and seeing double. He was there—and he wasn't—and as desire welled up in her again, she wished he'd hurry back. She even tried to get up and go find him, but when she stood up, her legs wobbled, and she quickly sat back down. Her head was slowly dropping to the table when suddenly a thunderous explosion rousted her from her stupor.

On stage, the electric piano exploded in a deafening barrage of noise and a shower of sparks. The keyboardist was thrown into the audience. Roadies fought the blaze with fire extinguishers and buckets of water while the mob gave in to panic.

Leah couldn't be sure what happened next, but somehow she got to her feet. Lucien floated toward her looking calm and reassuring as he herded her toward the door. Over her shoulder, the stage was a blazing pyre.

"What happened?" she asked.

Lucien shrugged. "Fucking staggering," he said as he led her out of the Veil and onto the street. Her ears were ringing, and her brain rolled around like a marble in her skull, but the predawn chill enlivened her once more.

"Let's dance," she giggled happily, but he just walked her to the Lamborghini. She got in and fondled him all the way to Westwood, where she finally passed out cold.

He carried her over his shoulder into the apartment and dropped her belly-first onto her bed. He fell asleep next to her, and when he awoke an hour later, he felt the old familiar stirring below his belt. He wanted her all over again. He nudged her to wake her up, and when she didn't respond, he wasn't really surprised. For someone who didn't drink, he mused, she'd completely polluted herself the night before. Between the 'lude he'd slipped her and all that cheap red vino, she'd be lucky to remember her name this morning.

"Leah?" he said. "Wake up, babe."

She moaned and rolled over, so he pushed her roughly, but still she slept.

"Dumb bitch," he sighed. He gave her a little kick, and when *that* didn't bring her around, he twisted his ponytail distractedly.

Not sure what else to do, he wandered over to her desk and picked up her Rolodex. Flipping through it, he noticed Kat's number and wondered if she looked as good at seven in the morning as she did in the movies. He decided to call her. When she answered groggily, he explained that he'd come by to pick up Leah for tennis—and found her incapacitated.

"Maybe you should come over," he said. "She looks kind of strange."

"You mean drunk?" Kat asked warily.

"Yeah—*really* drunk."

"I'm on my way," Kat said.

When she got there, it took the two of them several minutes to roust Leah from her stupor. When she finally came around, she stumbled to the bathroom and threw up while Kat and Lucien held her steady. Then Kat helped her into bed and told her to sleep it off. She was snoring loudly as Lucien and Kat said good-bye in the living room.

"Are you sure I can't make you some coffee?" Kat asked him.

"Maybe some other time." He'd briefly flirted with the idea of coming on to Kat, but Leah's little purge in the bathroom had put a damper on his romantic urges. "I've gotta run."

"Well, thank you for all your help," Kat said gratefully as he went out the door.

When he was gone, she paced the living room, wondering what to do for her friend. She was still pacing an hour later when Leah appeared from her bedroom. She looked terrible. Kat tried to get her to talk about the previous night, but she soon realized that Leah was totally blacked-out.

"That's it," Kat said decisively. "Get dressed. I'm taking you to Palm Springs."

"Swell," Leah muttered. "I could use a vacation."

"Forget the vacation," Kat told her. "You're going to the Betty Ford Center."

Crickets were chirping as Sam and Frank drove the bumpy road that led to the mission. In defiance of her doctor, Sam had insisted on coming to Togo. Frank had tried to argue her out of it, but she'd refused to listen.

"Clayton needs me," she'd said. "You can come with me, or I'll go alone."

They ended up going together. When they arrived at the mission long before dawn, dew covered the ground like a blanket of diamonds, and Vonga quietly ushered them inside. Clayton lay in his bed, surrounded by proteas and birds of paradise. The flowers that had been brought by the Africans were so vivid and alive that they almost seemed capable of breathing life into the dying man.

"Samantha, thank you for coming . . ."

"Don't try to talk," she said, touching his forehead. It was hot, and he seemed to cringe at her touch. But when she withdrew her hand, he shook his head weakly, and once again she rested her fingers gently against his gaunt face.

"Are you ill too?" he asked in a whisper. She nodded, and hot tears burst from his eyes. "I'm so sorry," he told her hoarsely. She clutched his skeletal hand and put her lips close to his ear.

"I have no regrets, Clayton." He looked at her uncertainly, and she smiled. "You gave me my life."

With great effort Clayton directed his gaze past the window. On the veranda, Frank stood, watching the morning's coppery sunlight wash across the mountains.

"He's a good man, Samantha?" She nodded, and the deep lines in his forehead disappeared. "Thank God," he breathed.

A rasping noise rattled in his throat, and he tried feebly to raise his head. She held his frail shoulders lovingly and urged him back onto the damp sheets.

"I love you, Sam . . ." His voice faded away.

"I love you, too."

His cracked lips formed a faint smile, and when she put her mouth to his, she knew he was gone. She wept softly, and when Frank came back into the room, he knelt on the floor beside her and took her in his arms until she couldn't cry anymore. At dawn, the Africans arrived with a simple wooden casket.

Sam's last good-bye was a handful of dirt, and then the Africans, along with Frank, filled the grave slowly and planted a small white cross in the newly turned earth.

On the way back to Lomé, Sam guided Frank through the bush. They drove across the wide savannahs and watched the peaceful herds of cattle and goats. When they came to the mountains, she led him up the steep slope of her favorite, the Queen's Crown.

At its peak, she made love to him while eagles soared

above. Afterward, she told him, "I have to do something for this place—and for Clayton. If it weren't for him, and for Africa, I might never have learned who I am. I might never have found a home."

She looked deep into Frank's eyes, and she saw that he understood.

Ideas were beginning to take shape in her mind as they made their descent, then hiked through the jungle that led to the sea. As they flew out of the capital, they watched the Queen's Crown disappear into the clouds, and they both knew they'd never be the same. They'd each left a piece of their heart behind, taking root like a sapling in the rich African soil.

Thirty-Four

DRIVING BACK FROM Palm Springs, Kat stopped off at the Holmby Hills estate. Pru was on the phone when she got there, but she hung up fast when she saw how upset Kat was. Kat filled her in on Leah's binge, and when she'd finished, Pru was furious.

"That's the last straw," she seethed. "I've had it. Mo was right."

"Pru, calm down—"

"I'm through with her. If she doesn't care about herself, why should *we* care about her?"

"Because she needs our help, Pru."

"We have helped her. For years. And what good has it done?"

"She was making great strides until this happened."

"But that's the point. Something always happens. She's a lost cause."

"Sugar, you don't really think that—"

"For God's sake," Pru said. "Leah has spent her entire life on self-destruct, and there's nothing we can do about it." When she saw the pained look on Kat's face, she looked at her impatiently. "Oh, forget it. I don't want to fight with you—Leah's not worth it."

The women said nothing for a moment, and then Kat broke the awkward silence.

"Truce?" she asked softly.

"I guess," Pru said. "Look, I'm sorry I came on so

strong. It's not you I'm mad at. It's Leah. It seems like even in a drunken stupor, she's calling the shots.''

"She won't anymore," Kat promised.

"Good, because we can't carry her to happiness. She has to get there on her own two feet.''

"I know," Kat said slowly. Eager to change the subject, she grinned at the new sprinkling of freckles on Pru's nose. "So," she asked, "how was Hawaii?''

"Fantastic! Great food, great sex, and a magnificent wedding gift from Mo. He bought me *Tropic of Danger*!''

"Hot damn!''

"I know." Pru smiled and her green eyes sparkled. "I'm so excited I can hardly stand it." Abruptly she frowned, and the sparkle disappeared. "If Leah had managed to keep off the sauce, I would have brought her in for the polish. Goddamnit, Kat, she's such a jerk.''

"Shush. You'll just get yourself worked up all over again. You know, you care about her a lot more than you let on, sugar.''

Pru rolled her eyes, but she didn't deny it.

"Now, then, tell me, dear friend, is there a part in the script for a woman, hint hint?" Kat prodded mischievously.

"She's fifteen, unfortunately.''

"Fiddlesticks! I'm already over the hill!''

"Not by a long shot, kiddo. Say, do you remember that kid, Will Avery?''

"Sure thing. He had a couple of lines in *Hawkeye*. He was good.''

"To put it mildly. This morning I saw some rushes of a film he did that got shelved. The movie was shit, but Will was dynamite.''

"I'm glad to hear it. He'll go far.''

"And he may do it fast," Pru predicted slyly.

"Are you thinking of him for *Tropic of Danger*?''

Before Pru had a chance to answer, Lucien's Lamborghini thundered into the driveway, and over the din, she quipped "He's baa-aack" in a little-girl voice. "God, teen-agers!" she said, throwing up her hands and looking heavenward.

Lucien entered the living room and smiled graciously at the women.

"Hi, you two."

"Hi, yourself," said Pru. "You look *trés* Eurotrash," she added, eyeing the pleated trousers and silk shirt that replaced his usual jeans. "I like it."

He smiled modestly.

"Lucien," said Kat, "I was going to call you. I wanted to thank you again for all that you did for Leah."

"Can we not talk about it?" he asked gravely. "I don't like to think about what could have happened . . ."

"Kat's right," Pru said. "You got a lot more than you bargained for when you made a date for tennis."

"That's true," Lucien agreed. "No offense to your friend, but I think I'll find another partner. Leah's a handful."

"She's a worthless bum!"

They all turned to see Mo in the doorway.

"Mo!" Kat gasped. "How can you say that?"

"Some people really want help," he answered slowly, as if he were talking to a child. "They should get it. The others can go to hell."

Kat stood up. Flushed with anger, she headed for the door.

"Just remember," Mo called after her, "nursemaids don't help anyone. They only kid themselves." The door slammed behind Kat, and the others stood in silence.

"You were rough on her," Pru said. Put off, she started to head back to her office, but Lucien stopped her.

"Wait. I have something to tell you," he said shyly. "I've enrolled in Jeff Morwood's school."

"You're giving up music for acting?" Pru asked.

"Staggering, huh?" Lucien turned to Mo. "I think I'm cut out for the movies. Don't you, Dad?"

"I think you're cut out to do anything you set your mind to. And stick with," he added pointedly. He thumped his son on the back, and Lucien trotted upstairs to study the monologue for his next class.

As soon as he was out of earshot, Pru sighed, "What an improvement. I'll take monologues over electric pianos any day! And he seems so enthusiastic—"

"Enthusiasm's fine," said Mo noncommittally, "but you need perseverance, too, and I'm not so sure he's got that.

Before rock and roll, there was kickboxing and race-car driving. Lucien has a hard time sticking with things.''

"Well, maybe acting will be the thing that takes," Pru said optimistically.

"Who knows?" Abruptly Mo reached out and took Pru's hand. "Baby, I'm sorry if you're troubled by what I said about Leah. But I want what's best for you, and what's best is not to wear yourself out saving people who don't want to be saved. If Leah wants to go under, then all the rope you throw her might was well be spaghetti.''

"I know," Pru admitted. "I just don't want to hear it.'' She patted his hand and rose from the couch, but in standing up, she felt a strange dizziness that made her sit right back down.

"What is it, baby? You look white as a ghost.''

She smiled wanly. "I'm fine, Mo. Just a little tired.''

"Well, maybe you should take it easy today.''

"I'll lie down right after I talk to Will Avery's agent.''

"Good idea." He kissed her cheek and grabbed his briefcase. "When I get back from the office, I expect to find you resting. And good luck with Will.''

"Cross your fingers," she smiled as he started for the door.

"You mean everything to me, Pru," he told her impulsively, blowing her a kiss.

Staggering, Lucien thought from his secret perch at the top of the stairs. *I don't know which of those two is more repulsive. He's a fucking barricuda, and she's the bimbo who couldn't see it if it was tattooed on her eyelids.*

Disgusted, he retreated to his room until he heard the sound of Mo's Mercedes taking off. Right after that, he heard Pru's footsteps on the stairs. She lumbered into her bedroom, and when it seemed that she wouldn't bother him for a while, he crept downstairs. He went into her office and began rummaging around. As he snooped among the papers on her desk, he found what he was looking for: a copy of *Tropic of Danger.* It was stamped CONFIDENTIAL.

He opened it to page one, and that was all it took to hook him. *Tropic of Danger* was spellbinding as it pitted its young hero against impossible odds—drug runners, hurricanes, and a cruel father. With each page he turned, Lucien grew more certain that he'd been born to play Buck, the lead.

He finished the script, then went to his room and began improvising the way he would play his character in front of the camera. He cracked open his Stanislavski book, then eagerly tore into one by Uta Hagen. He pored over the tiny print, looking for pointers and tips, but all he found were long incomprehensible passages. He threw down the books in disgust and realized he was on his own. But that was all right: in his heart of hearts, he knew he *was* Buck. No problem.

But then it dawned on him that there was one small snag. *What was that guy's name? Will . . . Will something.*

He was trying to remember Will's last name when suddenly he heard Pru moving around. He ran downstairs and put *Tropic of Danger* back on her desk and sauntered out into the garden for a smoke. *Whoever this Will guy is, he's disposable,* Lucien thought, flicking cigarette ashes into the birdbath. *And he can't hold a fucking candle to me.*

In San Miguel, Krysta knew that something was terribly wrong. It was obvious by the way Dr. Menendez carefully took her small, trembling hands in his large, steady ones. A warm breeze wafted through the courtyard, and Krysta shivered. Despite the heat, she'd been cold for weeks now. A chill was lodged inside her like an uninvited guest.

". . . The tumor is malignant, and it's too late to operate," the doctor told her.

It's too late to operate. Too late to operate. The words echoed through her brain . . .

"But that's ridiculous, Doctor. This is a simple case of *turista.* A couple of ampicillin, and I'll be as good as new."

"Señora, you are a very sick woman."

"You know," she said blithely, "you'd think I'd have learned by now not to get near the salads. Every year I come to San Miguel, and every year I get this—"

He touched her arm and looked searchingly into her eyes. "If you don't believe me, señora, perhaps you should go home. Perhaps there is a doctor there whom you will believe."

Suddenly a wrenching pain shot through her belly, and she doubled over in her chair. She fell heavily to the marble floor, but the doctor caught her and carried her to a low couch. He quickly filled a syringe with Demerol. He shot the painkiller into her arm, and she was numb within seconds.

A dream rose slowly, like steam from the frozen pond of her drugged sleep. A young mother held her newborn child, she took her bows on a Broadway stage, she turned away from a dark-eyed girl. She turned, and turned, and still the girl wouldn't go away . . .

She awoke with a jolt, and Dr. Menendez stood above her.

"A bad dream," he told her as he set down a tray of fruit juice and biscuits.

"Gracias, señor."

The following day, she was back in L.A., sitting in her internist's office overlooking Century Park East. Earlier that morning, she'd been run through a battery of tests, and she waited eagerly for confirmation that she was, in fact, suffering from an unusually severe case of Montezuma's revenge.

But when he slowly looked up from the lab report, she knew that Dr. Menendez had been right all along.

"It's pancreatic cancer—" the internist began.

She didn't listen after that.

Thirty-Five

PRU LAID A trail of rubber as she tore out of her driveway. She couldn't wait to get to work to see what the day brought. Since she'd married Mo just two weeks earlier, it was as if a good-luck spell had been cast over her. First *Tropic of Danger* came her way, and yesterday Owen Scott—the hottest director in town—had signed to direct. Everything was coming up roses. Everything, that is, except . . .

Impulsively she picked up the cellular phone. She punched the number that Kat had given her—and she'd tried to forget.

"Dr. Joan Ingalls," a woman answered crisply.

"Doctor, my name is Prudence Daniels—"

"Yes, of course. Leah's mentioned you."

"May I talk to her?"

"I'm afraid that's out of the question right now."

"But why?"

"Ms. Daniels," Joan said patiently, "if Leah were undergoing open-heart surgery, you'd understand why you couldn't speak with her just then—"

"Of course. But she's not having a bypass, for God's sake. She's just parked her butt in a country club while she dries out." The line was quiet while Pru asked impatiently, "Are you there?"

"Ms. Daniels," Joan spoke kindly, "Leah doesn't want to see you—or anybody—right now."

"But I'm her best friend!"

"Leah has to learn that she herself is her own best friend. Can you understand that?"

"Of course. But talking to me will *help* her."

As gently as she could, the doctor said, "Sometimes a person's friends don't help."

"I beg your pardon?"

"Friends can be very demanding. Their expectations are often more stressful than they imagine, and from where Leah sits, they're sometimes impossibly high—"

"So she picks up a bottle."

"You're very angry with her, aren't you?"

"Who wouldn't be? I'm sick and tired of wiping her off the ceiling."

"Is that how you think of it?"

"No—not really."

"Good, because Leah doesn't need any more critics in her life. She's already her own harshest critic, and with you making judgments, she'll never get well."

"Are you saying it's my fault she drinks?" Pru heard the shrillness in her voice.

"Of course not. Leah's *disease* makes her drink. She craves alcohol, and she won't stop craving it until she stops drinking. Then, eventually, the desire will recede. She'll put some distance between herself and the booze, and she'll start to see how it damaged her, how it made her feel like a bad person."

"But she's a great person!"

"She sees it differently. She remembers all the stupid, senseless things she did while she drank, and she thinks of those things as herself. Alcohol has been so much a part of her life that she can't separate what it is from who she is."

Suddenly Pru flashed on the image of herself, drunk and carrying on in front of Mercer Vaughn. Chills crept down her back at the memory. She felt sick—as she always did when she recalled it. And poor Leah! She had dozens of thoughts like that—memories tearing her apart.

"So . . . What can I do, Doctor?"

"Give her time."

"I'll try." When she finally spoke again, her voice was barely a whisper. "Do you think she'll ever get well?"

"It's up to her, but I can tell you this much: she's a hell of a fighter. And she's eight days sober."

"Thank you," Pru said softly. As she hung up, she thought miserably, *What a bitch I am, saying that Leah likes to be sick. Kat's right. I'm getting hard. Was I always like this?*

She remembered a warm September day, five years earlier. Standing at the bulletin board in MacGowan Hall, she and a dark-eyed waif had both grabbed at the same three-by-five card. They laughed when it tore like a wishbone in their hands.

"Kismet," Leah giggled. "Let's look at it together."

As they'd walked down Hilgard Avenue to the two-bedroom apartment on Weyburn, Pru had been instantly envious of Leah's svelte figure and her nonstop mouth. She'd never met anyone like her.

Of course they'd been unable to afford the apartment, but they'd signed the lease anyway, and then they'd hastily recruited Sam and Kat from their History of Cinema class. Sam had been Pru's choice. She had a silver Audi and great clothes, and she seemed like the type who didn't mind lending things; there was obviously lots more where that came from. Leah had favored Kat: "She'll draw men the way shit attracts flies. And she'll pass them around like the Hong Kong flu."

That had been the beginning of their foursome, and sometimes, when Pru felt fanciful, she imagined they were petals on a four-leaf clover, bound together to bring good fortune to each other. But it hadn't exactly turned out that way for poor Leah, she thought gloomily.

Pru arrived at the studio and was heading past the reception area when Drew, her assistant, turned the corner and ran right into her.

"Pru," he said. "I've been trying to reach you! Your phone's been busy forever. Did you forget your meeting? Come on, we've got to jet!"

Pulling Pru along, he broke into a canter, and they cleared the halls as they raced to her office. She was totally out of breath by the time Drew ushered her inside.

"Sorry, everyone," he mumbled to the gathering. "Ms. Daniels was caught in traffic." Pru took one look around the room and realized in an instant why he'd made such a fuss: she'd kept two casting directors, Owen Scott, and Will Avery and his agent waiting.

"So good of you to come," said Will's agent, Cookie Spender, in a nasty, nasal tone. Pru guessed she was too cranked up on cocaine to have time for tardiness. "I'd like you to meet Will Avery," she said.

When he stood to shake hands with her, Pru knew she'd been right about him. From his penetrating indigo eyes to his sun-streaked locks and easy smile, he *was* young Buck of the Everglades.

The casting directors handed him his sides, and he gave a magnificent reading. He grasped the material fully, made it his own, and when he'd delivered his last searing line, the others just sat there, stunned.

"That will be all," Pru said softly. "Thank you very much."

When Will and Cookie were out of the room, Pru looked at the others.

"Can we get him?" she asked breathlessly.

"I think so," one of the casting directors replied.

"Then get Business Affairs going on this," Pru instructed. The casting directors took off, and Pru slumped over on her desk.

"Are you all right?" Drew asked.

"Just recovering from that performance," she said. "What a knockout."

"You want a cup of coffee or something?"

"I'll get it," she said. She started to get up, but as she did, she swayed and quickly sat down again. Her head was spinning, and her stomach fluttered.

"Are you sure you're all right?" he asked again. Pru nodded and then stood up again, this time more slowly.

"I'm fine, but could you bring me some breakfast from the commissary? I think I need something to eat."

"Sure. What do you want?"

"You know, Drew, I think I'd like a corned beef sandwich with extra pickles and *lots* of mustard."

"A nourishing way to start the day," Drew kidded her.

"Go on," Pru snapped. "I'm starving!"

"Aye, aye, sir," he answered with a fast salute, but he'd hardly gotten halfway down the hall when Pru called out after him.

"One more thing. Jalapeño chips. Two packages, please," she ordered.

"Pru, if you don't mind my saying so, you're going to make yourself ill," Drew advised.

"Thank you, Doctor Drew," Pru retorted. "And make that three jalapeño chips. On the double. Or should I say triple?"

She spent the rest of the day on the phone. She'd definitely decided to shoot in the arboretum: she could save a bundle by making the film locally, and the arboretum had stood in for the Everglades in countless films.

There was only one hitch: it was unavailable after February 1, 1988, because major renovations were due to begin then. So, unless she felt like waiting, which she certainly didn't, she needed to shoot within the next three months. Everyone told her it was impossible to plan and shoot a major motion picture in ninety days, but Pru took their nay-sayings as a challenge.

After a marathon storyboarding session with the director, it was past midnight when she left the studio. Her mind was still buzzing with ideas when she got home, and she quickly dashed into her office to glance at a copy of the script. As she opened it, she noticed cigarette ash ground into the pages.

Lucien was the only one in the household who smoked. That meant he'd been in her office, uninvited, reading a script stamped CONFIDENTIAL. She fumed in exasperation.

That little sneak. She started to march upstairs to have it out with him, but then decided her time was better spent working. He'd just deny it anyway.

She opened the screenplay, found her place, and was still scribbling notes in the margins when the phone rang much later, close to three in the morning.

"Pru?" Her brother's voice sounded strange and distorted, like an echo barreling down a dark tunnel.

"What is it, Tony?"

"It's bad. You'd better come home."

She rushed upstairs to pack her bag.

Thirty-Six

THREE DAYS LATER, Kat was in her library, fluffing the pillow on the couch, when the phone rang. She'd just wrapped up an interview with Barbara Walters, and she waved good-bye to Barbara and the crew as she picked it up.

"Kat? Mo. I have to talk to you, doll. I feel like a real shit for what I said about Leah."

"To tell you the truth, I was fit to be tied."

"Well, listen. I sure as hell didn't mean to upset you, and I want you to know I'm awfully sorry. I apologize."

"I accept," Kat said promptly. "You're entitled to your opinion," she added diplomatically.

"Great. You're a doll. And hey, while I've got you on the horn, don't you owe me one?"

Kat was perplexed. "Excuse me?"

"Think back, if you will. Remember when you and my better half tried to bluff me on *College Craze*?"

"I remember. That was sure tacky of us—"

"Hey, water under the bridge. But like I said, you could make it up to me. Here's the thing. We're shooting a prestige picture for the kiddies—a real classy version of *Snow White*. It's our first G rating, and we want it to be real special."

"That's nice, Mo. Kids deserve better movies than the things that are around."

"My sentiments exactly! And hey, these baby boomers have disposable income pouring out of their diapers. So— how'd you like to be the fairy godmother?"

"Gee, I don't know, Mo—"

"Kat," he said somberly, "we're talking labor of love here."

"It does sound like a charming idea, but I'm pretty tied up with *Gambit*—"

"*No problema. Snow White* won't interfere with *Gambit*. Your part's pivotal—but smallish. Just a couple of days right here on the lot."

"All right, I guess so."

"Love ya, Kat. Thank you, thank you. I'll be in touch."

"Fine. And Mo? I'm very sorry about your mother-in-law."

"My what? Oh, yeah, it's a real shame. Cirrhosis—what a way to go."

"I guess you'll be flying up for the funeral," Kat said.

"Actually no. I think I can support Pru a lot better right where I am—"

"Of course. Well, I know you're busy—"

"You betsky, doll. Kiss, kiss!"

When Kat put down the phone, she felt the way she always felt after a conversation with Mo: a little winded, and slightly wary. Mo was one of those people who shook your hand and left you counting your fingers afterward. But Pru loved him— and for Kat, that was enough.

After Thelma's funeral, the mourners gathered in the church rectory for the wake. The twins sat with Hugh as he chain-smoked and nervously traced the fish-hook scars in his gaunt cheeks. Pru couldn't bear watching him, and when she saw her ex-husband enter the room, she quickly went to him.

"Thanks for coming, John."

He forced a smile and put a comforting arm around her shoulders. They walked outside to the rectory garden, where the autumn air was crisp and pine-scented. The apple and pear trees were heavy with fruit.

"It's lovely here," she said. "I guess you're happy to be back in Tahoe."

"I am, but there are times when I miss you—and your wild friends," he added with a smile. When Pru didn't return it, he asked her, "What's wrong?"

"One of my wild friends has really outdone herself this time," Pru sighed. "Leah's in the Betty Ford Center."

His face turned ashen. "What happened?"

"The usual. You know Leah."

John sighed deeply. "Do you have her address?"

She gave it to him, and they went back inside.

Later, as Tony drove her to the airport, Pru pulled her checkbook from her lizard bag. "Mom's hospital room must have cost a fortune," she said. "Let me take care of it."

"Forget it, Sis."

"But, Tony, I don't want you stuck with it."

"Don't worry about it. Mercer took care of it. He insisted."

At the mention of Mercer's name, Pru felt the color rise in her cheeks. She nervously twisted a strand of bright copper hair, and out of the corner of her eye she watched Tony for telltale signs of mockery or disapproval, but it was obvious he had nothing more on his mind than the road ahead. With a sigh of relief, she realized that he was completely in the dark about the scene she'd made with Mercer. Thank God he was a gentleman. Pru was grateful.

"Look," she said, putting her checkbook away, "please tell him thank you for me, will you? He really went beyond the call of duty."

"He always does, and I'll be damned if I can figure out why. I mean, I'm no deadbeat, but we're not friends or anything. We don't socialize outside of work, and we hardly see each other on the job. I run the hotel, he takes care of the other holdings, and basically we go our separate ways—"

"Strange."

"It is—he's a hard nut to crack. I sure haven't figured him out."

Pru frowned. "How can you put in all that time with someone and not get even a glimmer of what he's about?"

"Why are you so interested?" Tony asked.

She wasn't even sure herself. She'd had her chance with Mercer, and she'd blown it sky-high. Besides, she was a happily married woman. But still, there was something about him, something intriguing.

"Tony," she said slowly, "do you think Mercer would make a good investor in the movies?"

"So that's why you're interested! I knew you had to have something up your sleeve."

"You guessed it," Pru admitted. "Could you do me a favor? Could you feel him out for me? See if he's interested in high-risk ventures?"

He patted her knee. "Why not? Anything for my big sis." He pulled over at her terminal, and she kissed him good-bye. "You won't forget, will you?" she asked, giving him a warm hug.

"Not if I value my life, Pru."

He hugged her back, and she dashed into the airport to make her flight.

Thirty-Seven

THERE WAS NO letup in the hot Santa Ana winds that ravaged the city during the autumn of 1987. Even in October, the cruel breezes that bore down from Bakersfield made all of Los Angeles bristle with heat and frustration. Even at night, in Kat's hilltop house, the heat was relentless.

"You're brooding again," she said one evening as she kneaded Mick's neck and shoulders.

"It's the goddamned job," he said. "We're up to our eyeballs."

"You work too hard, sugar. You need to take some time off."

"I don't see the home boys taking time off. It heats up like this, and every goddamned punk in the city loads up his roscoe and hoses down the neighborhood."

His shoulders were so tense that working on them made Kat's hands ache. The veins in his temples pulsed frantically.

"You've got to relax," she said.

"How can I relax in this hellhole? You want me to just go with the flow?" he asked bitterly.

She kissed him lightly. Her lavender-scented skin tingled in his nostrils, and he breathed in gratefully. She smoothed his brow as he slumped back against her. "God, I'm crapped out," he said.

"Let's sleep on the deck tonight," she suggested. "It's too hot upstairs."

As they lay together, she wanted to make love to him under

the stars, but she knew there wasn't much chance of that happening. He'd been this way for weeks—a tortured, exhausted stranger—and she wondered how much longer it would go on. It was taking its toll on everyone. The previous week, he'd had to cancel two dates to take Misti riding. She'd been terribly hurt and angry. Between her mother's busy schedule and Mick's, Misti felt lonely and neglected.

As Mick slept restlessly beside her, Kat vowed to do better by her daughter. Fortunately, she had some help there. The *Gambit* producer had left over a salary dispute, and the project was temporarily up in the air. Meanwhile, Kat had some free time.

She decided to spend it with Misti and—just possibly—do a play. *If* the right play came along. She had to admit it; the prospect of stage work had been brewing inside her for months. She'd never had as much fun in her life as when she'd done her stint at the Westwood Playhouse, and she was longing to do live theater again.

That's what I'll do, she decided. As the hint of a breeze wafted up through the redwood slats, the moon rode high on the sable horizon, and Kat fell asleep beneath a blanket of stars.

In the morning, she got her agent on the phone. "Michele, I want you to find me a play."

"Get real, toots. What you want is exposure, not a handful of highbrows watching your *Masterpiece Theater* act."

"But I love the stage, and to be perfectly honest, I'd appreciate a little *less* exposure. Sometimes I wish people would just forget all about me."

"Oh, for God's sake, Greta, give it a rest."

"But I'm tired of skulking around Safeway in disguise. I look like one of those darn hijackers! And it doesn't do any good anyway—the reporters still rummage through my cart for their big scoop."

"Well, if you stopped shopping for groceries and started eating at Morton's like the rest of us, nobody would bother you. And they sure as hell wouldn't squeeze your cantaloupes."

"I'm not joking, Michele."

"You should be. You know damn well what it was like

before, when you had your precious privacy. It was tuna fish casseroles, waiting for the phone to ring, and dying to be a star. You wouldn't trade that for this, and you know it. So don't be ungrateful. It's unbecoming.''

''I'm not ungrateful. I just want a play. A stretch. A challenge.''

''Ix-nay, Kat.''

''What do you mean? I'm the boss!''

''Well, toots, you may be the boss, but I'm the brains, so what I say goes. Besides, when *Gambit* gears up, you won't have time for kvetching. And by the way, my ears over at the studio tell me they're going to announce a new producer in the next day or so.''

''I wonder who they'll get.''

''Whatever scum floats to the top when they test the waters.''

''Isn't it in my contract that I have some sort of input about who they hire?''

''Input yes, authority no. Jesus Christ, Kat, they're paying you five million dollars. What do you care about input?''

''I'd just like to be in control, for heaven's sake. *Gambit* started out as Tommy O'Toole's and mine, and then we let Infinity get its foot in the door, and now I feel like the Little Match Girl, just watching the party from outside in the cold. The studio's completely taken over the project.''

''Between you and me, that's the best thing that could have happened. Let the suits bust their asses while you take care of yourself. I know you're feeling pretty frisky, but you've been through a lot. You should still take it easy.''

''Why, you sweet old thing,'' Kat giggled. ''You're fussing over me like a mother hen.''

''Just protecting my investment,'' Michele answered brusquely. ''Now, listen. Get with the program. Enjoy your time off. Play with the kid. Or better yet, play with that Dirty Harry you've hooked.''

''Mick is not Dirty Harry.''

''Well, he ain't exactly Kojak, either,'' Michele said. ''I'm not ashamed to admit I wouldn't mind sharing a private cell with him. I'll bet he wields a mean set of cuffs.''

''Michele, don't be crude.''

"*Moi?* Anyway, toots, I hope you're luckier than most of us at finding a cop when you need one. Gotta go, my buttons are all lit up!"

Surrounded by potted palms and rubber plants, Leah sat on a floor pillow in Dr. Joan Ingalls's comfortable office at the Center. "What's wrong with me?" she pleaded. "Why am I such a goddamned corkscrew?"

"Maybe because you're getting well," Joan suggested. "The scariest thing in the world is to change."

"No. What's scary is to think I'm not changing at all. Every time I think I'm getting better, I wonder if I'll really be better when I'm out there in the world."

"Are you sure that's a relevant question for today?" Joan asked mildly.

"I guess not. I'm not going out there today. I'm going to Group."

"Right. So the relevant question is . . ."

"Will I get through Group?"

"Group's tough for you, isn't it."

"God, yes. When I first went, all I did was crack jokes, and everyone got down on me for that. So I stopped saying anything and just sat there, and of course everyone got down on me for *that*. So now I cry."

"And what do the others do when you cry?"

"Cathy holds my hand, and Robert hugs me, and Josh tells me what great work I'm doing. But all I feel is how messed up I am."

"Recognizing that you're messed up is a big step."

"Not for me. I've always known that I'm messed up. Just knowing doesn't cut it. I want to get better."

"Fair enough. How do we get you better?"

Leah thought for a moment. "For starters, I want to tell people how sorry I am." She paused uneasily. "But I'm afraid it's too late. No one calls, no one visits—"

"They're not allowed to, Leah. You know that." Joan moved down to the pillow next to Leah's. She looked her in the eye. "What if I did allow you a visitor?"

Leah looked at her skeptically. "I'd plotz."

"An honest answer," Joan laughed. She put an arm around Leah. "Let's try."

"I'm game, but I doubt that my friends have been beating down the door."

"For your information, several people have called, and they're all very anxious to see you."

"You're kidding." Leah's dark eyes widened. "Really?"

"Really. But I'll only authorize visits on one condition."

"Name it."

"Talk to them, Leah. Do more than make conversation. Speak the truth. Find the courage to change, and run with it. Agreed?"

Leah solemnly extended her hand. After they shook, she rose. "Wait," Joan said. "I almost forgot." She pulled a letter from her pocket. "This came for you."

When Leah saw the South Lake Tahoe postmark, she clutched the letter happily and took it to her room for a private reading.

From the window of their honeymoon suite, Samantha and Frank could see the Eiffel Tower, brilliant by night.

"It reminds me of you," Frank told her. "Strong and tall, with an iron foundation. But graceful too. More delicate than lace if you're looking from a distance."

"I'm glad you're not," she said. "Having you close is the reason I'm alive." She gazed across the sparkling City of Lights and sighed deeply. "It's wonderful to be here. And it's even more wonderful to finally have a honeymoon. Thank you for bringing me."

"It was the least I could do, after you were good enough to let that Elvis impersonator marry us."

She laughed, but it caught like a bone in her throat. She looked down sadly on the glittering city, and Frank warmed her hands in his. "It's your folks, isn't it?" he asked.

She nodded reluctantly. "I have to make peace with them. I can't leave things the way they are."

As if reading each other's mind, they both headed for the door at once. They went downstairs to the lobby of the beautiful old hotel, and Sam spoke to the concierge about sending a cable to Greece. It was a simple message: "I need to see you. Please reply."

When that was taken care of, they strolled across the Latin Quarter hand in hand. They shared a midnight onion soup in a tiny bistro on the Boulevard Saint-Germain, then walked back to their hotel for another moonlit evening in each other's arms.

The days and nights flew past, and still no message from Santorini.

Each day they had together was a precious gift—they both knew that—and they refused to let her parents' silence sabotage their happiness. But even so, when the morning arrived that they were due to fly back home, they decided to extend their trip another few days. Sam told herself she wanted to take more pictures, but in truth she was waiting for a cable— one that never arrived.

The phone rang insistently as Kat groped for it.

"Kat? Michele. Sorry to wake you—I've got some bad news."

Kat drowsily raised herself on one arm to listen.

"The new producer on *Gambit* is Nestor Gramsky."

"Yuck," Kat said groggily. "He's ruined every studio in town."

"I know. The guy couldn't run a hamster wheel. Someone must owe him a huge favor."

"At our expense," Kat said tightly. "He'll ruin the film."

"I know he will. And it gets worse."

"I'm listening."

"He wants you out."

"What?" Kat sat bolt upright.

"Can you believe his nerve? He says you lost your looks."

"Hog wallow! I never looked better. My scars are completely healed."

"I know, but Nestor claims the original contracts are null and void. I'm about to call the little twit and shove the phone down his throat."

"Wait, Michele."

"For what? The scum needs his lights put out."

"I think I know what this is all about," Kat said thoughtfully. ''The other day I was having lunch with Tommy at the commissary, and everyone was talking about that Playmate of the Year, Wendy What's-her-name—''

''I remember her. Tits you couldn't climb with a fireman's ladder.''

''That's her. Anyway, they were saying that Wendy and Nestor are a hot item these days. Maybe that explains why he wants me out of the picture.''

''To give his bimbette the part!'' hissed Michele. ''Goddamnit, Kat, we're going to sue him for ten times your salary! No one pulls this on Michele Gendelman and gets away with it.''

''Now, don't get your knickers in a twist,'' Kat said soothingly. ''I was getting frustrated about *Gambit* anyway. Infinity was asking Tommy for all kinds of ridiculous rewrites, and I could feel the whole project running through my fingers once they started making demands. To be perfectly honest, I'm relieved to be out.''

''Well, keep your relief to yourself, toots, because we're taking Nestor to court, and we're going to win a settlement that will make your five-million-dollar salary look like pocket change.''

''You're a real little muskrat, Michele, and I sure do appreciate it, but I don't want to spend the next ten years in judge's chambers. Let's just let it go and move on.''

''Not on your life, toots. You are going to bleed this sucker dry—whether you like it or not. Gotta go!''

After she hung up, Kat snuggled back into bed. With *Gambit* and its headaches out of her life, she smiled as she fell asleep.

She dreamed of musty dressing rooms, colorful pots of greasepaint, and rickety old costume racks rolling through dim halls. Harried dressers and frantic prop men screamed at each other with lungs that wouldn't quit—until the curtain opened.

Boldly she strode out from the wings—and then she woke up. She sang in the shower for half the morning.

Thirty-Eight

As soon as her plane touched down at Burbank Airport, Pru—still dressed in her mourning suit—rushed to the studio. When she saw what Mo had done on her behalf, she was stunned.

"You shouldn't have!" she exclaimed.

"Are you mad at me, doll?"

"Of course not! You're a prince! You've done everything but train the crocodiles!"

"I knew you were under the gun, so I figured you wouldn't mind if I took care of a few things."

"Are you kidding? I go away for three days, and when I come back you've got my little swamp epic practically camera-ready. Thank you so much, darling."

She reached out to plant a kiss on his balding pate, but he ducked away with a wide grin. "Get the lead out, baby. Your head's on the block here."

He went over the contracts with Pru while she took a swig from a bottle of Pepto-Bismol and then gazed admiringly at the work he'd done to put *Tropic of Danger* together in record time. Permits and waivers were all set to go, and the screenplay was polished to a high gloss.

"You must have fed steroids to the script doctor," she said with admiration. She scanned a couple of key scenes. "This is letter-perfect," she sighed.

"I'm glad you like it," Mo said. "I just wanted things to go smoothly—after all you've been through."

He watched with concern as she took another dose of Pepto-Bismol. "That bad, huh?"

"It comes and goes. I'm all right."

"Maybe you should see a doctor, baby . . ."

"It's nothing. You know me, I always get the jitters before a shoot. Remember *College Craze*—"

"And how," he said with a wink. Goosing her playfully, he told her, "If you're sure you're all right, I've gotta run back to the office. Apparently the *Roman Holiday* remake has turned into more of a Roman massacre. The director's called twice this morning. The two leads are locked in their suites at the Cavalieri Hilton, waiting for their lawyers to arrive."

"Oh, no," Pru sympathized. "Have you closed down production?"

"Yeah—and it's costing me more than the goddamned space program. The whole shoot's up on blocks while these prima donnas sit tight and order up room service," he fumed. "My lawyer's on his way to Rome now. That ought to pick up the pace."

"Good," Pru said. As Mo started to leave, she caught his arm. "I'll see you at home for a midnight snack," she added lasciviously.

"I'm drooling already, doll. *Adiós*."

All afternoon she was in meetings, conferring with the director, the production manager, and the head of the accounting team. The costume designer threw not less than four tantrums, and as if that weren't enough, the Friends of Animals picketed the building. They were threatening to sue if any alligators were abused during filming. Pru personally met with them in her office and assured them of the animals' humane treatment. She stayed behind her desk the whole time, however; she didn't want them seeing her alligator pumps.

By the time the matter of reptile rights was taken care of, it was well past eight, and Pru called it quits. Driving across town, she barely had time to stop off at Chalet Gourmet before it closed. She bought a huge piece of châteaubriand, new potatoes, a Bavarian torte, and another bottle of Pepto-Bismol.

* * *

Hasta la bye-bye. Lucien crushed out his cigarette. He turned off the *Hawkeye* cassette he'd been watching, then threw the remote across the den as he thought of Will Avery's one-note performance in the film. *The guy has about as much talent as a trained seal.* Even in his tiny role, Lucien thought, he practically brought the entire picture to a grinding halt.

Pru's really got a death wish if she hires that zero! Lucien shook his head in disgust. Will Avery was a hack and a flash in the pan. Any airhead could see that. And speaking of airheads . . .

He couldn't help it. He had a soft spot for Pru's dingbat buddy. What a cutie she'd been—and dumb. He liked that in a woman. If she hadn't been so snookered that night at the Veil, he might have had some trouble on his hands. But bless her wasted little heart, between the 'lude cocktail and all that wine, her eyes had been tied in bows, and he'd pulled off quite a fast one. Bang, zoom, pow to the moon.

He went upstairs and worked on his newest monologue in front of the mirror. The teacher had told him there were a lot of problems with his interpretation, but Lucien knew that the old fart was just envious. He read the lines a few times, rehearsed them to his satisfaction, and went downstairs for something to eat. En route, he got sidetracked at the sight of Pru's wide-open office: you just never knew what interesting tidbit might pass across her desk.

He was shuffling through a stack of Will Avery stills, wondering what the big deal was, when he heard footsteps behind him.

"Just what do you think you're doing?" Pru asked angrily. Her green eyes flashed. "Get out of here," she ordered. But he didn't.

"Hi," he said amiably.

She crossed her arms in front of her and studied him coldly. "What are you doing in my office?" she asked.

"Trying to call you," he lied, patting the telephone. "I wanted to let you know I have an acting class tonight, and I won't be home for dinner—"

"Well, next time," she said sharply, "please use another phone. God knows we have enough of them in this house."

"I'm really sorry," he said contritely. "I should have respected your privacy."

"Yes, you should have. I happen to know that you've been in here before, and if I catch you in here again, I'll speak with your father."

"Over and out," Lucien said humbly. "No more calls from here. I promise." He looked at his Rolex and smiled sunnily. "I'd better jet—my craft calls."

Despite herself, Pru was impressed. "You're really working hard at it, aren't you?"

"Like a dog," he said modestly.

"That gives me an idea," she said, feeling more kindly toward him. "If you want, you can come to the studio sometime and sit in on a couple of rehearsals. You'd learn a lot."

Like hell, he thought. *Those lame-os could learn from me.*

"Why, thanks, Pru. I'll take you up on it."

He left, and as she heard him pull out of the driveway, she took another swig of Pepto-Bismol and reached for the Rolodex. Spinning it like her own personal wheel of fortune, she tied up some loose ends before dinner.

After a lot of brainstorming with Frank, Sam had decided to make a documentary film about Togo. Funded by UNESCO, the film would be used to raise money for various projects in West Africa.

Sam and Frank were in New York, meeting with a group of their United Nations sponsors, when a cable arrived at their hotel. It came from a lawyer in Athens who regretted to inform Sam of her parents' death. They'd been killed in Santorini in an automobile accident a few days earlier.

"I have to go there," Sam said. Frank reached for the telephone.

The following day, they arrived by helicopter on Santorini just as the sun was setting. The sea circled the island in a sparkling necklace of reflected light. Shepherds led their flocks home from the hills, wives fed the fires in their thatched huts, and tourists swarmed the cobbled streets, shopping for woolens and pottery.

Sam and Frank walked through the village and climbed up a winding road to the Devanes' hilltop villa. Grape arbors and wild roses studded the road with color. Finches filled the redolent almond branches with their noisy trills. At the gate, Sam led the way up the rocky path to the whitewashed house.

As the sprawling villa rose ahead of them, she felt a tightening in her throat, and her stomach churned when she reached the huge olivewood door.

"I can't," she whispered.

"Then we'll turn around." Frank started to steer her back down the path, but she hesitated.

As she reached for the brass knocker, she thought how lonely the villa looked, how dead and empty. The lemon trees were barren, the path needed sweeping, and the dark windows of the house gaped like missing teeth.

Just as the sun sank into the ocean, the door to the servants' cottage slowly creaked open. An ancient peasant woman scurried toward the visitors. Her black eyes were bottomless pits of sorrow, and she wrung her hands as she approached Sam and Frank.

"Magdalena," Sam said softly as she kissed the old woman's weathered skin. Magdalena pulled a key from the pockets of her black dress, and she led the couple inside the house.

Everything was just as Sam remembered, but there was an overwhelming stillness to the large, airy rooms. From the kitchen, Magdalena brought a decanter of retsina and, along with it, a thick envelope. It was stamped with the return address of the same Athens lawyer who'd sent Sam the cable.

"It's their will," she said, opening the envelope and quickly scanning the document. She tossed it aside. "I'm rich," she said without enthusiasm.

Magdalena tapped her shoulder and beckoned the couple to follow her outside. They made their way through an overgrown garden, and the old woman pointed across the estate, toward a stone wall overlooking the cliffs.

Sam thanked her. She led Frank along the windswept footpath toward the wall. They made their way carefully as darkness descended, and finally they reached the place that Magdalena had pointed to. There, high above the sea, Edward and Polly Devane lay buried. Snowdrops grew in white patches around the grave, and Sam knelt to pick one. She brought it to her face, breathed in its delicate perfume, and ran the soft petals along her cheekbone.

She looked back down the path. Magdalena pulled her black shawl across her thin shoulders, then disappeared inside the house.

Frank opened his arms, and Sam rushed in. The wind swirled around them as her sobs mingled with the cries of the gulls overhead. Bowing their heads against the wind, they turned away from the dizzying heights of the cliff and started back toward the house.

Along the path, she stopped to pick an olive from a tree. It was a lustrous dark fruit—but deadly poisonous until it had been soaked in saltwater. She squeezed the beautiful nugget until its lethal juices ran through her fingers.

"The Devane tree bears bitter fruit," she said wretchedly.

"That's all in the past, Samantha. There's no time for bitterness."

She looked at him uncomprehendingly at first. Then, slowly, she gazed into his wise eyes and nodded.

He swept her into his arms, and they clung together as the ocean's silvery mist showered them with diamonds. Shot through with silver and gold, Sam's hair blew wildly as the wind gained momentum.

"Let's go back," she whispered.

Effortlessly he lifted her and carried her across the threshold of the kitchen door. She seemed to float in his arms as he climbed the stairs and carried her into their candlelit bedroom. A roaring fire blazed in the hearth, and as they came together in her parents' bed, it creaked and rocked beneath the power of their love. The house which had been filled with sorrow was now resplendent with joy. By the time they blew the candles out and covered the fire, they'd chased despair from the ancient whitewashed walls.

They spent three days making plans before they flew to Dakar to begin work on the UNESCO project. Frank wanted to wait longer so that Sam could rest up for the trip, but she wouldn't hear of it.

"I haven't got time to rest up," she told him. "It's now or never."

In Dakar, they hired a skeleton crew and flew to Togo to

begin the shoot. In the wild, Frank was heartened to see Sam thrive. While he spent his days scouting upcoming locations, she worked long and arduous hours with the crew. They met up in the evenings, and every night around the campfire, Frank saw the same hell-bent woman he'd first fallen in love with. She wasn't following doctor's orders—or anyone's. Fully aware that she was working against time, she shot the documentary in less than two weeks, trekking across the lowlands and jungles as she photographed Togo's rich and varied wildlife.

On their last night of filming, as they lay together in sleeping bags by the dying campfire, Sam leaned wearily against Frank's chest.

"I couldn't have done it without you," she said.

"That's a crock," he murmured, ruffling her hair.

A jackal howled in the distant darkness, and she held him tightly. The last embers of the fire burned to ash, and his breathing became regular as she listened contentedly. She was happy for every moment she had with him. Even now, as a hush fell across the jungle and stars crowded the deep black sky, she was almost unwilling to abandon him for sleep.

Thirty-Nine

"Dammit, Misti, when I say no, I mean no!"

"But, Mom, all my friends do it!"

"All your friends take limousines to Century City and spend the day getting permanent waves? You've got to be kidding. For heaven's sake, you're twelve years old!"

"I know that, Mom. I'm a young lady now, and I ought to be able to spend Saturday having fun with my friends."

"But I don't approve of those friends."

"Well, I don't approve of Mick O'Reilly."

"You don't even give him a chance."

"Sure I do—and he stands me up every time."

Kat, the actress, didn't show how that stung. "We're not talking about Mick," she said. "We're talking about you, and I'm saying no, you can't go driving around Century City with a carful of spoiled brats!"

"They're the only friends I have, Mom, and I can't help it if their parents give them chauffeurs."

"I know," Kat sighed unhappily. "It's just that they're all so . . . sophisticated . . ."

"I can handle it."

"But what if you can't, Misti? What if someone offers you coke, or gets fresh—"

"You should talk."

"Excuse me?"

"You know what I mean. You didn't do such a swell job of handling my father when he got fresh, did you?"

"I made some mistakes," Kat answered carefully.

"Like having me?" Misti taunted. Her violet eyes were defiant, but her voice wavered.

"Stop that. You know I love you more than anything in this world. I won't have you talking like that!"

"Jesus Christ, Mom—"

"Don't swear."

"Mom, all I want to do is go shopping with my friends. I promise I won't get knocked up by some hillbilly—"

"How dare you speak to me like that? Go to your room. Now!"

Misti slunk out of the kitchen, and Kat, trembling, poured a cup of coffee.

"You two fighting again?" Marie came waltzing through the back door with a basketful of cilantro from the garden.

Kat nodded miserably.

"You know," Marie said, "you've got to give her some space. She's growing up."

Kat stared incredulously at her mother. " 'Give her some space'? This from the woman who practically sat in my lap whenever a boy came to visit?"

"You gotta change with the times," Marie said, and shrugged. "Let her take the limo and fry her hair. What's the harm? Besides, don't you feel just a little bit silly coming down on her about perms? Girl, your cleavage has cut across the cover of every magazine in the country."

"All the more reason to be careful with Misti."

"I was careful—and look where you ended up. Barefoot and pregnant. No, honey, if you want to be careful, be careful with the things that count. Listen to her. Be there for her." Marie set down her basket and hugged her daughter awkwardly. "You've got a lot going on right now, loving your man and being a good mother. It's a handful, but you'll manage."

Marie was stroking her daughter's hair when Mick walked in.

"Hello, ladies," he said tiredly.

"Land's sake, you look like the devil bit your butt," Marie said.

"Just another long night in the cesspools." He smiled

wearily, then called upstairs, "Misti? You around?" She came downstairs, still scowling. "You feel like taking a ride?" he asked her. "The equestrian division got a couple of new ponies and I thought we'd take them out for a test drive."

"Sure," Misti said, her bad mood quickly forgotten. "I'll go change." As she bounded upstairs, Kat told him, "Thank you. That's nice for her."

"I could use a spin myself. Change of pace from that hell-hole downtown. Goddamned crazies . . . Pardon my French, Marie." With a heavy step, he left the kitchen, shaking his head.

"That man's in trouble," Marie told Kat.

"I know."

"Well, the best I can do is make him a home-cooked meal," Marie said. She rummaged in the cupboards and pulled out her Chinese cooking equipment. "Wok on the wild side," she announced. "That's my motto."

She was dictating a grocery list to Kat when they both heard a tiny "psst." They looked up, and Misti stood in the doorway, dressed for riding.

"I'm sorry, Mom," she said softly.

"Me, too."

Kat held her close.

Krysta promised herself she wouldn't take a pain pill that night: she needed a clear head. Standing on the terrace of her Santa Monica condo, she watched the sun slip into the dark water. Clouds slithered like eels across the sky, and she wondered how many evenings she had left. The doctor had said six months at most; she knew it would be far less.

Night fell. It was chilly on the terrace, and she went inside. She was standing in the kitchen, thinking she should eat, when the pain hit. She was seized with a cramp as sharp as a labor contraction. She stumbled to her bedside table and forgot all about her promise as she swallowed two Percodans. Breathing deeply, she waited for the familiar floating sensation. Soon she felt airborne, as if the pills were a magic carpet, and with a sleepy smile she let them carry her far away from her agony. . . .

An idea drifted foggily into her mind. She pulled a step-stool into her closet and climbed it, then poked around behind hatboxes until she found a worn leather album. It was dusty and looked as if it might disintegrate in her hands as she lifted it from its hiding place. She carried it to her bed and opened it to a page full of faded snapshots. A dark-eyed baby girl lay in her cradle . . . took a wobbly step . . . lapped an ice-cream cone as she stared unblinkingly into the camera.

Krysta cried out as a sudden blade of pain cut through the Percodan. Tears splashed across the photographs until the dark-eyed child receded and dissolved. Sobbing uncontrollably, Krysta finally understood what she had to do.

The scent of nasturtiums perfumed the October air as Leah walked back to her room one evening after Group. It had been a good session, and she was feeling lighthearted as she headed across the lawn.

When she got to her room, she sat at her desk and reread Sam's most recent letter from Africa.

". . . We leave for Nairobi in the morning, where we'll mix and score the movie. Some days I get tired and have to sleep a little extra, but most of the time we go gangbusters. Since it's hard to call, I don't even try. I just thank my lucky stars to be alive. Life is a gift. Don't you agree? XXX, Sam."

Leah tucked the letter back in her drawer, then changed into a nightgown and sat before her mirror, brushing her hair one hundred strokes. As she faced herself, she practiced the exercise they'd learned in Group. She looked carefully at her image in the mirror and tried very hard to like what she saw. She stared into her lustrous brown eyes until she got a glimpse of their intelligence. She focused on her slim neck until she couldn't help but recognize its grace. Then she cocked her head slightly and noticed for the first time that her chin was strong: it had resolve, it had character.

She turned out the light and climbed into bed. When her head hit the pillow, she looked out her window. The stars formed a twinkling net across the night, as if God and the angels were afraid of falling. But Leah, who had already fallen so far, wasn't fearful at all. She took the plunge willingly and fell into a deep, untroubled sleep.

Forty

PRU SHIMMIED INTO her pantyhose and pulled her Donna Karan caftan over her head. She was just plucking her pearls from her gynecologist's desk when Dr. Cole returned.

"There's nothing wrong with you," she said with a smile. "You're pregnant."

"Damn," Pru sighed, yanking her pearls into position. She scowled in the mirror as she painted her lips with the same bright shade of red that highlighted her hair. "Isn't there someone I can sue? How about those jerks at Ortho?" she asked, thinking of her diaphragm. "Next time I'll buy Japanese."

"Look, Prudence, you're just surprised," Dr. Cole said.

" 'Surprised' is not the word, Doctor. Try 'damned annoyed.' " She picked up her briefcase.

"Don't you want to discuss it?" the doctor asked.

"There's nothing to discuss," Pru snapped. "I'll see the receptionist on my way out, and we'll set up the—procedure."

"Are you sure?"

"Absolutely," Pru answered, heading for the door.

Outside in the parking lot, she fumbled for her car keys and told herself to stay calm. She could have the abortion the day before Thanksgiving, then rest over the long weekend before the shoot began.

Cursing the mai tais and moonlit Hawaiian beach that had gotten her into this mess in the first place, she drove across town, waved gaily at the studio guard, and swung into her parking place. As she marched into the elevator, she vowed to put the whole fiasco behind her. Thank God it was a cinch to fix—or so she'd heard.

As she rounded the corner to her office, Drew stood in the hallway looking harried.

"Your stepson is waiting inside, Pru." He nodded toward the closed door.

"Not again," she fumed. "What does he want this time?"

"Search me."

"Can't you get rid of him?"

"Maybe with a SWAT team," Drew said.

"Please try, pretty please." She looked at her assistant wearily. "I had enough of him last night at Michael's," she said. "He had the nerve to hint that he should replace Will in *Tropic of Danger*. I almost choked on my free-range chicken."

Drew patted her shoulder and handed her a fistful of phone messages, which she gratefully stuffed into her briefcase.

"I think I'll use Mo's suite," she whispered, heading for the elevator. "Where you-know-who won't look for me."

Cooling his heels in her outer office, Lucien was eavesdropping on the entire conversation between Pru and her assistant, and when Drew opened the office door, he hastily leaped backward. "I was just leaving," he said. "Will you do me a favor and tell Ms. Daniels when she gets here that I couldn't wait any longer?"

"I'll be sure to pass along the message," Drew said in a businesslike tone.

"*Ciao,*" Lucien said casually. As he stepped out of the office, the phone rang in his wake, and he overheard Drew answer, "Yes, of course, Mr. Avery. She's been expecting your call. Let me buzz her—"

In the hallway, Lucien slammed the heel of his hand against the wall. He stormed past the reception area and marched outside to his car. Stepping on the gas, he raced to the closest freeway ramp, where it felt good to bring the Lamborghini up to speed. He cruised along the Hollywood Freeway sucking a joint, and when the Hollywood turned into the San Berdoo, he figured what the hell and went along for the ride.

The day was scorching, the sun was climbing, and Guns n' Roses were burning up the tape deck as he coasted at eighty. He drank tequila from his silver flask, and he honked at trucks to get out of his way as he spend down the freeway toward the desert.

What a fucking wasteland, he sighed. *I wish I had some company.*

No sooner had he made his wish than inspiration struck. He sped into Palm Springs and checked in at the Spa Hotel. In his suite, he took a long shower, tied his pony tail with a gold-and-lapiz bolo, and slipped into his Tony Lama cowboy boots.

Dressed to kill, he thought, studying his reflection in the mirror. Then he went to his car and cruised down scenic Bob Hope Drive to the Betty Ford Center.

They knew him there. He'd had a girlfriend at school whose mother made the Center her home away from home, and Lucien had passed many hours in the guest lounge while Tisha played dutiful daughter.

"Mr. Blake?" he heard the receptionist ask.

He walked to the desk and, with the kind of somber smile he knew they appreciated, signed his name in the visitors' log.

"Ms. Sirk will see you now," the receptionist said. An aide led Lucien down a carpeted hallway to the lounge. When he walked through the doorway, Leah rose from the couch and went to him.

"What a nice surprise," she said. "Especially after what I put you through. Kat told me you were the one who found me passed out. Lucky you. I'm sorry, Lucien."

As she spoke, he was blown away by how great she looked. The last time he'd seen her, she'd had her head in the toilet. What a sight! But now her skin was radiant, her black hair fell down her back like a rushing waterfall, and the sparkle in her gypsy eyes was dazzling.

"Anyway," she said with a warm smile, "it was sweet of you to come." She sat down on the couch and patted the seat next to her.

"I wanted to see you," Lucien told her, sitting down.

"I've thought about you a lot." He slid closer. "You look staggering, Leah."

"Staggering's always been my forté." She grinned, then noticed his Tony Lamas and gave a low whistle. "Not bad, cowboy."

"Thanks. How are you, anyway?" he asked.

"Good. And getting better." She nodded slowly. "I have to tell you, Lucien. You seem so young. I guess it's just that I've aged." She studied his unlined, barely lived-in face. "How are you?" she asked.

"Getting by," he answered evenly. He didn't seem to want to talk, and she found herself wondering why he'd come.

"Is everything all right at home?" she asked.

"Cleaver City," he replied.

"Well, if it's not," she said carefully, "you know we can always talk about it, right? Here at the Center, I'm learning a lot about how important it is to open up—"

Spare me, thought Lucien, lighting a cigarette and walking to the window. *I didn't drive a hundred miles to hear a sermon.* He took a deep drag and leaned against the sill.

"Anyway," Leah continued, "I just have to make sure you understand that I'm truly sorry for any trouble I caused you."

"You already said that." He flicked ash into one of the potted geraniums on the sill, and looked down at her on the couch.

"Look," he said brusquely, "you really don't have to apologize anymore." He paused. "You want to take a walk? Get some air?"

She nodded and led him out onto the lawn, past the dormitories and out toward the tennis courts. It was too hot to play, and the courts were abandoned. The only person in sight was a gardener riding his lawn mower off into the distance.

"Shit, it's hotter out here than it was in the lounge," Lucien said as they stood under the shade of the awning near the courts.

"If you want we can go back inside and get something to drink," Leah suggested.

"There's no need to go in." He paused dramatically. "I've got something right here."

He bent over and took the silver flask from its hiding place in his boot. He held it out to Leah, but she just stood staring at him in disbelief.

"Are you out of your mind?" she asked him.

He ignored her and drank from the flask. When he'd finished, he wiped his mouth and again offered it to her.

"Just one. Enough to wet your whistle."

Leah's blazing eyes bored into him like bullets. "You're really an asshole, you know that?" She turned and strode away from him, but he quickly caught up.

"For chrissake, Leah, there's not even enough to get drunk," he said, holding it out to her. "Maybe you'll just get a little friendlier," he added. "Remember how it used to be between us—"

"You moron!" With a flick of her wrist, she sent the flask flying. "I think it's time for you to go."

She started back toward the Center. "By the way," she called out over her shoulder, "don't bother to come back, because if you do, I'll have them throw you out."

Bitch! Lucien thought, watching Leah disappear down the walk. *You'll be sorry. Count on it.*

Krysta nervously crossed and recrossed her thin legs. She tried to read a *Bazaar* that someone had left in the waiting room, but she couldn't concentrate.

Finally, she heard her name called. "Ms. Bennett?"

Still not sure that she was doing the right thing, she walked to the desk. Pain was cutting her in half as she stood before the receptionist, but she couldn't allow herself a Percodan: she needed her wits about her.

". . . Leah's in the waiting area now if you'd like to go see her."

Krysta followed the aide to the same lounge in which Leah had met with Lucien earlier that afternoon. As she walked through the door, Leah regarded her warily. After her run-in with Lucien, she wasn't exactly in the best of spirits.

"Thank you for seeing me," Krysta said. Her arms hung like sticks at her sides, and her black sheath seemed a size too large, but with her lustrous auburn hair and cool white skin, she was still the same beauty who'd commanded the halls of UCLA. Next to the deeply tanned, leathery aide, she was a bolt of silk in a stable.

"I'm sort of tired," Leah apologized as she shook Krysta's hand and the attendant disappeared.

"I can come back another time," Krysta said quickly.

"I didn't mean it that way. I just wanted to let you know, I'm not exactly great company right now. But I'm glad to see you. It's nice to know that people care."

"I do." She paused uncertainly. "You're probably wondering why I'm here."

"Well," Leah said, "I wasn't exactly the teacher's pet. I couldn't have acted my way out of a traffic ticket."

"But you made us all laugh."

"The class clown," Leah murmured. "But that's a past life," she added. "We don't like court jesters here at the Center. We go for the heart, not the funny bone."

"I see," said Krysta.

Another spasm of pain cut through her abdomen, and she breathed in sharply.

"Are you all right?" Leah asked.

"Fine," Krysta answered, sitting down carefully on the couch. "Leah," she began, and she wished with all her heart that she was simply reciting lines. If only she were playing a role right now; if only she were reading a script. But this was no stage, and the only spotlight that fell on her was Leah's watchful gaze. She took a deep breath. "There's something you have to know."

Leah leaned forward, listening.

"I knew your father many years ago," Krysta began.

"And you never mentioned it?"

"I couldn't."

"Why not?"

"I was afraid I'd say something—"

"Say what?" Leah asked. She'd begun to have a bad feeling about Krysta's visit; all of a sudden she wanted it to end.

"I'm so sorry," Krysta mumbled. "Leah—your father and I . . . we were friends . . . more than friends—"

Leah's heart shot to her throat. She thought she'd choke as she whispered, "Don't say it. It can't be."

"I'm your mother," Krysta blurted.

''No!'' Leah bellowed. ''No!'' She flew across the lounge, hurling herself into the corner and sliding down the wall in a flailing heap. ''No!'' she screamed. An aide rushed in, but Krysta got to her first and tried to grab her. Leah spun from her arms and ran to the window. She pushed her fist through the glass.

It shattered everywhere, and Leah picked up the biggest shard. It glinted and gleamed with light as she held it to the soft flesh of her arm. Krysta tried to wrestle it away from her, and as they fought, they were both soon covered with blood. The aide finally knocked it from Leah's hand just as Joan came running from her office. She took Leah in her arms.

''You're going to be fine,'' she said calmly. She led her hysterical patient out of the room.

Krysta sat with a handkerchief wrapped around her hand as Leah's cries echoed from the hallway. Standing in the wreckage of the dayroom, Krysta looked at the blood on her hands—Leah's blood, and her own. Blindly she stumbled to the rest room. Under the ghastly fluorescent light, she stared with horror at the face of Medea in the mirror.

Forty-One

THE DAY BEFORE Thanksgiving, Pru got up early and padded across the Berber carpet into the bathroom. At first she thought it was just the flattering morning light, but then, when she peered closely into the mirror, she had to admit it: her skin was as pearly pink as the chamber of a seashell. She stepped out of her velour bathrobe and rested her palms on her thickening waist, and to her great surprise, a smile crossed her face: the curves she'd battled most of her life were lovely and graceful if she only looked. Her ample breasts were beautiful, and so were her generous thighs.

"Putting on weight, baby?" Mo asked as he stepped into the bathroom. "I guess you'll have to cut back on the midnight snacks." He grinned, slapping her behind.

"I'm just fine," Pru answered curtly. Even to her own ears she sounded a bit sharp, and she quickly reached out to Mo and kissed his thinning crown. "Sorry, darling," she said contritely.

"I guess you woke up on the wrong side of the bed," he said, then stepped into his shower. She walked into hers, and as she lathered bath gel on her milky white shoulders, she looked down at the slight fullness of her abdomen and gave it a little pat. She felt strangely exhilarated as she stepped from the shower, dried her body, and gently tugged the tangles from her wet mop of curls. The color in her cheeks was as red as her fiery mane, and she went to her closet for the kelly-green bolero that would perfectly complement her skin and hair. She was pulling it off the hanger when a loud knock at the bedroom door startled her.

"Who is it?" she called out.

"Lucien."

"Hang on," she said irritably as she threw on her robe. Mo was just getting out of the shower, and his rotund waistline was wrapped in a towel as Pru opened the bedroom door.

"You're up early," she said. "Especially for someone who came roaring into the driveway at three in the morning. That was some entrance you made."

"Sorry," Lucien apologized. "I got in late from the Springs." He tilted his face toward her. "Can't you see my tan? I've really been working on it."

"Maybe you should try working on a job," Mo said as he plucked the tie from his valet.

"Lighten up, Dad. When I start landing roles that were written for Tom Cruise, you'll be eating crow *en croute*!"

"Spoken like true Eurotrash," Pru muttered.

Lucien ignored her and held out his open palm to Mo. "Mind if I use the Jeep? The Lamborghini needs a tune-up."

Mo sighed and tossed him the keys.

"Staggering, Dad. Thanks." He turned to leave, and when Pru said a perfunctory good-bye, he made a point of not looking at her as he closed the bedroom door. His snub wasn't subtle, but Pru was in far too good a mood to let her spoiled stepson get her down.

"Are you free tonight?" she asked Mo with her most engaging smile. Before he could answer, the phone rang. He picked it up, listened impatiently, and snapped, "Put him through." He scowled as he listened for a long time, then said, "I'm on my way." He slammed down the phone and quickly stepped into his closet.

"Can you phone Roz?" he called out. "I need a flight to Rome."

"Rome? Why?"

"Because that goddamned little prick Victor Field is about to walk off the picture."

"But can't the producer stop him? Can't you send your lawyer?"

"Already have. Now it's time for Victor to find out who he's fucking with."

Pru called Roz, then sat heavily on the bed and watched Mo hurl clothes into a bag. "Mo—" she began.

"Not now," he barked, but as quickly as he'd done it, he turned to her apologetically. "I'm sorry, doll, it's this god-damned shoot—"

"I understand. I was just wondering how long you'll be gone."

"A couple of days if all goes well. A couple of weeks if Victor decides to play hardball."

"A couple of weeks! That's a long time, Mo . . ."

"For chrissake, do you think I don't know that?" She burst into tears. "Oh, shit, I'm sorry, baby." He sat down on the bed and put his arm around her. "I didn't mean to take it out on you," he said.

She blew her nose. "I know. You're under a lot of pressure."

"You seem to be, too," he said kindly.

"Not pressure, exactly."

"Are you kidding? There's *Tropic of Danger*, and your loony sidekick, and I know Lucien's no small load. Hell, he's a goddamned redwood. It's no wonder you're so edgy—"

"Not edgy," she corrected. "I'm just very emotional," she said pointedly.

The phone rang again, and Mo answered it. "Roz? . . . Thanks . . . I'm out the door."

"I'm coming with you," Pru said as he zipped his suitcase closed.

"To Rome?"

"No. To the airport."

"But why, doll?"

"There's something I have to tell you."

As they scrambled into the limo, Pru checked to make sure there was champagne in the tiny refrigerator. Then she snuggled up next to Mo, who was going through his briefcase.

"Honey?" she said softly.

"There it is!" he exclaimed as he found Victor's contract and began to study it.

"Honey?" Pru said more loudly this time. When that failed to get his attention, she nudged him in the ribs.

"Yes, doll, what is it?" he asked, still not looking up from the contract.

"Mo, darling, I'm pregnant."

He dropped the contract. His eyes opened wide, and he took her hands in his.

"What do you think, darling?" She reached for the fridge and the chilled Roederer, but the look on his face made her pause.

"Mo?" She watched him uncertainly. "Talk to me," she said.

"No wonder you wanted me around," he told her. "If you haven't been through this before, you don't know what to expect."

She searched his eyes. "What do you mean?" she asked, her voice rising.

"Calm down," he said kindly. "I'm told that root canals are worse."

"Worse than what?" she mumbled, but she already knew the answer.

"What did you say, doll?"

"Nothing," she whispered. A single tear ran down her freckled cheek.

"You'll be fine," he assured her. With two fingers, he pushed the corners of her mouth into a smile. Her mouth complied, but her heart was broken. "When is it?" he asked.

She looked at him blankly.

"When's your appointment?"

". . . Today," she answered faintly. Her head was turned to the window as she looked at the world outside, rushing irretrievably into the distance.

She held back her tears until she'd let Mo off at the airport. Then she told the driver to hurry.

"I'm late for my doctor's appointment."

In Santa Monica, Krysta stood at her balcony rail, looking out at the sea. Her head was ringing, and her stomach was a solid wall of pain. But her mind was intact—as clear as glass—

and it was the part of her that hurt the most. How could she have told Leah? Why hadn't she left well enough alone?

As the ocean swallowed the sun, gulls circled overhead, and in their cries, she heard Leah screaming. The truth hadn't saved her: it had made her want to die.

The water seemed to reach up and pull down the last light. Darkness fell, and she remembered the fateful September afternoon when Leah walked into her classroom and blew the lid off the neatly wrapped parcel of Krysta's past. She'd thought she'd never see her child again—she vowed to stay away—but there was dark-eyed Leah. She was unhappy even then, and it filled Krysta with despair to see her joke helplessly with her friends about dates gone bad and scripts going nowhere. There were times when Krysta had been forced to leave the room rather than pull her daughter into her arms. But she'd known it wouldn't be right to tell her.

How could I? she asked herself as she clutched the rail and rode out the pains that cut through her gut like razor blades. When the last wave ended, she dragged herself back across the terrace. The phone was ringing when she pushed open the sliding door.

"Ms. Bennett? This is Joan Ingalls—Leah's doctor. I need to see you right away."

Pru strode through the lobby of the medical building and flung open the doors. She stepped outside into the warm sunlight and basked in its glow as she paused, wondering which way to turn.

She didn't know where the maternity shops were in Beverly Hills, so she simply strolled until she found one. She went inside, figuring she'd just browse a little, but when she left an hour later, half the inventory went with her.

As she drove across town to the studio, she picked up the car phone and called Kat. "I've just blown a small fortune at Great Expectations," she announced.

"Sugar, I'm so happy for you! When are you due?"

"June. Can you believe it?"

"I'm just surprised it took this long! You've got 'Mom' practically tattooed on your forehead. You'll be a wonderful mother."

"I will?"

"Of course—you were born to bounce kids on your knee."

"I was?"

"That—and run a multinational entertainment empire."

"Kat, you're so sweet—"

"And so excited! What does Mo say?"

"He . . . doesn't know. He's in Rome—something came up."

"Well, he'll be tickled to death. Holy smoke, this is the best news I've had in ages."

"Thanks, Kat. Oops, I just pulled into the studio. Time to chop wood. I'll talk to you later, okay?"

As soon as she put the phone down, it rang again.

"Ms. Daniels, this is Dr. Ingalls—at the Betty Ford Center—" Her voice was grave.

"What is it?" Pru asked anxiously.

"Leah needs her friends now—very much. Would you be willing—"

"Name it, Doctor. Is she all right?"

"She's in shock."

"What happened?" Pru asked. As she listened to Joan's explanation, she sat parked in her space at the studio. Praying that no one would come up to her car, she cried silently with her head against the steering wheel.

When she finally walked into her office, she phoned Kat and told her what she'd learned.

"My God," Kat whispered. "Poor Leah."

"I know. Listen, Joan says it would be good if we could go out there. I was thinking we might do something for Thanksgiving."

"I'll meet you at the Chalet. Half an hour."

Pru cleared her desk, left a few last-minute details in Drew's capable hands, and told him, "The next time I see you, we'll be shooting a movie!"

The Chalet was a zoo on the afternoon before Thanksgiving, but Pru and Kat paid no heed to the crowds as they piled all the trimmings onto a fresh tom turkey that sat like a king in their cart. As Pru heaved a case of Perrier onto the bottom rack of the cart, Kat acted quickly to grab it from her.

"Don't you know you're supposed to take it easy, sugar?"

They walked down the aisles in companionable silence until Kat suddenly exclaimed, "There it is!" and reached for a jar of Marshmallow Whip.

"Remember my sweet potato pies?"

"They're better than any man I've ever had," Pru said with great seriousness.

They went back to Pru's designer kitchen and spent the afternoon preparing a banquet so rich it brought tears to Pru's eyes.

"You really are emotional," Kat said as she dabbed Pru's wet cheeks with her apron. They didn't finish cooking until almost midnight, but Pru sent Kat home early to get some sleep. Then, while she waited for the sweet potato pie to finish baking, she went upstairs and carefully hung up her new maternity clothes.

Forty-Two

IT WAS NEARLY dark outside when Joan ushered Krysta into her office and they both sat down.

"How is she, Doctor?"

"Badly shaken. She's been dealt quite a blow."

"I'm so sorry—" Krysta faltered. "When I decided to tell her, I had no idea it would hit her like this. I thought it would help her to know the truth—"

"Look," Joan said impatiently, "for your own reasons— and I can't begin to imagine what they are—you decided to purge yourself of your guilt by dumping it in Leah's lap. Isn't that true?"

"No!"

Joan stared at her in disbelief. "Ms. Bennett, I don't think there's any point in continuing this discussion." She rose from the couch, walked to the door, and held it open for Krysta.

"Wait," Krysta stammered. "I'll tell you." Joan shut the door, but her expression remained dubious.

"I came here," Krysta began, "because I wanted Leah to stop hating herself. I knew that if I told her the truth, she would realize that everything was my fault, not hers." She paused, clutching her throat as if each spoken word cut her breath short. "Don't all children feel somehow responsible when their parents die?"

Joan nodded.

"Well, I wanted Leah to know that she wasn't responsible. I wasn't dead—and she wasn't to blame."

Krysta felt a sharp knife cut deep into her belly. She clawed at her armrests and continued speaking even as the pain brought tears to her eyes.

"I didn't tell her earlier because I knew she would despise me. So I stood by and let her despise herself instead. I wonder which was worse," she said bitterly, "my silence for all those years—or telling her the truth when it was too late."

She buried her face in her trembling hands. When she looked up, Joan was watching her warily.

"Why, Krysta? Why now, after all these years?"

Krysta looked out the window at the darkening mountains that stood sentry over the foothills below.

"I'm dying." She pursed her lips into an ironic smile. "For once in my life, I can afford to do the right thing." She stared across the desert at the gathering clouds. A storm was brewing in the west.

"I'm so sorry," Joan said softly. She gripped Krysta's hands. "Does Leah know?"

"Of course not!"

"Are you going to tell her?"

"After everything else? Never!"

"Never is a long time," Joan said.

"You won't tell her, will you?" Krysta's voice was shrill. Joan handed her a tissue.

"No, I won't tell her. Here, dry your eyes."

Thunderclaps echoed off the mountains. The storm clouds moved quickly across the sky, and the rains came in blinding slate sheets until the desert seemed to be awash in tears.

"Are you ready to see her?" Joan asked. Krysta coaxed a faint smile across her haggard face.

"Send her in," Joan said quietly into the intercom. The door slowly opened, and Joan left as Leah came in.

"Hello, Krysta."

Leah stood in the doorway, nervously twisting her braided hair.

"Leah . . . How are you feeling?"

"Pretty strange. It's not every day I witness the miracle of resurrection."

"I want to tell you how sorry I am," Krysta said. "I had no right to tell you."

"You had no right to leave me. How could you walk out on your own child?"

"I was young and immature. You were better off without me."

Leah gave her a withering look. "No one is better off without her mother."

"You were, Leah. I couldn't raise you. I was nineteen years old. I wasn't married—" She wanted desperately to touch her daughter, but she didn't dare try.

Leah went to the window and watched the rain come down. "Try not to lie," she said. "Did my father want to marry you?"

". . . Yes."

"And what did you say?"

"I said I wasn't ready."

"I see. What were you waiting for? The truth, Krysta."

"I—had to prove myself as an actress . . . and I couldn't be tied down. It was different then: marriage or career, not both. I knew that if I married your father, I'd be—unfulfilled."

"Oh, Christ, not that old groaner. So you took off."

"You would have been miserable, Leah, with an angry, frustrated mother—"

"How fucking considerate! You were thinking of *me* when you wandered off the face of the earth?"

"Yes, I was thinking of you."

Leah spun around and looked at her defiantly. "Don't insult me," she said in a low, dangerous voice.

"Leah, it's more complicated than you can begin to imagine. I was young and scared to death. You know what they say about babies having babies? Well, that was me."

"Not quite, Krysta. You weren't a baby—you were a ruthless little trouper who bailed out for the big time."

"I didn't intend to leave you for good," Krysta murmured.

"I see. It just turned out that way while you weren't looking."

"I wanted to tell you years ago, but your father was against it."

"That's right—put the blame on dear old, dead old Dad."

"I'm not blaming him. It's just that when I started doing pretty well for myself, I asked him if we should tell you, and he said no. He felt we should leave well enough alone."

"He was right," Leah said slowly.

"Yes, I can see that." Krysta picked up her handbag. Slowly she walked out the door and into the dark hallway.

Leah watched her dissolve in the darkness and fade to black.

Forty-Three

AT NOON ON Thanksgiving, Leah was waiting on the lawn when Pru's limousine pulled up. Mick, Kat, Pru, and Misti embraced her, and then everyone got busy unloading the bounty. As they set up the picnic in the shade of a giant date palm, Pru approached unsteadily with the last load—four homemade pies.

"It's a good thing I've squirreled away some Mallomars," Leah said gravely. "We have five people . . . and only four pies—"

"We have seven people!" Pru announced.

Stepping aside, she pointed with a flourish to the grassy knoll behind her, and there, fast approaching, came Sam and Frank. Together they embraced Leah, and she laughed until her face was streaked with tears.

"Samantha," she said. "The divine Devane!" Then she turned to Frank. "Are you two as happy as you look?"

"Happier," Frank said.

"And you came halfway around the world just to watch Pru strap on the feed bag?"

"Very funny," Pru muttered as she unmolded the salmon mousse.

"I can't think of anything I'd rather watch," Sam said.

"Thank you," Pru giggled.

Leah shrugged. "Taste is a matter of taste."

Pru gave her a withering look. "Cool it, Shecky, and let's eat up." She mounded a heap of mousse onto Leah's plate.

Everyone dug in, and except for the sounds of chewing, all was quiet.

"It sounds like a cow pasture," Leah remarked.

"This is delicious," Kat said.

"Thanks," Pru answered. "How's the cuisine around here?" she asked Leah somewhat incoherently; her mouth was full.

"Well, we've got the four basic food groups—and then there's the chocolate group," Leah answered. "When people get sober, they turn to candy bars in a big way."

"When you get out of here," Pru said between bites, "you call me up any time you want to binge, and that's an order."

"You bet . . . I always knew that if things didn't work for me as a lush, I might have a future in diabetes."

Kat touched Leah's arm and asked her quietly, "Are you holding up okay, sugar?"

"A lot better than I ever would have hoped."

"But still," said Pru, watching her closely, "the recent revelations must have hit you like a semi."

"Make that a Minuteman," Leah admitted unabashedly. "But I'm all right. Joan and my group have been incredibly supportive. And I'll tell you one thing—as much as I loathe Krysta, I'm glad I know the truth. I've learned I can handle it."

"Bravo," said Sam.

"I second that," Kat chimed in.

"You know what they say at Jane Fonda's Workout, don't you?" Pru asked sagely.

"No, and I'll bet you don't either," Leah laughed.

"No pain, no gain," Pru recited. "So there."

Leah looked horrified. "Christ," she said. "You, of all people, are the one person I counted on to ride out the fitness craze."

"Guess again," Pru said. She flashed a mysterious little grin as she hoisted the turkey platter at Frank. "Come on," she said. "Let's carve this sucker."

Later, when the Thanksgiving meal was demolished and everyone felt relaxed and sated, Pru set down her fork and looked happily at the others.

"This is what I call afterglow," she sighed.

"Well," said Leah pointedly, "if Jane Fonda were here, I guess we'd all start laps, huh?"

"I found one," Kat smiled. She rested her golden head against Mick's thighs.

Leah hopped to her feet. "Come on, Pru." As she pulled her up, kicking and screaming, she asked, "What's the matter? I thought you were on the front lines of the Fight Against Fat."

Pru grinned. "Not exactly . . ."

Leah feigned astonishment. "You mean you're not in training for Seoul?"

"If you must know," Pru said, pausing until the other women's eyes were upon her, "I'm in training for a baby."

Sam let out a whoop that must have been heard in Fresno. She scrambled to her feet and spun Pru around, and then the rest of them tackled her.

"Gently," Kat scolded. As each friend embraced her, Leah grinned. "What a lucky kid. Three doting godmothers!"

"That's right," Sam agreed heartily. "And I'll be the one who teaches her to fly a plane!"

"Not a man?" Leah asked, out of Frank's earshot.

"You're terrible," Kat said, and shuddered. "I'd better get the menfolk out of here, before you embarrass them." She busied Frank and Mick with the cleaning up, then began helping Misti clear away the pies.

Pru stopped her. "What's your hurry?" she asked, reaching for the Boston cream. "I shouldn't—but I guess it's all right, now that I'm eating for two."

"Officially," said Leah.

"I'll ignore that," Pru said as she daintily licked a patch of whipped cream from her fingertips. Next she had a rematch with the rhubarb cobbler. "Kat," she said, "this is the most obscenely delicious little indulgence I've ever eaten."

"I know," said Kat. "It's Marie's."

"That woman can cook," Pru said with deep admiration. "Remember that dish she made for my wedding? Szechuan okra! I thought I'd died and gone to Mr. Chow's."

"That's my mama," Kat said. "East meets Dixie."

"Well, the South will rise again if Marie has anything to say about it."

"You know," Kat said, "Marie's at home making another Thanksgiving dinner for tonight. Why don't you stop by?"

"I really couldn't," Pru smiled, her freckles sparkling in the sunlight. "What time?" She licked her fork clean and settled back against the date palm.

Watching Kat and Sam cover the pies with foil, she suddenly remembered her conversation with Lucien the night before. He'd gotten home late, just as the pies were coming out of the oven.

"Leah," she said. "I almost forgot to tell you. Lucien sends Thanksgiving greetings."

"Tell him I returned the sentiment," Leah answered through clenched teeth as she shoved garbage into a trash bag.

"We're getting along fairly well these days," Pru remarked as she scraped plates. "Since he took up acting, he's started showing some interest in what I do down on the lot. Lord knows I'm not crazy about having him hang around, but at least he's off the streets."

"Great," Leah said, twisting a tie to close the full bag.

"I think Lucien's cute," Misti piped up as she helped them. Pru patted her on the head and smiled.

"I'm afraid he's spoken for, kiddo. He's got himself a girl friend."

Leah wondered where he'd found her. Transylvania?

"He's taken up with Mo's secretary," Pru continued.

"Roz?" Leah was astounded. "She's a dinosaur!"

"Not Roz. Her assistant, Raven. What a scream—she comes to work in leather minis with garters hanging past the hem."

"Sounds like Lucien's Perfect Ten."

"I think you're right, kiddo. Their first date was only a couple of days ago, but she asked him to her parents' for Thanksgiving. They must deserve each other," Pru sniffed. "Between you and me, I was relieved she had him over. Otherwise I might have felt guilty enough to invite him along with us."

Leah gulped and asked quickly, "Have you told him about the baby?"

"Not yet," Pru answered uneasily. "I think I'll wait for his father to come back." She paused uncomfortably. "Mo will be pretty surprised himself. As far as he knows, I had an abortion."

There was an awkward lull in the conversation as everyone took a moment to digest this latest bit of information.

"Well," Kat said, "he'll be pleased as heck when he finds out you didn't."

"I'm sure you're right," Pru said heartily. She glanced at her watch as a sweet autumn breeze swept away the heat of high noon. "I told Joan we wouldn't stay too long," she said. "We'd better start packing things up."

As the others began loading the hampers and carrying them to the car, Leah pulled Kat aside. She pointed toward the parking lot, where Mick was hoisting the ice chest into his trunk. Even from a distance, it was impossible to miss those hardworking biceps.

"Kat," said Leah, "I hope you don't intend to let him get away." Kat shifted uncomfortably, her violet eyes downcast.

"Lighten up," Leah told her. "I think it's great that you and Mick are an item. *Comprende?*" Staring so far into the distance that she might have been scouting for a wagon train, Kat bobbed her head. "What's eating you?" Leah asked.

"Nothing. Really. Honestly. I swear." Kat nervously bit her lip.

"I get the picture," Leah said. "You're worried about how I fit into all of this."

"A little," Kat admitted, staring at the ground.

"For God's sake, Kat, will you please talk to me, not to your cleavage! How many times do I have to tell you—Mick's a friend."

"I know you've said that, sugar. But that was before we got so darn serious," Kat said miserably. "You didn't realize, and neither did we, that things might get—out of hand."

"Oh, I had an inkling," Leah said slyly. She gently tugged Kat's face toward her own, and she wouldn't let up until Kat finally met her gaze. "Are you going to marry him?" she asked.

"I don't know—"

"Why? Are you afraid that I'll flip out when you and Mick take a walk down the aisle?"

"I don't think that," Kat protested.

"Yes, you do, and I don't blame you. But guess what? My days of flipping out are behind me, knock on wood, and if you decide to marry Mick, the only person happier than you two will be me."

Kat smiled at her with lustrous eyes.

"Good girl," Leah said. "And now that that's settled, will you please do me a favor and stop treating me like a god-damned orchid? I'm tougher than I look." She swatted Kat's rear. "Now get out of here before you miss your ride."

As the others gathered around her to say their good-byes, she realized she'd never spent a happier Thanksgiving.

Forty-Four

THE FIRST DAY of the *Tropic of Danger* shoot went much better than Pru had dared to hope. Will Avery brought depth and conviction to the starring role, Owen's direction was impeccable, and the lush foliage of the arboretum proved to be a viable stand-in for the Everglades.

The only wrinkle occurred late in the afternoon, when a clamp on the boom popped loose during a take, and the whole thing fell dangerously close to Will. Luckily, he saw it coming and ducked out of the way, but it rattled everyone on the set. Pru gave the sound crew a good talking-to, and they promised to check the equipment more carefully in the future.

After they wrapped for the day, Pru was inching westward on the Santa Monica freeway when her phone buzzed.

"Pru? It's Lucien."

"Oh, hi. What's up?"

"I just wanted to thank you for letting Raven and me come to the shoot."

"No problem. Besides, Raven's supposed to be there. She's working."

Lucien ignored the dig. "Well, anyway, it was staggering, and I don't think it's premature to say you've got a megahit on your hands."

"Thanks, Lucien."

"And Will Avery is terrific."

"I know. He's really something."

"What a great guy, Pru—and what a great artist. I couldn't believe his intensity. Just watching him really gives me something to shoot for."

"Well, I'm glad you enjoyed yourself, but listen, I have to run now. The traffic's unbelievable."

She'd no sooner gotten rid of him than the phone buzzed again.

"Pru? It's me, Tony."

"Hi, kiddo. What's shaking?"

"A lot. Remember you asked for the poop on Mercer?"

"Of course. I thought he had investor written all over him."

"Well, I think you may be right. I finally rounded up the file—it's really an encyclopedia—of his interests and holdings, and I was amazed at how diversified he is. I'm so wrapped up in the hotel that I lose track of everything else, but he sure doesn't. He's got his fingers in every pie you can imagine, and from the looks of it, he's always open to new ventures."

"Hmmm. Has he done anything in entertainment before?"

"Not movies, but get this—one of his companies bought that TV station you used to work at."

"TWSP?" Pru asked.

"Bingo."

"But TWSP was owned by Bud Sinclair for years. And he sold it to some big consortium, Fischler and Associates, out of New York."

"Fischler and Associates *is* Mercer," Tony laughed.

"Wow. Small world."

"Yeah. And the thing about Fischler is, they're into high returns, which means high risks, which means you. So just say the word, and I'll set something up."

"It's worth a shot, don't you think, Tony?"

"Absolutely."

"Thanks . . . And now"—she paused theatrically—"can you keep a secret?"

"Scout's honor."

"I'm going to have baby."

"Fantastic! Just think, I'll be Uncle Tony. When, Pru?"

"June."

''Well, that's just about the best news I've heard in ages. Mo must be in fat city.''

''Actually, he's in Rome.''

''At a time like this? What a putz.''

''It's my fault, Tony. I told him without a whole lot of warning—''

''Who needs warning?''

''Well, he was surprised. He thought we were going to work together—''

''It sounds to me like you're working together just fine.''

''Not like that, Tony. Mo and I have a sort of partnership—''

''So, have a baby, too!''

''He's already got a son, and the studio takes up so much time—''

''For chrissake, Pru—listen to yourself. You're making excuses for him.''

''Stop it. You're acting like he's a jerk, and you don't even know him. If you'd come to my wedding—''

''I would have if you'd given more than ten minutes' notice. Maybe I should have met this guy before you took the plunge. What kind of asshole finds out he's going to be a father and hops the first plane out of town?''

''He'll change, Tony. I know he will.'' Her words were strong, but her voice wavered.

''Well, you know best,'' he said, backing off.

''He'll come through, Tony. Really.''

''Sure he will.'' In a lighter tone he asked her, ''So, what do we do about Mercer? Reel him in?''

''Let me sleep on it. I've just begun the shoot, so I'm swamped through Christmas.''

''Well, just let me know, Sis. And keep in touch, okay?''

''You bet . . . And, Tony? Thanks.''

She'd hardly put the phone back in its cradle than it rang again.

''Grand Central,'' she answered.

''Hi, baby, it's Mo.'' His voice crackled and sputtered.

''Darling, I can hardly hear you,'' she said.

''I can hear you fine.'' The connection began improving

as he continued. "I just called to find out how your first day went."

"It was great, Mo. How's Rome?"

"A headache. I'm ready to throw that moron Victor Field in the Tiber. If he weren't such a goddamned great actor, I would. I'm tired of paying these guys a million bucks for the privilege of baby-sitting them.

"Listen, doll," he continued. "I love you, and as soon as this thing clears up, I'm outta here. I may stop at Pinewood to check out the miniseries, but that'll just take a sec, and then I'll be home."

"You're going to London?" Pru asked, barely assimilating the news.

"Just a pit stop. Besides, once things start heating up on your shoot, you won't even know I'm gone."

"But I miss you, Mo!"

"I miss you, too, baby, but duty calls!!"

The connection began to falter again, and all she heard was a faint *"Ciao"* as the line went dead.

"Sugar, you're putting me on!" Kat sat down with a thud on the edge of Michele's desk. "They settled for *more* than my original salary?? I don't understand."

"You don't have to understand, toots. All you have to do is take the money and run."

"But how did they decide on ten million dollars?" She sank back in her chair and stared wide-eyed at her agent.

"It's got a string attached. You have to promise not to litigate."

"I never intended to litigate. I was relieved to be off *Gambit*."

"We know that—but they don't. They want a guarantee of no lawsuit, and they figure all those zeroes after the ten ought to buy your promise."

"You bet," Kat said with a grin.

"Good. Now, then, there's one other thing." She shuffled through some memos. "Here it is . . . Liliane down at the Shubert called, and she wondered if you were interested in a play."

"What is it?"

"Some old warhorse, *The Women*."

"You're kidding, that's a great play!"

"Forget it, toots. Do you have any idea what they pay at the Shubert? I'll starve! I'll lose my table at Morton's. They won't know me at Chinoise!"

"But Michele, it's my career."

"And it's my ten percent."

"For heaven's sake," Kat said. "You just made a million dollars this morning. Isn't that enough?"

"Not on your life."

"Well, I sure admire your honesty, but for just one minute can we forget money and talk about the play? Who's directing it?"

"Lee Rogers."

"She's wonderful!"

"She's an *artiste*, for God's sake. She'll direct with such goddamned sensitivity that they'll be turning away in droves."

"Shush," Kat chided. "When does it open?"

"Right after the New Year."

"So soon?"

"They're already in rehearsal, but they've had a dozen snafus, including the fact that they had to let Tawny Crawford go."

"Why? She's a big star."

"And an even bigger cokehead."

"Poor thing . . . I know this sounds horrible, but what part was she playing?"

"Mary."

"Oh, please, Michele, I've got to do it!"

"Jesus Christ," Michele sighed.

Kat leaned close to Michele's face. "It's a play that speaks to women," she said. "It's important, and I've got to do it."

"Spare me," Michele groaned. "Next you'll be doing telethons. Good Lord, woman, this is a business, not a philanthropic society."

"It's also an art form," Kat said testily.

"Art who? Hollywood is not a Paris salon. This is the jungle, and you've got to be a tiger."

"Well, listen up, Tiger Lady," said Kat, who surprised

both Michele and herself with the sharpness in her voice. "Either you call Liliane and make an appointment, or I'll do it myself. Is that clear?"

"As clear as the space between your ears."

The phone buzzed, and Michele picked it up. "I said no calls," she barked. "Oh, all right, hang on." She handed the phone to Kat. "It's the Fairy King himself."

Kat looked puzzled.

"Your esteemed *Snow White* director."

Kat scowled.

"Don't you want to speak to a true *auteur*?" Michele asked. "A man of artistic brilliance, integrity, and courage? Not to mention temper tantrums."

"Quiet . . ." Kat whispered through giggles. "He'll hear you."

"So what? He knows he's a spoiled brat who's never once brought a film in on time. Or within budget, but my Gawd—he's such a geeeeeenius!" With a snooty pinch of her nostrils, Michele handed the phone to Kat.

"Hi, Ken." As she listened, her face fell.

"But, Ken, I thought I'd finished. . . . You didn't like the curtains? You want to reshoot the whole thing? . . . Oh, all right, of course it's your vision, Ken. . . . Yes, artist to artist, I understand. . . . Right. Cheerio to you, too." She hung up the phone and looked at Michele miserably. "This little favor to Mo is turning into my life's work. Ken thinks Snow White's christening needs a different mise-en-scène."

"Whatever that is." Michele rolled her eyes. "Tell Ken he can kiss my mise-en-scène."

Kat shook her head unhappily. "I'm back on the set tomorrow at six A.M. . . . I sure hope we get it right this time. We've already done a hundred takes, and that pink mist he sprays everywhere makes me break out."

"The wages of Art," Michele said knowingly.

"Shoot!" Glancing at her watch, Kat leaped to her feet. "I'm late!" She tore downstairs to the parking lot and drove to Burbank Airport in record time.

Mick was waiting when she got there. He threw his bag into the trunk, hopped into the car, and gave Kat the most enthusiastic kiss she'd received in weeks. As they clutched each other like a couple of teen-agers, he whispered, "God, I've missed you." He swept the honey-blond hair from her shoulders and kissed her exposed throat.

"It's only been a day," she murmured.

"That's a day too long, babe." They kissed again, and Kat felt weak. "Let's get out of here," she said.

As they zipped through traffic, he told her about his mysterious junket to Bakersfield. He'd kept mum before—he'd wanted to check things out first—but now he was ready to spill.

He wanted to buy a horse farm, and after meeting with breeders and bankers, it looked as if he just might pull it off.

When he'd told her the whole story, he asked uncertainly, "You don't think I'm crazy, do you? Chucking it all to raise ponies?"

"I think you're smart, Mick. And brave. How many people know what they really want—and then go after it?"

"Sounds good," Mick said. "But not everyone will see it that way. Hell, a lot of guys on the force will call me a quitter."

"Do you listen to them?" she asked.

"Well . . . Shit, no!" he laughed.

"Good, because I never heard of a quitter who gets up every morning for eighteen years and puts his life on the line. That's a lot to be proud of, sugar. But now you owe it to yourself to put your dreams on the line, too."

"You really think so?"

"Cross my heart." Her eyes were on the road, but she knew he was smiling as he leaned across the seat.

"In that case," he asked, his voice warm in her ear, "will you do me a favor?"

"Name it," she replied, and her fingers grazed his thigh.

"Take me downtown—I'm quitting the L.A.P.D."

"Hot damn!" she cried as she made a very deft, very illegal U-turn. "Now that you're not a cop anymore, I guess I can drive like a hot-rodder!"

As they hightailed it downtown, she knew that tonight would be an evening to remember.

Forty-Five

December 12, 1987

Dear John:

Congratulations on your poem! There it was, staring back at me from the centerfold of The New Yorker! *I'm so proud—and so touched that you dedicated it to me. Thank you.*

Life goes on here—Joan, Group, and the possibility of parole. My "mother" has finally stopped calling. I guess she's taken the hint at last. I suppose in some sense I have to thank her. If it weren't for the havoc she's wreaked, I'd probably be too happy for my own good.

Brace yourself. I've started a novel. It's hard work, and some days it doesn't feel like writing as much as wrestling the devil . . . But I'll spare you the details.

Can you believe it's almost Christmas? When I was a kid, I didn't like to be wished "Merry Christmas" or "Happy New Year," because I always thought that would jinx it. It was too much to ask, if you know what I mean. But now, in the spirit of leaving old habits and superstitions behind, let me close by wishing us both *a very happy holiday. And may our paths cross in the New Year. Be well, take care, and skip a stone across those emerald waters for me.*

Love,

Leah

AN ELECTRICAL FIRE broke out on the set of *Tropic of Danger* one dreary December morning. Will and two other actors were standing near a coil of wires that overheated, and it was only Will's quick reflexes that kept the three men out of harm's way: he shoved them aside before anyone was hurt. The crew had no trouble putting out the small blaze, but even so, Pru was shaken by the mishap, and she shut down production for the day.

As Will walked off the set toward his trailer, she caught up with him. "Are you sure you're all right?" she asked.

"I'm fine, but that was a close call."

"Come on, we'll get you inside, and I'll find a doctor."

"Pru, I don't need a doctor!"

"Look, you've had quite a scare, and I say you need one." She settled Will onto his sofa and made tea while he looked on.

"It's funny," he said. "My agent told me you were a real ballbreaker, but ever since we started working together, you've been super."

"Come on, drink this," she urged as she handed him a steaming mug.

"I want you to know," he said between sips, "how much I appreciate all you've done—giving me this chance, and being so supportive."

"It's easy, Will. You're doing a wonderful job."

"And so are you—"

"Hey, it's a mutual admiration society," Raven chirped as she poked her head into Will's trailer. "Sorry to interrupt, Pru—I just wanted to let you know I'm heading back to the studio. I have to fax Mo the daily log."

"The way he's keeping tabs on the set," Pru muttered, "you'd think we were building a nuclear reactor here."

I wish he were half as concerned about me!

"Hi, Pru!" Lucien stuck his head in the trailer, and as his hand rested on Raven's leather-covered derrière he beamed at Will. "You were staggering, man."

"Thanks," Will said.

"Speaking actor to actor, you blew me away."

"I didn't know you were an actor, Lucien."

"I'm still studying," Lucien said modestly, "but it won't be too long before the whole world knows!"

"What a terrific attitude you have. Keep it up," Will encouraged.

"I will," Lucien promised, grinning.

"Babe, we'd better get going," Raven said.

"Hasta la bye-bye," Lucien said to Pru and Will as he led Raven away from the trailer.

"Nice guy," said Will, but Pru just frowned.

Misti was out of school the week before Christmas, and she dreaded every minute of her vacation. *What kind of fun am I going to have hanging around the house with Mom and Mick?* she asked the reflection in her vanity-table mirror. *Now that they've decided to get married, they're more kissy-face than ever. Yucko! It's like living with a couple of lovebirds—except when it's people, you can't cover the cage.*

"Misti! Look out your window!"

She turned from the vanity, and there, hanging from a date palm, was Mick with a big goofy grin on his face.

"What do you think?"

The tree was strung with twinkling lights, and on the ground below, a wooden Santa and eight reindeer leaped across the lawn. Mick flipped a remote, and the reindeers' noses lit up while Santa waved and stiffly shouted "Ho, ho, ho" in a tinny voice.

Totally grosso, Misti thought.

As she turned away from the window, shaking her head in disgust, her friend Shelley Kreinberg came into her room.

"What a circus," Shelley said.

"Shut up," Misti snapped.

"Chill out, girl. I was kidding—I think it's cool the way Santa talks."

"I think it sucks," Misti muttered.

The girls exchanged gifts—they'd bought each other the same CD—and as they sat down on Misti's bed to listen to Madonna, there was a rapping on the door. Misti thought it was her mother, who'd been holed up all week learning lines for her new play.

"Come in."

The door opened, but it wasn't Kat—it was Santa Claus.

"Ho, ho, ho," said Mick from behind his snowy beard. "I thought you two might like some of these." He set down a tray of eggnog and homemade cookies, and Misti looked at him with murder in her eyes. But he just smiled at Shelley and said, "Merry Christmas."

"She's *Jewish*, Mick."

"But thanks," Shelley piped up, "and a Merry Christmas to you."

"You kids enjoy," he said. Still all smiles, he backed out of the room, the pillow in his red jacket slipping as he walked. As soon as he closed the door, Shelley burst out laughing while Misti wished she could crawl in a hole and die. Here she was, trying to fit in with her cool L.A. friends, and along comes her mother's jerko old boyfriend. Her cheeks burned with humiliation.

"I love your dad," she heard Shelley say.

"Get real, Shelley. Besides, he's not my dad."

"You know what I mean. Anyway, he's fab. I can't believe these cookies he made for you," she said as she took another buttery bite. "My father wouldn't know how to buy cookies at Gelson's, let alone *bake* them," Shelley declared. "You're really lucky."

"Are you kidding? He's moved in here and taken over."

"They always do, but at least Mick's a cool guy. You could do a lot worse, Misti. I have. Four times."

The album ended, and Shelley stood up.

"I'd better go," she said. Misti walked her downstairs, where she was forced to wait impatiently while Mick cut down a sprig of mistletoe that he'd hung in the foyer. He quickly wrapped a satin ribbon around it and handed it to Shelley with a flourish.

"Thank you so much," Shelley gushed. Misti looked the other way as her friend gave Mick a peck on the cheek.

Gag me with a spoon!

"Merry Christmas!" Shelley said as she skipped out the door to the limo that was waiting. Misti started to head upstairs, and when Mick stopped her to give her a sprig of mistletoe for her bedroom, she glared at him and swatted it out of his hand. She marched upstairs and slammed her door loudly.

Kat came running to see what was the matter, but Misti called out, "Just leave me alone!" Kat came in anyway and sat on the edge of the bed.

"I know you're doing a lot of adjusting," she said, "and I'm here if you want to talk about it."

"There's nothing to talk about. I'm fine."

"Do you know how much I love you, sugar?"

"Yes, Mom. I'm not mad at *you.* I just don't like the way Mick's wormed his way in here. It's not our house anymore." She pointed outside at the gaily twinkling date palm. "It's *his*!"

Kat took her daughter in her arms, and Misti sat stiffly, refusing to cry, as Kat told her, "This is your house, honey, and mine and Grandma's—and now Mick's, too. I'm sorry if it takes some getting used to, but that's the situation."

"Well, the situation sucks."

"Misti, watch your language. If you don't like it, then it's up to you—and all of us—to make it better. If we work together, we'll make a fine family."

"We're already a fine family—just the three of us."

"Of course we are. But Mick will make it even nicer."

"Gross."

"Shush, Misti. I guarantee, if you give Mick a chance, he won't let you down. Now, come downstairs—it's suppertime."

After dinner, Mick and Kat took off without a word, and Misti was furious because she'd wanted her mother's help in selecting the right outfit for Christmas Eve services the next day. She went to bed angry and hurt, fell asleep with her headphones on, and woke up groggily some time later. The house was quiet.

As she sat up, she saw in the moonlight that there was blood on her sheets.

My period! She could hardly believe it. She'd never been quite convinced it would happen to *her*. Eagerly she scampered down the hall to the master bedroom; she couldn't wait to tell her mother. But just as she was about to knock, she heard squeals and giggles on the other side of the door.

They're screwing! Right when I need her!

She walked silently downstairs to the bathroom, found a box of Kotex under the sink, and put one on the way Kat had coached her several months earlier. Tears streamed down her cheeks as she stood in the bathroom and listened to titters and thumps coming from her mother's bedroom. *That's it! If they don't need me, I don't need them.*

Stealthily she went upstairs, dressed warmly, took her savings from her piggy bank, and crept downstairs without so much as a backward glance.

Upstairs, Kat giggled as she watched Mick struggle with the Apple computer he'd bought for Misti. "Jesus Christ," he groaned, "what the hell is a grappler?"

"Shhh," Kat cautioned. "We'll wake her up."

"There's an idea. She'll probably know how to put this thing together—before I blow it up."

Kat laughed softly. "We're in over our heads," she whispered.

Finally, just before dawn, they got the thing hooked up with the printer. All they needed to do was plug it in. They hid it in Mick's closet and fell into bed.

An hour later, Marie's screams woke them up.

"What is it?" Kat cried as she and Mick raced into the hallway. Marie pointed a trembling finger at Misti's empty bed. She announced in a dull voice, "My baby's gone."

Forty-Six

ON CHRISTMAS EVE, Leah walked back to her room after
lunch. Through her window, the snowy peaks of the mountains stood like angels on the tops of flocked trees.

She looked down at her desk, at the present Krysta had
sent. At first Leah had refused it, but when Joan opened it
and told her what it was, she relented. In the end, she wasn't
sorry. The gift was an old leather album, full of photos from
Leah's childhood. There were also pictures of Krysta's family—relatives Leah had never known. Looking at their faces,
Leah saw—at last—where she'd come from. She saw Ray,
too, looking carefree and young with his arms around
Krysta.

She was picking up the album, to have another look, when
an aide appeared at her door. "There's someone to see you,
Leah."

She frowned. "Really? No one signed up."

"Surprise!" Pru's freckled face bobbed behind the aide
and she rushed right in. "You'd better sit down," she said.
"I have some rather shocking news."

As Leah sank warily into an armchair, Pru laughed. "No,
no, no, this is shockingly *good* news."

She flung *Variety* onto Leah's lap. It was opened to the
film review. Leah read it over twice before looking up.

"There must be some mistake," she said.

"There's no mistake." Pru shook her red mane. "You did
it, kiddo! *Variety* loves you. Everyone loves you. We did great

in last night's opening, and the studio's predicting a twelve-million-dollar weekend.''

"People will pay twelve million dollars to see our movie?"

"No, silly, they'll pay five bucks. But it adds up." She pulled *The Hollywood Reporter* from her bag and read aloud:

" '. . . Screenwriter Leah Sirk has really done her homework with *College Craze*. She deserves a Ph.D. in Phunniness for her lively mix of farce, satire, and wit, and if my guess is right, Ms. Sirk will be writing her own report card from now on.' "

Leah plunged her head between her knees. "I'm either going to faint or throw up," she moaned. Pru knelt in front of her and snapped her fingers. Slowly Leah raised her head. "Tell me this is really happening," she begged.

"If it's not, kiddo, we're both in the same dream, and the chances of that are highly unlikely."

As she helped Leah up, Leah suddenly realized, "You're the one who's pregnant, Pru. I should be taking care of you. Here, have a seat—"

"Thanks, but I'd better run. Gotta get home."

"How romantic," Leah sighed. "Your first Christmas with Mo."

"Without Mo, you mean. He managed to come down with some virus in London, and I'm afraid he's sitting out the holidays at Claridge's."

"Pru, that's terrible. So it's just you and Lucien?"

"He's off in Acapulco with Raven."

"Well, then, why don't you stay in the Springs tonight, and we'll spend Christmas together."

"You're on," Pru said promptly. "I thought you'd never ask. But I'd better skedaddle into town and make sure there's room at the inn. This berg's crazy at Christmastime. And shoot"—she glanced at her watch—"that only leaves me six hours to shop."

"Hold on," Leah protested. "You don't have to do that—"

"Kiddo, telling me not to shop is like telling the Pope not to wear that pointy hat."

"Gee, I never thought of it that way. In that case, you'd better hustle, before the Church of I. Magnin closes its doors and you're left outside with all the other sinners."

"Merry Christmas, ladies." Joan walked in with a hundred-watt smile. "Did you tell her, Pru?"

"Not yet," Pru said. "I didn't want to burden her with too much good news at once."

"Get your coat," Joan told Leah. "You're on furlough."

"I can go out?" Leah asked incredulously. Then she looked at Pru. "You sly fox."

Joan patted her shoulder. "Have a ball, Leah. You've earned it."

They shot downtown to Palm Canyon Drive, and as they got out of the car, Leah noticed something that made her gasp: the marquee on the Palm Canyon Theater read *College Craze*.

"I could plotz," Leah said in a hushed voice. She stared dumbly at the crowd buying tickets. The line snaked all the way around the corner, and when Pru asked her teasingly, "Wanna go to the movies?" she tore down the street and took her place with the others.

"You shop," she told Pru. "I'll see you in two hours."

"No, ma'am," Pru laughed. "We're in this together!"

"But, Pru, you must have seen it a hundred times!'

"Sure, with Industry audiences full of ass-kissing toadies. Now I'm going to see it with Jane Q. Public."

As the line moved and they got closer to the box office, Pru looked at the prices on the board and shook her head. "Who are they kidding?" she asked in her loudest, most obnoxious voice. "Six bucks! Only in the Springs. Boy, this had better be worth it!"

Once they'd bought their tickets, they made a beeline for the concessions stand, where Pru wryly asked the counter girl, "How much for the whole thing?" They decided on a tub of buttered popcorn and enough chocolate to raise Hershey stock a quarter of a point. Then they settled into their plush velvet seats—Leah was on the edge of hers—and waited for the curtain to rise.

The Muzak stopped, the lights dimmed, and the soundtrack kicked in with a wallop. As the credits rolled, four young women dashed about in a tiny apartment, plucking lingerie from the bookshelves and stirring a bubbling brew in a plastic garbage can.

"All killer, no filler," one leggy beauty announced, and on that note, the film began. In the dark, Leah sat rigidly, her gaze locked on the screen. Her mouth was slightly open, her stomach in knots as the film unreeled. Around her, the audience was laughing, but she didn't seem to notice: her eyes were up *there*.

While she watched the movie, Pru watched the crowd.

They're not even getting up for popcorn! she realized.

When they laughed in all the right places, she began to relax, and by the last third of the picture, she was thoroughly enjoying herself. Near the end, right after a scene that had the audience practically weeping with laughter, Leah leaned toward Pru, and without taking her eyes off the screen, she whispered, "You brought me here on purpose, didn't you?"

"Shut up and watch the movie," Pru whispered back.

When it was all over and the lights went up, the crowd cheered and applauded—and Leah just sat there with her mouth hanging open.

"What do you think?" Pru asked.

Leah stared at the huge white screen they same way she used to stare at a blank sheet of paper in her Olivetti.

"Talk to me," Pru said almost desperately.

Leah looked at her, and a lazy smile stretched across her face.

"What do I think? I think it needs work."

"Oh, kiddo," Pru moaned. "Won't you ever be satisfied?"

"Of course not. It can always be better. Right?"

"I don't see how. There wasn't an empty seat in the house. But if you're still not satisfied, well . . . we'll just have to give you a crack at the sequel."

As they walked outside, the usher was putting a sign up over the box office: TODAY'S PERFORMANCES SOLD OUT.

"Hallelujah," Pru crowed.

She linked arms with Leah, and they strolled along Palm Canyon Drive, stopping to listen to the afternoon carolers in front of Maxim's. While the pure, clear notes of "Silent Night" rang through the balmy air, a desert breeze ruffled the women's hair. Pru brushed a strand from Leah's face and saw that her dark eyes were lustrous with tears.

Forty-Seven

ABOVE NICHOLS CANYON, the black sky was shot through with lightning. Thunderbolts echoed across the valley as storm clouds opened and dumped their glistening deluge. Squalls sent Mick's Santa Claus flying across the backyard, and the date palms shook helplessly, their branches torn away by the raging tempest.

Where are you, Misti? Please God, keep her safe!

"Kat? . . . Kat, honey, it's Mick." Marie handed her the telephone.

"I've covered the baby beats," he said tersely. "I'm on the Strip, then heading up to Hollywood Boulevard, but there's no sign of her."

Holding the phone limply, Kat tried to make sense of Mick's words. A palm frond smashed against the bedroom window and she screamed in terror.

"Babe, are you all right?"

"Oh, Mick, she could drown in this rain."

"I'll find her, don't worry. But I've got to warn you, it won't be long before the press gets wind of this."

"I can handle the press. Just please don't let anything happen to her!"

"Babe, I'm tearing this town apart, but it takes time."

"What about the Greyhound station?"

"Covered. I've got a guy from the force staked out there. What about you? Did you come up with any more friends?"

"I've called everyone in her phone book, and Shelley gave me a few names. She thought maybe the Galleria—"

"I've already alerted their security people."

"And what about Century City?"

"Ditto."

"The movies maybe? My God, where could she go in this storm?"

"Not far, babe. Listen, I'm going down to the Beverly Center, and then I'll hit the city buses. Meanwhile, look around—there's got to be something."

Kat climbed the stairs and went into her daughter's room. She'd already ransacked the drawers and read Misti's diary— but she'd found nothing, not a clue. She looked at the walls: spelling medals, Madonna posters, a couple of photos of Shelley. Despondently she sank to the bed and picked up a well-worn brown velvet pony as she looked out the window at the howling storm.

Sobbing, she buried her face in the pony's mane—and then it hit her.

Dropping the pony, she rushed downstairs and through the kitchen as Marie stood at the wall phone, blowing a police whistle into some reporter's ear. "Where are you going?" Marie called, but Kat was already halfway to her car.

She raced east through the rain until she finally reached the dark, soggy slopes of Griffith Park. The observatory shone like a beacon as she drove up the deserted road. Blinded by rain and fog, she crawled up the steep road that led to the stables. By the time she reached the paddock, the road was mud.

She stepped from the car into a foot of water, then stumbled toward the stable as torrents fell like chain mail across her back.

"Misti!" she screamed into the long black tunnel of the enormous barn. "Are you here?"

There was no answer except for the horses' snorts and stomps, but far ahead—and just barely visible in the distance—a sliver of light ran across the floor like a vein of gold in a mine. Kat staggered through the doorway and groped her way into the barn. As she got closer to the light, she saw that it was a lantern.

Next to it stood the shadowy figure of Misti. She was holding a saddle almost as big as herself.

Yelling her daughter's name, Kat lurched toward her. When she reached her, she pulled Misti into her arms, and the saddle fell with a thud. She stroked the child's tangled, wet hair as she collapsed with relief. On her knees she whimpered, "Thank God you're safe." Her tears ran down Misti's shoulders until she was pushed away.

"Why are you here?" Misti asked coldly.

"Sugar," Kat sobbed. "I was scared to death."

"Why? You have Mick."

"Misti, I love you more than anything!"

"More than Mick?"

"It's not the same, and you know it. You're my daughter."

"So what?" Misti asked accusingly. "Last night when I needed you, you were screwing Mick—"

"How dare you talk to me like that!" Kat stood and gripped Misti's shoulders fiercely. "In the first place, if we were 'screwing,' it would be none of your business. And in the second place, we weren't. We were wrapping Christmas presents."

Misti studied her mother indifferently and fingered the bit in her hands. Behind her, a chestnut filly whinnied impatiently.

"She sounds hungry," Kat said.

Misti nodded and expertly pitched a forkful of hay into the stall. She filled the feed bin with oats, then dragged the hose in from the paddock to fill the water pan. While the filly ate, Misti groomed her with long, sure strokes.

"I didn't know you knew so much about horses," Kat said.

"There's a lot you don't know about me," Misti answered. As she combed the filly's tail, she gave her mother a withering look. "You don't care enough to ask."

"We'll talk about that later," Kat said firmly. "Right now I have to call Grandma and Mick."

"Of course," Misti said sarcastically. "Mick the dick must be worried sick," she chanted. Kat seethed at the smirk on her face.

"Dammit, Misti, what you did was wrong!"

"What *I* did? I'm not the one who's an unfit mother!"

Kat slapped her across the cheek and sank to her knees, sobbing. "Goddamnit," she choked. "Don't you know I'd die if anything happened to you?" She sobbed uncontrollably, venting all the panic and terror of the day. When she couldn't shed another tear, Misti knelt beside her and embraced her.

"I'm sorry, Mom. I shouldn't have run away."

"But I drove you to it," Kat said dully. She held her daughter tightly and kissed the top of her head. "I'm sorry, too."

"Can we just forget it?" Misti asked. "I won't do it again. I promise."

In the light of the flickering lamp, Kat turned Misti's shining face up toward hers. "Good, because if you do, I'll skin you alive. Don't you know that without you my life's not worth a mangy dog's hide?"

"You say that now," Misti whispered, "but when we get home, there's so much happening—"

"Too much. It's time to take stock of things. I've been so wrapped up in myself . . ." Kat shook her head. "What a dumb cluck I've been. Thoughtless and self-centered—"

"Hold it, Mom. You're not that bad. I know you love me— it's just that I feel left out sometimes."

"God, I'm such a fool."

"No—you're okay. You should see my friends' parents. They're really screwed up. Compared to them, you're Cosby."

"Thanks, sugar."

"Not that you couldn't use some improvement," Misti was quick to add. "I mean, I don't want you to get a swelled head!"

Kat smiled and helped Misti up. "Come on—we've got to get home."

The sky began clearing as they drove across town. When they got home, Marie ran outside to meet them, and moments later, Mick called. When he heard the good news, he came home right away, and as soon as he'd swept Misti up in his arms and bombarded her with kisses, there was hell to pay.

He marched her upstairs to her bedroom and closed the door behind him.

"No more bullcrap, young lady. The way I see it, I'm the dad, you're the daughter, end of story."

"You're not my father."

"I'm better than a father—I'm a volunteer. I deal with your garbage even when I could look the other way. You should be flattered, kid. I'm only up here yelling at you because I feel like it."

Misti looked at him skeptically. "Mom says you looked all over for me. Did you really go downtown, and to the Strip, and even to Venice Beach?"

"I sure did—and if I'd found you instead of your mother, you wouldn't be able to sit for a week."

"Well, then, I'm glad you didn't find me—but I'm glad you're here." She smiled at Mick and took a step closer. "Do you want to help with a surprise for Mom . . . ?"

On Christmas morning, Kat was surprised to find herself on the back of a young mare who had more horsepower than a Ferrari. Traveling at what she figured had to be close to the speed of light, Kat hung on for dear life as she flew through the surf on Malibu Beach in the wake of Misti and Mick. By the time they finally stopped in Zuma, she was looking over her shoulder to see where she'd left her stomach.

"So here we are," she said as she gingerly sat down on the sand. "At least I think I'm here." The trio ate hungrily from a lavish picnic prepared by Marie, and afterward Misti leaned back against a log and asked, "Mom, remember a long time ago when you said you'd buy me a horse?"

Over her head, Kat winked at Mick. They'd decided not to announce his plan until it was firmed up. "I told you we'd see, Misti." Kat daintily held out a carrot for her mount.

"Well, I need a horse," Misti stated flatly. "Look!" she exclaimed as the mare nuzzled Kat's hand. "She's nuts about you."

"Well, I'm not nuts about her." After only an hour of riding, she was walking like a wishbone, and she even let go with some cowboy curses as she climbed stiffly into her saddle and waited for the others to mount up. "Let's get this show on the road,'' she ordered, and as they rode back to the stable, all she could think of was a nice long soak. The lather! the suds! the perfumes and oils . . . she couldn't wait to wash away the smell of horse.

But as tired and sore as she was, she couldn't help but take pleasure in the fun her daughter was having. Speeding along the water's edge, her yellow hair streaming behind her, Misti held the reins taut in her hand, and she rode with purpose into the wind.

Forty-Eight

PRU WAS LYING on her king-size bed, gently rubbing her belly, when the telephone rang.

"Happy New Year!"

"Happy New Year, Mo. Long time no see."

"I miss you, doll, and when I get back, we'll go out on the town—just the two of us—and I'll make this up to you. Got that?"

"Got it."

"You sound sort of down, baby. What is it?"

"I wish you were here."

"Likewise, Pru, but the show must go on, right? As soon as I got over that damned bug in London, they needed me back in Rome again. What can I say?"

"I understand. It's just that I thought that's what we hired lawyers for—to strong-arm those little creeps like Victor Field—"

"Lawyers can't do it all, baby. You've been in this racket long enough to see that the ambulance chasers screw up more than they fix. In this business, you've got to have finesse. You've got to make the actors think that coming around to your way of thinking was their idea. You know what I mean—you must have similar problems on *Tropic of Danger*, right?"

"Not really. Everyone's been an absolute gem. I can't complain about a thing."

"Well, you're a rare bird, then. Me, I've got a list of grievances a mile long, and they all start with Victor Field. That guy's so low he could look up a snake's asshole. And speaking of assholes, how's that kid of mine—uh—ours?''

''Lucien's great, and I've got to hand it to him, he's been nothing but gracious in your absence. He and Raven made a lovely midnight supper for a few of us last night. We had a wonderful cioppino, and Raven made a coconut cake that I have to admit I would have run away with if I weren't already attached.''

''Sounds good.''

''It was great, except that poor Will Avery got a little tight and damn near drowned in the pool. We were all inside listening to music, and I swear, if Lucien hadn't wandered out to the pool and seen him there, well, things could have ended pretty badly.''

''Holy shit. How scary.''

''It was. So let's not talk about it anymore.'' Massaging her tummy with almond oil, she realized she had to take the plunge. ''Mo,'' she said. ''I wanted to tell you this in person, but I'm just too excited to wait. So here goes:—We're having a baby.''

''Prudence''—his voice was tight—''that's not what we decided.''

''*I* decided, Mo.''

''What do you mean, you decided? Everything was all set.''

''I know, but I couldn't go through with it. And, Mo, I've never been so happy in my life—''

''Who the fuck do you think you are? We already discussed this. We agreed that Heliotrope is the only baby you and I need—''

''Mo, Heliotrope isn't a family—it's an empire.''

''I don't care what you call it, Pru. It's everything I've ever wanted, and I brought you on board because I thought you wanted it too.''

''I do, but I want more—''

The line went dead. Pru dropped the phone in its cradle. She gripped her knees and wept, muffling her sobs in the sleeve of her silk kimono.

Not a goddamned baby! Lucien left his post at Pru's door. He went to his room and drove his fist through the wall. Then he walked downstairs and out of the house.

The roar of the car's engine jolted Pru from her crying jag, and she rose slowly, walked to the mirror, and dropped her kimono as she stood before it. Her growing belly made her smile, and she looked like a pudgy little Buddha as she studied herself in the mirror.

"Happy New Year," she wished to the person inside her. She thought sadly of Mo and his resistance to the things that mattered most.

He settles for so little, she thought with a shudder. Then she drew a bubble bath and wondered what to have for dinner.

The air was chilly off the Potomac, and while Sam slept, Frank started a roaring blaze in the fireplace of their hotel suite. When she awoke, he stuck a thermometer in her mouth, and she tapped her fingernails against a pillar on the canopied bed, waiting impatiently until Frank read aloud her temperature.

"One hundred point two," he said. "Forget it."

"You've got to be kidding."

"We're not going, Sam. I'm calling Dr. Ross."

"That's ridiculous. Tonight is the premiere—the *premiere*—of *Sanctuary*. David Rockefeller and Jane Goodall are going to be there. Along with most of Washington and the UNESCO board of directors! How can I miss it?"

"You've got a fever."

"It's nothing. I'll take a couple of Excedrins and get dressed."

"You can't, Sam."

"Watch me." She swung gracefully out of bed and scampered to the window. "Look, Frank, it's snowing!" Flakes as big as cotton balls fell in lazy drifts across the duck pond below, and the branches of cherry trees bent beneath the weight of their fluffy white coats.

"We'll build a snowman before breakfast!" she exclaimed, but as she darted across the bedroom, he caught her in his arms.

"Not so fast, lady."

"Don't, Frank." She wrestled free only to be pulled back to the bed by her husband. "Oh, I get it," she said slyly, "you have something else in mind." She pushed the rumpled sheets aside and lay back on the bed, pulling him with her.

"Sam, this is no time for kidding around—"

"Who's kidding around, sweetie?" she murmured as she brought her face close to his. Gently, he pushed her aside.

"I've got to call," he said, "and tell them we're not coming."

"We're coming all right," she whispered as she hooked her feet behind the small of his back. She nibbled at the hair on his chest as her hands found their way inside his shorts.

"Don't, Sam. I'm calling the doctor."

"Why don't you let me decide?"

"Because you'd rather roll around in the hay than look after your health."

" 'Look after my health!' I'm dying, Frank, and living like a nun isn't going to change that. Besides, right now I feel fine—and it's high time you felt fine too! Do you realize how long it's been?"

"I'm not counting, Sam."

"Well, you would if you weren't such a goddamned saint."

"Physical exertion puts a strain on your heart."

"Frank, you haven't touched me in two weeks."

"It's a small price to pay."

"Bullshit. No one can afford to live without love. If you try, you'll just end up running off with the first floozy you meet at my funeral."

"Don't be morbid, Sam."

"Death is morbid . . . Shit," she said, ignoring him and glancing at her watch on the nightstand. "We're late. You shower, and I'll call the doctor, just to put your mind at rest."

"Good." As he walked toward the bathroom, she suddenly leapfrogged onto his back and kissed his neck. She ran her fingers down his chest and below his flat belly.

"Goddamnit," he growled. She quickly brought his hand to her forehead and whispered, "See? My fever's down." It was true: she felt cool to the touch. She swung down from his back and kissed him, and this time he didn't resist. He let her lead the way to the bathroom. She knelt and drew a bath as her tongue's caresses fired his loins. Steam rose around them in swirling clouds.

He took her from behind on the thick pink carpet and her back arched as he rode her, driving her pelvis gently into the rug. When she came, he was still hard. His breath was quick, and the sweat trickled down the small of her back as his fingers urgently explored her flesh. Once again he brought her to a pulsating climax, but this time he was coming, too.

Afterward, he kissed the soles of her feet and she murmured, "Now do you believe me?"

The thermometer proved her right: her fever was gone. It was her spirits that soared.

It was snowing when they left the Kennedy Center, and the wind across the river was sharper than glass. *Sanctuary* had been received with wild enthusiasm, more than Sam had dared to expect.

"You're a hit," Frank told her.

"I can't believe it," she said.

"Well, the folks at UNESCO believed it. You raised them a bundle in just one screening. Wait until they take it on the road!"

She closed her eyes and saw schools and clinics and wildlife parks in the jungle. When she opened them, he was grinning. "You did it," he said.

"*We* did it, Frank. It's as much your film as mine."

He stooped over to kiss her; her lips were cold from the snowflakes.

"Make love to me again tonight," she whispered.

He drove carefully through the icy streets back to the hotel, and by the time he pulled into the garage, she was fast asleep. He lifted her out of the car, carried her up to their suite, and undressed her in the dark. Gently he pulled the blankets and comforter over her, knowing that one day she would lie like this—and never wake up. He fell to his knees at her bedside and wept silently.

Forty-Nine

THE LAST DAY of the *Tropic of Danger* shoot was miserable and cold. It began with one of those stormy mornings that cause mudslides in Malibu, floods across the Valley, and slick, treacherous freeways from San Diego to Santa Barbara.

In the arboretum, rain fell steadily on the tarp-shrouded set, and lightning flashed angrily above the cypress trees. Ferns and foxfire trembled in the gales that stormed through the park, and anything that wasn't nailed down was in danger of flying off every time a high wind whistled through the set.

The only good thing about the storm was that it added a lot of free "atmosphere" to the production. Howling winds— and trees valiantly struggling against them—added frenzy and terror to the final scene that was being shot, a scene of Buck lost in the Everglades. As the crew set up lights and laid tracks for the camera, Pru scanned the raging sky and realized that the storm was actually serendipitous: it provided a much better look to the picture than she could have gotten from Special Effects.

Holding on to an umbrella that spun crazily in the wind, the director, Owen Scott, set up a tricky shot with the cameraman. As they blocked it out with the camera, other crew members bustled about and Pru went over some notes with the continuity supervisor.

Will stood alone behind a cluster of cedar trees and got into character. Although the scene had no dialogue, Will did his usual Method preparation. He was a very committed artist—and this morning his commitment was driving Pru crazy. His scene was physically challenging and possibly dangerous, and Pru had originally asked for a stuntman. But Will had insisted on doing it himself.

"Let's make it real," he'd argued earlier. "If I do it myself, the camera will pick up on it, and the scene will be authentic."

Will's reasoning sounded like a lot of Actor's Studio gibberish to Pru, but when Owen said he'd go along with Will's wishes, she realized she was outvoted.

"Action!" the director called, and Will began his lithe movements through the wind-churned greenery. The camera tracked behind him as he padded through the dense undergrowth and foraged a creek full of alligators.

"They don't look tranquilized to me!" the script supervisor whispered to Pru.

Will's athletic prowess carried the scene beautifully, and although the take was long—almost four minutes—it was going perfectly when Will reached his last obstacle, a steaming, sucking swamp of "quicksand" cooked up by the F/X crew.

Will looked about the jungle for a way to cross the muck, spotted a hanging vine, and crawled up a slippery embankment to reach it. Then, in the capper of the shot, he grabbed the vine, kicked off, and sailed in a perfect arc across the quicksand.

But just as Owen was about to say "Cut and print," an odd snapping sound broke through the silence on the set, and suddenly Will screamed. The vine broke and hurled him twenty feet down into the chemical pond. His shrieks rose from the vapors as crew members flew into action.

They plunged poles into the simmering swamp and yelled at Will to grab them. But in his panic, he thrashed about wildly and didn't seem to hear them. Meanwhile, a grip tore off his jacket and dived into the pond while an F/X engineer turned off the eddies and vapors. The sludge stopped churning as the grip paddled to Will and pulled him out of the chemicals.

Pru ran to his side with the first-aid crew.

"Jesus," Will muttered. "What happened?"

"The rope broke," Pru told him.

Will sat up, and Pru covered his bare shoulders with a blanket. She stood by while the medic examined his legs and arms. "You're okay," said the medic. "Nothing's broken."

"Thank God you got out of the pond in time," the F/X guy added. "That shit's not something you'd want to take a bath in."

"How do you feel?" Pru asked him softly.

"Scared."

As she pressed a mug of coffee to his lips, Owen looked him over. "You okay, kid?"

"Fine," said Will, and for the first time since she'd known him, Pru had the distinct impression that Will was acting.

The assistant director trotted up and grinned. "You did great, Will. We got the shot."

"We almost got the shot," Owen corrected.

"Are you kidding?" asked the other man. "They'll save that last beat in the cutting room. We got the arc over the quicksand, and it was beautiful."

"It really was, Will," Pru said quietly as she led Will to his trailer.

"You don't think we should do it again?" he asked.

"Are you serious?"

"Well, shit, Pru, I want it right."

"I know you do, but it's fine."

"How can it be fine? The last part's missing, the part where I clear the quicksand and land on my feet."

"Don't worry about it. Like the A.D. said, the editor will patch it together."

"No way," Will declared. "I don't make patched-together movies. Let's do it again."

"Listen to him, Pru," Owen said as he caught up with them. "Will's right. It could be better."

Pru shook her head and looked at the two men defiantly. "I'm the boss, boys, and I won't have Will endangering himself—or anyone else—all over again. Once is enough," she snapped.

"No offense, Pru, but you're missing the boat this time around," Will said quietly. "We've come this far, and we're nuts not to get it right." He stopped dead in his tracks. "I'm not leaving this set until we've got ourselves a perfect take."

"You heard him," Owen said.

"I don't believe you two," Pru shot back.

"Come on, Pru, what are the chances of the rope breaking twice?" Will asked. "One in a million? Come on, we'll set it up, and you can climb up there and check it out for yourself."

"Absolutely not."

"Then call my agent," Will informed her.

"Mine, too," Owen interjected. "We've got ourselves a whopping case of creative differences."

"I don't believe this," Pru exclaimed. "I'm trying to be a humane, caring, compassionate producer, and you're telling me I should risk your lives in order to get a lousy shot."

"A great shot," said Owen.

"Amen," Will added. "This is a movie set, not a playpen. Let's take some risks and see what happens." As he took Pru's arm and led her back to the set, Owen called out, "Okay, people. One more time."

Crew members scurried to their positions, and this time Owen personally supervised the hanging of the vine. When he declared it ready to go, Pru insisted on having a look. She rode the crane into the sky, grabbed the vine, and suddenly shoved off. She went swinging through the air and across the pond, and the crew applauded as she landed on her high heels. She let go of the vine, straightened her skirt, and grinned.

"Be my guest," she told Will.

"Just one sec." He ducked behind the cedar trees to get into character while Pru looked high above the set, at the rope she'd just ridden.

Did you like that, baby? she asked the tiny trapeze artist inside her. She was marveling at her skill and daring—not to mention sheer stupidity—when suddenly a finger tapped her on the shoulder. She twirled around.

"Lucien, you startled me."

"Sorry, Pru. I just wanted to say hi and tell you how sorry I am."

"About what?"

"I heard the crew talking about what happened."

"Everything's dandy," she replied irritably.

"But today's shoot was the big scene, and now that you've lost it—"

"We didn't lose it."

Suddenly Will stepped forward from the cedar trees. Lucien's jaw dropped when he saw the young actor.

"Are you okay?" Will asked. "You look as bad as I did a few minutes ago." When Lucien stared at him in puzzlement, he asked, "Didn't you see what happened?"

"No, of course not, I just got here."

"Oh, I thought I saw you earlier this morning."

"No way," Lucien said. "Raven and I were in her trailer. She's showing me how to storyboard."

Sure she is, Pru thought. *On the last day of the shoot!*

"I didn't know you were interested in storyboarding," Will said politely.

"It's crucial to learn every aspect of the business," Lucien pontificated.

"Well," said Will, "you've sure got a swell teacher right here in your stepmom. She's the best." Pru smiled as Will gave her an affectionate hug.

"Yeah, she's staggering," Lucien said heartily, flashing white teeth in a grin.

"Places," Owen called, and Will hurried to his·mark. This time the take was perfect, all the way through.

"Holy shit, we got it!" Owen sighed as the crew burst into applause.

Pru embraced her director and star.

"So, was it worth it?" Owen asked Pru. She just grinned. Then she stepped onto a crate so that everyone could see her.

"Listen, kids," she called out. "Can you believe we shot this baby in six weeks? You're all the greatest, and since this is my last opportunity to boss you around, here goes. Get your butts to Trumps, and let's wrap this up with a party!"

The cast and crew cheered wildly, and as Pru stepped down from the crate, she realized that Will and Owen had been right all along: second best wasn't good enough. It was worth taking risks to get what you really wanted.

Pru walked off the set a smarter woman.

Fifty

IN SCREENING ROOM A on the lot at Heliotrope, Pru and a few key crew members watched the last batch of dailies from *Tropic of Danger*. Even patched together on a grainy black and white print, the footage was riveting.

"I can live with it," Pru said happily. She and Owen went into the hallway and shook hands.

"I hope we'll make more pictures together," he said.

"Count on it."

"Remember how the smart money said we couldn't pull it off?"

"I remember," Pru chuckled. "And I won't let them forget."

"Hey, Pru!" Drew waved a phone as he ran to meet her. "You've got a call. It's Tony—he says it's important." He handed her the phone.

"Pru? Brace yourself. Remember when you wanted me to find out about my boss as a possible investor, and I told you I'd do some digging around?"

"Sure."

"Well, I did, and one thing led to another." Tony hesitated. "It sure as hell wasn't what I expected . . ."

"Tony, whatever it is, just tell me," Pru said, looking at her watch. "I'm a little bit swamped here."

"Okay. I came across a file that I think you'd be very interested in. It's a bank account right here in Tahoe."

"So?"

"So, it's all in code!"

"Gee, Tony, I don't think my ticker can stand the excitement. Excuse me while I check into Cedars—"

"Shut up and listen. Obviously the account's in code because Mercer intended to keep it a secret. Does the date April fourteenth mean anything to you?"

"Of course—it's my birthday," Pru said.

"And December twenty-fifth," Tony continued. "That's no mystery." She could hear him shuffling papers. "But what about June twelfth?"

She had to think a minute. "I don't know—wait, my college graduation . . ." Her stomach lurched as random pieces of a familiar puzzle swam dizzily in her head.

"That's right. And what did you receive on that day?" asked Tony.

"A cashier's check for five thousand dollars." Her temples pounded. "Tony," she said carefully, "the money came from Mercer. It had to."

"The numbers spell it out," Tony agreed. "He gave you forty grand over the years."

"That son of a bitch!"

"What are you talking about? Forty grand is quite a chunk of change to give someone."

"He didn't give me anything. No one gives a stranger that kind of money. He owed it to me. I know it."

"But that's ridiculous, Pru."

"Oh? I suppose you're going to try to tell me he was throwing around small fortunes out of the goodness of his heart."

"Maybe he was. Maybe he's some kind of a crackpot."

"Oh, Tony, for God's sake, wise up. Your boss is a businessman, not a philanthropist. He had reasons for paying me off—and I intend to find out what they are."

"Look, maybe we should just forget it. You know, bury the dead."

"Tony," she cut him off, "you told me before that Mercer owns Fischler and Associates. Do you know what that means?" She already knew the answer. "I'm coming up there," she said.

"I don't think that's such a good idea. Leave it alone, Pru. Let it go."

"Let it go? Are you crazy? Mercer Vaughn has been playing games with me, and I want to know why. So do you, or you wouldn't have called in the first place."

"Don't open a whole can of worms, Pru."

"I have to. When someone pulls my strings, I'm entitled to an explanation."

"Most people would be satisfied with the forty grand," Tony said dryly.

"Well, I'm not most people, am I?" She hung up the phone and rang Drew. "Book me a flight to Tahoe, on the double."

"There's no need to announce me," she said as she barged past Mercer's shocked secretary. She threw open the doors of his inner sanctum and slapped a check onto his ebony inlaid desk. He didn't give it so much as a glance but instead looked Pru in the eye as he rose and extended his hand. She ignored it.

"You bastard."

"Nice to see you, too, Ms. Daniels. What a surprise."

"I'll bet."

"What brings you by?" he asked politely.

"That," she said with a toss of her head toward the check. It was made out to Mercer Vaughn, for the sum of $50,000.

"It's what I owe you," she said. "With interest."

"I'm afraid I'm a step behind, my dear."

"Don't 'my dear' me, Vaughn. You know exactly what the money's for—and it's time you told me. If I'm going to be in some jerk's pocket, I'd damn well better know what the hell for."

"Ms. Daniels, I don't have any idea what you're talking about."

"Oh, I think you know exactly what I'm talking about," she said shrilly.

"Look, I hate to be rude," he said, "but you're cutting into my very valuable time."

"My time's valuable, too. But I'm not leaving this office until I get some answers."

"For the last time," he said quietly. "I'm afraid I must ask you—"

"Spill, Vaughn. Neither of us is leaving this room until you do."

Mercer heaved a sigh and looked out the window at the verdant forest in the distance. The sparkling green water beyond the trees was the color of Pru's flashing eyes as he turned back to face her. She stood with arms folded and legs apart, and the set of her jaw was formidable.

"Please have a seat," he said. She sat while he paced. He rubbed a graying temple as he glanced in Pru's direction.

"I'm waiting," she said.

Choosing his words carefully, he spoke. "I suppose I'd better start at the beginning . . ."

"That would be nice."

"Ms. Daniels, if you're going to be sarcastic, there's really no point—"

"I'll decide what the point is! You just talk."

"All right. A few months before my eighteenth birthday, my father was arrested and tried on charges of extortion, racketeering, and attempted bribery. Three weeks after I turned eighteen, he was sentenced to twenty years in the federal penitentiary at Joliet—"

"I don't see what this has to do with anything—" Pru interrupted.

"You asked me to talk, so let me," he said sharply.

"I was just a kid when I inherited the family business. I'd been all set to go to Cornell, but instead I stayed in Hoboken and gradually learned the ropes from Pop's boys. I also learned just how low he'd sunk."

Mercer paused uncomfortably, and Pru felt a fleeting pang of empathy as he groped for words.

"I hated the business. I hated the filth and the greed, and I decided to set it straight. I came out to California and told the boys that we were going to turn the old rackets into legitimate businesses."

He smiled sadly at the memory.

"They nodded their heads, but behind my back it was business as usual. I was still a greenhorn then, and I didn't have any idea what was going on. If I had, maybe your father wouldn't have gotten hurt.''

Pru frowned in puzzlement.

Mercer explained. ''I thought I could go straight overnight. I bought parking lots. They were legal, and they made money fast. We were in the black, we were playing by the rules, and I could sleep at night.'' His voice was bitter as he remembered. ''There I was, thinking we'd cleaned up our act, and all the time my men had kept up all the old rackets on the side: extortion, loansharking, drugs.''

A glimmer of understanding began to take hold of Pru.

''Late one night I dropped in on a club I owned, and there was some trouble outside in the alley. I went out, and two of my gorillas were smashing a guy's face.''

''My father,'' Pru whispered.

''Your father. A petty gambler who owed maybe a few hundred bucks—and there he was in a pool of blood, his face carved up like a pumpkin.'' Mercer looked at her steadily. ''That night changed me. I couldn't merely pretend to be a good guy any longer. I had to do more than make the right noises. It was a matter of life and death. Your father taught me that, Ms. Daniels—for which I owe him.''

''And so you paid him.''

''For twelve years your father took my money, but it didn't do him any good. He gambled it all away. Then one day I saw your name in the *Tahoe Tribune*. You were a National Merit scholar and the valedictorian of your class. I did some checking around and decided that my money would help you more than your old man. So I sent you a check.''

''And I got my first installment of blood money,'' Pru said.

''Save your sarcasm, Ms. Daniels. I didn't ask you to listen to this. You came barging in here and demanded to know the truth, and that's what you're getting.''

''Fine. Just promise me you'll cash my check, and I'll be on my way.'' She rose from her seat and faced him. ''Do you have any idea what I feel like, knowing that my entire career was predicated on the fact that you bought a TV station and gave me the top job? It had nothing to do with my talent, and I'll never know if I could have made it on my own.''

"That's crap. I didn't buy TWSP because of you. It was a solid investment that I would have picked up whether you worked there or not. And once I did, I had to get rid of Shirley Sampson: she was running the place into the ground. You took over because the board determined that you were the best choice. I had nothing to do with their decision."

He pushed the check across the desk toward Pru.

"Please don't ask me to take your money." A pained smile lifted the corners of his mouth. "You put it to better use than I ever could have. You went to college—where you did yourself proud—and then on to graduate school, and now you're doing exactly what you set out to do."

"I should have done it on my own," she said quietly.

"You could have," he told her. "In your sleep. From the day I read about you in the paper, success was written all over you. But please—indulge me. Let me believe I had some small part in your triumph. Let me think I did something right for a change, and that my money served a useful purpose." Her eyes followed him to the window, where he stared out as he spoke. "I've seen so much dirt in my life."

He opened the jacket of his silk suit and Pru flinched: he was wearing a shoulder holster that held a Walther revolver.

"For a long time it was normal to wear one of these. Thank God I don't need it anymore—there hasn't been an attempt on my life in several years—but I keep it to remind me of where I've been. Just like I keep tabs on you—to show me where it's possible to go."

He went to the window just as the streetlights flickered on. They gave his face a yellowish cast.

"Tony doesn't know that I made sure he got a job here. You probably hold that against me, too. But he's a hard worker, and he's risen on his own steam. Do you believe I ruined his life the way I ruined yours?"

Tears glazed Pru's green eyes. "I'm so sorry," she heard herself say in a small, barely audible voice.

On wobbly legs, she stood up and fled his office.

Fifty-One

OUTSIDE KAT'S BEDROOM window, the new moon hung like a scant smile in the wintry dark. Kat traced the worry lines in Mick's brow.

"What's wrong?" she asked him.

"Nothing. Go to sleep, babe." But she knew by the tremor in his voice, and the deep shadows beneath his eyes, that he was lying. It was two o'clock in the morning, and he hadn't slept at all. Finally she turned on the light.

"Tell me, sugar. What's got you so upset?"

"I told you. Zip. I swear."

She turned to him, and he twisted a tendril of her luxuriant hair. "Go back to sleep," he said, kissing her forehead.

"Not until you quit your pussyfooting around and let me in on your life."

He sighed and rolled over. "Good night, babe."

She shook his shoulders until he turned around and faced her. "It's money, isn't it," she said. "I heard you on the phone with the bank."

He raised himself on one arm. "Then you know," he said. "My financing won't stretch as far as I thought it would. I'm priced out of the market."

"The California market," Kat corrected. "The most expensive land in the country, right?"

He nodded wearily.

"But what about cheaper land?"

"No way, babe. This is where you are, and this is where

I'm staying. Those commuter marriages are for the god-damned yuppies.''

"I agree, sugar. But what if I decided I don't want to be here?''

As he looked at her in bewilderment, she jumped out of bed. She raced out of the room and reappeared an instant later with a stack of brochures. She fanned them out on the comforter, and he gazed appreciatively at the colorful photos of rolling hills and deep green valleys.

"Shangri-la, babe.''

"Actually,'' she told him, "it's West Virginia. Remember all that money I got for not making *Gambit*? Well, I'm going to use it to build a theater, a drama school, and a playwrights' retreat.''

"But why?''

"Because I love the theater, Mick. Not the parties, or the money, or the hype. I just love the work—and that's what this place will be about.'' She settled back in the crook of his arm. "Will you come with me, Mick? You can raise your horses, and I'll raise my actors, and we'll have a high old time.''

He swept the brochures off the bed and took her in his arms. When they finally parted, she smiled impishly. "I'm so glad you said yes. How can I thank you?'' As if to answer her own question, she reached under the covers and felt Mick come to life in her hands. He pulled her warm body to his and kissed her eager mouth.

His hand slid down her belly until it rested in the soft vee between her legs. She rolled over on her back and drew a shallow breath. He probed her gently with one finger, and as she closed her eyes, he pushed another inside. His fingers fluttered like butterflies and Kat moved easily against them. Without disengaging his hand, he ducked beneath the covers, and while his fingers moved slowly inside her, his mouth brought her to the verge of orgasm.

She flung the covers back and drew him up to the pillow. "You've got that down to a science,'' she sighed giddily as she straddled him. From atop his chest, her view was magnificent. It was everything she'd hoped for—the massive shoulders, the hungry eyes. She drew him in, and as her

honeyed hair fell around his head, his mouth once again
sought hers. He cupped her buttocks with loving hands, and
soon they were coming together, sharing a kiss that would
last until morning.

"Christ, Lucien, you scared me to death!"

Pru's heart pounded like the distant surf as she reached for
a lamp in the foyer of the Malibu beach house. In the darkness stood the shadowy figure of her stepson, who was up at
bat with a fireplace poker. But when he heard Pru's voice,
he put it down.

"Sorry, Pru, I thought you were a prowler." He turned
on the lights, and Pru sank onto a rattan couch, her pulse
still racing. Only after a few deep breaths did she collect
herself enough to notice her surroundings, and when she did,
she was lucky not to go into cardiac arrest.

The beach house had been completely redecorated: on the
walls hung huge, abstract paintings that vaguely resembled
entrails. They were done in clashing color schemes of peach
with purple and rose with canary.

"My God," she gulped.

"Staggering, huh? Do you like them?" Lucien asked eagerly, and it was then that she understood his paint-splattered
overalls.

"You did these?"

He grinned proudly, and for a brief moment her heart went
out to him: his paintings were unspeakably bad. Like his
music—which she'd heard—and his acting—which, thank
God, she'd only heard *about*—this last pursuit was an obvious
dead end. The paintings were so ugly and amateurish that she
just wanted to hang sheets over them. She closed her eyes
while Lucien hovered.

"Honestly, Pru, what do you think?"

"Honestly, I don't think they're very good." She was too
tired to mince words; it was after midnight, and she'd just
flown down from Tahoe. After her confrontation with Mercer, she'd come to the beach house because she needed some
privacy and a place to think. And what had she found? Lucien—and eight Rorschach tests flung like highway accidents
across the living room walls.

"You don't like them?" he asked.

"Maybe I just don't understand them, Lucien—" Wearily she closed her eyes. "I'm sorry—I'm just very tired and out of sorts. It's been a long day—"

"I know what you mean. I've been painting since the sun came up."

"Then you ought to rest. We'll talk in the morning."

"Yeah, I think when you see them in the light—"

"Lucien," she snapped irritably, "daylight won't make any difference." As soon as she'd spoken, she regretted the harshness of her tone. "I'm sorry—" she said, but he'd already rushed out the front door. It swung behind him as he ran down the beach, into the moonless night.

"Lucien," she called out, her voice lost in the thunder of the surf. "Lucien, I'm sorry, please come back." She slipped on her sweater and ran down the beach after him, but he was lost in the darkness, and after a while she turned back toward the house. She left him a note on the kitchen table—"I'm sorry, let's talk"—and then dragged herself to bed.

As he walked along the beach, he saw her bedroom light go out. Cursing her ignorance and vulgarity, he wondered what he could do. She was ruining his life. First there was Will, and then she got herself pregnant with a baby that no one wanted, and now—out of jealousy and spite—she was trying to tell him his paintings were no good.

It was hard to believe that she had everyone else eating out of her hand; even Raven thought she was "ultra nice." Why was everyone so stupid when it came to Pru?

As he walked along the beach, his gazed locked on the brightest star in the night sky, and he wished upon it feverishly for Pru to get a taste of the pain she dished out. He asked the night for justice, and above him the stars wrote their answer in light: swords, arrows, and an ancient hunter burned through the black sky. Lucien walked down the beach to Devil's Point, and in the wailing wind and the hammering surf, he heard at last the answer to his prayers.

Fifty-Two

SINCE MONDAY NIGHTS were dark for *The Women*, Kat drove out to the Springs at a leisurely clip. She had all day to spend with Leah, and there was no pressure to get back in time for an eight o'clock curtain.

When she arrived at Leah's doorway, Leah quickly closed the big leather-bound book she'd been looking at.

"What's that?" Kat asked.

"Something Krysta sent," Leah answered curtly. "Nothing I want to talk about." She moved quickly to the bureau and scooped up the bouquet of flaming desert poppies she'd picked that morning. She handed them to Kat.

"By way of congratulations," she said. Kat looked bewildered. "Now, don't be coy with me," Leah went on. "I read the papers. I can't believe you didn't tell me about your reviews!"

Kat shrugged modestly.

"Admit it," Leah said. "Even that sleazeball misogynist from the *Herald* couldn't pretend you weren't great."

"He said the entire production was great," Kat corrected.

"He said you were inspired."

"Well, sugar, I take it with a grain of salt."

"You just don't know how to accept a compliment, Kat. But be that as it may, just as soon as I get out of here, I expect to see your play front row center."

"I'd like that, Leah. You won't believe the women I'm working with. They're all fantastic."

"That's terrific."

"It is—and they've all been incredibly supportive about my project in West Virginia. Debra Winger's going to be my first actor-in-residence."

Leah embraced her. "It's amazing what's possible now. Can you imagine Marilyn Monroe trying to launch her own theater group? God, they would have stuffed another fistful of pills down her throat."

"They did," Kat said sadly.

"It's incredible what's happened in twenty years," Leah said. Pushing Krysta from her thoughts, she added, "We owe a lot to our mothers."

"Our daughters, too," Kat said. "I sometimes think if it weren't for Misti, I'd be holed up in a trailer park wondering what might have been."

Leah looked at her askance. "I seriously doubt that. The only trailer you were meant for was the one with a star—and 'Ms. Winter'—embossed on the door."

"Applesauce! I wasn't meant for anything until Misti came along and gave me purpose."

"How is Misti?" Leah asked.

"You'd have to ask her horse. These days, she spends most of her free time at the stables. She wants to learn everything she can in order to help Mick set things up."

"Sorry to interrupt," an aide looked in on them. "Mail's here." He handed Leah an envelope.

"It's from Sam," she said.

Hola, sweetie!

It's been awhile, hasn't it? Don't ask me where I've been, because I'm not sure I know. Since the premiere, UNES-CO's been flying us hither and yon to promote the film and pass the hat.

I love the work, but apparently my heart doesn't. My doctor's axed the rest of the winter's travel. I caught a pretty nasty cold in Chicago, and—please don't spread this around—it's been hard to shake. Some days I wonder how long my luck will hold out.

For the time being, we're in New York, shooting public-

interest spots. Compared to airport-hopping, it's absolutely Club Med. Frank's been appointed to the board of the World Health Organization, and even though it's bit of a grind, we have some time to ourselves. When we do, I try to view my illness as a bargaining chip: it's amazing how much nookie you can get when your husband knows you won't be around forever!

Please forgive the gallows humor, although you—of all people—can probably appreciate it. God knows if I couldn't laugh now, I'd really be in a state. Lying in state . . .

Anyway, this city is wonderful. Even now, in the bitter cold, I can't get enough. Every morning we tramp a mile uptown from our hotel on 44th Street to WNET. Frank always bugs me to take a taxi (I guess he wants me to save my strength for the boudoir!), but I say forget it. I look up at those bedroom eyes, through the freezing, sooty air, and I start singing, "I love New York!"

God, I wish you could be here with me. I miss you, sweetie.

> *Love,*
>
> *Your prodigal sister,*
>
> *Sam*

By February, Mo was still dragging his heels in Europe—this time on a U.S./French coproduction—and Pru had to face the truth: she didn't miss him at all. Neither did she miss his churlish son.

Lucien was in Paris with Raven; she was working as a production assistant for Mo, and he was studying painting. At that unpleasant thought, Pru shuddered for the art world, but at least he was out of her hair. And not a moment too soon, either. The day he left—right after her trip to Tahoe— he was sulky and hostile, and Pru was grateful when he climbed into the limo and took off.

She spent her days in postproduction on *Tropic of Danger*, and during her evenings she hit the baby shops. Her own baby was kicking up a storm, which never ceased to amaze her. She was also amazed by how well she slept at night. Pregnancy was an even better cure for insomnia than sex, and her troubles with Mo and Lucien easily gave way to contented exhaustion.

Early one morning, she groggily awoke to the sound of the telephone ringing on her bedside table. She groped for it as she pulled the sleeping mask from her freckled nose.

"Pru Daniels?"

"I think so," Pru muttered.

"Michele Gendelman. You sound like hell."

"I appreciate it, Michele. What's up?"

"I just thought you'd want to know—the Academy nominations are in, and Leah's been nominated for Best Original Screenplay."

Pru sat up, stunned. "You're kidding! My God, that's fantastic. I can't believe it! Michele, thank you so much for calling."

"Believe me, hon, I have an ulterior motive. Tell me, is it really true that your pal has no representation?"

"Michele, let's talk about this later. I have to go!"

She raced to the studio, where Drew was waiting for her, holding the fax and beaming. She looked at the other names in nomination—all heavy hitters—and she knew right away that Leah couldn't possibly win . . . but what a shot in the arm!

And what perfect timing, she thought. *Leah comes home today.*

She drove to Palm Springs in a state of exultation. She thought she'd burst as she waltzed into the cafeteria at the Center, but before she could surprise Leah with the good news, she faced a little surprise of her own.

"John!"

He and Leah looked up from the hot fudge sundae they were sharing. "Hello, Pru." He stood awkwardly and Pru looked bewildered as he reached out to shake her hand.

"I—I should have told you," Leah said, her eyes darting back and forth between Pru and John.

When Pru failed to shake John's hand, he slowly withdrew it. But suddenly she grinned and threw her plump arms around him. "You two," she said, shaking her head but smiling her approval. "I should have known. Sit," she told John as she pulled up a chair. "Listen. Whatever you were talking about will just have to wait."

Running her finger through the hot fudge sundae, she barely sampled it before she pushed it out of the way.

With elaborate slowness, she handed Leah the fax. Leah's mouth opened in shock as she read it, then she passed it to John. He scanned it, pulled her to her feet, and twirled her about as they both screamed with delight. When he put her down, she pushed the wild mane from her face and clutched the fax to her breast.

Pru picked up a spoon and helped herself to the half-eaten sundae. "So, kiddo, what do you think?"

"I think I've lost a lot of respect for the Academy of Motion Picture Arts and Sciences." As Pru polished off the sundae, Leah frowned. "I wish I'd tightened up the second half."

"Well, it was tight enough to buy you a seat at the Dorothy Chandler Pavilion, so give it a rest," Pru ordered.

"Can I help it if it could have been better?"

"Yes," said John and Pru in unison.

"Leah," asked Pru, her eyes the color of money, "do you have any idea what kind of buckaroos you can get for a script now?"

"Jesus . . . maybe I can pay for all of this," she said as she looked around the Center.

"From now on," Pru told her, "you can write your own ticket."

"Actually, I'd rather write a novel."

"A novel! Don't you dare," Pru wailed. "You're hot, Leah. You should be making deals as we speak."

"But I don't want to make deals. I just want to work on the book I've started."

Pru threw up her hands. "John! Talk sense to this woman."

John shrugged. "She doesn't need our advice. She's got a great book inside her."

"And all I have to do is write it!" sighed Leah. She threw John a questioning look. "Can I tell Pru?" she asked. "Don't bother to say no."

John flushed with embarrassment. "Leah, it's nothing—"

Leah waved at him dismissively. "John's won the Yale

Younger Poets Award—and he's been offered a teaching job at New York University.''

"That's wonderful,'' Pru congratulated him. "So why don't you look happier?'' she asked shrewdly.

"We've been going back and forth all day,'' he admitted. "Leah says I should take the job, but I'm afraid New York's not for me.''

"You've never even been there!'' Pru protested.

"I've never been there because I've never wanted to be there,'' he answered. "I think Tahoe's about as big a town as I can manage.''

"You think,'' scoffed Pru. "You'll never know until you try.''

"I tried L.A.'' he said pointedly.

"L.A.'s nothing like New York,'' Leah jumped in. "My dad and I used to go there a lot, and it was great. In New York you don't have to drive, and there are all sorts of plays and museums, and no one goes to the supermarket in a bikini. New York makes California look like the Planet of the Apes.''

"But in California a person can commune with nature,'' John protested.

"When you need to commune with nature,'' Leah said, "there's always Central Park. It's more wild than you'd care to imagine. And, of course, you can always go to Connecticut. It's absolutely overrun with trees.''

John looked at her skeptically.

"Besides,'' she continued, "you also need to commune with other writers. It's important to hang out with people who care about the same things you do—and I'll bet you don't run into many of those in Tahoe.''

"That's true,'' he admitted.

"Yoo-hoo. Can we decide John's fate later?'' Pru asked impatiently. She glanced at Leah. "What time do you fly the coop?''

"As soon as Joan signs me out''—she slit her throat with her finger—"I'm on my own. I'll have Six-twelve Weyburn all to myself.'' She stood up reluctantly. "I'd better go pack. You wait here, and Pru, why don't you order something? I'm sure you could use a little pick-me-up,'' she said, looking pointedly at the empty sundae dish.

Once she was gone, Pru didn't waste any time. She looked John in the eye. "What's going on between you two?"

"We're friends."

"John, I wasn't born yesterday. This is me, Prudence. The Grand Inquisitor."

"All right," he said slowly. "To tell you the truth, I wouldn't mind being more than friends, but I'm deliberately hanging back. The last thing Leah needs is some pushy guy coming on to her."

"True, but you're hardly the pushy type, John. You're the pully type. My God, I still cringe when I think of how I tore you away from Tahoe and dragged you down to L.A. without even asking what you wanted."

"Don't dwell on it," he said. "I sure as hell don't. After we broke up, I did a lot of thinking. I realized how passive and irresponsible I'd been. By letting you make our decisions, I'd set you up to take the rap when things didn't work out. Pretty crummy, huh?"

"Nothing you could have done without my help," she said.

"Maybe. But the point is, I don't hitch rides any more."

"Good for you," she said thoughtfully.

"But I wonder if it's good enough for Leah," he said. "She has such guts—and hell, I'm the guy who can't even muster up the courage to leave Tahoe again."

"But I thought you just said you didn't want to leave. You love Tahoe."

"Sure I do, but it's not that simple. It's not only that I love Tahoe—I'm scared to try new things."

"That's my fault," Pru said dismally.

"No, it isn't. Getting me out of my Tahoe rut was the best thing you could have done for me. I was so in love that I actually got past my fears and went, and we ended up having some good times together."

"When?" she asked. "I don't recall that we ever took our gloves off."

"It wasn't that bad, Pru. Believe me, I'm grateful you got me off my front porch."

"But isn't that exactly where you're heading back to?" Pru asked boldly. "Good old Tahoe—where the living is easy?"

"Maybe not." Suddenly John stood up. There was a look of unshakable resolve on his face as he kissed her cheek.

"Do me a favor, will you? Say good-bye to Leah for me."

"What?"

"She'll understand. I've got to split." Abruptly he took off.

Annoyed by his bad manners, Pru shrugged and went to find Leah.

"Knock, knock," she said at her door.

"Come on in," Leah said. "Where's John?"

"Back at the ranch, I guess. He just bolted."

"That's odd." Leah frowned. "It's not like him at all."

"I'm beginning to wonder what John is like," Pru said. "I think you're a good influence on him, though."

"I hope so, because he sure is on me—"

"Do you know what I hope?"

Joan appeared in the doorway.

"I hope I don't see you again, Leah. Not here, I mean."

Leah took a step toward her. "You won't." She grinned and looked around the room, startled. "Did I say that? Was that vote of confidence my own?"

"It'd better be," Joan told her. "You sweated blood to achieve it, and I don't think you're about to lose it again. Right?"

"Now, Joan," Leah said patiently. "Of course I will. Let's face it. Confidence isn't my strong suit, and every day I will certainly lose some. But I'll gain some, too. It will all even out. And besides, whatever happens in the confidence department, I won't pick up a drink again as long as I live. Because if I do, I'll die."

Pru closed her eyes as Leah's word sank in. When she opened them, Leah and Joan were embracing. Pru picked up the suitcase, and the trio headed for the parking lot.

Joan leaned in at Leah's window and kissed her good-bye. She waved until they were out of sight. Once they got on the desert highway, Pru stole a glance at Leah and saw the pink glow of sunset blush her cheeks.

To the west, a rainbow straddled the horizon, and the lavender sky deepened to purple as they made their way home in the gathering dark.

Fifty-Three

As a THOUSAND heart-shaped balloons floated upward in the morning sky, Leah caught Kat's bridal bouquet. The other guests cheered while she stared dumbly at the roses and baby's breath as if she'd never seen flowers before.

"They won't bite," Kat whispered. Then she and Mick ducked their heads and dashed through a storm of rice on their way to the limo. Because of *The Women*, the newlyweds only had time for an eight-hour honeymoon, but Pru had promised them one to remember. She had stocked the beach house with everything from caviar and champagne to massage oil, and she hired a security squad to ensure the couple's privacy. She also stashed Lucien's paintings in the attic so that Kat and Mick wouldn't suffer from motion sickness as soon as they walked through the door in Malibu.

"Get the lead out," she told the newlyweds as they entered the limo and hugged Misti one last time. Then they were off, clanging Beluga cans down the canyon road.

With the bride and groom gone, the wedding guests got their second wind and went back for more of Marie's home cooking. She'd slaved for a week, and the effort was well worth it: her southern-fried Szechuan, as she fondly called it, was an unqualified success. The guests lapped up her soy-cured hams, dandelion greens stir-fry, rhubarb dim sum, and even a batch of corn liquor (Mick's pals from the L.A.P.D. pretended not to notice).

Leah was on her third piece of corn bread when Misti tapped her on the shoulder. "You've got a phone call."

"Who could it be?" Leah wondered out loud.

"I didn't ask," said Misti primly, "but it's a man, and he sounds nice."

"Gee, do I know any nice men?" Leah asked as she took the phone.

"Leah? Happy Valentine's Day."

"John!"

"Listen, I'm sorry I ran out on you in Palm Springs."

"Me, too. It's not your style to be so rude. I hope."

"It's not. It's just that there was something I had to do. Listen, can you meet me?"

"Gee, I don't know . . ."

"Come on."

"Oh, all right. Where?"

"New York."

"New York? I thought—"

"Don't think. *Act.*"

"Gee, John. I don't remember your being so . . ."

"Assertive? Only when it matters. Look—hop on a plane. I'm at the Algonquin."

Leah put the phone down, and before she had a chance to change her mind, she headed for the door, still clutching the bridal bouquet.

Pru was one of the last guests to leave the reception. She'd cried like a baby from the first note of the wedding march straight through to the kiss. Then afterward, in the midst of so much love and commitment, she'd been forced to question the nature of her own marriage. She hadn't seen Mo in nearly three months.

As she drove through Beverly Hills, she thought about her parents: two empty, pathetic people who'd wasted their lives on their respective addictions. Pru had seen firsthand the price they paid, and what scared her was that Mo—for all his power and success—was also an addict. In his own sophisticated, glamorous way, he was as hopeless as any other junkie.

He's a slave, thought Pru. *And I want to be free.*

She wondered if some benevolent fate had sent Mo to her

as a warning. He was her future—unless she changed her ways.

She felt the baby stir, and she realized that this was the first step in a new direction. Babies weren't career moves—they demanded huge amounts of time and attention—but that didn't matter, because as much as Pru loved her work, the baby touched places inside her she'd never known were there.

As she pulled into the driveway, she suddenly understood that she could love her job without being its Siamese twin. That was where Mo had been wrong. She shuddered as she thought of the vast emptiness of his busy life.

Resolutely she walked into the house and sat down at her desk. Although she had no idea when he'd come home—he was still in Europe—she knew that when he did, she wouldn't be there.

"Dear Mo," she wrote, "I'll see you at the office."

She dropped the note on his pillow and grabbed some clothes. She went to the garage, climbed into her old red Mustang, and turned the key in the ignition. Even though she hadn't used the Mustang since Mo gave her a BMW, it started up perfectly.

She patted the dashboard and drove to the Westwood apartment, where Leah now lived solo. She found the old key still on her key chain. She unlocked the door, kicked off her high heels, and sat back contentedly, inhaling the heady scent of freedom.

Late that night, John met Leah in the elegant wood-paneled lobby of the Algonquin Hotel, and he quickly sat her down at a cozy table in the lounge. He still hadn't kissed her, but he'd hugged her so hard she'd gasped, and now they sat together, waiting for coffee, as he told her he'd fallen in love.

"Really?" she asked, her throat tightening.

"It's true. New York is *fantastic*!"

"No!" she said, her dark eyes wide with mock surprise.

"This morning I walked down to the Village, and everything was so damned stimulating I thought I'd bust. I saw it all, Leah! People you can't imagine."

"I can," she drawled.

"It was like someone pulled the pennies off my eyelids."

He gripped her hand excitedly. "I called my principal, Leah. I resigned."

"That's wonderful news. You'll love it here."

But you won't be in California! she despaired. *At least in Tahoe we shared a time zone.* Hiding her disappointment, she flashed him her whitest smile and put her hand on his arm.

"Congratulations, John. You've made a wise move." Suddenly weary, she stifled a yawn. "Sorry," she said. "The flight wore me out."

He quickly paid the tab, signaled the bellboy, and led her into the elevator.

"I called Sam," he told her. "We'll meet them for dinner tomorrow."

"Great." *But what about tonight, cowboy?* She was more than mildly curious about the sleeping arrangements by the time the elevator opened upstairs.

"You're just across the hall from me," John told her. He showed her into her room, tipped the bellboy, and stood with his hands in his pockets as he asked her if everything was all right.

"It's fine—just fine," she said awkwardly.

"So—I'll say good night, then." He hesitated, but when she turned away without protesting, he left quietly and closed the door behind him.

Doesn't he like me? she wondered forlornly. She undressed, then put on a sexy little black teddy that she just happened to have packed—for emergencies. *Another Valentine's Day Massacre,* she thought miserably as she settled into a troubled sleep.

Across the hall, John paced nervously as he mulled over what Joan had told him when he visited the Center:

"She has to take charge of her life. In the beginning, she'll try to get other people to do that for her. But it's not what she needs."

I'm what she needs, he thought. *And God knows I need her. But it's got to be her move.* He climbed into bed and turned off the light, but didn't sleep for a long time. Her voice, her eyes, and the sound of her laughter kept him awake until almost dawn, and when he finally did sleep, she crowded his dreams.

She knocked on his door bright and early the next morning, and they bounded downstairs and onto the streets of New York. The housing office at NYU gave them a list of apartments for rent, and they decided to go look at the one that was closest, over on MacDougal Street.

It was large and had a great view of the park. There were high ceilings, built-in bookshelves, and an alcove that was perfect for a study.

"I'll take it," he told the super. He wrote out a check on the spot, and afterward they walked to the White Horse Tavern to celebrate. When they'd had their fill of burgers and fries, they headed uptown to the Museum of Modern Art.

They spent the afternoon beneath Monet's water lilies, and when the museum guards finally gave them the boot, it was time to meet Sam and Frank.

They rendezvoused at a quiet French bistro on Sixty-first Street. Leah and John were already seated by the time Sam and Frank rushed in. Sam was rosy and red-nosed from the blustery evening, and Leah was pleased to see her with such high color. But her hopes for Sam's health were quickly dashed when Sam removed her cashmere overcoat and Leah saw that she'd dropped more than a few pounds.

The weight loss didn't seem to affect her outlook, though. Her silver eyes sparkled as she quickly demanded, "Tell me every dirty detail of Kat's wedding. Can you believe that damned doctor refused to let me go?"

Leah could, easily. The color in Sam's cheeks had already faded, and Leah was appalled to see that her usually tanned skin was frighteningly pale. Throughout dinner, as she prattled on about the wedding, she watched Frank carefully, and in his brooding gray eyes, she knew Sam's time was running out.

When the plates were cleared, Sam pulled out the plans for a hospital that *Sanctuary*'s profits would pay for. There were other projects in the works as well, and poring over the blueprints, Sam spoke of Togo's bright future as easily as if she would be a part of it.

Under the table, John reached for Leah's trembling hand,

and when she looked at him gratefully, he reached for her other one. She clung to him tightly and tried not to notice the way's Sam's collarbone jutted through her silk blouse.

After coffee and dessert, the party broke up. Sam wanted to go on to the Blue Note to hear some jazz, but Leah could read in Frank's tense expression that it wasn't a good idea. "I'm exhausted," she insisted, and the couples parted reluctantly.

As they drove down Broadway, John took her hand. "I know it tears you up," he said. "But don't forget, that lady's lived a hundred lifetimes in just this one."

Leah smiled and blew her nose into John's handkerchief. "You're right. It's not as if there are things she hasn't done."

When they got to the hotel, they settled into the lounge for cocoa. Leah wasn't ready to go up to bed, and she secretly hoped that if she gave herself a little time, she might even find the courage to make a play for John. She knew it was what she wanted, and she sensed that he wanted it, too. But for some reason he was leaving the ball in her court.

It was just as well, she decided. It was never too soon to try out newfound social skills. She vowed to seize the day, and in this case, the night. She could almost hear Joan cheering her on as she slipped her hand into John's.

"Let's go upstairs," she suggested. From the speed with which he paid the check, she knew she'd done the right thing.

Before heading for the elevator, they stopped off to collect their messages. Leah went white as she read: "Call Joan. It's urgent."

When she got upstairs, her breath was short. John stood behind her, his hands on her quaking shoulders, as she got through to Joan.

"Leah, Krysta is sick. Will you come?"

"Right," Leah said tightly. "Is that all?"

"She's dying. This is your last chance."

"Let her die," Leah choked. "I hope she finds what she's looking for in hell!" She slammed down the phone and fell sobbing into John's arms. She couldn't be sure how long she cried, but when her tears finally subsided, her throat was parched.

He brought her water, and as he patted her forehead with

a damp cloth, he told her softly, "You'll regret it all your life if you don't go to her now."

"But I hate her. She hurt me in ways I never dreamed were possible."

"She'll hurt you more if you let her go like this. Say good-bye, Leah. For your sake, don't let her haunt you. She will if you don't face her—you know that. Every time you close your eyes, you'll see her staring back at you."

"I do now," Leah whispered.

"Then you know. It can't go on forever, can it?"

Leah shook her head slowly and got up from the bed. John helped her pack.

"I'll come with you," he offered as she zipped her flight bag.

"No. You've got the Yale dinner tomorrow night—"

"It's no big deal. I'd rather be with you."

"Thank you," she said. "But I'm going alone." She raised herself on tiptoe and kissed him full on the mouth. In that first kiss, she tasted the wine she'd always been searching for—and never found in a glass. It left her a little drunk and breathless as she quickly stepped back and whispered, "I have to go."

"Let me come," he whispered.

Shaking her head, she kissed him once more, then turned and walked out the door.

Fifty-Four

LEAH FOUND KRYSTA'S hospital room and stood before the closed door, wondering if she should enter. It wasn't too late to turn away, but in the hush of the corridor, and in the silence of her heart, she heard a voice deep inside her—deeper even than her pain. It told her to open the door.

"You're here," Krysta whispered, her chestnut hair damp with fever. Her skin was translucent, paler and more waxen than the white blooms that stood beside her bed. The room was filled with flowers from students and fans, and among their brilliant colors, Krysta looked as faded as an old photograph.

Leah sat on a chair next to the door.

For a long time, they didn't speak. Leah stared past the window. The sun burned through the early-morning haze, and bare trees rose from the mist. As their branches blurred, she wiped her eyes and got up to leave.

She went to the door and turned the knob, then stopped.

She looked back. Sunlight struggled against the fog and won. It washed across Krysta's face, and she seemed to shine from inside.

In a small voice breaking with emotion, Leah shattered the silence.

"I have so many questions . . . Mother."

Krysta's pain-filled eyes opened wide. Leah's hand dropped from the doorknob. Feebly, Krysta raised her arms. She held them up, outstretched and trembling. She waited. With tentative steps, Leah crossed the room, closing the distance between them.

For three days, they talked. Krysta answered Leah's questions in a flood of memories and tears. It did her good, and she rallied briefly, long enough for Leah to take her home.

From her terrace in Santa Monica, they watched the sun sink into the ocean and the moon rise in its place. They talked a lifetime in the hours they had left, and often Krysta told her, "This is more than I ever hoped for."

The day she died, she made a final request, and reluctantly Leah opened her notebook. She read aloud from the novel she was writing. It was rough and raw, but Krysta listened with a smile on her face as if she were hearing the voices of angels.

"Your father would be so proud," she said when Leah finally closed the manuscript. She gripped her daughter's hand, and in her last gaze there was no more pain, and no fear.

March came in like a lion and went out like a mosquito. It was so unseasonably hot that Pru often dragged Leah to the beach for a late-afternoon swim. Leah hated the water—it made her seasick just to look at it—but Pru loved it. With her extra layer of prenatal fat, she was particularly bouyant, and now that she was almost six months pregnant, she floated like the *Queen Mary*.

"At work, I'm more like the queen bee," she told Leah.

In Mo's extended absence, she captained the helm of the studio, oversaw *Tropic of Danger* in postproduction—as well as several other projects—and somehow made time for Lamaze classes. But it was lonely being the only single parent in class, so Leah often went with her. At first Leah was a little put off.

"They treat the whole thing like an Olympic event," she protested.

"Or like the Oscars," Pru retorted.

"Shhh . . . You promised you wouldn't bring that up. I've already got enough trouble sleeping."

They both knew that the source of her sleepless nights was John, and Pru took the no-nonsense approach with Leah.

"Shit or get off the pot, kiddo. That'll cure your insomnia
. . . and here, put the pillow under my back."

As she and Pru practiced the Lamaze techniques, Leah had
to admit that the relaxation methods really worked, and within
a few weeks, she was enough of an expert to pass them on
to Kat. The actress was so revved up between *The Women*
and plans for her theater center that she, too, needed help
relaxing.

In the last week of March, however, Kat's life became a
little less chaotic. Her stint with *The Women* ended, and she
passed on her role to Amy Irving. Although it was difficult
to say good-bye to the cast, she was glad for the time off.
She and Mick flew to Charleston and began combing the lush
countryside for their respective projects.

Kat had been gone only three days when she called Pru at
sunup and chirped into the phone, "I've found it!"

"This had better be good," Pru muttered.

"Morgantown! It's gorgeous, you can hear yourself think—
and George Washington slept here!"

"Well, I'm sleeping here, Kat—"

"Shoot, I always forget those darn time zones. I'm
sorry—"

"It's all right. Listen," she asked warily, "do they have
running water?"

"Sugar, don't be silly. It's right down the road from Washington, D.C., and it was here before anyone ever heard of
Beverly Hills. Mick and I are buying adjoining parcels."

"Great," Pru said, "I know quite a few actors who'll be
right at home on a stud farm."

"Now, Pru!" Kat laughed. "Don't you dare put a damper
on my enthusiasm."

"I'm sorry, kiddo, but I cannot in good conscience enthuse
over a place where there's no Mr. Chow . . . no Michel Richard . . ."

"Land sakes," Kat scolded. "When Marie gets here, she's
opening a restaurant—the Waggin' Dragon—and I bet they'll
come all the way from Richmond to taste her soy-cured hams
and Peking grits."

"Stop it," Pru wailed. "You're making me hungry."

"Well, sugar, I've got just the cure for that! I'm bringing

you back a chocolate chess pie that'll make those sissy croissants of yours look like possum drops.''

She was right, too. When Pru picked her up at the airport, the aroma of the pie made her so delirious she could hardly hold on to the wheel. And it tasted even better than it smelled. By their third piece each, Pru and Leah were convinced: there were worse fates than having Kat in West Virginia. At least they could always drop by for dinner.

"This must be insulin shock," Leah murmured as she polished off the pie with Pru and Kat.

"I've got a jelly roll in here somewhere," Kat said as she ransacked her suitcase. "Here it is!" She pulled out the genuine article: hand-beaten sponge cake with homemade huckleberry jam.

"Eat your heart out, ladies."

And they did.

The Oscars were less than a week away, but Pru was so wrapped up in marketing *Tropic of Danger* that she hardly noticed. She was at odds with the company that had cut the trailer, she hated the print campaign, and she was tearing her hair out over the tie-ins. Her only pleasures, it seemed, were the weekly Lamaze classes and her brand new hobby, househunting. She loved driving around and seeing what her hard-earned money could buy. She wanted her child to have a huge yard and pretty garden, and since 612 Weyburn didn't even have a flower box in the window, she was looking at houses in Brentwood and in the Valley.

The Friday evening before the Oscars, she was on her way to look at a place in Sherman Oaks. At the busy intersection of Sunset and Beverly Glen, traffic had slowed to a halt, and as Pru looked around, she noticed Lucien's girl friend in the Mercedes convertible next to her. At first she didn't recognize Raven. Instead of the pasty-faced punker who'd hung out with Lucien, she was now a deeply tanned, blond California girl who used the down time at the traffic light to pump a set of weights.

"Raven!" Pru called, and when the young woman heard Pru's voice over the driving beat of Michael Jackson, she smiled and waved her dumbbell.

"I thought you were in Paris," Pru said.

"Didn't work out." Raven shrugged. "Lucien thought it was ultra cool, but I got sick of all those French people. I mean, they speak French fluently, and it was just over my head."

"Anyway, I told Lucien we should travel or something, but instead the bastard dumped me, so I came back here with André."

I'll bet, thought Pru.

"Who's André?"

"A stunt man. We're ultra happy," Raven beamed, "and last week, when I ran into Lucien, he was so weird that I was glad we broke up—"

"Wait a minute. Did you say Lucien's here?"

Raven nodded. "I ran into him at the Palm—oops, traffic's moving!" With a cheery smile and a little wave, she roared off shouting, "Catcha later!"

The heavy traffic and dense smog occupied Pru's thoughts all the way to the Valley. She felt as though she were driving straight into the sun until she finally made a right turn on Valley Vista and entered the leafy, tree-lined suburb of Sherman Oaks. She followed her broker's directions through the winding, shaded streets, and when she pulled up at last at a charming Spanish Colonial, she was excited once again.

While Pru poked about in the closets and cupboards of the Spanish Colonial, Lucien used his Gold American Express card to slip into 612 Weyburn. He wasn't looking for anything in particular; he just felt like touching base with Pru. But when he ransacked her briefcase and found some paste-ups for the ad campaign for *Tropic of Danger*, he was reminded all over again of how she'd shafted him.

He carefully put the paste-ups back in the briefcase and then explored Pru's bedroom. It was a real step down from the boudoir she'd shared with his father. He thought she was a real idiot for blowing Mo's scene. Did she really think she'd get away with it?

As he wandered into the other bedroom, he noticed a stack of hand-crocheted baby blankets that were piled on a small white chest of drawers. In the corner, a white bassinet was still covered with plastic. As Lucien walked toward it and

looked into the empty cradle, he thought of his poor, pathetic
father.

He walked stealthily back through the apartment. His mind
was a jumble of possible plans, and he sifted through them
as he prepared to leave. But just as he was about to open the
front door, the handle turned, and he leaped into the closet,
out of sight.

He heard the door open, and a familiar voice called, "Pru,
are you home?" Sneakers padded right back into the kitch-
en, a silence followed, and then the sneakers padded out the
same way they'd come in. Lucien waited until the door handle
turned. Then he popped out of the closet and had a look in
the kitchen.

There was a note on the table: "Pru, we have got to shop!
Monday's coming up fast! Love, L."

Leah! Staggering!

A slow grin crawled across his face. He turned and walked
out, leaving the apartment exactly as he'd found it.

On Saturday, Pru picked up Leah in Santa Monica, and they
went to lunch at the West Beach Café. Pru ate the Cobb salad
"without the Cobb." She'd dreamed the night before that she
showed up at the Oscars in a loosely pinned bedspread.

"And I took up two seats at the Dorothy Chandler Pavilion," she lamented.

"Pru, you're gorgeous, and come Monday night you'll
blow those anorexic ingenues right out of the theater. So
lighten up."

"Easy for you to say, Leah. You're already light. Besides,
you could show up in your bathrobe and steal the show."

"Well, I just might show up in my bathrobe if we don't
do some serious shopping this afternoon."

They made tracks to Beverly Hills, and a few minutes after
two, Prudence parked in a lot south of Wilshire.

"Let the games begin," she said solemnly. "We'll start
with underwear."

"Underwear?" Leah protested.

"In case you're hit by a car—you know that," Pru replied
tartly as she steered Leah to the escalator at Neiman-Marcus.

"They have the best selection of silks here," said Pru. "Of course, they're not all hand-stitched—"

"Not hand-stitched!" Leah cried in mock despair.

"Behave yourself," Pru ordered as she pushed Leah onto the escalator. Looking across the panoramic first floor, Leah's eyes rested on the men's department, which was featuring unstructured Italian suits and baggy trousers.

"That stuff reminds me of Lucien," Leah said. "How is he, anyway?"

"Beats me," Pru shrugged. "He's back from Europe, but he hasn't been around to bug me. Yet."

"Do you want to hear something truly trashy?" Leah said wickedly. "But you have to promise not to get mad, because I wasn't in my right mind. Okay?"

"I'll bet I know what it is."

"No way."

"You fucked him, right?"

"How did you know?"

"An educated guess, Leah. He was within a fifty-mile radius."

"Are you mad?"

"Mad? No. Disgusted? Yes." She moved in closer. "Was he good?"

"He's hung like a horse and has more energy than Santa's reindeer."

"Big deal." Pru smiled slyly. "Leah, my dear, you are in for quite a treat with you-know-who."

"You mean . . . ?"

"None other. But first you have to say the word—and I hope by the year 2000! Guys like John don't wait around forever."

"You're right . . . Oh, look," Leah cried, and she pointed excitedly. "There's my dress!" She dragged Pru off the escalator and over to a mannequin in the evening wear department. The model wore a strapless lavender gown with a narrow skirt and butterfly back.

"Perfect!" Leah exclaimed. "Wrap it up!"

Next Pru found a very roomy but flattering velvet Empire gown, and then the real work began—shoes, bags, and wraps. Fortunately, Pru knew every shelf and rack on Rodeo Drive, and by four o'clock, their mission was accomplished. To celebrate, they settled into La Scala Boutique for a gooey dessert and espresso.

"Just a little something for the road," Pru said gravely. "I don't want my blood sugar getting low." Now that she knew she had plenty of room in her Oscar gown, she could see her way clear to a Napoleon. "Doctor's orders," she explained to the waiter.

At five, the two friends walked back to Pru's Mustang, piled it full of the day's purchases, and took off toward the beach. It was a beautiful afternoon, and scenic Sunset Boulevard was much prettier than the freeway. Leah and Pru chatted about hairstyles and makeup, and Pru was just reminding her friend of their Monday appointment at Joseph Martin when a hairpin curve suddenly appeared before them.

Pru expertly pumped the brakes as she guided the Mustang. But something happened: there was a snap, and then a loss of control.

The car careened dizzily as she turned the wheel in vain. There were no brakes and no steering—nothing but forward thrust. The car lifted off the road. Sparks flew from the engine, the air turned black with billowing smoke, and broken glass cascaded down the dashboard like water breaking through a dam. Over their screams, the women heard the sound of metal tearing.

Fifty-Five

"IT'S A MIRACLE we're alive," Pru said thoughtfully as she stared at the cast on her ankle.

"Try not to think about it," Leah advised her.

"Can you believe the baby's fine?"

"The kid's a survivor—like you. And I managed to make out all right too. Not a cut or bruise to mar my white shoulders tomorrow night."

"I've gotta say, we really turned up trumps this time," Pru remarked. She directed her gaze heavenward. *"Muchas gracias,"* she sighed.

As she made herself comfortable on the funky old couch in the Westwood apartment, she traced an ancient stain in the upholstery and smiled faintly. "Borneo Boomerang," she said.

"Here, finish your pizza," Leah ordered. "You need to keep up your strength."

"For what? I think this ankle is going to keep me out of the next performance of the Joffrey Ballet."

"Well, it's not going to keep you out of the Dorothy Chandler Pavillion. You're my date, crutches and all, so eat up and then let's get our beauty sleep."

Pru dutifully ate the last crusts of pizza.

"God," she groaned, clutching her stomach. "Call me Barfarella." She took a last sip of Diet Coke, and Leah helped her hobble off to bed. Leah tried to sleep, too, but she was

still shaken from the accident. It was hours later before she
finally fell into a restless slumber.

*A blinding fire leaped before her, its flames licked her
eyes. Screams, and echoes of screams, unfurled through the
dark. Sparks sputtered, a car went flying, and a stage collapsed. Pru cried her name, and the singer onstage was
thrown into the audience. The car exploded, the nightclub
burned. Everywhere there was fire and fury, and through the
rubble, Lucien walked. Through the flames, Lucien smiled,
his mouth a deep black well.*

Leah woke up screaming.

"It was just a dream," Pru called to her, hobbling into
her room. She shook her until she finally awoke.

"My God," Leah stammered, sitting up. "It was so real!"

"No, kiddo, it wasn't real." In the scant light of dawn,
she gently pushed Leah's head back onto the pillow.

"I was there," Leah whispered. "It wasn't a dream."

"Try to get some sleep," Pru urged. "I'll stay in here
with you." She crawled into Kat's old bed and listened in
vain for the sounds of deep and regular breathing. As the sun
rose steadily above the mountains, they lay in wide-awake
silence. When Leah finally spoke, there was a tremor in her
hoarse whisper. "The nightmare, Pru—Lucien was in it."

"I don't doubt it," Pru said. "He's in my worst nightmares, too."

"We were being so crazy," Leah continued. "We were
out of our minds."

"That's just the way dreams are, Leah."

Suddenly Leah sat bolt upright in bed. "No!" Her brown
eyes flew open. "When you were in Hawaii, he took me to
a nightclub. It's hard to remember—I must have gotten really
shellacked—but he did something there. Something terrible." She closed her eyes, and her brow furrowed in concen-
tration as she tried to recall what had happened. "That's it,"
she exclaimed. She looked at Pru in horror. "He messed
around behind the stage. He screwed up some wires, I think,
and all of a sudden, a fire broke out."

Pru frowned. "An electrical fire . . . We had one on the
set of *Tropic of Danger*. It damn near killed Will Avery."

Leah got up and scrambled to Pru's bed. "Listen," she

said, clutching Pru's arm. "The singer who got hurt was a guy Lucien hated. I remember now. Lucien wanted his job."

"And he wanted Will's job," Pru whispered. "My God, there were so many accidents on that set. And Lucien was always there, hanging around. He was hanging around the pool, too, the night that Will nearly drowned."

Leah tightened her grip on Pru's arm. "Do you think he could have messed with your car?" she asked fearfully.

"I don't know," Pru answered. "But I'll tell you this much. It's high time we found out what Lucien's up to."

She threw off the covers and reached for her crutches. "He hasn't called me since he got back from Europe," she said. "That's strange—he always wants something."

"Do you think he's lying low on purpose?"

"Maybe, Leah. Come on."

They dressed quickly and drove to Holmby Hills, but the house stood empty, so they shot west to Malibu. They arrived at the beach house just after ten and parked behind the oleanders.

Lucien was in the driveway, leaning over the engine of the Lamborghini. His sinewy back glistened in the sunlight as the women approached. The pounding surf drowned out the sound of Pru's crutches as she sneaked up behind him.

"Long time no see," she said.

He twirled about and went white as the blood drained from his face. "Pru," he stammered. "Leah—"

"Surprise!" said Leah. "*Staggering,* huh?"

Lucien's hands shook as he closed the hood of the car. "What brings you by?" he asked, staring out at the ocean.

"We want to talk to you," Leah began. "Some strange things have been going on—"

"Fuck off!" With a single sweep of his arm, Lucien knocked both women back into the bushes. He jumped into the Lamborghini and peeled out of the driveway. The women were still helping each other out of the hedge as he disappeared in a cloud of smoke down the Pacific Coast Highway.

"Are you all right, Pru?"

"I'm fine," she answered, balancing on her crutches. "Let's have a look around."

They walked into the house, and the first thing that struck

them was the new painting over the mantelpiece. It was one of Lucien's, all right—garish, violent strokes of color—but this one wasn't like the others.

"It's me," Pru gasped.

Beneath her hideous, bloated face, Pru's belly was swollen like a milkpod. A fetus floated in the black sea of her uterus, and the entire canvas was slashed down the middle like a corpse about to be autopsied.

"My God," Leah breathed. They left the house quickly and drove down the highway to the first phone they saw.

"I'm calling the police," Leah said.

"Wait! What if they don't believe us?"

"Pru, you saw for yourself—the guy's wacko."

"We know that, but the cops don't. And what do we have for evidence? Bad feelings? Modern art?"

"You're right. Forget the cops." Leah dialed Kat's number.

"Kat, we have to talk to Mick."

"What's the matter?"

"Please, Kat. Where is he?"

"Out riding with Misti."

"Can you find him?"

"I can try. Are you sure you're all right?"

"Just find him, Kat—and send him to Joseph Martin's."

As Leah hung up, she shuddered. When she got back to the car, Pru said heartily, "Don't worry, kiddo. We scared him to death. He'll probably crawl right back under his rock, and we won't hear another peep out of him."

"I hope you're right . . . Pru, do you think he really could have done those things?"

"I'm sure of it. But I'm also sure he won't try again. You saw how he ran from us. He's a coward, and now that he knows we know, the gig's up."

Leah look unconvinced. "I don't think so," she said. "I think he'll try harder."

In a show of bravado for her friend's sake, Pru vehemently shook her head. "He's history," she vowed. She put an arm around Leah's trembling shoulders. "I promise, Leah. Now, just try not to think about it, okay? Mick will find him and put his lights out."

Speaking with far more conviction than she really felt, she reassured Leah all the way to Joseph Martin's.

They were late for their appointments, but the whole salon was running late because of the Oscars. They changed into their velour robes and sank back in a calfskin couch.

Beautiful women were everywhere, soaking their feet in whirlpools, touching the mud as it cracked on their faces, and sitting like Coneheads under the hair dryers. Leah tried to read, but finally put the magazine down.

"How dangerous do you really think he is?" she asked. Pru didn't like the fear in her voice. It was more than Leah should have to handle.

"Listen," Pru said. "You saw what happened. We confronted him, and he took off. He's afraid of us, kiddo, and don't you forget it."

Leah smiled wanly. "You're right, Pru. But I still wish Mick would call."

Abruptly Pru's hairdresser tapped her on the shoulder and she nearly jumped through the window. "Lorenzo," she sputtered. "You surprised me."

"Ready to go wild?" he asked with a smile, and he led her off.

Moments later, Mick burst through the door of the salon and sent an excited little ripple through the clientele. Leah and Pru pulled him into a tanning booth. Pru dragged Lorenzo with her, and he combed her out while she locked the door and faced Mick.

"Listen," she said, and she told Mick everything she knew.

Later that afternoon, the two women were driving home from the salon when the car phone buzzed. Pru listened intently, then thanked Mick for all his help.

"They've got him," she told Leah. "They picked him up for speeding, but he's got enough outstanding warrants that they'll be able to hold him for a while. Mick says that'll scare him. He'll break down in no time, and whatever he's been doing, the police will find out about it."

"So that's it?" Leah asked, glancing sideways at Pru.

"That's it," Pru assured her. "He's the cops' headache now."

"Thank God." Leah collapsed with relief against her bucket seat as she pulled the car up in front of the Westwood apartment. Suddenly lighthearted and carefree, she helped Pru inside. They hit the bathroom and stood together in front of the mirror, dodging elbows the way they had when they first moved in together.

"Watch it," said Pru. "You could blind me with your mascara wand."

"I can't believe we're still vying for space in this dinky mirror," Leah laughed.

"We won't be for long," Pru reminded her, trying to balance herself against the sink while she dabbed eyeshadow on her lids. "Just as soon as I close the deal in Sherman Oaks, I'll be a Valley Girl. But you know, I'll miss the old homestead. There's something special about it. Our first apartment—"

"Pru, snap out of it. This place is a dump."

"But it's our dump."

"Prudence Daniels! Don't tell me there's a sentimental streak in your nature!"

Just then the doorbell rang. "That must be Will," Pru said, touching up her eyeshadow. "Can you get it?"

Leah walked to the living room and opened the door.

"No!" she shrieked.

Pru came hobbling out of the bathroom.

"My God," she cried. "John!"

Leah kissed him as he swept her off her feet and spun her through the air. "Ummm . . . kiss me again," she told him when he set her down. Pru discreetly limped into the kitchen and happily devoured a slice of chocolate torte as she eavesdropped on their conversation.

"I have to say something," Leah announced breathlessly. He nuzzled her neck, and when she started to lose her train of thought, she steadfastly pushed him away. "First, I have to get this off my chest. Sit down."

Pru peeked through the door as John sat.

"I'll make this short and to the point, and please don't interrupt, because I've been practicing for a month—"

He pulled her down on the couch.

"Wait . . . Please . . . John, I'm crazy about you and—I wonder if you'd like a roommate."

"Holy shit," he whooped. "Do you know how long I've been waiting to hear you say that? I promised I'd wait until you were ready, in your own time, but I have to admit, I came out here to do some gentle prodding."

"Prod away," she giggled. He threw open his arms and she sailed right in, and when Pru saw the kiss that ensued, she blushed.

The doorbell rang again, and this time it was Will. "Sorry I'm late." He whisked them into the studio limo, and along the way they stopped on Melrose. Will jumped out at Deluxe Tuxedo, disappeared inside for just an instant, then loped back to the limo with a tux in hand. Unfortunately it was powder blue. "This was all they had left," he apologized.

As John changed clothes in the car, Leah stole furtive glances at the man she was going to move in with.

But what she saw, in a flash of Jockeys, was plenty. He finished dressing, and she slid close to him. They necked in the back seat like teen-agers all the way downtown.

Inside the Dorothy Chandler Pavilion, Leah led John and Pru to her block of seats, and she was handing Pru's crutches to an usher when a hush rippled through the gathering crowd. Leah looked up the aisle, and a shimmering figure waved happily.

"Kat!"

Kat bounded down the aisle, almost tripping on her satin gown as she rushed to embrace her friends.

"Leah, you look gorgeous!" She pried open Leah's clenched fist and pressed a penny into her sweaty palm. "For luck, sugar. Not that you need it."

"Where's Mick?" Pru asked.

"He'll be along. He wanted to clean up after chasing Lucien all over the canyons."

It was getting close to showtime, and Leah was wondering how she'd endure the next three hours, when she heard someone calling her name. She turned around and craned her neck.

"Sam!" she exclaimed. She leapfrogged over her seat and

profusely apologized to the row behind her as she scrambled past them. She and Sam embraced.

"I can't believe you made it!" Leah cried.

"Don't tell my doctor," Sam whispered. She was thinner than ever, but radiant.

"You look wonderful," Leah said, and she meant it.

The orchestra grew silent, Chevy Chase took the stage, and Leah grew light-headed with anxiety. More than once, she felt herself drifting away only to return to earth when Pru nudged her.

Halfway through the show, Kat had to leave—she was a presenter—and a moment later, Leah flinched when Pru suddenly gasped out loud.

"Mo?"

Leah looked up, and there he stood. His tuxedo shimmered like fresh tar as he beamed at Pru and groped his way toward her. "Daddy's home!"

"I—I don't believe it," Pru whispered while Leah gaped.

"I missed you, baby." As he leaned over to kiss her, his fingers rested lightly on her belly, and Pru pushed them away.

"It's over, Mo."

"Lighten up, doll. Let's enjoy the evening."

He made himself comfortable in Kat's seat while Pru raised her eyebrows at Leah. His hand found his way to Pru's lap, and she turned to him angrily. "Don't you know I've moved out?"

She placed his hand back in his lap. When he reached out and draped his arm around her shoulders, she shook it off and started to give him a piece of her mind, but suddenly she stopped short.

Deafening applause filled the theater as Kat and Will appeared from the wings. In her rippling blue satin gown, Kat seemed to float across the stage, and Leah thought that she, too, might float away. She gripped the edge of her seat.

Kat and Will read the names of the nominees for Best Original Screenplay, and then Kat fumbled with the envelope.

"The winner is . . ."

She took forever to rip the paper, and when she finally did, an eternal moment passed before she raised her head high.

The smile on her face was brighter than a thousand suns as she cast aside the microphone and shouted, "Leah Sirk!"

Sam pounded her back, and the audience thundered with applause as Leah rose unsteadily. She'd hardly gotten up when she suddenly leaned back down and kissed John. Then she pulled Pru up. "You're coming with me!"

She dragged Pru kicking and screaming down the aisle. Will was waiting at the stairs, and he made Pru look lighter than a feather as he lifted her onto the stage. Kat embraced Leah and handed her the gold statuette. Then she walked her to the podium. The ovation died down, and the room grew silent as the terrified winner set her Oscar in front of her.

The spotlight shone in her eyes as she groped for the hands of her friends. Kat and Pru stepped slightly forward, and Leah wove her fingers through theirs as the crowd waited. She took a deep breath, but still felt paralyzed and short of breath.

"Members of the Academy . . ."

She looked across the audience. There was nothing but privilege and fame in that room, nothing but power. The smug faces were all in place, and so were the false smiles.

She thought of Ray—long gone but never forgotten. She felt his impossible presence beside her, and suddenly she realized why she hadn't prepared a speech.

Ray wrote this one for me, she thought.

She gazed out at the rustling, expectant crowd. Her dark eyes—her father's eyes—bored into them as she tilted her face toward the light. Unblinking and unafraid, she spoke.

"Thank you very much for this great tribute." She paused. "I accept it in honor of my father, Raymond Sirk."

The audience rustled. Murmurs rippled through the theater, and Leah waited, unmoving, for silence to return.

"Ray Sirk lived in a dark time," she said when it was quiet, "and although his worst efforts far surpass my best, no one rewarded him. No one even tolerated him . . ." Her voice splintered and broke, but she didn't stop.

"Tonight," she continued, "I would like to believe that in giving me this very special, very unearned award, you are also giving it to Ray. He would accept it gladly—as long as it carried with it the promise of no more witch-hunts."

She faltered, and Pru and Kat gripped her hands tightly. "So . . . in his name, and in the names of all the other blacklisted writers, I gratefully accept this award."

A shocked silence fell over the crowd as she stepped back from the mike and Kat and Pru guided Leah across the stage.

"Leah!"

A voice rang out through the darkness.

Sam was on her feet, shouting Leah's name, and so was John. Frank stood next, and then Mick, and their impassioned applause spread like wildfire, sparking others to cheer and stand. As Leah wiped the tears from her eyes, she looked out into the sea of faces before her and realized they were all standing, all cheering.

Dazed and disoriented, she clung to Pru, and as she looked at the Oscar for the first time, she could have sworn that in its golden face, her father smiled up at her.

Fifty-Six

JUST ABOVE SUNSET, Spago was nestled like a treehouse in the Hollywood Hills. Lights twinkled in the bushes that surrounded the chic restaurant, and tempting aromas of garlic and basil wafted through the evening air. Klieg lights threw long arms of illumination into the darkness as the best and the brightest of the glitterati made their way inside. Except for the pesky paparazzi who lined up like a firing squad outside the door, the post-Oscar fête was strictly A-list.

"Are you sure we're invited?" Leah asked uncertainly.

"Are you kidding? They've already dubbed you 'the conscience of the industry,' " John answered.

"Every party has its pooper," Leah said with a shrug.

She breathed deeply and followed after John and Will as they helped Pru up the hill to the airy little bistro. Unfortunately, Will wasn't much help: as soon as the press spotted him, they swarmed like locusts.

"Leah! Pru!"

Sam was waving from just inside the restaurant. Pru batted a few reporters with her crutch as she led her little band past the maître d'.

"Here," Sam cried, heading for a lovely table in the front room. It stood next to an enormous window with a stunning view. A balmy breeze drifted in from the ocean, and the lights of the city sparkled below like buried treasure at the bottom of the sea.

"Glamorama!" Leah sighed, looking out the window at

the evening sky. "This is what I call Star Wars!" They all
sat down.

"We can talk here," said Sam, which was true. Compared to the rest of the gala, their corner was relatively calm:
the hard-core schmoozers hung around the bar, the photo
hounds guarded the entrance to the palace, and the buffet was
swamped. But in the corner Sam had staked, the women could
almost hear themselves above the noise of the party.

Beyond their table, a pianist sat at a baby grand, and the
tinkling melodies of all the great show tunes swirled like
bright constellations of sound in the candlelit restaurant.

Sam winked at Frank, who was amiably arguing politics
with some people at a nearby table. Pru hit the buffet and
returned with enough food to open her own restaurant.

"Make mine a double," she remarked as she bit into a
piece of goat cheese pizza. She was about to sample the
grilled chicken when she abruptly set it down. She leaned
forward and squinted, crinkling her freckled nose. She
pointed at the entrance. Kat and Mick were arriving. Kat,
with her saint's face and sinner's body, left the whole restaurant breathless. Flashbulbs went off everywhere, but even in
the explosion of all the blinding lights, Pru was able to make
out a familiar figure trotting behind her friends.

"Look what the Kat dragged in," she muttered.

Mo waved to the crowd roguishly as he stepped inside the
restaurant, and he wasted no time in pushing Kat into Liz
Smith's outstretched arms.

"Isn't she the prettiest little fairy godmother you ever
saw?" Mo beamed.

"We're all terribly excited about *Snow White*," Liz gushed.

"It'll blow the top off *E.T.*," Mo promised. He paused to
find the right words. "It's a fairy tale with teeth!" he declared. He might have continued all night promoting his latest project, but he happened to spot the person he was looking
for, and quickly dashed over to Leah.

"Leah! Congratulations! I always had you pegged for a
winner! Call me, doll. Yesterday!" Abruptly he turned to
Pru. "We must talk."

"Not now, Mo. If you'll excuse me," she said tartly, "

think I'll go to the ladies' room and hang out with the coke-heads.''

Mo started to follow Pru as she hobbled away, but John nipped that in the bud. ''Shall we have a word outside?'' he asked. He stood up, and his imposing figure—even in a powder blue tux—cut Mo down to size.

''Catch you kids on the flip side,'' Mo said hastily. He backed off and quickly disappeared into the crowd, and Leah went to retrieve Pru. She found her in the bathroom, steaming.

''Don't let him get to you, Pru. He's not worth it.'' Leah handed Pru her crutches, and they elbowed their way through the throng of lively women. At the bathroom door, they met Sam coming in. She looked almost skeletal in the harsh light of the makeup mirrors.

''Are you all right?'' Leah asked.

''Between us?''

Pru and Leah nodded gravely, and Sam pulled them as far from the crowd as she could. She poked in her evening bag for a bottle of pills and dropped a capsule down her swanlike throat while her friends watched anxiously.

''I get fevers,'' she said matter-of-factly. ''And I can't keep any weight on.''

She looked around the bathroom at the women who were eyeing her with envy.

''They're wondering how you stay so thin,'' Leah said bitterly. She took Sam's arm. ''Let's go home.'' She steered her toward the door, but Sam shook free.

''I'm not an invalid, and I wouldn't miss this party for the world.''

''Leah's right.'' Pru stifled a very loud yawn and patted her mouth several times. ''Let's call it a night.''

Sam scowled and shook her head. ''Knock it off, Pru. You're not tired and neither am I. So let's party.'' As Sam resolutely led her friends back to their table, they passed by the huge wood-burning pizza oven. Pru wrinkled her nose and sniffed with delight.

''They're going to roll me out of here tonight,'' she laughed.

At the bar, Kat managed to duck out of an ''Eye on L.A.''

interview. She met the others back at the table. "Having a good time?" she asked.

"The food's so-so," Pru answered as she speared a fresh steamed clam.

"Have some more," said Mick. "You look a little peaked," he teased. He pushed his plate toward her.

"Thanks, Mick. And listen, thanks for this afternoon, too." She leaned in close to him. "Leah was scared to death until you nailed him. You really saved the evening for her. I appreciate it."

"No sweat. My friends had fun playing hide-and-seek with his Lamborghini."

"What did he say when you took him in?" Pru asked.

"Plenty, I'll bet. But I'm not sure. I didn't hang around to find out. I'm no longer one of L.A.'s finest."

"Yes, you are," Kat cooed in his ear. Their love life was a constant delight since Mick turned in his badge.

"Shoot!" Kat cried out, startled by a paparazzi whose long lens nosed her between the shoulder blades.

"Get that camera out of here!" barked Leah to the brazen photographer. "Go hang around the bar. Look, there's Arnold Schwarzenegger and Maria Shriver. Go bother them."

Pru seconded the suggestion, then headed back to the buffet, and when she returned, the four women huddled over a fistful of caviar shimmering in a nest of angel hair pasta. Their forks flew and their tongues wagged.

"So you're going to New York with John," Sam sighed. "Isn't it romantic?"

Leah blushed. "It should be quite the love nest—us and nine million cockroaches."

"It will be perfect," Pru insisted.

"Hell, if it's even bearable it'll be a step up for me."

"You've climbed a lot of steps this year," Sam told her.

"It's worth it for the view," Leah said, and smiled.

Pru suddenly squealed. "It's kicking!" she announced.

The others put their hands to her belly, and sure enough, they could all feel the new life within.

Staggering, thought Lucien. *Fucking staggering.*

From his hiding place in the thick bushes outside the restaurant, he shook his head in disgust. It was hard to watch her all night like this, laughing and pigging out with her crazy friends. But soon it would all be over.

A squad car wailed in the distance, and he had to laugh. *How could those assholes expect to hold me? They didn't have shit. Maybe their scare tactics work on some people. But not me—and not my old man's lawyer!*

He ran his fingers down the cold metal barrel of his hunting rifle. He hoisted the rifle onto his shoulder and tucked his head close to the trigger. He aimed, and the rifle sight framed Pru like an old-fashioned portrait.

Sit still, bitch, and don't you dare head for that fucking buffet again.

Between her trips to the trough and her dumb friends getting in the way, Lucien hadn't been able to get a line on Pru all night. Every time he had a clear shot, she fucked it up, or one of her friends ran interference. He wouldn't mind blowing away any of those bimbos—especially Leah—but that would spoil Pru's surprise.

His legs began to cramp from crouching for so long, so he decided to get up and stretch for a minute. He climbed down from his hiding place and crept around to the back of the restaurant. He looked out over the twinkling city and felt a oneness with its energy. The lights pulsed with him, the power surged inside him.

He returned to his prayer position at the window. But as usual, Pru was obscured by her friends. Sam and Kat darted back and forth, and fucking Leah was hanging all over some dude. She was practically sucking the lips off his face.

I guess I taught her a thing or two! But goddamnit, this shit could go on all night. Fortunately, I've got nothing but time . . .

Once more Lucien trained his rifle on Pru's table, and this time he was pleased to see that Leah and her boyfriend had finally unglued themselves. Now that they'd parted, he could see straight to Pru.

He raised himself a fraction of an inch and snared Pru's face in the cross hairs of his rifle sight. He lowered the rifle a tiny bit, just enough to hit the bull's eye.

* * *

Not more of those damned paparazzi! Sam thought irritably.

She squinted to get a better look at the dark figure right outside the window. It moved slowly, then stopped altogether, and too late she saw the barrel of a rifle.

"No!"

As Lucien fired, she flung herself headfirst across the table. In midair, she took the bullet that was meant for Pru, and she dropped onto the table as Frank cried out. Leah screamed, and John and Mick tackled Pru. They broke her fall as she crashed to the floor on top of them. The music stopped, and all hell broke loose.

With Mick scrambling after him, Lucien rose up from behind the shattered window and climbed onto the sill. Towering above the crowd, he aimed again and fired—

But this time the bullet spun dizzily out of control.

It flew harmlessly into the ceiling as a second gun, across the restaurant, fired a single shot.

Lucien clutched his chest. He lurched, lost his balance, and slumped forward. His blood spilled a shiny red sea onto the white floor.

Across the panic-stricken restaurant, a tall figure dropped his pistol on the bar.

"Dear God," Pru wailed as she rocked Sam against her breast. Sam's blood flowed across Pru's belly and down her legs. Frank's hand over her heart couldn't stop the bleeding. Her mouth was deep and silent, a chasm dug by pain, and her lips trembled as Leah mopped the sweat from her brow.

Kat held her bloody hands. "You're okay, sugar," she said softly.

Frank lifted his fingers from her fading pulse and leaned over her. His rough skin rested on her smooth cheek, and his lips met hers.

"You're going to make it," he whispered. She raised her face to his ear, and the gurgle in her throat grew louder as she struggled to speak.

"I'll always love you," she said so softly it might have been his own thought.

The women made her comfortable. Pru's evening wrap became her pillow, and the ice in Kat's drink cooled her burning face. Leah tore the butterfly back from her dress; gently she laid it like a comforter across her friend. Samantha's wide pewter eyes took in each of the faces before her. Her head rested in the crook of Frank's arm.

"Will you tell my doctor that that damned bug didn't kill me after all." She managed a weak smile. "I love you, sweeties."

An ambulance cried somewhere in the night, growing louder as it hurled through the dark. Frank gathered her fingers in his.

"Kiss me," she murmured. Their lips met, and the last breath she would ever draw mingled with his. Her head dropped back into the palm of his hand, and her eyes closed.

For a long time Frank didn't move.

Then he carried Sam outside to the ambulance.

Mick led the women away. They stepped carefully over Mo, who knelt above Lucien and stared in puzzlement at his son's frozen grin.

As Pru headed for the door, she heard someone call her name. She looked around, and then she saw him, standing at the bar.

"Mercer?" She walked slowly toward him and leaned her blood-splattered cheek against his chest. He guided her past the police lines and reporters. They got into his car, and the others followed.

In their black cocoon, cut off from the crowd and the din, she looked at him questioningly. "I had to see you again," he answered.

"Can we leave now?" she asked dully.

He shook his head. "The police will want to talk to me, Pru." His voice was barely a whisper. "I shot Lucien."

At the West Hollywood police headquarters, the three women made their statements. Outside the station, the press clamored and tried to push their way inside, but John and Mick held them at bay.

Once the police report was filed, the women were free to leave.

"I'm staying," Pru told the others.

"Are you sure?" asked Leah. "Maybe you should come with us."

"Leah's right," said Kat. "This could take a spell. They'll have some questions for Mercer, and you're already dead tired."

Pru shook her head. "I'm staying."

"All right then," Kat said. "Take this." She wrapped her beaded jacket around Pru's shoulders.

Leah placed a cup of steaming coffee in her cold hands. "Frank wants us to help him with the arrangements—" she said vaguely.

Pru nodded. She watched from the window while her friends left the building and plowed through the field of reporters.

Pru waited. She couldn't be sure how long: time expanded and shrank like a pulsating star in the wake of the rifle fire. All she knew was that the coffee was cold, and the tears were dry on her face, by the time a door swung open down the hall.

Mercer stepped into the light.

She rose on her crutches and limped toward him. He ran to meet her, and his mouth seized hers, but she stepped back and turned away. He pulled his hand out of her tumbling red hair.

"I wanted to thank you. For everything," she said. Her green eyes were downcast.

"I came here to ask you to marry me, Pru . . . I guess that wasn't such a good idea."

She rested her hands against her soft belly.

"I don't think so," she said kindly. She wasn't ready, and maybe she never would be. "You could give me a lift, though," she told him.

Dawn rose behind the Hollywood Hills, and her child fluttered inside her as Prudence headed home.

Epilogue

ON A BALMY June evening, Pru delivered a hefty baby girl, Samantha Devane Daniels. The day that Pru brought her home from Cedars-Sinai Medical Center, Samantha's godmothers arrived from the East. Kat brought Queen Anne's lace from the hills surrounding Morgantown. Leah came empty-handed: she had finally learned that her friendship was the greatest gift she could bestow. For this wisdom she had many people to thank, including her fiancé, John.

In July, the Morgantown Players unveiled their first production, and critics lauded Kat's achievement. That same month, Leah finished her novel. It was the bittersweet love story of two well-meaning people who couldn't make their relationship work. Leah dedicated it to her parents, and in doing so, she put the past to rest.

Pru read the manuscript in one sitting. When she finally persuaded Leah to adapt it for the screen, neither of them dreamed that *High Hopes* would earn Weyburn Productions its first of many little gold men.

At summer's end, the three women rendezvoused in Dakar. Frank drove in from upcountry, where he was heading a UNESCO project, the Devane Memorial Hospital.

The foursome flew to the highlands of Togo. There, Sam's beloved Queen's Crown rose highest among the mountains. In the early morning, the friends climbed the rugged face that Sam had trekked so many times before.

On the crest where she had once made love to her husband,

they looked down across the scarlet slopes blanketed with flame trees. Emerald valleys plunged beneath their feet as Frank opened the sterling urn.

With a single gesture, he cast Sam forever into the wind. Sown like a thousand seeds, she fluttered across the plain, over the jungle and the wide savannah far below. As the north wind carried her toward the sea, a lone eagle spired and soared in her wake.

Sunset flowed like a lavender river across the blue horizon. The women turned and linked arms with Frank. High overhead, the African sun warmed their backs as they made their way down from the mountain.